TREASURES, DEMONS, *and other* BLACK MAGIC

TREASURES, DEMONS, AND OTHER BLACK MAGIC

Published by Old Man in the CrossWalk Productions 2014
Vancouver, BC, Canada
www.oldmaninthecrosswalk.com

Library and Archives Canada
Doidge, Meghan Ciana, 1973 —
Treasures, Demons, and Other Black Magic/Meghan Ciana Doidge — paperback edition

Cover image & design by (2023 -) Damonza.com

ISBN 978-1-927850-17-6

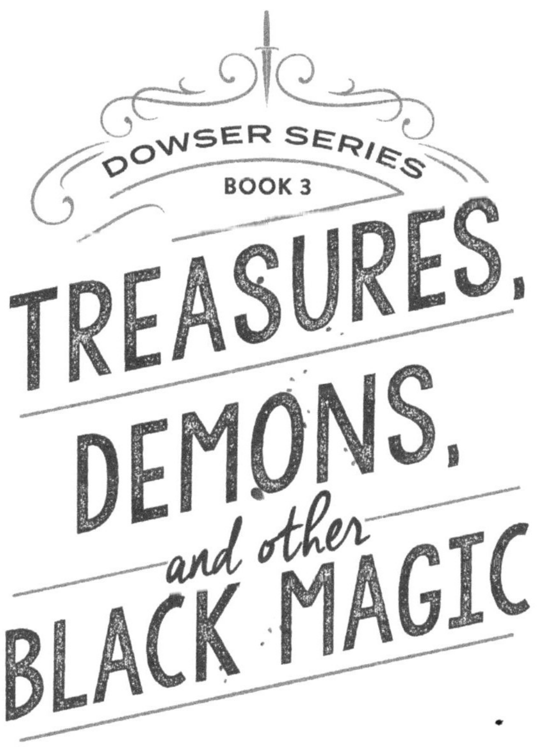

Treasures, Demons, and Other Black Magic

MEGHAN CIANA DOIDGE

For Michael
If I have to fight demons I'm glad I do so
by your side

I hadn't set foot in the human world for more than a few hours in over three and a half months. Sure, I was stronger and faster than I'd ever been before, and I had a shiny new sword, but I was seriously chocolate deprived. I don't recommend quitting cold turkey. And the new sword was a problem — to my mind, anyway. It represented all the expectations of a powerful father and a new otherworldly life. A life that wasn't the one I'd worked so hard to build. It also represented the responsibility I had to bring my foster sister Sienna to … what? Justice? I didn't know if that was even possible. What I did know was that Sienna wouldn't stop, and that I couldn't just leave everything up to fate and destiny … or maybe I was. Maybe I was doing exactly what I was supposed to be doing. If you believed in that sort of thing.

I just hoped that before the chaos and mayhem renewed, I'd manage to get my hands on some chocolate. It didn't even have to be single-origin Madagascar. I was utterly prepared to lower my standards.

Chapter One

With one hand on the invisible knife at my hip and one hand twined through the wedding ring charms on my necklace, I stepped out from the golden magic of the portal onto the shores of Loch More. Yeah, Loch More, as in Scotland.

The ground underneath my feet thrummed with wild magic and untapped power. Supposedly, all the grid points around the globe — where natural magic reigned — teemed this way. Too many thousands of years ago for me to comprehend, the guardian dragons set up a network of portals anchored at these points. I gathered the portals were rather helpful when it came to saving the world, which the guardians did constantly.

Thankfully such responsibility wasn't my duty. No, my focus was much more personal.

I drew a little more of the shielding magic from my necklace, and the hair on the back of my neck settled. I unclenched my teeth. The land around me glowed — I could see for miles in all directions — but not with any specific color of magic. Rather, all the natural hues of the earth were intensified. I could actually see magic in the air I breathed.

I'd expected snow, seeing as it was the first week of November, but there wasn't any. I wondered if that was like people who didn't know Vancouver expecting it to snow there all the time, which it hardly ever did. Unlike the rest of Canada.

The sun was low in the sky. I'd misjudged the time, which reminded me I also wasn't sure of the exact date, though I'd tried to keep a rough calendar based on my infrequent calls home. My sleep schedule was erratic, now dictated by exhaustion rather than the rotation of the earth.

Time moved oddly in the dragon nexus. At least three and a half months had passed while I'd trained, studied, and pretty much did anything to avoid the fate waiting for me in the Sea Lion Caves, but it felt like more and less all at the same time. I supposed that was what destiny felt like … or was that inevitability?

Memories of the terror my sister, Sienna, had created in the caves along the Oregon coast — which, ironically, were a tourist attraction for some people — had melded over the past months with the bloody vision that Chi Wen, the far seer, had shared with me. A vision that showed my loved ones slaughtered on an altar. A vision that had stopped me from following Desmond and Kett back through the portal and kept me training like a woman fueled by vengeance. A vision, mixed with a memory, that had me formulating a plan.

The portal snapped shut behind me, leaving me alone for the first time in a very long time. Maybe as alone as I'd ever been. That was an odd thought.

Anyway, to the point. The shores of Loch More looked like any other lake surrounded by rolling green hills in the late afternoon light of a sunny, crisp day. So pretty. A really, really vibrant green, and seemingly in the middle of nowhere.

Actually, this was the middle of nowhere. It was my second visit. I was seriously glad to see the empty pickup truck parked about a dozen feet away at the edge of the single-lane dirt road. I really hoped it wasn't a standard shift. I might have forgotten to include that specification in my request. Yeah, look at me, Miss Plan-And-All-That.

I took a step toward the truck, my supple leather knee-high boots crunching the grass. It was obviously colder than I thought it would be. I could have put a jacket on over my leather getup, if only for show. Though to get my hands on a jacket, I'd have to seek out humans, and that was contrary to the objective of this brief excursion. I wasn't interested in getting into a situation where Chi Wen's horrific vision of the future had a chance to manifest. I was dodging destiny today ... and caves ... and loved ones for that matter.

So yeah, a jacket would have been a good idea. The dragons believed in training — and fighting, actually — in laced leathers. If I'd tried to change before leaving, I would have tipped my hand. Thankfully, I still had my trusty Matt & Nat satchel. My katana — a gift from my father — nestled between my shoulder blades where I wore it slung across my back. The two-handed, single-edged sword was easily accessible over my right shoulder. Its twenty-eight-inch blade was deadly sharp. The sword had been commissioned specifically for me — well, the alchemist part of me — and created as an empty vessel into which I could channel and store magic. The responsibility that came with such a gift weighed on me heavily, and I'd put my current plan into action only two days after Yazi had presented the sword to me.

Yazi was the warrior of the Guardians. Also, my father. My newly found father, who I'd never known and was still trying to get to know in between his guardian duties and my training schedule. He wanted me to train and train and train until I was strong enough to actually stop a train. Pulou the treasure keeper wanted me — rather obviously — to treasure hunt with him. And Suanmi, the fire breather, wanted me out of sight and out of mind. The six other dragons hadn't really weighed in, but I'm sure they would — given a hundred more years or so. Time held little meaning for any of them.

Guardians were perpetually swamped saving the world from whatever threatened it with extinction. Some, I'd heard, frequently disappeared for years, deeply entrenched in their duties. Others, like my father or Baxia the rain bringer — who dispelled tidal waves and hurricanes if she was capable — moved from territory to territory as called upon. Chi Wen, the eldest guardian, didn't seem to comprehend time at all — whether it was a single day or a week or a month. But, if it wasn't for the nine of them, I didn't think humanity would have made it through … well, anytime.

Ignorance — and I speak from a deep understanding of the concept — was definitely bliss.

A chilly gust picked the blond curls up off the back of my neck, bringing with it the earthy, floral scent of witch magic. I paused, my hand once again on the invisible jade knife at my right hip. Actually, it was the sheath — a gift from Gran — that was spelled to make the knife invisible, not the blade itself. That blade was the length of my forearm, hand carved from jade I'd found along the Fraser River on a hike outside Lillooet. The knife, along with the necklace of wedding ring charms I never took off, were the first magical items I'd made, even though I had no idea that I was an alchemist at the time.

A young woman, her hair a fiery mass of wavy curls, became visible as she stepped out from a witches' circle a few feet to the left of the front of the pickup truck. She was about my age, gazing at me with muted green eyes that stood out against her pale skin. She wasn't at all beautiful — her nose too big and chin too small — and yet she exuded an earthy sensuality. Men would shoulder by me to get to her any day.

"Hello, witch," I said. "Impressive cloaking spell."

The redhead nodded. "It's a family thing," she said. "Rooted in the rocks of our ancestral land." She gestured around her. "Amber Cameron, granddaughter of Mauve, Convocation secretary, at your service." Her accent would quadruple her heartbreaker status.

Okay, then. The witch's magic was dim compared to the power of the portal and the grid point, hence my not picking it up right away. She carried the earthy base that identified her as a witch. Against that, her own magic was sugared, vanilla tones but not sickly sweet … brown sugar toffee, maybe? Also, the witches' Convocation had a secretary? Like, to take notes and distribute minutes?

"It's a portal, then," Amber stated rather than asked.

I didn't answer. She was younger than I'd first taken her to be. Maybe closer to nineteen. She was wearing the most gorgeously comfy green Aran cardigan. It was long enough to cover her ass and well-worn jeans. I wondered if she'd be up for a trade, except she was about four inches shorter than me and had no hips to lament.

"I … Normally my brother would come." She stumbled over the words. "He's older and the duty is his. But he's away at university."

My silence was unnerving her. I felt bad about that and very unlike myself, but I wasn't going to blather about dragon magic. Not that dragons were a secret or anything. They were relegated to myth status due to rarity, not mystery. I'd only met a dozen or so myself in the last three months, while living in the dragon nexus that was supposedly their home base.

"The request was for a drop off only, not an escort," I said, trying to be nice but firm about it. I'd studied up on the protocol of such things before coming. Major portals — ones that lay over the grid points — often had a guardian who oversaw them. Only dragons — or half-dragons in my case — could open and pass through portals unaccompanied. Pulou, the treasure keeper, could create portals and temporary doors other than the ones that lay over the grid points, but enlisting his help would have alerted my father to the fact that I was leaving, if only temporarily. It was past time that I started cleaning up some messes.

"Yes. Yes," Amber answered. "I know, but you left too much money."

"That's a poor excuse for breaking the rules." Yeah, that was just who I was these days — boring, dependable, and on task.

"You are … you can … you're a witch. Jade Godfrey, granddaughter of Pearl, the Convocation chair." I'd signed my name to the request. It felt deceptive not to. "A witch who walks through portals?"

"Sure," I answered. "Let's go with that. I really don't have time to —"

The golden, fresh magic of the portal blew open behind me and I groaned inwardly. Damn, I'd taken too long.

I turned in time to see Drake tumble out of the glowing doorway and onto the grass about ten feet behind me. The thirteen-year-old was incapable of simply walking anywhere. He spent every hour of the day charging around. His dark hair fell across his almond-shaped eyes, and he brushed it away as he righted himself. He was grinning ear to ear at me.

"Found you!" the fledgling guardian declared. The portal snapped shut behind him. "Second guess, still pretty good. I was going to try Shanghai, where Yazi and I got the sword, but then I remembered that sorcerer you were looking for."

Damn it.

"Drake," I hissed. "Get your ass back through that ..." I faltered. I hadn't actually confirmed it was a portal to the witch.

"Nope." The thirteen-year-old barreled the last ten steps to my side.

The red-haired witch meeped. Yes, meeped. Even if she couldn't taste the magic rolling off Drake like I could — all golden honey-roasted salted almonds and steamed milk — he probably looked otherworldly to her.

Drake and I were dressed practically identically, in black laced-leather vests and pants. His were more broken in than mine, though, and his gold broadsword was more obvious across his back. He was as tall as my ears now and had easily grown an inch a month since we'd first met — and fought a demon together — in the dragon nexus. I figured he'd be six feet in a matter of months. His shoulders and feet were already too wide for the rest of him. Like a puppy, actually. Give him a couple of years and he'd be as formidable as any of the guardians. I'd seen him try to eat an entire roast pig by himself. Yeah, dragons liked roasting things, mostly fowl. Not that I'd ever found the nexus kitchen or managed to get my hands on any chocolate, no matter how many times I tried. The nexus wasn't a labyrinth or anything. Given that it housed nine of the most powerful beings on earth, it was actually deceptively small — unless you knew where you were going. Yeah, I couldn't wrap my head around that either.

Just at the thought of chocolate, I began jonesing. I was seriously deprived. I really wouldn't recommend going cold turkey. Hell, I wouldn't recommend going one day without some sort of chocolate-imbibing, let alone three and a half months.

"He's thirteen," I snapped at the red-haired witch. If she got any more awestruck, she'd melt into a pile of goo. That would be annoyingly sticky.

"Hello!" Drake cried. Unhelpfully, he was grinning at Amber like she was his new favorite toy. His voice was far too loud for the quiet of the countryside.

I put on my stern face. I'd had a lot of practice with it now, specifically with Drake. "I mean it."

"Nope."

"Drake."

"If I go back, I tell everyone you've left. You've got maybe twenty-four hours before Branson comes looking for you. Want to shorten it?"

Double damn. Branson, the sword master, was our trainer. He was a dragon, but not a guardian. Yep, not all dragons were guardians. As far as I'd figured out, there were less than fifty nonguardian dragons worldwide. Branson had been in line for Yazi's guardianship … or seat … or whatever, but was severely injured before he could take on the mantle of the warrior. Technically we had tomorrow off — one day of rest every nine days — so I'd known I'd be able to get away fairly cleanly. Until Drake followed me.

"So we're hunting the sorcerer?" he asked hopefully.

I sighed. Rock? Hard place? Meet my head.

"Sorcerer?" Amber asked. "You seek Blackwell?"

"It doesn't concern you, witch," I said, still attempting to be firmly polite. I was quickly losing control of this situation, and I wasn't even ten steps into it.

"Well, you'll be heading to Blackness Castle then," she responded archly. "And I can direct you better than that iPad you had me put in the glove box."

"Fine," I said. "There just better be treats in there as well." Yeah, I'd put that in the request. So? I knew myself that much at least.

"Fudge," the witch said. "Chocolate. A family recipe."

I rewarded her with a blinding smile. She managed to not stumble back from the wattage of it, but I sensed it was a struggle as I made a beeline for the truck and went hunting for the offered fudge. It would be insanely sweet. Probably enough to give me a headache. But I found all fudge too sweet, and still I was desperate to get it in my mouth. Um, yeah, I was aware that said a whole lot about me beyond the fact that I was craving chocolate.

"You're a witch?" Drake asked the redhead.

"Amber Cameron, granddaughter of Mauve, Convocation secretary."

Drake bowed to her formally, as if he'd just remembered his manners. "Drake, ward of Suanmi, the fire breather. Apprentice to Chi Wen, the far seer."

Amber's jaw dropped. She had no idea what he was talking about, but it still impressed her. People were so like that. Not that Drake didn't have an impressive pedigree. But why was it that the things we didn't have or didn't understand impressed us, even as the wonders we knew seemed ordinary and even trite? If only Sienna had been happy, content with her life and magic —

I yanked open the passenger door of the pickup as I shoved the 'if only' out of my thoughts. We were so far beyond 'if only' that it wasn't funny or sad anymore. It was just time. Time to stop.

"Show me a spell?" Drake asked.

The witch managed to raise her chin a little at this request. I guessed Drake wasn't so awe-inspiring when he wanted to see magic so badly he asked for it. Amber had no way to understand that the fledgling didn't play Adept power games. At the peak of the power pyramid, dragons had no need for such posturing.

She shrugged and stepped sideways into her witches' circle. She disappeared. I could still pick up traces of her brown sugar toffee magic, though, now that I had the taste of it.

Drake whistled as he paced around the circle. Now that I looked closer, I could see that it was a ring of smallish stones. Ancestral stones, Amber had said. That would be a bitch to lug around, but it was obviously super effective.

However, even shiny new magic couldn't distract me from chocolate. If I was quick enough, I might be able to get my hands on the fudge without Drake noticing. I really didn't feel like wrestling him for it. His boundaries and strength weren't well defined. As in, he had endless strength and absolutely no boundaries. He was a fledgling guardian raised by fully actualized guardians. At twenty-three, I was the only person Drake knew who wasn't a hundred years older and stronger than him. Dragons weren't big breeders. Presumably, saving the world from utter destruction every other day got in the way of that … a lot.

How the hell was I going to get him back through the portal?

I insisted that Drake sit in the bed of the pickup truck, which was open rather than canopied. I was worried his magic would fry the iPad, then the truck's engine.

Driving on the left side of the road was discombobulating enough, I didn't need the distraction of the truck breaking down.

I didn't manage to shake the witch either. I needed to work on my solo intimidation factor. No one wanted to hang around when I was flanked by a vampire and a werewolf. Well, no one aware of their own mortality … so that would have excluded Drake. Yeah, I missed Kandy and — as odd as it was to admit — Kett. Last time I'd managed to check in, Kandy was in Portland leading the pack hunt for Sienna, who'd escaped the Sea Lion Caves with Mory in tow. Mory was still missing, presumed dead by anyone who'd known Sienna for more than half a minute. We didn't talk about it though, and I — as always and forever — held out hope for the necromancer's safety. I had no idea where Kett was and no way to contact him. The portal magic fried cellular phones. And Desmond? Well, I hadn't tried to contact the alpha of the West Coast North American Pack, and I thought it was best left that way.

Drake didn't mind being in the open air, though I had to pull over and berate him for jumping in and out of the truck while we were moving. This maneuver had startled Amber so badly that she actually shrieked, then wept a little when the adrenaline surge wore off.

I felt sorry for the witch, even though she'd forced herself on me. She claimed she'd have to walk over an hour to get home if I didn't drive her, and that she would therefore freeze to death.

The urge to scream, then cry when around crazily high-powered Adepts doing crazily high-powered feats didn't ease over time. I'd just always had cupcakes, chocolate — and now — dogged focus with which to smother my terror.

Amber twisted her fingers through the ties of the drawstring bag in which she'd collected her ancestral stones. Earthy, sweet magic thrummed underneath her hands.

"The stones are unique," I said. "Are they passed down through generations of your family?"

"No," Amber replied. "When it is time, we walk the land. If the stones speak to us, then we collect them."

"When it's time? Like a rite of passage?"

"If you like." Amber shrugged, not looking up from her entwined fingers. She was embarrassed, perhaps by her reaction to Drake's maneuver.

"So the stones are natural to the land? Specifically around the grid point?"

"Yes."

"But they taste of your base magic. The magic you must share with your family."

Amber looked up at me. Yeah, even in the old country — as Gran called anywhere overseas — tasting magic was a rare ability. "They do? Like what?"

"Brown sugar toffee, with a hint of something floral, maybe."

"Thistle?" Amber asked.

"I don't know if I've ever smelled thistle before. Why that?"

"It's the family emblem. For austerity."

"That makes sense," I said. "Can you cast without the stones?"

"Of course," Amber replied. Her nose went out of joint at the suggestion, which informed me that her magic was at its strongest when tied to the stones.

It was fascinating. I'd spent dozens of hours in the dragon library, soaking in as much magical theory as I could in between training sessions. Yet, still there was something new to learn from a witch family that was generationally tied to the magic of Scotland and the Loch More grid point. Six months ago, I had no real idea about the magical world I'd been sheltered from — or rather, denied, according to Sienna.

"How much farther?" I asked.

"The Cameron lands stretch from and through Loch More," the red-haired witch replied proudly. She gestured to either side of the still empty but now paved single-lane road. Green hills and more green hills — some spotted with seemingly spray-painted sheep — stretched as far as my eyes could see. I didn't ask about the sheep. I was having a hard enough time maintaining control of the situation without admitting ignorance as it was.

"Would you prefer to walk?" I asked sweetly, not even remotely interested in managing a junior witch who was breaking the rules of etiquette all over the place. Things like cellphones and cars couldn't pass through a portal — the intense concentration of magic fried electronics — so dragons had contacts who facilitated their movement through the human world when necessary. Though I understood it was rare that actual guardians ever needed such things.

"Ten more minutes," Amber answered.

Silence fell between us. I'd been away from humanity for over three and a half months, but I had no real interest in chatting. I just wanted to get to Blackwell, and ... well ... move forward from there.

I also wanted to get my hands on the iPad to check what time it was in Vancouver. It had been at least two weeks since I'd spoken to Gran or my mom, Scarlett. And I thought ... well, I hoped there was some tiny chance that Mory was home safe and sound, exactly where she would have been if I'd turned her away from my apartment. She'd come to me seeking information about her brother's murder. Her brother, Rusty, had been magically drained and killed by my sister. Yeah, it was a sordid tale. I desperately wanted the fledgling necromancer safe and sound, and not in the clutches of my evil foster sister — cue dramatic music — and not possibly dead. Possibly? Hell, most likely dead.

"Is he going to do that again?" Amber asked, meaning Drake jumping in and out of a moving vehicle. She'd seen the stunt in the side-view mirror the first time, and she kept nervously glancing there now.

"Probably," I answered. "He's still distracted by the fudge. He's never had it before." I'd had to give up the fudge in order to placate the fledgling. Life was all about compromises these days.

"Is he … is he a dragon, then?" Amber asked.

"Yes." No point in lying about it. Her family had a history — most likely an actual chronicle — that must have passed down the guardianship of the Loch More portal and detailed who they were guarding it for.

"You called him Drake."

"That's his name."

"Then he is not a guardian? Not one of the nine?"

"Not yet." Even a witch in the middle of nowhere Scotland knew more about the Adept world than I had six months ago. Or she was just way quicker at putting things together.

"But you … you are a … witch?"

"Sure."

"But not really?"

"It's fine then, in Scotland, to ask an Adept about her magic? Not a breach of etiquette?"

Amber lifted her chin defiantly, but looked away from me. "You asked about the stones."

"You offered the information freely."

Amber nodded, letting the topic of my magic drop.

The rolling green hills to either side of the road really did seem to go on forever. But then, I wasn't too sure of the speed limit so I wasn't driving terribly quickly. Sheep and cows were abundant now, but there was a lack of cars and homes. Or rather farms, I guessed.

"Blackwell —" Amber began to say.

"Also not an acceptable topic of conversation." I cut the witch off.

"It's just that the Camerons have an understanding with the sorcerer."

"Hear no evil? See no evil?"

"Sorry?"

"Nothing," I answered. "A lot of the Adept seem to have agreements with this particular sorcerer."

Amber nodded. "He is powerful, and he keeps to himself."

"I'm not asking you to come with us to Blackness Castle."

"I'm … I'm offering." The witch set her hands and eyes on the pouch containing her ancestral stones.

"That would be rather foolhardy of you."

"But it is my duty. You called upon me as your guide —"

"So guide us. Do you know how to work the map app in the iPad?"

"Of course."

"Your help is greatly appreciated."

Amber set her jaw but nodded her head in acceptance of my terms. I got that the junior witch wanted to see what was going to happen at Blackness Castle. But I wasn't going to be responsible for anyone getting hurt ever again. I still had errors and omissions to clear up and correct. I wasn't adding Amber to the list.

Drake, though. Well, as far as I'd seen, Drake was indestructible.

We dropped the witch at the end of a long driveway leading to a house that looked like a manor. Given the area, I'd been expecting a farmhouse.

I pulled away, leaving the pouting redhead at the front gate as Drake decided to climb into the passenger seat. Yes, while the truck was moving.

Amber's jaw — seen in my rearview mirror — dropped as Drake opened the door and swung himself into the seat.

I immediately tucked the iPad into the pouch on the driver's-side door in an attempt to save it from Drake's magic. "Show-off," I muttered.

Drake laughed and started digging through the glove box … looking for more food, I imagined.

"Don't touch that," I said, as Drake pulled out the cellphone I'd requested from Amber.

"Ah," Drake said, doing his best Chi Wen impression without actually realizing he was doing an impression. "A cellular phone."

Suanmi was the fledgling's actual guardian. His parents had died in some terrible fire, though what fire was capable of killing a dragon, I didn't want to know. Chi Wen was Drake's mentor. The fledgling was destined to wear the mantle of the far seer once Chi Wen was ready to shed it, sometime in the next hundred years or so. Yeah, I'd been living it for three and a half months, and it was all still mind-boggling for me.

"I was going to call my mom," I said with a sigh, holding my hand out for the phone. Drake tossed it to me. Technology held no fascination for the fledgling, probably because nothing actually functioned around him.

I tried turning the phone on. It started to boot up, so maybe I'd gotten lucky —

"Will the witch follow us?" Drake asked. Then he stuffed something in his mouth so quickly that I couldn't actually identify it as food.

"I hope not," I answered.

"It is foolish to hope for an outcome you know will not happen."

"Oh, thank you, sage one."

Drake grinned. He popped something else in his mouth, chewed, and then swallowed.

Gum. He was eating gum.

"Stop that!" I snapped. "It's gum. You're just supposed to chew it."

Drake frowned. "What good is that?" He ate another piece.

"If you get sick, I'm not carting your ass around."

"I never get sick," Drake declared with utter confidence.

"You're hanging with me, kid," I said. " 'Never' just went right out the window."

Drake looked at me seriously for a moment — probably working through the window reference — and then broke into a broad grin. "I hope so, warrior's daughter. Never is a boring word."

Jesus. "Suanmi is so going to kick my ass," I muttered.

"That would not be good," Drake said, all serious now. "I fear you would not survive such an assault, but the fire breather rarely resorts to physical confrontation."

"Helpful."

"You are welcome."

"I was being sarcastic."

"I know." He didn't. He'd picked up the lying-but-not-really-lying thing from me. It wasn't as endearing a trait as I would have thought.

"So we meet the sorcerer and then what?" Drake asked. "Are we saving the necromancer?"

I sighed. The thirteen-year-old knew way more about my life than he should. But then, he'd been my constant companion for the last three months, and he asked a lot of questions.

"I hope so." I glared at the fledgling, daring him to pull out one of his sage sayings. He just smiled back at me, content for the moment. That calm would probably last for another thirty seconds.

"Maybe we'll have to storm the castle," Drake said gleefully.

And the calm was gone.

"At least I have a dragon," I said, knowing it was wrong to play along with Drake but desperately trying to channel some of his lightness. "You need a dragon to storm a castle, don't you?"

Drake threw his head back and laughed. It was a mannerism I thought he might have adopted from my father, Yazi, but one he embraced with abandon.

The truck engine stalled … then caught … then stalled again. I took my foot off the gas.

"Stop it," I said to Drake. Yeah, I said that to him a lot. It didn't seem to have any lasting effect.

He snickered. "We could get there faster on foot."

The engine caught again.

"You could, maybe. But the swords would be rather obvious out in the human world."

"What would the humans do if they saw swords?"

"They'd wonder. They'd ask questions."

"But we need not answer them," Drake insisted.

"This is why they don't let you out of the nexus yet," I said. "You can't just go blundering around in the world you're spending your entire life training to protect."

"You blunder just as much as me!"

"More, probably. But I can't bulldoze entire mountains in a single breath."

"Neither can I, though I don't understand 'bulldoze.' I assume it is bad."

"We're here to rescue, not to destroy, is what I mean."

"I don't destroy."

"But you don't create." The words were out of my mouth before I thought them through.

Drake fell silent. I forgot how young he was, all the time.

"I'm sorry —"

"No, alchemist," Drake interrupted. "You create. I protect. I understand."

"Okay."

"We are careful of the humans."

"And others."

"Yes, I will be careful."

"My version of careful, not yours."

"Your version?" Drake cried. "You would barely give me permission to breathe, you're so docile."

"Did you just call me docile?"

"Yes. Did that anger you? Perhaps we should fight?" the fledgling asked hopefully.

I shut my mouth and clenched the steering wheel. I didn't like getting my ass handed to me by a thirteen-year-old on the training floor ... or off it.

According to the Google Maps route that the witch had plotted, the drive was only supposed to take us two more hours in a fairly straight line. I could make it through two hours, couldn't I?

If the truck didn't break down first.

Chapter Two

Blackness Castle was — literally — a castle. As in, built out of stone, with towers and one big wall running the perimeter and everything. I mean, I wasn't sure what I'd expected — the word 'castle' was in the name, after all — but I'd never actually seen a castle in person before. Forgive me; I'm from Canada. I was impressed by the Parliament Buildings in Victoria.

"There's a freaking gate," I said.

"It looks like a boat," Drake said.

I rolled the pickup truck to a stop in the gravel-filled area in front of the wide front lawn that ran the length of the castle. I swiveled to look at the fledgling guardian incredulously.

He was peering up and out of the windshield at the castle. "What? The two towers ... north and south look like the stem and stern. It's long and narrow and it juts out into the water."

"Yeah," I muttered. "A really big stone boat."

Drake shrugged. Freaking dragons were impossible to impress.

Night had fallen right around the time the fledgling guardian's tummy had started growling. Drake didn't complain and I didn't stop for food. I also pushed the gas tank so much we might have been rolling in on fumes, which was fine because Drake was right. If we really needed to leave in a hurry, we'd probably get away quicker on foot.

The half moon was bright in the dark, clear sky, though it had rained for portions of the drive. A low stone fence branched off from the high castle wall to form a sort of front yard. The castle was set back, looking — as Drake had already said — as if it was floating in the Firth of Forth behind it.

It was impossible to tell from this vantage point if anyone was home. I couldn't see any lights on in the towers.

"So are we just going to knock on the front door?" Drake asked.

"Yeah. I think it's behind the castle gate, but that was the short version of the plan."

"What's the long version?"

"It was more of a plan B. You know, if he doesn't answer the door."

"We break it down."

"Yeah. Well, I break it down."

"And now you have me."

"Great," I said, casting a long look in Drake's direction. The fledgling grinned back at me, as if the idea of breaking into the powerful, potentially evil sorcerer's castle was like ice cream and video games for him. Maybe it was. There didn't seem to be any other dragons Drake's age around the nexus, nor did there seem to be a formal school or anything. Just our trainer Branson, who barked drills at us and let us loose in the library.

"Where are all the other fledgling guardians?" I asked as I opened the truck door and stepped out into the cool night. Nothing like a little friendly banter to lighten our short walk toward the deadly magical onslaught that potentially awaited. I wasn't underestimating Blackwell ... well, not again, at least.

"There aren't any right now," Drake said. "Baxia will be the next guardian to choose her successor, and she doesn't need to do so for another two hundred years or so."

"What about Yazi's nephew or niece?" I hadn't met my younger cousins; I'd just hunted through my family tree wondering if my three-century-plus-year-old dad had any other children. He didn't. Guardians, it seemed, didn't breed often. I'd also tried to find information about guardian succession in the nexus library without any luck. I had no idea how potential guardian dragons were selected, how they ascended, or why each guardian then wielded unique magic beyond their inherent strength, agility, and invulnerability.

Drake shrugged, strangely silent as he followed me around the front of the truck. I let it drop.

The stars were clustered densely overhead, and I wondered what they would say about the next couple of life choices I was about to make. You know, if I could read stars.

"We only have twenty hours," I whispered, urging myself forward. I could take whatever the sorcerer could throw. Hell, I'd been training my ass off in anticipation of this moment for three months. Well, not this moment exactly, but a moment probably much, much worse. Blackwell had a thing for me. He was a collector, the same as Kett and I were collectors. Sienna was only interested in destroying ... as far as I could tell, at least. Sienna, not Blackwell, was my ultimate target.

"Yeah," Drake said, but I couldn't remember right away what we'd been talking about. Then I picked up my own train of thought.

"Branson might not have come for me, you know," I said. "If you hadn't followed."

Drake shrugged. The moonlight glinted off the hilt of the gold broadsword behind his shoulder.

A shadow disengaged from the low stone fence that stretched behind Drake. My jade knife was in my hand before the taste of her magic hit me … bitter yet refined dark chocolate … more berry than citrus.

"Kandy?" I whispered.

Drake slipped behind me but didn't draw his sword. It was a well-practiced move. We'd determined early on that if he was behind me, my dowser senses were more accessible. By 'we,' I mean Branson figured it out. So Drake followed while I led. The fledgling hated it, and I wasn't a big fan of having that sword behind my back either. It wasn't exactly a precision weapon.

The shadow stalked toward me. Teeth flashed, their white enamel caught momentarily in the moonlight. Next thing I knew, I was running, then crushing a green-haired werewolf in a massive hug.

The werewolf in question gave as good as she got. If I wasn't half-dragon, my upper arms and back would have been seriously bruised.

"Kandy," I cried. I had missed her so much I forgot any and all decorum, not that I ever had much.

"Dowser," Kandy murmured as she buried her face in my curl-covered neck and inhaled. "You smell the same. That's good."

I pulled away from the hug to look at her. Even in the moonlight, I could see her green hair wasn't as perfectly dyed as it normally appeared. And she was slimmer than usual. More wiry than her typical litheness.

"You, however, do not look the same, dowser." The cool voice spoke from off to my right. "And it's not just the sword you carry or the new ability to wield it that is evident in your body."

Kett. Surrounded by Drake's and Kandy's magic,I couldn't taste the vampire's magic at all, but I could feel the life debt bond he owed me. It hung between us in the darkness like an unsprung trap. I didn't have to see him to know he would be untouched by the three-and-a-half-months that had passed.

"You've teamed up with a vampire?" I teased Kandy as I stepped back from our hug.

She shrugged. "He was here when I arrived."

"Oh? What brings you to Blackness Castle, Kettil, Executioner of the Conclave?" I asked mockingly. Vampires never did anything that didn't benefit them directly, though they were also all about the long game, so maybe I was missing something.

"I came directly from Portland," Kett said, not answering my question at all. "Blackwell was obviously the best lead to the black witch's whereabouts."

Kandy snorted. "Would have been nice of you to share that info, vamp."

"You've been here for three months?" I asked.

Kett didn't answer.

Kandy growled with frustration. "We can't get in."

"We can," Drake said from behind me.

We all turned to look at him. Even Kett stepped into the moonlight to lay eyes on the fledgling guardian. I still wasn't sure how the vampire collected shadows around him so thoroughly. He was dressed in his typical cashmere sweater and atrociously expensive jeans combo.

"I thought it might have been a dream," Kett murmured. His voice was unusually heavy with emotion.

"No such luck," I said.

Kett turned his ice-blue eyes on me and smiled. That should have probably scared me even sillier than I already was, except I welcomed it.

God, I missed my life. Even the terrifying parts, it seemed.

"You brought a dragon to storm a castle, eh, Jade?" Kandy peered over my shoulder, jumping to a conclusion about Drake's identity that must have been informed by Desmond's recounting of the events in the nexus. Kett wasn't chatty as a rule, and I'd had to keep our couple of phone conversations very short.

"You wouldn't expect anything less, would you?"

"Nope." Kandy grinned her patented predator grin. "I'm glad you're alive."

"Ditto, babe. Ditto."

I hadn't wanted to drag anyone — not my mother or Gran or Kandy — any farther into Sienna's mess than I already had, so I'd kept my mouth shut about my plans. But I was more than pleased that the green-haired werewolf was back by my side. And the vampire, of course, though I never quite knew what would happen the moment our interests diverged.

"Artillery fortified," Kett said. "The defensive spur to the southwest is the main entrance."

"Just point, vampire," I said. Only five minutes into our reunion, I was already snapping at him for being way over my head all of the time.

We were standing by the pickup and gazing at Blackness Castle. Surveying would be a better word, maybe, except I really had no idea what I was looking at.

Kett raised his hand to indicate a stone walkway to the far left of the castle. "He'll reside in the central tower," he added.

"The wards are impressive," I said. I'd scanned the length of the castle's nooks and crannies, and couldn't see any weak points in the magic that protected it and kept us out.

"Yes," Kett agreed. "But I wouldn't expect anything less of a sorcerer with Blackwell's lineage."

"Did you stop by the bakery for cupcakes?" Kandy asked. The castle neither impressed nor intimidated her. That unending confidence was the hallmark of most werewolves — but it was especially prevalent in Kandy, who was a pack enforcer.

"No time," I answered. My employee Bryn had graciously taken over my shifts in the kitchen. Todd, the espresso wizard, eagerly stepped up to full time. And my mother, Scarlett, was doing the bookkeeping. Cake in a Cup was my baby. Tending to it had been the first phone call I'd made, the first moment I'd made it out of the nexus — after letting my Gran know I was alive, of course. She wasn't too inclined to take Kett's and Desmond's word on that. "I was worried that bouncing in and out of the nexus would draw too much attention."

"Cupcakes? What are cupcakes?" Drake asked.

Kandy looked at me as if I was a complete stranger with two heads. "The dragon doesn't know what cupcakes are, Jade?" she mock-whispered. "Your world really is collapsing."

"On hold is a more accurate assessment … I hope."

"Maybe Blackwell has a kitchen," Kett said.

Now it was our turn to stare at the vampire, who might just have made some sort of joke. He looked back at us all with his cool demeanor firmly in place. It was quite the poker face, but it brought me back on topic, which might have been Kett's point.

"Is Blackwell inside?"

"Haven't seen him," Kandy said.

"Yes," Kett replied at the same time.

"He could be popping in and out with that amulet of his," I said. Blackwell wore a ruby amulet that tasted — to me — like sour cream and butter on a baked potato rather than his own earthy cabernet sorcerer magic. The amulet was an exceedingly rare transportation device, most likely created many hundreds of years ago by an alchemist far more powerful than I was. I gathered this artifact was also renowned among collectors — Kett had identified it by my brief description alone. Blackwell had called it his "most precious possession." It was also how he'd fled the Sea Lion Caves like the utter coward he was.

Kett shook his head and turned his gaze back to the castle.

"The vamp doesn't think the sorcerer would leave with us out here," Kandy elaborated.

"Too much to protect," Kett murmured. His anticipation was marked, though maybe it was just the tingle of pleasure I felt from the life bond that colored his tone. That was new, unexpected, and disconcerting. I wondered if Desmond felt that same sensation through our life debt bond. I really hoped not, but seeing as he'd felt my pain when Sienna tortured me, he'd probably felt my desire afterward as well. Since then, I hadn't taken the necklace off in Desmond's presence. I never took it off anymore, not even in the shower. If it wasn't for my necklace, I doubt I would have survived … well, Sienna. Actually, I still didn't know if I would survive my sister.

"Any visitors?" I asked. My voice was louder and sharper than I'd intended. I meant had Sienna shown up. The sudden silence that fell between us told me they knew who I meant. The mere mention of her dampened our easy camaraderie.

"No," Kandy said at last.

"Did you knock?" Drake asked.

The green of Kandy's magic rolled over her eyes as she grinned at the fledgling guardian. "Yeah, we knocked."

Drake nodded, very serious. "Plan B, then?"

"What's plan B?" Kandy asked.

I turned to the green-haired werewolf and grinned at her. The smile stretched my face as if the muscles were unused to the expression. "We huff and we puff —"

"And we blow the door down," Kandy said with an edgy chuckle.

"Artillery fortified," Kett repeated.

"You think Blackwell has guns set up?" Guns weren't something I'd considered. Magic screwed with such weapons so much that a sorcerer of Blackwell's power should find them utterly useless. And while just shooting Sienna from afar was a lovely — if bloodthirsty — daydream, she shielded herself with so much magic that a crossbow or bullet wouldn't get within a foot of her. Bullets — if Blackwell had somehow circumvented how magic screwed with guns — might work against Kandy, though. Silver bullets, specifically.

Kett didn't answer, which was typical when he didn't know an answer … or considered it beneath him.

"What about outer defenses and perimeter spells?"

"Disabled," Kett said. He sounded so pleased with himself I was surprised he didn't wink at me.

"Yeah, and no scaling the walls," Kandy said. She ran her hands over her arms as if remembering something nasty. I could hear her wolf in her voice, probably manifesting along with the thickening tension. I felt it too.

"A month is a long time to be away from your pack," I said quietly.

Kandy shrugged. "The fledglings must be avenged."

My stomach bottomed out. She meant Jeremy, who Sienna killed with Blackwell's sacrificial knife, and whose blood raised one huge, nasty demon. And she meant Mory.

"Have you heard ..." I couldn't bring myself to ask — again — if Mory was dead.

"No, dowser," Kett said. "But the necromancer lives." His cool tone instantly soothed me. I liked the soothing part, but I didn't like the instant part. Since when did I feel comfortable around Kett? He liked to go all fangy and blood-lusty in tense situations ... like this one.

"Do you have actual confirmation?"

"She wears a necklace constructed by you. She lives."

"You don't know." I choked down the emotion threatening to close off my throat. "You don't know that the necklace will ... can ... withstand three months of whatever Sienna's been doing."

Kett inclined his head, then turned his attention back to the castle.

I hated being potentially right about such a thing, more than I hated being wrong about everything else. Why had Sienna kidnapped Mory in the first place? For collateral? Even if it had been a spur-of-the-moment thing, why hadn't she abandoned the necromancer as soon as she'd gotten clear of the caves? Or — as dreadful as the thought was — why not kill Mory and leave her body on Gran's doorstep or by the bakery to further torture me?

Kandy touched my shoulder, just lightly. But I could feel the brush of her dark-chocolate magic, and I welcomed the taste along with the gesture.

The castle intimidated me. I could admit it. I'd come through the portal all cocky and focused, and had immediately gotten derailed by Amber and Drake. Now, standing before the centuries-old structure, I was waffling. I was more unsure of my 'find Blackwell/find Sienna' plan with Kandy and Kett at my side than I'd been without them. Having them here made the last months far more real than that time had actually felt in the day-to-day living of it.

"We came all this way. Maybe Blackwell will play nice if we ask nicely?"

"He does have the hots for you," Kandy agreed. "But what if — faced with all four of us — he decides to pull more of those demons out of his pocket?"

"Demons, yeah!" Drake cried, utterly delighted at this possibility.

"One doesn't collect those kind of demons, werewolf," Kett said without turning away from the castle.

Kandy mimed ripping off the vampire's head and kicking it like a football behind his back.

"That was a greater demon," Kett continued. "I wouldn't have thought Blackwell was powerful enough to call it forth."

"He seemed surprised himself," I said. "Right before he ran like the utter coward he is." And with that terrible memory on the edge of my mind, I turned my reluctant feet toward the main entrance.

Kett stepped up to follow, just behind my left shoulder. "Fighting a coward is a very different prospect."

I nodded.

Kett stepped sideways into the shadows as we moved past the low fence and stood before the spur, as he had called it. The latticed iron gate, which was barely illuminated in the moonlight, loomed before us. It was wide enough that — if it stood invitingly open — we four probably could have walked through abreast. However — closed — it was secured at the top, bottom, and to each side into the thick stone walls and roof of the spur. Even Kandy, as slim as she was, wouldn't find an opening wide enough to slip through.

"There'll be traps," I said. "Even if he agrees to let us in voluntarily. He likes to hide spells in things, boxes and such." I directed this last caution to Drake, who was practically vibrating directly behind me. I took a deep breath and reminded myself the thirteen-year-old was invulnerable. If I tried to make him stay in the truck, he'd probably get into worse trouble than he would surrounded by Kandy, Kett, and me. Or so I hoped. I had a bad habit of being wrong. Like, a whole lot.

"You got any chocolate, Jade?" Kandy whispered.

"Just your magic, Kandy."

"That doesn't help me," Kandy bitched, but I could hear that she was smiling.

I stepped forward until I was an arm's length from the outer wards. Those defenses seemed to be attached to the stone of the curtain wall rather than placed in the yard itself. I reminded myself of the power of Amber's ancestral stones. This was Blackwell's ancestral home. Being a sorcerer, he couldn't access natural magic the same way a witch could. But this castle had been in his family for generations. Yeah, the dragon library was extensive and detailed. It was finding the information that had taken the time. Digging through handwritten chronicles was way more intensive than Googling. Anyway, Blackwell's magic would be potent here.

I opened my dowser senses to the magic of my three companions, breathing in Kett's cool peppermint, Kandy's bitter chocolate, and Drake's honeyed almond. I firmed my offensive stance — left foot forward, right foot back with more weight on the ball of the foot than the heel — and ran my fingers across the knife at my hip.

I twined the fingers of my left hand through the wedding ring charms of my necklace.

I could do this. Blackwell might be able to take on any one of us solo, but four together were pretty darn intimidating. Castle or no castle.

Of course, I was deliberately not factoring in that Blackwell owned the world's foremost collection of magical artifacts — well, apart from the dragon cache. That was an unknown bitch. This collection ranked high on the dragon watch list, and it usually took the end of the world to get the attention of one of the nine. Speaking of bitches, Scotland was under Suanmi's protection. One look at the fire breather and Blackwell would give up his best friend. Too bad Drake's guardian hated me, and that anything below nuclear annihilation was beneath her notice.

Then Kett laughed. He was enjoying himself, maybe even feeding off my anxiousness. I wrapped my hand around the hilt of my knife as his pleasure and anticipation hit me through the life debt bond he owed me. Well, that was new. Of course, I hadn't actually been in the same room as him since extracting the bond to save him from the cleansing of the dragons.

I laughed, deep in my throat and quietly. The vampire's confidence was infectious. What was the point in being immortal — he was thinking — without a challenge?

"Okay," Kandy said. "Now you're both being really creepy."

"Power up, wolf," I said. "It's time to dance."

Kandy laughed. "I like it when you dance, dowser."

"Everyone likes it when Jade dances," Kett said from the shadows to my left.

"Is it like when she fights?" Drake asked. "Because that's pretty cool."

"Hush, youngling," Kandy said. "The elders are being inappropriate."

I laughed again, lighter and more freely this time. Then I pulled my knife from its invisible sheath and flung it at the wards that covered the gate before me. The knife crashed against the magical barrier with a blue-streaked crack of energy.

"Knock-knock, sorcerer!" I called as the knife boomeranged back into my open palm. Yep, the blade returned to me at mere thought now. This newly refined trick made me rather difficult to disarm. "Time to come out and play."

"Yeah, or we'll huff and we'll puff and we'll blow your castle down," Kandy cried, repeating the story book mantra from before.

I laughed. The anticipation of the fight invigorated me. I itched to draw my new sword, to press my strength against another's. To be beaten and get up. Or to triumph. I was game for either.

Who the hell had I turned into?

"Jade Godfrey." A voice floated out of the darkness behind the latticed metal gates on the other side of the wards. "To what do I owe the pleasure?"

"You invited me, Blackwell," I answered. "You know, before you colluded to murder two innocent teenagers and aid my sister in draining my magic."

Blackwell stepped forward into a wash of moonlight that just touched the gate. His pale face appeared to be slashed to pieces by the iron latticework. His dark hair and clothing blended into the night. The effect was creepy to say the least.

"You must know, dowser, that was never my intention. I was blinded —"

"A sorcerer of your lineage and power was blinded by a half-witch in a blood frenzy?" Kett's voice cut through the shadows that hid him. "That is difficult to believe."

Blackwell flicked his eyes to my left, but he didn't seem to be able to see the vampire. "I was blinded by the thought of opening the portal, especially after I knew what it was. And, indeed, by the promise of your magic, Jade. The promise of a dowser of your obvious power." His hand lifted to touch his chest, just briefly. I gathered he wore his precious amulet beneath his dark sweater, but I couldn't feel its magic through the wards. "Nothing more or less."

"Take down the wards, Blackwell," I said. "And I'll give you a taste."

Blackwell tilted his head, assessing me. Then he grinned. "It's unfortunate that you come to me so heavily guarded, dowser. Otherwise, I'd gladly take you up on that offer."

"Scared of the vampire and the werewolf?" I said, goading him. "They didn't stop you before."

"But they are not all who stand with you, Jade Godfrey," Blackwell replied. "The wards block me from fully understanding, but you have a third with you as well."

"Perhaps that's my magic you feel."

Blackwell laughed. "You're a tease, Jade." His use of my first name was intimate. I didn't like it at all.

"This is so boring!" Drake complained. His voice was shockingly loud against the quiet banter Blackwell and I had been trading. "We can crack the wards. Right there." The fledgling shoved his arm by my shoulder and pointed to the base of the gate. "Let's get to the tricks. You'll have tricks, won't you, sorcerer?"

Drake pulled out his broadsword. The gold of the blade caught the moonlight. Dragons were big on gold and jewels, and flash in general.

I sighed.

Kandy laughed, low, husky, and full of anticipation. "I like this boy, Jade. I'm glad you brought him to play."

"I didn't bring him willingly."

Blackwell was staring at the thirteen-year-old boy standing in his walkway. Drake was clad identically to me, in black, well-worn laced leathers minus the knee-high boots. The get-up had to look like a Halloween costume on both of us. The wards would block Blackwell from feeling Drake's full power, but the sorcerer wasn't an idiot.

I sighed again. I, too, had seen the edging around the gate where the wards had been opened and closed for centuries. Worn spots. The sorcerer had been remiss in his upkeep, which was odd when he must have expected visitors. More likely, he thought too highly of himself, or maybe he wasn't able to perceive the weakness in his own defenses. Perhaps he needed to be cut down to size …

Again, who the hell was I?

I was angry. So angry at Blackwell that I could barely contain it beneath my polite upbringing.

"Perhaps the sorcerer would prefer we didn't break his wards?" I asked mockingly. "Perhaps I should offer a parley?"

Blackwell shifted his gaze back to me. "You have no authority to do so."

"Do I need a badge of some sort? No, let's forget that silly being-nice idea. Perhaps the sorcerer would like to face me one-on-one? We're evenly matched, aren't we, Blackwell? Will you test your spells against my knife?"

Blackwell eyed my jade knife as I twirled it in my right hand. I knew he found it shiny and unique. It was one of a kind, after all, but would that be enough to entice him?

No.

Blackwell stepped back into the darkness of the spur entrance. I couldn't feel anything beyond the wards of Blackness Castle, but I was sure he was gathering as much magic as he could muster.

So we went in.

Chapter Three

Okay, it wasn't that easy.

Before anything else happened, Kandy — in a blast of shifter magic — transformed. I'd seen her in wolf form before, but this was different. Now half-woman, half-werewolf, she towered over the three of us, all long-toothed, razor-clawed, and furry, but still on two legs. This was Kandy's version of Desmond's half-beast, who I referred to as McGrowly. A few shifters had the ability to combine their beast and human forms. This hybrid was stronger and more resistant to magic. She — still clothed in a stretched-out tank top and ripped jeans — wasn't quite as hideous in this form as McGrowly was. She was a sleeker monster, but still nightmare inducing. If, you know, she didn't happen to pretty much be my best friend in the entire world.

"Whoa," I said. "I see I'm not the only one who's been practicing."

Kandy snapped five-inch-long teeth at me and laughed. At least I thought she laughed. It wasn't a joyful sound.

"Too cool," Drake said.

Kandy pointed one three-inch claw at me. Yes, she still had opposable thumbs — which were also clawed — as well as pointy wolf ears sticking out of her still-dyed green hair. "Owe. Witch. Cupcakes." She choked the words out of-not-quite human vocal cords. McGrowly's ability to converse in this form was obviously something he'd refined further than Kandy had.

"You name it, you got it." I turned back to the gate, scanning the edges where the magic had thinned. Well, it was more like wear spots. Worn layers that had built up like crumbs at the corners of a cookie jar.

Deciding that the worn magic was easier to access at the bottom, I laid down on my stomach, facing the gate, and took a deep breath to prepare myself ... not that breathing would make the pain any easier to bear.

I slid my jade knife along the flagstone walkway underneath the gate.

The magic of the ward resisted, of course. Pain streaked up my arm and through my neck, trying to get out my mouth. Multicolored sparks exploded before my eyes and I tried to blink them away. Then — the pain increasing with every inch — I slid my knife along the bottom edge of the gate, severing the ward's connection to the stone of the walkway.

It was kind of like carefully slicing a cupcake in two after you've already iced it, so you can add filling. Except cutting cupcakes usually didn't rack me with pain.

I had cut through about a foot of the ward before I started screaming. I had to force myself to continue. This wasn't the type of magic I could absorb or displace and be done with. It shifted, fighting my intrusion. I tried to shield myself further with the protective power of my necklace, but it still felt like every nerve in my arm was on fire.

I'd cut through and along about two feet when Drake stepped on either side of my shoulders and reached down to curl his fingers under the tear I'd created.

"Not yet, fledgling," Kett said. "Let the alchemist sever the sides, and then we will all step in and distribute the backlash."

Drake wasn't big on listening ... or on waiting around for others to open a door for him. He jammed his fingers underneath the ward and the lattice iron gate, and with a bellow that hurt my brain, he wrenched the gate up and open.

The ward magic — centuries strong — lashed around the fledgling guardian, who fell to his knees under the assault. This effectively trapped me underneath his legs. With another grunt, Drake lifted the gate above his head.

Kandy flung herself forward and underneath, then rolled — back down, feet upward — to take the weight of the gate on her legs.

With a moan, the fledgling dragon collapsed forward. Kett caught him before he crushed my head, set him off to the side, and then stepped forward to help Kandy hold the gate.

I rolled to my feet, grasped Drake underneath the shoulders and — squeezing between Kandy and Kett, who were vibrating with the pain of holding the compromised wards open — ducked underneath the gate while dragging Drake after me.

I hadn't taken more than two steps into the spur, as Kett called it, before he and Kandy had dropped the gate behind them. The ward didn't fully snap back into place.

"We've damaged it," I whispered. "Two feet of clearance at the bottom now." Kett and Kandy couldn't see magic as well as Drake and I could.

The fledgling dragon attempted to sit up but didn't make it.

"The fledgling probably has the extra magic cycling through him right now," Kett said. He sounded bemused and impressed. I wasn't sure the ward magic or Kett's doubly raised interest was healthy for Drake.

"Give me a mo ..." Drake muttered.

I propped him up against the wall. He looked okay, just woozy. His magic looked and tasted as usual. "He's undamaged," I said.

"Good," Kett said. "He can follow. We must press Blackwell at once."

"There's a ton of magic ahead," I said. The stone walls of the entrance jogged immediately left.

"Yes," Kett said. "The spur is doglegged to force intruders to place their backs to the caponier. The passage is also exposed to attack from the parapet on the upper walk. Also, note the gun batteries —"

"English," Kandy growled through nastily fanged teeth.

I was seriously glad the werewolf had broken before me. I hated to admit that I had no freaking idea what Kett was saying ... like with every second word out of his mouth, as always. Doglegged? Caponier? Parapet?

"See those holes in the wall?" Kett enunciated each word, treating us like the idiots we were.

"Yep," I answered. Kandy simply snarled and flexed her claws.

"They are places where the castle's defenders would have attacked intruders."

"Right," I said. "Avoid stepping in front of the holes."

Kandy's size was a liability in the narrow, tall stone passageway, but she stepped forward and ducked underneath the first of the 'gun batteries.' Lanterns flared as she passed, perhaps triggered by her magic. Helpfully, this further illuminated the walls and corners for me.

I knew from experience that Kandy and Kett could already see well in the darkness.

"Pockets of magic everywhere," I said. "Try to not touch anything."

Kett nodded and stepped so far into the shadows between the lanterns above us that he practically disappeared. I could still taste his magic, though, and feel the life debt bond. I wondered if he could ever fully hide from me again.

"Drake?" I asked. "Do you need some help?" I wasn't actually sure I could lift him. He was way heavier than he looked. Epically heavy for a thirteen-year-old. I thought it was a dragon thing. I'd never managed to knock Branson off his feet in training, though I had some spectacular bruises to show for my attempts.

"Right behind you," Drake murmured sleepily.

I sighed. Kandy and Kett were turning again — I could feel their magic shift as they moved — and I didn't want them to get too far ahead. I should be leading, given that I could actually see magic way better than Kett. Kandy was almost completely blind to it, though I gathered she could smell certain magic ... like mine.

I reached over Drake's head and pulled his sword out of its scabbard. I laid the blade across his lap and wrapped his hand around the hilt. He clenched his fingers obligingly.

"Right behind you, warrior's daughter," he said with a grin. The title made the bottom drop out of my stomach. It was weighted with all the responsibility that also imbued the gift of the sword across my back.

Then Kandy screamed. Well, yowled, as if she was in terrible pain.

I stood, spinning away from Drake and dodging defensive magic as it exploded around me — Kett was right about the gun batteries. I dashed through the zigzagged stone passageway until I rounded the corner into the courtyard.

"Kandy?" I cried, unable to see anything besides the large central tower looming beyond. The spur and the curtained wall were open to the night air.

"In the guardroom to your right." Kett's cool voice slid out of the shadows ahead of me.

I swiveled and peered into the darkness. As if reacting to my movement — or, rather, my magic — a light spell shifted over me. Bars crisscrossed a doorway that seemed to lead to a small stone room. Thick silver bars.

Within the room, Kandy was hunched down. Her hands were pressed to the ground before her, her back arched in pain. Her skin rippled as I watched her shed her half-beast form for her human skin. She was still wearing her stretched-out tank top and ripped jeans, but now her exposed skin was covered in nasty red slashes.

"Silver," I whispered. "He expected werewolves."

"One has been camped in his front yard for weeks," Kett murmured. He was closer now, immediately to my left where he always stood. This position kept him guarding my weaker side and out of the way of my knife, which I wielded with my right hand. It had only taken three and a half months of dragon training to figure out why he always positioned himself that way.

Kandy lifted her head. Her eyes gleamed with the green of her shapeshifter magic as she snarled at me. "Move your ass, dowser. Before Blackwell uses the amulet."

"He won't abandon his collection," I said. I had the sorcerer pegged.

"If it is here," Kett said.

"Why else would he hole up here and need these defenses?" I countered. But I knew Kandy and Kett were right. I'd already left Drake behind, and I was now going to leave my werewolf friend trapped and in pain. This was who I was now. I didn't have to like it. I just had to do it.

I stepped away from the guardroom doorway, turning toward the central tower. Blackwell might have expected retribution from the shapeshifters for Jeremy's death, but he had no idea what I was capable of.

"He's on the other side of the tower," I said, not bothering to lower my voice. "Outside, not in."

Kett nodded in my peripheral vision and stepped left as I branched off around the right side of the tower. I kept about ten feet away from the stone walls. They glistened with a magic that was different from the wards we'd just broken through. I didn't know its purpose or function, and didn't have time to study it. The Blackwells — if that wasn't just a completely made-up surname — had spent centuries fortifying their home.

Everything could be broken, though, or so I was learning. Promises, hearts, lives ...

Blackwell went for the vampire next. It made sense that he would try to take Kett out, assuming I was the weaker opponent. It was still rude, and maybe a touch misogynistic.

The spell he used, however, was brilliant.

We'd circled the central tower and met with what appeared to be a well between us. Then we stepped toward the open expanse of courtyard in the direction of the north tower, where I was sure Blackwell had retreated.

A whirling fog rose out of the well beside Kett and spread out between us. It enveloped the vampire without a sound. No, not fog. A gray cloak of magic that reeked of day-old, cheap red wine — overly sweet and nausea-inducing. This was not the refined, earthy cabernet that I associated with Blackwell's magic.

"Kett," I hissed.

The vampire didn't answer. He didn't step out from the fog, which just sat like a malevolent cloud beside the well.

It was a containment spell of some sort. Really impressive, and troubling because I couldn't reach into it or even slash at it with my knife without some concern of getting sucked in or injuring Kett. I couldn't injure the immortal, but it probably wasn't a good idea to mix his blood with any spell, especially one this … well, gray.

"Your protector is unharmed," Blackwell said as he stepped into a pocket of light ten feet in front of me. He flicked his fingers, and more light spells floated in from their resting spots on the curtain wall to illuminate the area around us.

"You going to stand up and fight now, sorcerer?" I taunted. Yeah, I was still pissed off about the demon and Jeremy's death. I was always going to be pissed about that, even after I kicked Blackwell's ass.

The sorcerer responded by throwing a black mass of magic at me. It was a weak, underhand toss.

I slashed this unknown spell — by its taste, a variation of the fog that had encased Kett — out of the air with my knife. I twisted sideways as the magic dissipated around me.

Blackwell's eyes widened. Yeah, the knife was pretty impressive.

"My sister might be evil through and through, but at least she hits me with everything she's got. Hell, she set that demon on my ass without even blinking. And she supposedly loves me. What's your excuse for holding back, Blackwell?"

The sorcerer flashed a grin at me as he spun another spell in his hands. I couldn't pinpoint the source of his power. He wore the amulet around his neck, but he wasn't drawing magic from it. I wondered if it was the castle itself, and that was an unpleasant thought. Its stone walls were long and high, and they were coated in massive amounts of magic.

"You're too valuable to truly harm, Jade Godfrey," Blackwell said.

He tossed the second spell at me. I stepped into it, thrusting my knife into the sparkling black mass of its magic instead of slashing. It took an extra pulse of my power, an extra breath to collapse this spell. Again, cheap red wine coated my mouth. I wanted to spit to clear the taste, but it wouldn't be ladylike — so I swallowed and promised myself a dark hot chocolate chaser.

"Why is your magic black?" I asked. "Shouldn't sorcerer magic be blue?"

Blackwell lost the grin. I had that effect on men these days … or this entire year, actually. I just had to open my mouth.

I could feel Drake moving behind me, near Kandy. I didn't want the fledgling stepping into this fight.

I lowered my knife, deliberately making myself vulnerable, and smiled brilliantly at Blackwell. "Let me give you a hint. I like it rough and ready. I don't like to screw around. Make your play or lose me forever. Because when I lay hands on you, you'll wish you'd shot to kill."

Blackwell's lips twisted and his spell hit from two different directions. The asshole could double cast, which was a real bitch.

The magic blasted me back to hit the curtain wall — six feet or so of thick stone. Later, I was rather proud to see I'd managed to crack it with my head, except at the time I felt like my skull was crumpling into exploding stars of magic.

This wasn't the fog spell that had enveloped Kett. Or maybe it was but it couldn't find a hold on me, so it left twisting rivers of pain in a wreath around my body as it tried to settle.

I slid down the wall to my feet, but then my knees buckled. Blackwell's dark magic swirled around me. Now that I was enveloped in it, I could see that it was actually dark blue edged with black. I hunched over as it seared me.

"Not so lippy now. Are you, little witch?" Blackwell taunted as he stepped closer. A nasty, thin-lipped smile stretched across his face, but his pupils looked like liquid pools of the same dark magic that swirled around me. I blinked and the effect was gone, but I remembered … I remembered Sienna, and how the black magic had slowly taken over her eyes from the pupil outward.

I arched back and up as the pain collected all along my spinal column. My breasts and martial arts-slimmed waist were now on full display.

Blackwell's smile widened into a toothy leer.

Then I channeled all his magic into the katana slung across my back. This was the blade's purpose — aside from lopping off heads, of course. It had been waiting patiently for me to push a spell into it, even as I'd waited patiently for Blackwell to step closer.

"I missed Halloween, sorcerer," I whispered. My knife was at his neck before he'd even registered that I'd moved. "Trick or treat."

Blackwell covered his surprise and swallowed against the press of my blade. "Treat."

I laughed, though I wasn't actually amused.

Drake and Kandy stepped up behind Blackwell. Kandy, who was still in human form, wrapped her hand around the back of the sorcerer's neck. "I owe you," she whispered up against his jugular vein.

"Look at the little witch now," I mocked. "And I didn't even bother drawing the sword."

Blackwell held my gaze steadily. Beaten, but brave. Or overly confident, maybe. He knew we needed him … for now.

I sighed and lowered my knife. "The vampire?" I asked.

Blackwell turned to look over his shoulder toward the column of fog that still held Kett. Except his gaze hit Drake and didn't move farther.

"W-What?"

Sorcerers could see or feel magic to various degrees, like I could. They had to in order to exercise their power. They couldn't just tap into the natural magic of the earth as most witches did … though some, like Sienna, chose to build their power through blood magic. The governing body of witches — the Convocation, of which my grandmother was the chair — seriously frowned on blood magic users. It was the sacrifice part of it that really irked them.

"The vampire," I repeated. I was getting ready to prod the mute Blackwell with my knife when a snarling mass of chaos clawed its way out from the fog.

"He figured it out," Blackwell said with a shrug.

I really, really hated it when powerful people shrugged about the workings of magic.

The snarling mass — all red eyes, fangs, and claws — swiveled its white blond head toward the sorcerer, then leaped at him like a terrifying mutant vampire cat.

Drake stepped into this projection of fury — his movement a blur even to me — and snatched the insanity out of the air, slamming it to the stone at his feet.

"Jesus … Mother of God," Blackwell breathed.

"You've got that backward, asshole," Kandy said.

Drake pressed his foot to Kett's chest. The vampire, who apparently had some sort of beast form like the shapeshifters, writhed and snarled. His claws shredded Drake's leather pants.

"Stop that!" I snapped. "You'll hurt the fledgling!" Yeah, I was suddenly everyone's mother ... well, all the monsters, anyway.

Kett stilled and closed his blood-red eyes. He shuddered and recaptured his humanity ... or at least his typical ice-carved countenance.

My heart was pounding in a way that it hadn't during the confrontation with Blackwell. I had momentarily thought Kett had gone rogue — not that I knew whether rogue vampires took that form — and that we'd have to put him down. He might have torn Blackwell and maybe even Kandy apart if Drake hadn't been here to intervene.

"There's a reason for everything," I murmured.

"So you have been listening during your lessons with Chi Wen, warrior's daughter," Drake said with a grin. "Nothing happens without purpose. It is just the why that is obscured."

I grinned back at him, crazy pleased that he was here, but not wanting to admit it and reinforce his rebellious behavior. He didn't need to think that every choice he made was fated.

"Warrior's daughter," Blackwell echoed. He was obviously trying to put everything together, but I wasn't interested in helping him out.

Kett opened his ice-blue eyes and locked his gaze to Drake's, who kept grinning as if this was all a game ... and it probably was to him.

Drake lifted his foot off the vampire, who — in one fluid movement — stood at my side.

We three turned to look at Blackwell. Kandy still had her hand wrapped around the back of his neck. It was probably dangerous to be touching the sorcerer skin to skin. Kandy would risk death to avenge Jeremy, though, so I didn't caution her. Blackwell seemed neutered, his eyes constantly shifting between Drake and me.

"All right?" I asked Kett under my breath.

He nodded, but then shuddered again as if remembering something. I gathered that the fog had a psychological component. Impressive spell. Dangerously simple. Blackwell's finesse with magic just pissed me off more.

"Do we actually need to ask the questions, Blackwell?" I said.

"I will not provide information if my life is forfeit."

I sighed. I hated it when the Adept got all wordy and formal. There was magic in words. Words that I wasn't particularly versed in.

Kett inclined his head, agreeing to something. Blackwell nodded in response, but he still didn't speak.

"Sienna!" I snapped. "She's not here."

"No," Blackwell answered. "And I do hope it stays that way."

"Do you know where she is?" I was even more pissed that he'd made me ask. It sounded too close to begging once the words left my mouth. I also didn't like how much anger I was capable of, and that my capacity for it kept growing. I knew what I had to do, but I didn't like it for one second.

Standing before Blackwell was the next step in killing my sister.

"No," Blackwell answered.

I felt relieved, then felt guilty over that relief.

"But," the sorcerer continued, "if you are as powerful as you seem, I can give you a clue."

"What is the price of this boon?" Kett asked with a sneer. I don't think I'd ever seen the vampire sneer before. None of us liked the sorcerer playing us ... and yet here we were trading moves.

Blackwell smiled, and I saw something in his face that reminded me of how Kett had said that the sorcerer would make a good vampire.

Blackwell would give me the means to hunt my sister, but in exchange I'd have to — somehow, I just knew — make him more powerful in return.

I met Kandy's gaze. The green-haired werewolf nodded her approval, though her rabid anger was evident in the sharp lines of her unnaturally elongated jaw — her wolf was eager to follow through with the kill.

"Show me," I said. And that was all it took to make the deal. I felt the magic hanging between us, making me itch. "But next time we meet, Mot Blackwell, all deals are void."

Blackwell stopped smiling. "I shall endeavor to not cross your path ... warrior's daughter." He tested out the title, which seemed to scare and excite him at the same time. Then his gaze flicked to Drake.

The sorcerer was a devil in deep disguise. I just hoped what I was about to hand him didn't come back to bite me in the ass ... or harm anyone else.

I sighed.

Blackwell inclined his head and stepped toward the central tower.

Magic vibrated off Kett and Drake. They, at least, were having a blast. The vampire had a short-term memory tonight, probably by choice.

"Don't touch anything," I said.

Kett laughed. Jesus, he was changeable. He was already anticipating laying eyes on Blackwell's collection. It was probably the only reason he was here. Forget rescuing Mory.

The fledgling dragon was just as excited about going inside the castle. He was hard to impress but easy to please.

"I want to break his neck," Kandy muttered as she stepped up beside me.

"Next time," I said. The words came from some place deep within me. I'd just voiced some bit of fate. I was half-dragon after all. Fate was a dragon thing.

Chapter Four

The central tower of Blackness Castle was larger inside than out, which I was coming to understand was not unusual in the Adept world. Or at least not unusual in the world of the Adept I'd seen over the past three months in Europe and Asia. The castle's magic was old. Not as old as it had tasted in the dragon nexus, but way older than Gran or even Kett's magic tasted. Yeah, I could identify magical age by taste now.

Blackwell led us through an inner magical ward that looked like it was embedded in the stone walls — they glistened blue — rather than just coating the outer edges. The entranceway appeared to vault all the way to the roof of the tower. Oil paintings lined the wide, stone stairway that branched off from the main doors and curved up to the second floor. A massive magically suspended glass chandelier spiraled into the center of the room. I was already getting tired of being impressed by the evil asshole even before he opened a large set of thick wooden doors that were strapped width-ways by tarnished metal. He did so as a grandiose gesture that wasn't unfounded, because spread out beyond the doors was a museum's worth of magical items.

More chandeliers suspended by magic flared as Blackwell stepped into the gallery. The room was round, but every few feet an alcove — some curtained but none empty — jutted out like a tooth on a massive gear.

As I stepped into the room, I had a sense that we might not actually be in Scotland anymore — or, more specifically, that this room might just be a cog in a great machine that could start twisting and rolling at any second.

Yeah, it wasn't clear to me either.

I thought it was the magic that threw me. I'd become accustomed, though not comfortable, to the constant magic surrounding me in the dragon nexus. So much so that the presence of Kett, Kandy, Drake, and Blackwell beside me now was completely manageable. The extra shielding of my necklace helped, of course.

But Blackwell's treasures — totaling maybe hundreds of artifacts — were a different type of deluge. Each painting, statue, or piece of jewelry was carefully hung, placed on a pedestal, or grouped together on shelving units. Each one was protected by a micro ward, for lack of a better way to describe it.

I stepped toward the pedestal nearest me. Runes flared blue along the edges of it, perhaps in response to my magic. A small box crusted with emeralds and diamonds sat on a velvet cloth in a warded circle.

Gran also used runes on some of her wards. Specifically, on the complex wards that protected the entry to my bakery. They were complex because they had to read a person's magic and allow them to pass or not, then were doubly complex because they had to adapt quickly whenever I granted entry to an Adept.

Runes were usually used in the writings of sorcerers, as a way to anchor their spells or pass their knowledge along in written form.

Anyway, the point was that each of these artifacts emitted a hint of magic — and a hundred hints of magic, each subtly differently flavored, was a lot to absorb.

Kett stumbled when he entered the gallery beside me. It was the first unintentionally ungraceful thing I'd ever seen the vampire do. His cheeks infused with red. He was blushing like a human. I looked away from his dismay, completely uncomfortable with this sudden appearance of humanity. As always, I preferred to know what to expect with Kett. His distant coolness and his fugue-like states were uncomplicated and understandable. Now, here, he'd been as overwhelmed by the sensation of magic as I was. Somehow, perhaps because I tasted magic more adeptly than the vampire, I was able to hide my reaction better.

I eyed Blackwell, who was smiling at me like a proud father showing off a talented child. I scanned the room, noting the different flavors of magic that created the individual wards. Blackwell's treasure hunting was obviously a hereditary trait. Many of the wards were constructed not by him alone, but by Adepts who shared his underlying magic.

"It's an impressive collection, sorcerer," I said. "I assume it's one of your newest additions you want me to look at?"

Blackwell nodded, but before he could indicate the way, I stepped by him through the first rows of artifacts and moved toward the center of the gallery.

I could taste Blackwell's magic up ahead — the rich, earthy cabernet he emitted, not the day-old cheap wine of the fog spell. The difference was worth investigating but wasn't on today's to-do list.

Drake scanned the gallery almost systematically as he followed behind Kett and me. There was no hint of his ever-present grin on his face now. Dragons weren't big on this sort of accumulation of power. Blackwell was lucky that Pulou, the treasure keeper, wasn't with us. I wondered what rules the dragons followed. Could they just seize Blackwell's collection, or did they need cause to do so? And if they could, why hadn't they done so already?

Kandy stayed by the entrance with her arms tucked behind her back. Smart wolf. She couldn't see magic like Kett, Drake, and I could. I imagined she didn't want to tangle with any more of Blackwell's spells. She still had the silver burns that I'd seen on her skin in the guardroom. They were fading now, but she usually healed much more quickly.

Blackwell had a dark edge. If he decided to not be gentle while surrounded by these many magical objects, we'd definitely be more than bruised.

Something caught my attention, and I paused to stare at a curtained alcove to my far right. A few statues of various origins and materials stood between it and me, but I could clearly taste the pulse of magic hidden within the alcove — stronger than anything outside it. Blackwell's magic overlaying something …

"Here," Blackwell said. He rested a prompting hand on the back of my shoulder. I slowly turned my head to look him in the eye. His nose was even with my forehead. He didn't remove his hand … in fact, his smile widened.

I felt my own smile spreading deliberately across my own face in response. Then I did something I'd never done aggressively before. I reached out with my alchemist power and grabbed a bit of Blackwell's magic from where his hand rested on my shoulder. I gave it a tug.

My stomach churned as the taste of red wine flooded my mouth. But Blackwell's reaction was worth the nausea. He blanched and snatched his hand away from me.

My don't-touch-me point made, I raised an eyebrow and inclined my head to indicate I was ready to move forward.

Blackwell rubbed his thumb across his palm and looked at me thoughtfully. That little power play might have been a bad idea. I mean, he must already get that I wasn't just a witch with an affinity for dowsing, but maybe it wasn't a great idea to display unusual powers to a collector. I was already on Kett's shelf. I didn't need Blackwell's rapt attention any more than I already had it.

"Just here," Blackwell said as he stepped by me to draw my attention to a long wooden table in the very middle of the gallery. A circle was carved into the stone floor all around it. A straight-backed chair — also made out of solid, chunky wood — stood at one end, but this wasn't a dining table. It looked like a workstation. Or, rather, a place to collect bits and pieces of objects, jewels, and other knickknacks.

My fingers immediately itched to surf the magic of the broken items, to pluck out the glimmers that called to me and make them into a new whole.

Cool fingers brushed against the inner wrist of my left hand. Kett, cautioning me. I looked up from the table to find Blackwell watching me far too closely.

"Your magic is very intriguing, Jade Godfrey," the sorcerer said. "I do wish we were convening under better circumstances."

I opened my mouth to rip his head off over those 'circumstances,' but Kett brushed his cold fingers against my wrist again.

I clamped my mouth shut and clenched my hands. It was interesting that the sorcerer could see my magic, as I couldn't. I often wondered if I tasted more like my mother's witch magic or my father's dragon magic, or if I was some unique taste altogether.

I stepped over the carved circle that encircled the table. Within it, I caught a glimpse of inactive runes.

The vampire followed me over the ward line, but Drake didn't. I guessed that this inactive ward snapped into place if anything went wrong when Blackwell was inspecting the pieces he laid out on the table. By 'wrong,' I was thinking magical backlash that could potentially harm the collection. Or interact with it badly.

Again, I itched to touch it all, wondering what he did with the bits he deemed useless. In my hands, they could be made whole again. To him, they were probably garbage.

A wooden box, eight inches square, sat before the single chair at the end of the table. Blackwell circled to stand before it. He opened the lid and looked up at me expectantly.

I circled in the opposite direction until I stood by Blackwell, with Kett practically glued to my side.

A silver circle some six-and-a-half inches across was nestled in the chest. A different rune — or so I guessed, as it wasn't a language I could read — was carved every two inches or so into the silver band. What looked like rough-cut diamonds were embedded into the metal between these runes.

"Silver doesn't hold magic well," I said, thinking out loud.

"It's platinum," Blackwell said.

Ah, silly me.

"The diamonds are huge." The gemstones looked as if they'd been chiseled out of the earth and simply crammed into the platinum band by raw, brutal alchemy. I wasn't the only one who made magical objects, but there wasn't a long list of people who could do so. Actually, according to the dragons, I might be the only one currently living. Yeah, that wasn't overwhelming at all.

"It's a collar?"

"A circlet, I believe," Blackwell answered. There was something lurking in the smoothness of his tone that I didn't want to identify or even know about.

The circlet or headband didn't emit any obvious magic, but still I hesitated to touch it. It was almost as if it repelled me … or more like it was a small, malignant void just sitting pretty in its wooden box. A tiny black hole in the guise of a jeweled coronet.

"Will it harm me?"

"You tell me."

Asshole sorcerer.

"Have you touched it?"

Blackwell shuddered at this question. So that was a yes.

"I don't like it." I directed this statement to Kett, who was standing so close to me I could see his magic dancing in his skin. This display always reminded me how far the vampire was from human. He was like animated magic … or maybe the corpse of his previous self reanimated by magic, with its memories and thoughts intact. But 'reanimated' wasn't the perfect word …

"Yes," Kett answered. "I can see."

"Tell me what it is. What its function is, dowser," Blackwell said. "And I will set you on your sister's trail … if you're up for it."

I wasn't sure if he meant identifying the object or hunting Sienna, but I really wasn't up for either. Of course, I did a lot of things I didn't want to do these days.

I reached out and hovered my hands over the circlet. Nothing happened. Always a good start.

I lowered my hand, but at the last second, I chose to avoid touching the circlet. I pressed my finger into the velvet cushion in the very center of the platinum circle. Blackwell really had an unhealthy thing for plush fabrics with heavy naps.

I exhaled. Nothing happened.

I inhaled, about to lift my finger and actually touch the band, when a pulse of multicolored magic spread from carved rune to gem to carved rune all around the circlet.

Then the magic clamped down on my finger.

I screeched and yanked my hand back. The feeling instantly dissipated. The glow faded from the runes.

"What color was the magic?" Kett asked.

"All colors. You couldn't see?"

Kett nodded. He was just questioning his senses, I guessed.

"But I think the runes and gems color the spell," I said. "Not the … alchemist who created this."

"Created what?" Blackwell asked, eagerness edging his tone.

I was fairly certain Blackwell already had his suspicions. But instead of answering, I reached out and pressed my fingertips to the outside of the band, carefully not touching the runes, gems, or inside edge. I lifted the circlet from the box.

I gazed through the circle as if it were a window. The magic didn't try to grab me again. I hesitated to tell Blackwell any of what I was tasting, but I felt compelled by the bargain we'd struck in the courtyard.

"Hold it like this and it won't affect you," I said, turning to pass the circlet to the sorcerer.

He carefully placed his fingers next to mine until he held the full weight of the platinum band.

"It's deceptively light for something so terrible," I said.

"Yes?" Blackwell lifted the circlet and looked through it as I had. For a moment, the inner edge caught the reflection of the sorcerer's eyes, and I had to look away from the yawning chasm of greed I saw there.

"Do you have others?"

Blackwell hesitated, but then said, "No."

I looked at Kett, who always seemed to know when people spoke the truth — maybe he noted their heart rates — and the vampire nodded.

"What is it?" Blackwell actually seemed to have an excess of spit in his mouth.

I turned away, sweeping my gaze across the parts of the gallery I hadn't walked through. Drake was leaning against the stand of a smiling Buddha. I almost cautioned him from doing so, but then stopped myself. Obviously, the micro wards didn't bother the fledgling guardian. His deceptively casual stance was probably for Blackwell's benefit, because the fledgling was as unsettled as I was. Now that I was looking for it, I noted that a number of the alcoves had their curtains drawn, and a few pedestals were draped with red velvet. It bothered me that Blackwell didn't have his entire collection on display. I was going to have to walk away, to hand him more power, and take his clue in order to save Mory and stop Sienna.

And that was my ultimate responsibility.

I offered Drake a sad smile. He shrugged in response, bowed his head, and turned to walk back to Kandy at the front entrance.

"You understand that such a thing as this would not hold me, Drake, or Kett for very long. But we would be terribly angered by its use."

Blackwell nodded. I was fairly certain he was barely listening to me. He was just waiting for the punch line.

"It's a dampener," I finally said, not looking at Blackwell as I spoke. Kett stiffened — though I wouldn't have thought that possible — beside me. "A magical suppressor, as far as I can tell."

Blackwell expelled a breath. Then, smiling to himself, he carefully placed the circlet back in the chest.

"It drains magic?" Kett asked.

"No. Is that even possible? I think it just holds it in place."

"Rendering the Adept human," Blackwell said. I really didn't like the barely contained glee evident in his tone.

"Maybe," I said. "Or maybe it simply stops them from using their magic, which is why it wouldn't hold a vampire for long." Vampires were made of magic, or at least Kett was to my eyes. The dampener — placed on a vampire — would have nothing specific to grab a hold of and then restrict.

Blackwell turned to look at me. His hand was placed possessively on the lid of the wooden box. "And why is that, dowser?" the sorcerer asked.

I smiled. "That information isn't part of our deal, sorcerer."

Blackwell inclined his head.

"Now for your part," Kett said.

Blackwell nodded. "We'll need to go to the library."

"Lead the way," I said.

Blackwell tucked the wooden box underneath his arm and headed back the way we came.

I tried to not worry about the information I'd just traded. I tried to not worry about what was behind all the curtained alcoves. The treasures contained in this room no longer dazzled me. I just hoped that Blackwell was so careful and jealous that those treasures never left the confines of their wards and these stone walls.

Though, honestly, for a moment, I did think about pulling out my sword and destroying everything in my path. It was a silly but compelling thought.

Instead, I laced my fingers through Kett's cool ones and stared at the midpoint of Blackwell's back. The familiar peppermint taste of the vampire's magic filled my senses, clearing my sinuses of all the other magic in the gallery.

This wasn't the worst thing I was going to have to do to get through this Sienna debacle. But it saddened me to think about how Blackwell might use that circlet.

I freed myself from Kett's fingers and stepped from the gallery. Drake, Kandy, and Blackwell had already exited before Kett and me. Blackwell raised the ward over the door as I passed. Stupid sorcerer. I'd already tasted this magic, and it wouldn't hold me at bay anymore if I wanted in.

I'd be back, I promised myself. When and why and how, I didn't know. Except that the circlet didn't belong in Blackwell's collection.

Blackwell led us diagonally across the main entrance and then up a twist of circular stone stairs that were way too narrow and confining for my taste. McGrowly would have had to walk at an angle to get his shoulders through. Coming down was totally going to be worse.

As immediately as he sprang to mind, I determinedly avoided thinking about Desmond Charles Llewelyn, Lord and Alpha of the West Coast North American Pack. I hadn't even heard his voice in the last three and a half months, because I hadn't called him. I didn't like the way the life debt bond I owed him compelled our so-called relationship. And magic or no magic, I didn't need any of it interfering with finding Mory and stopping Sienna.

Instead of thinking of my would-be shapeshifter lover, I imagined how Kett would be full of information about the narrow stairs making it easier to defend the castle. Forcing intruders into single file would mean that a single sorcerer on the top landing could pick them off one by one. But would Adepts who could scale walls or tear down doors ever be stupid enough to get trapped like this? Castle living was so not for me.

Neither was the library. It smelled musty and dusty and like moldy leaves. By the gasp that emanated from the vampire, I gathered that Kett felt the complete opposite.

I scanned the bookshelves that stood double my height around the edges of the walls and within curtained alcoves. Replace the pedestals with shoulder-height lengths of shelving and the red velvet curtains with royal blue, and this room was a duplicate of the gallery below. Except for the fireplace and seating area on the far curved wall. And the obviously magical picture-framed window overlooking the wide, moonlit river below.

Blackwell's reading nook ... how cute. The fireplace didn't seem to have a proper chimney or vent — more magical showing off. I was beginning to understand Gran's conservatism when it came to magic. Throwing it around was flashy and wasteful.

"Your sister Sienna took — stole — two items when we parted ways in the caves," Blackwell said as he made a beeline for the reading area. "I would like them back."

"What, pray tell?" Yeah, I got he was Scottish, not English, but I wasn't above mocking him.

Blackwell continued forward without answering, which was okay. I was accustomed to being ignored by my elders when I was being mouthy.

The stone floor was covered by a thick Persian rug in front of the fireplace, which blazed to life as Blackwell passed by it. The rug was incongruent with the Victorian-looking love seat and chair, and I avoided stepping on it.

Kett began listing toward the bookshelves as we passed by. I kicked him in the calf with a back flick of my foot and he righted himself.

Blackwell stepped into the alcove positioned to the right of the magical window, and I turned to look at the room I'd just passed through.

Kandy, once again, stayed by the door. Her arms were crossed and her face grim. Unhappy wolf. Yeah, me too.

Drake peered at the fire for a moment — dragons loved watching magic in action — but he quickly grew bored and paced around looking at the books.

Blackwell stepped back out from the alcove with a leather-bound book in hand. He passed it to me and then waited expectantly.

Great. Another test, was it?

I sighed. The book's black leather binding looked new. The title was embossed in gold along the spine but not on the front cover. *The Book of Demon History on Earth*.

"Catchy title," I said.

I flipped the book open. It was filled with pages and pages of cramped, black-inked handwriting that — by firelight, anyway — was incomprehensible. I flipped a few more pages. The author had also included sketches of demons, symbols — runes, I guessed — and weapons. The chapters were chronological by date and seemed to begin in the fourteenth century.

"I don't get it," I said. "Its magic is dim. This isn't a book of power."

"The book is not the original, of course," Blackwell said. He was back to watching me intently. Normally that would bother me — I wasn't some science experiment — except this time I knew he was waiting for me to piece something together.

"Sienna stole the original? Why would —"

I stopped flipping. I recognized the wickedly curved knife depicted on the page I now held open. It was the blade that Sienna had used to murder Jeremy.

"You hire a duplicator?" Kett asked. Blackwell intrigued Kett far more than I liked. But then, I wasn't the vampire's keeper. In fact, I really hoped to never meet his keeper.

"Seems prudent," Blackwell answered.

As I understood it, Kett was turned, not born, which meant that some other vampire's blood had animated his corpse. And blood heeded blood. Yep, Kett's master would be a terrifying being, who the vampire would have to obey in all things. At least that was what the limited number of books on vampires that I could find in the dragon nexus said.

"Duplication," I said. "A duplicator." Yeah, I was a bit behind.

"Yes," Blackwell said.

"But he or she cannot duplicate the magic within the pages."

"No."

"Because magic can't be created or destroyed," I said. "So the duplicator borrows from the original?"

"A small amount," Blackwell answered. "Not enough to diminish the original —"

Kett snorted. I'd never heard him make such an indelicate noise.

Blackwell shut his mouth and grimaced.

"What was the second item?" I asked, already knowing the answer.

"Actually, it was the first." Blackwell tapped the sketch I'd recognized.

The knife. But did Sienna still have it? It had been in Mory's hands the last I saw it — covered in Jeremy's blood. But Sienna had Mory.

Kandy had managed to save my mother, who'd been magically depleted from holding the demon at bay, but not Mory. The werewolf had protected the more vulnerable, as she should have, but lost the necromancer and the knife. I'd have to call Scarlett to confirm that Mory hadn't dropped the knife after I dragged the demon through the portal. It wasn't something I had reason to ask before. Unless Kandy knew.

"How is any of this supposed to help me find Sienna? Why would she want this book in the first place? She's not a sorcerer."

"It's not that kind of book. It's merely information. Some would call these accounts fairy tales."

"Yeah, I know all about Adept bedtime stories coming true. I'm still waiting on the elves to show."

"Really?" Blackwell asked, very interested in this possibility.

"No, sorcerer. That was sarcasm. So this helps me how?"

"The book is a duplicate," Kett prompted me, but not unkindly.

"So what?" I asked. They gave me a minute. "You think I can track the original with this one. What are you smoking?"

Blackwell furrowed his brow. He was as unhip as the vampire when it came to slang.

"Fine. Even if I could do that, I'd have to be near the other book, and if I was that close, I'd taste Sienna's magic first. You know, with all the blood magic and mayhem in her veins."

Blackwell shrugged. "I have no idea why your sister wanted the book or what she plans on doing with it. Other than the obvious."

"It's a history of demons. It's not like they're walking the earth. They've been vanquished back to their own ..." I looked to Kett, hit with a completely irrational and impossible realization. "Mory ..." If Sienna had stolen Mory's necromancy powers, would she think she was capable of raising vanquished demons?

The vampire tilted his head thoughtfully. He liked to hedge his bets, which was fine by me. One of us had to be rational when it came to Sienna, and it wasn't going to be me.

My sister already had a taste for manipulating the dead. She'd used Hudson's corpse — my would-be boyfriend and Kandy's pack mate — to try to kill Kett six months ago. But demons, according to my father, Yazi, came from another dimension and dissolved into ash when vanquished. Necromancers needed a dead body in order to reanimate it, didn't they?

I glanced back at the entry that accompanied the picture of the sacrificial knife. "Dorset Street. London. 1888."

"Three demons," Blackwell said. "Summoned by an ancestor of mine. He died in the attempt. I believe the humans attributed his sacrifice to their Jack the Ripper myth."

'Sacrifice' was the completely wrong word to use for murder. Why was I just standing here chatting with this asshole? Right, Mory.

"She's not that powerful," I said to Kett. "She was only able to raise that demon in the Sea Lion Caves, because he" — I spat the word in Blackwell's direction — "laid the spell. With this ... she'd be combining completely different types of magic. It's impossible, isn't it?"

Kett, who was reading the entry over my shoulder, didn't answer. I couldn't bring myself to try to focus on the cramped writing. My mind was reeling, actually attempting to not put the pieces of the Sienna puzzle together.

My stomach churned but I forced myself to speak the fear growing there. "But we know what she does to become more powerful."

"I imagine there are a few sorcerers in London," Kett said, but to Blackwell not me.

"Yes," Blackwell answered. "Why?"

"They're in danger," I said. "She's going to need the power of a sorcerer to raise a demon."

"Please," Blackwell said, actually chortling.

"My sister kills the Adept for their power," I said, grinding the words between my teeth.

"Fleeting power, if she ever —"

"Her specialty, before she went dark, was binding magic."

Blackwell blanched. "She's figured out how to steal, then retain and utilize different types of magic?"

"Yes. I'm surprised she hasn't come back for you."

Blackwell jutted his chin at me, about to protest, but I cut him off.

"She currently has her hands on a necromancer —"

"Then the necromancer is dead," Blackwell said. His blunt assessment cut into the bubble of hope I was holding for Mory. "She'll need a powerful sorcerer if she's trying to do as you suspect. Not that I could even fathom it being possible to summon vanquished demons even with the power of a necromancer combined with a sorcerer. Not only would the magic be incompatible, but vanquished demons simply no longer exist in this world."

"Can you give us a name?" Kett asked.

"Yes." Blackwell turned away to a writing desk in the corner by the alcove and put pen to parchment.

The power of a sorcerer, a necromancer, and a sacrificial knife all in Sienna's hands. Plus the location of a successful demon summoning …

"My sister is trying to raise vanquished demons," I said. Saying it out loud didn't make it any less ridiculous or unthinkable. Unfortunately, it also didn't make it untrue.

"So it would seem," Kett said.

"You don't have to be so pleased about it," I muttered, trying to find my protective layer of snark even as my heart clenched, then began to race. "Three vanquished demons."

"Yes," Kett said. His smile widened and red rolled across his ice-blue eyes. "And you with a pretty new sword to break in." His eyes flicked to the hilt of my katana slung behind and sitting slightly above my right shoulder.

Yeah, great. Hanging with immortal and often-bored beings was so going to be the death of me.

Chapter Five

Southern Europe, or maybe it was properly called 'Western Europe,' was the territory of the guardian Suanmi, aka the fire breather, aka Drake's actual guardian. Using a portal at a grid point seemed innocuous enough that it wouldn't get Pulou's attention. Using that same portal to try to get into London via another portal almost exclusively used by Suanmi was a very stupid idea.

I had planned to return to the nexus immediately after confronting Blackwell, and from there formulate a plan — based on whatever info I'd managed to get from the sorcerer — to confront Sienna. Now, knowing my sister might be in London with Mory, I felt I needed to press on, plan or no plan. But my twenty-four-hour pass was so going to run out, like in just over twelve hours.

Thankfully, they don't check passports between Scotland and England. Unfortunately, that meant being confined in a vehicle with three other powerful Adepts for seven hours, not including bathroom breaks. I wasn't sure my dowser senses could take it, but our swords would be impossible to conceal on a plane and rather obvious on a train. The idea of Kett confined to a plane forty thousand feet in the air was a whole other level of concern, though he was currently in Scotland and had previously been in Vancouver, so he must fly. Maybe he had access to a private jet exclusively used by vampires.

"We could buy some yoga mats," I said to Kandy as we walked to the edge of the front lawn of Blackness Castle. Kett had disappeared into the dark night, and I could only guess that Blackwell was watching us from another magical window higher up in the central tower.

"Things are super weird if you're jonesing for yoga rather than chocolate," the green-haired werewolf said.

"No, we could wrap our swords —"

"I'm not wrapping my sword in a yoga mat," Drake interrupted. He was as affronted by this suggestion as any easily distractible thirteen-year-old could be.

"Does he even know what yoga is?" Kandy mock whispered.

"Yeah," I said. "Eastern philosophy is highly regarded in dragon training. No mats, though."

I really didn't like standing with my back to Blackness Castle. I really hoped I had guessed correctly that Blackwell couldn't cast anything nasty at us through his own wards. The sorcerer had led us out of the castle without a word, but he was going to be totally pissed when he examined the mangled wards at the front gates.

Drake was balancing on the low stone wall while Kandy and I waited for the vampire to return. That was assuming he was going to return promptly … I never really knew with him. He might fall into one of his fugue states.

"I don't like leaving it like this, but I'm glad to be out of there," Kandy said.

"Same here."

"He is nothing," Drake said. "A speck of darkness in a beautiful world." The fledgling guardian, steady as the wall itself, was practicing one-legged crane kicks now.

"That's very dragon of you, Drake," I said.

The thirteen-year-old grinned at me. "Your cares are interesting to me, warrior's daughter. I'm looking forward to the demons."

"The point is to stop Sienna from raising them. If raising them is even possible in the first place."

Drake shrugged, then pivoted to practice his kicks leading with the opposite leg.

"He doesn't sound like any thirteen-year-old I've ever known," Kandy said. She was watching Drake intently.

"I'm not sure he's ever been around any other fledglings. He's the youngest dragon I've ever seen. I don't think they procreate much." Plus, Drake's mentor — Chi Wen the far seer — was ancient. As in, nine-hundred-plus-years old. The old Asian man loved to smile but he wasn't big on words, play, or the latest trends. I gathered his seer power was rather all consuming.

Kandy's eyes flared green and she darted forward. I had my knife in my hand before I realized what the wolf was doing. She silently aimed a spin kick to the back of Drake's right knee. A breath before she made contact, Drake bounded into the air, tucking both legs up and away from Kandy's blow. Then, twisting in the air, he grabbed her still-outthrust leg and flipped the werewolf — actually, spun her sideways like an airborne top — onto her back on the grass.

I didn't think Drake had access to any of those seer powers yet. But man, sometimes he moved like he did.

The air whooshed out of Kandy's lungs.

"Ha, wolf," Drake said. "I heard you moving. You must learn more stealth."

Bad thing to say to a werewolf. And, judging by his grin, completely intentional on Drake's part.

Kandy snarled and rolled forward to crouch on the balls of her feet. Silent and deadly … just not to the fledgling guardian.

"There's no point, Kandy," I said. "You can't get the upper hand when he's in the zone. Try next time he's eating."

Completely ignoring me, the werewolf launched herself at the fledgling. They flew backward onto the grass beyond the wall, moving, swiping, and kicking in a blur.

Kett pulled up in a luxury silver SUV. Mercedes, maybe. I wasn't big on cars, but I could identify an OPI nail polish color in a single glance.

"Be careful with the werewolf," I yelled over my shoulder at Drake. Kandy would be pissed at me for cautioning Drake, but werewolves weren't immortal — unlike the fledgling guardian's regular wrestling partners. I wandered over to the passenger side of the SUV and climbed in beside Kett. "What took you so long?"

"He wards his garage. Then I had to choose one," the vampire replied mildly. His gaze was on the blurred tussle on the lawn.

"I don't like just leaving," I said. "Stealing an SUV isn't enough."

"I have taken the vehicle because it will be fortified against magic, and will have a better chance of getting us to London without breaking down," Kett replied.

Oh, okay. I was clearly the only one of us still lusting for Blackwell's blood. The fact that the other person in this conversation was a blood-lusting vampire didn't reflect well on my mindset.

"You will have many years to return," Kett continued, turning to regard me in the darkness of the SUV. "You will never need to regret time, alchemist."

"That's verging on philosophical for you."

"Not at all. It is merely a statement of fact."

"Fine. Blackwell can wait. Sienna ... or specifically, Mory can't ... if ..."

"The fledgling necromancer is alive. She wears your necklace. You have now forced me to repeat myself."

"Well, it's bound to happen once every hundred years or so," I snarked. Kett didn't laugh but that wasn't unusual. "Still, Sienna might have found a way —"

"Eventually, yes. But your sister is busy. Hiding from the witches and the shapeshifters is no easy task. She is lucky that the Adept are so secretive. I imagine no one has even thought to inform the sorcerers of London to be on watch."

The SUV dipped as Drake climbed into the back seat behind Kett. "I like the wolf," he declared.

Kandy climbed into the back seat beside Drake, behind me. Her eyes were still blazing with the green of her shifter magic.

"Of course you do," I replied to Drake. "She wishes she was thirteen too." The fledgling and werewolf were covered in mud and had mats of grass in their hair. I was rather gleeful about what this mess would do to the interior of Blackwell's pristine vehicle.

"I hated being thirteen," Kandy said, and then didn't bother to explain further. The werewolf had retrieved a bag from somewhere and was digging through it for a change of clothes. "We're going to need some food."

Kett scoffed and put the SUV into gear.

"I'm surprised you're coming with us, vampire," Kandy continued. "The castle seemed like your idea of Disneyland."

Kett didn't bother answering as he turned the vehicle toward the main road.

"I've been to Disneyland," Drake declared. "It wasn't all that."

"You have not been to Disneyland," Kandy said.

"Haoxin took me, last year. Right after she ascended. That way, Suanmi would have a more difficult time punishing her."

"I have no idea what you're talking about."

Haoxin was the cute-as-a-button, swathed-in-silk guardian of North America. She was also the guardian nearest to Drake in age, if a hundred-year spread counted as near.

"Listen, wolf," Drake said, channeling the tone of the far seer, "and you will hear many —"

Kandy punched Drake in the gut, then groaned while shaking out her hand. Drake started giggling.

I tuned them out.

The dashboard clock declared the time to be 2:23. It was pitch dark, and I wondered if the no-driving-at-night-with-the-interior-lights-on applied to vampires. Or if that was just for the oncoming traffic. Either way, I was glad for any feeble excuse to not read Blackwell's *Book of Demon History*. Though not as glad as for whatever cellphone package the witch, Amber, had prepaid on my new phone. I had signal. So I made some calls. Mom and Gran first. They'd want an update, and someone needed to know we were heading into London.

Traveling with Drake in an SUV was difficult. I figured out pretty quickly that the thirteen-year-old was unaccustomed to being confined and motionless for long periods of time.

Even with Kett speeding like a demon between towns, we weren't going to get to London very quickly.

The vampire didn't seem to have an issue with driving on the left side of the road. 'Speeding like a demon ...' Where did that phrase even come from? Were demons particularly speedy? And what human would survive an encounter with one and live to coin the phrase?

Food, and more wrestling sessions with Kandy at each gas station we stopped at, finally lulled Drake to sleep. He wanted to spar with me, but I was fairly certain that swords would attract way too much attention. Getting a too-large, bright green hoodie onto Drake the first time we stopped was enough of a battle that I worried the station attendant might start texting or tweeting about us. The hoodie covered his laced leather vest, if not the pants. I opted for a navy hoodie emblazoned with a red plaid lion rampant — that was according to Kett on the 'rampant' part. Drake's hoodie had the image of a sword in place of the 'T' in 'SCOTLAND' printed across the chest, and I was fairly certain that was the only reason he eventually agreed to wear it.

The sun rose, though we were clearly driving into an overcast day, and I begrudgingly hauled out the demon history book. Kandy and Drake were snoozing in the back. Kett donned dark sunglasses despite the fact that the SUV windows were tinted.

"We have no idea if we've even guessed correctly," I muttered as I read through the entry that accompanied the sketch of the sacrificial knife. Kandy and Scarlett had confirmed that the knife had been in Sienna's hands the last time they saw it. "She could be in Bora Bora. And if Mory's ... alive ... how did Sienna get her to London?"

"It's a logical leap," Kett answered. "She had the knife and a necromancer. Why steal the book? Out of everything in Blackwell's collection, why steal that book unless she intended to do something with it?"

"Sienna doesn't think things like this through ahead of time," I said. "Maybe she was just borrowing the book to read it, and then got her hands on the knife. Do demons even have shades or ghosts? Can Mory communicate with a being destroyed over a hundred and twenty-five years ago?"

"With the sacrificial knife to anchor the magic, and the power of a sorcerer drained ... perhaps," Kett answered.

I'd tried the phone numbers Blackwell had given us — three names in total that he deemed powerful enough to fulfill Sienna's requirements — but hadn't gotten answers or voice mails. Of course, it was rather early in the morning.

"So, the summoning," I said, referencing the book. "According to this story —"

"Chronicle."

"Fine, chronicle. The summoning took place in the White Chapel district."

"Similar timing to when the Jack the Ripper killers hunted there — perfect cover for the sorcerer."

"Blackwell's ancestor. Evil runs in the family."

Kett didn't respond. His definition of evil was far different from mine. In fact, I wasn't sure he bothered to define such things anymore.

"Jesus, the stupid sorcerer who wrote this included the incantation."

"Even if he uncovered an accurate accounting, the exact words have little meaning."

"Still. It's a focal point."

Kett shrugged. Yeah, it definitely irked me that immortal beings rarely seemed concerned when it came to magic.

"Killers?" I asked, backtracking to his previous comment. "Why say killers?"

"At least three of the murders were a rogue vampire who took glee in not hiding his kills. It was reckless and undignified."

"Reckless because it drew your attention?"

Kett smiled but didn't answer. I knew he was referred to as 'the executioner.' I knew he investigated — or, rather, judged — vampire crimes, which were pretty much limited to the don't-be-messy-with-food classification. What I didn't know was how old Kett was and how long he'd been the executioner for the Conclave — the governing body of the vampires. He was cagey about his age like some guys were about how many people they'd slept with, as if the number was so large it might scare off any serious relationship potential. For the human male, not the vampire. I had no idea why the vampire shared what and when he did.

"How many people did Jack the Ripper kill?" I asked.

"Eleven if you count them all. Five are usually agreed upon."

"But three were vampire kills?"

"Yes."

"And at least one …" — I referenced the book that sat open on my lap — "… on November 9, 1888, was the sorcerer's doing."

"According to a book written by sorcerers."

"Right."

"There was also the human the authorities referred to as the Torso Killer, who was active at the same time as the Ripper."

"Oh my God, stop talking. I don't need to know."

Kett laughed, a sound that was becoming a more regular occurrence for the vampire. Maybe I was humanizing him … and maybe that thought was a slippery slope.

"November 9th," I said. "What day is today?"

"The morning of the eighth."

"Would the connection — if any of this is actually possible — be stronger on the anniversary?"

Kett shrugged, but even before he did so, I knew I was asking the wrong questions. "Whether or not this can be done doesn't matter."

"No."

Because all that mattered was what Sienna wanted to attempt and what she would do to make her desires come true. It was a game. An accumulation of power, but to no end. Just for fun. Sienna wasn't in it for the long term. She never had been.

"She expects to be caught."

"Of course," Kett answered, never taking his eyes off the highway in front of us. As the morning dawned and we had neared the border of England, the traffic had increased. Kett was only able to speed like a half-demon now, which was ironic for multiple reasons I didn't have the brainpower to address at the moment. Such as, supposedly vampires had been created from demons, "by God," according to Kett. Yeah, I was still full-on ignoring that tidbit.

"Why do it then? Why do any of it?"

"To see what she can do." Kett's cool but matter-of-fact statement actually made me shiver.

"What she can destroy."

"Or who." Kett turned and looked at me then. I couldn't see his eyes through his sunglasses.

"She loves … loved me," I whispered. The words sounded weak and hollow coming from my mouth.

"Perhaps," Kett said. He returned his attention to driving.

I felt like crying, but I forced the feeling into the dark place in my heart where I stored all things Sienna now. I couldn't even remember the sound of her laugh, or the secrets we'd whispered to each other, or the life we'd shared. It was all mixed into the remembrance of the gritty, sour taste of her corrupted magic, and the black veins that etched her face.

I took comfort in the taste of the magic of the trio that surrounded me, closed the book and my eyes, and tried to sleep.

I'd never been to London, England. Actually, I'd never been out of North America. As we hit the traffic of the city, the crazily narrow streets, and the confusing street signs, I instantly wished I was home, cupcake in hand and trinket in the making.

London was insanely large. True, the biggest city I'd ever been to was Los Angeles, and that sprawled for miles. But London was huge and full — full of people, buildings, overpasses and roundabouts, and shops. Lots of shops.

This ... this was utter chaos. In a human way, though — not in a blood-and-magical-mayhem way. That was entirely different, and actually — sickeningly — not as overwhelming as it once had been.

Drake, of course, was unimpressed. It was his second visit after all.

I'd pulled out the iPad and hot-spotted it to my phone at Kett's request. Google Maps guided us effortlessly — avoiding one-way streets but not the bumper-to-bumper — into the heart of London.

At least that's what it looked like on the map. I actually had no idea where we were.

"Was that ... was that London Bridge?" I asked.

"We're looking for Waterloo," Kett answered.

"What? No. I mean, I didn't know it was an actual thing ... you ... know ..." I shut my mouth and pointed the way to Waterloo Bridge.

We crossed the bridge and miraculously didn't get caught endlessly in the traffic circle on the other side. I was seriously glad that Kett was driving.

Without further direction from me, the vampire made a left and then two right turns. He slowed the SUV as we came up to a grand building, stone-tiled in cream. It ran the length — and, I assumed, width — of the city block, and was constructed with columns and everything.

"Um, the sorcerer we're looking for lives in a palace?" I asked.

"It's a university. A college actually," Kett answered. "Blackwell was unsure of where his colleague resides, but you should be able to find him before class."

"The great and powerful sorcerer we have to protect from Sienna is a student?"

"A professor in biomedical sciences."

Okay, I was aware that I was only sounding more and more stupid every time I opened my mouth, but I was baffled by the idea of a sorcerer also being a professor. Call me prejudiced, I guess. I stared at Kett.

He raised a pale eyebrow at me. "Forensic analytical sciences," he elaborated. "He and I have met previously. It's best if you go on alone."

Kandy chortled in the back seat. All vampires had a long list of enemies. I wasn't sure they bothered to keep any other lists, actually.

"I'm sorry. You want me to waltz into a massive college, find some sorcerer, and convince him that a black witch might show up and try to drain him? Why the hell should he believe me?"

Kett smiled. "Use Blackwell's name. And Jade, the sorcerer will get one look at you and buy anything you're selling."

Kandy snorted and climbed out of the SUV. The noise of the city filled and rebounded around the cab. I'd never known I'd be so sensitive to such things.

"I'll need to announce our presence in the city to the Conclave elder who resides here in London," Kett said. "The fledgling guardian may come with me."

"Excuse me?" I asked. "I might be dim but I'm not that stupid. Drake doesn't need to be in on any elder vampire meetings —"

"As you wish." Kett turned away from me to stare out the front windshield, and I briefly thought I might have hurt his feelings ... like he had feelings.

"College professor sounds boring," Drake said. "Vampire elder sounds much more interesting."

"Exactly," I said. "Get out."

Drake laughed and climbed out of the SUV.

"I guess we'll have to leave our swords here," I murmured. I hesitated as Drake stepped away, and wondered if I should attempt to repair the obvious breach between Kett and me.

"You'll have your knife ... as well as your werewolf and your dragon."

Yeah, Kett was pissed, but what the hell? I was already in so much trouble — or so I imagined — because Drake was tagging along with me in the first place. I didn't need to ask for more. I maybe had minutes left on my twenty-four-hour pass. Even though time moved differently in the nexus, Branson was sure to notice when Drake and I didn't show up for training. I just hoped the sword master went to my father, Yazi, with news of our escapade, because I really didn't want to face Suanmi.

"What does he ..." — I consulted Blackwell's list — "... what does Edmonds look like?"

"You'll taste his magic before you see him."

"Fine." I climbed out of the SUV. Kett pulled away before I'd managed to slam the door shut — yeah, like the brat I was. If I'd been human, that maneuver might have broken my wrist. Pissy vampire. I wasn't accustomed to him being quite so volatile.

Kandy turned around from surveying the building and campus. "King's College has one of the largest zebrafish facilities in the world," she said. "This is the Waterloo Campus, but they have a bunch of campuses in London."

I stared at her.

"You're not the only one with a web browser on her phone," Kandy said with a grin.

"Let's go there first," Drake said. "I've never seen a zebrafish."

This was just a grand vacation for everyone but me ... and the pissy vampire. Kett didn't seem to like London at all, because there was no way I was capable of rousing his iciness that much on my own. If I had any sense at all, that should have scared the hell out of me.

Chapter Six

"Professor Edmonds?" I rapped my knuckles lightly on the partially open door that helpfully bore a plaque reading 'T.R. Edmonds.' Of course, as Kett had snottily suggested, I'd tasted the sorcerer's magic all the way from the stairwell to the third floor.

A man about forty-five years old looked up from his computer and squinted at me through round tortoiseshell glasses. His wool jacket actually had suede elbow patches.

"Yes? What can I ..." Edmonds removed his reading glasses to get a better look at me, but it wasn't my blond curls or ample assets that snagged this extra attention. Nope, the sorcerer had eyes only for my magic.

Dropping all the professor pretense, Edmonds stared at me — open mouth and everything — and then smiled as if I was a perfectly wrapped birthday present. And maybe I was. Just not for him.

Impatient as always, Drake stepped around me and into the small office, which was barely large enough to contain a sofa in one corner and a desk with two guest chairs in the other.

Edmonds lost the smile. He rose almost reverently and stared at Drake. His hands were palms down, flat on his desk. His shoulders slumped slightly forward. Yeah, Drake was the eighth wonder of the world.

Sure the fledgling's magic — all honeyed, salted almonds and steamed milk — was impressive. But once you'd laid eyes on a full guardian like my father Yazi, or the treasure keeper Pulou, it was easier to take Drake's magic in stride.

Kandy gave me a shove with her shoulder to nudge me out of the way of the door, which she then closed behind her.

Edmonds tore his eyes away from Drake, who was rather rudely ignoring the professor to examine the bookcase, then looked back at the werewolf and me. He reached for something on his desk that looked like a carved dowel of dark wood, but before he could close his fingers over it, Drake was holding it.

"Oh!" Drake said. "A wand!"

Edmonds stumbled away from his desk. He hit the back of his head against one of the diplomas hanging behind him, hard enough to crack the glass and dislodge it from its hanger.

Drake — once again moving too quickly to track — caught the picture before it hit the floor.

Edmonds now began gasping like he might be having a stroke.

"Drake," I cried. "Stop doing that!"

"What? Being nice?"

"Snatching things out of the air."

"Oh, sorry." Drake looked at Edmonds, who now seemed calm enough to at least take air into his lungs. "Sorry, sorcerer."

Drake placed the diploma and the wooden dowel back on the desk. Then with over-exaggerated slowness, he walked around and back to my side.

Kandy snickered. I sighed.

"I apologize, professor," I said. "We didn't mean to startle you."

"No. No. I — I —" Edmonds loosened his bow tie.

I guessed the professor getup and gig were cover. Too bad Edmonds didn't seem to have the Indiana Jones alter ego to pull it off.

"My name is Jade Godfrey. These are my friends, Kandy and Drake."

Edmonds nodded but once again fell into staring at Drake. I wondered if I ever looked that ... well, that moronic when I saw or tasted new magic.

"Blackwell gave us —"

Edmonds darted for the dowel. Runes carved along it flared at his touch. Drake shifted, probably to snatch the wand again, but I simply held my hand forward, palm facing the sorcerer.

"We're only here to ask you some questions about a witch, my sister Sienna, who we believe is in London."

Edmonds narrowed his light brown eyes at me. More magic bloomed in the wand. It was a fairly cool way to harness his sorcerer powers, but kind of silly looking.

"Probably not a good idea to grab the wand again," I said, clearly and deliberately addressing Drake. "It might sting you."

Drake tilted his head to look at the wand for a second. "I doubt it."

The fledgling guardian's nonchalance didn't help Edmonds calm down.

"We aren't here from Blackwell —"

"And you aren't a witch," Edmonds said. He wasn't completely sure where to point the wand. Three of us against one runed stick. Even if he could cast three spells at once — which I seriously doubted — he wouldn't even make it to the door of his narrow office without one of us laying hands on him. Unless he managed to kill us. Dragons were as immortal as a being could get

— even more so than vampires in my mind. If it wasn't for Drake's parents being dead, and the obvious limp that kept Branson as a trainer rather than a guardian, I would have thought them to be utterly indestructible. I, however, was a half-witch, and therefore not immortal at all.

"Whether I'm a witch —"

"You said you were looking for a witch, your sister. Therefore you'd have to be a witch, but your magic isn't like any witch I've ever known."

"I have a rare dowsing ability."

"You're one of Blackwell's collectors." Edmonds spat the other sorcerer's name like he didn't even want the memory of saying it in his mouth.

"I'm not," I replied as calmly as possible, though being thought of as Blackwell's chattel rankled me. "I'm simply Jade Godfrey, granddaughter of Pearl, chair of the Convocation. I bake cupcakes for a living."

This admission only deepened Edmonds' frown. "I'm not the Adept liaison in London."

"We have questions and perhaps a caution, nothing more. Our presence in the city will be brief, hopefully, and another of our group is making sure we're welcome." At least, I really hoped that was what Kett was doing.

Edmonds lowered the wand and sat. He kept it in hand, though. He straightened his bow tie and smoothed his hair, which was starting to recede. "Blackwell," he said, "is not a name to evoke lightly."

"You give the sorcerer far too much power with your deference," Drake said. His gruff tone was so unlike a thirteen-year-old that I had to stifle a laugh. Kandy snorted.

The sorcerer shook his head at our indifference. "He's an outlier, as his family has always been. But more so for the last decade."

"And yet," I said, "when asked to provide a list of sorcerers powerful enough to draw the attention of a blood magic-crazed witch, he gave yours at the top of a list of three."

Edmonds nodded but didn't seem to soften on Blackwell. Which was fine with me, as I certainly wasn't a fan either. "This witch is your sister?"

"Yes."

"My condolences. Witches have a more difficult time holding the blood lust at bay. Sorcerers are naturally distanced from its consuming effects." Edmonds thoughtfully rolled the wand beneath his fingers on the desk.

"That makes sense," I said.

Edmonds inclined his head. He was still having a difficult time keeping his eyes from Drake, who'd pulled some books off the shelf and seemed to be glaring at the words rather than reading them.

I sat in one of the two guest chairs. Kandy leaned against the door, always the protector.

I could tell that Edmonds desperately wanted to ask about Drake but wasn't going to. All of the Adept were secretive, which was probably a safe default position when outnumbered by human kind, like a million to one. But also, most Adept seemed to think that asking for information and receiving it put them under an obligation. Thankfully, I'd decided that was an antiquated belief — when it suited me.

I pulled the leather-bound book of demon history out of my satchel.

Edmonds' eyes lit up as I placed the book before him on the desk. "Not the original, I'm afraid," I said.

"Ah, that is a shame."

I opened the book to the entry that chronicled the demon rising in London in 1888. "Professor, have you been visited by a witch — she might call herself Valencia — in the last three months?"

Edmonds stilled. The hand not toying with the wand was already halfway across the desk. He wanted to touch the book. He probably also wanted to know what this visit was all about, but he didn't want to give up any information if he could get around it. As I was quickly figuring out, and as Gran had always cautioned me, this was typical sorcerer behavior.

"This witch is interested in demon history?" he asked.

I smiled. Edmonds wanted more information before giving any himself, but I wasn't in the mood for Adept games. The only times I really liked to play were on the dance floor, in my bakery, and in bed. Unfortunately for me, none of those locations were likely to be anywhere in my immediate future.

I leaned forward. My necklace dangled slightly away from my chest in this position, and it immediately caught Edmonds' attention. "I'm not here to trade information or bargain for power," I said, keeping my tone even and polite. "I would prefer to be in my bakery making cupcakes in Vancouver, BC, Canada. Instead, I'm in England hunting my sister, who is killing Adept to drain and harness their powers. She has kidnapped, and most likely killed, a young girl. A necromancer who was under my protection. It is my understanding that she has this original book and this knife ..." — I tapped the sketch of the weapon in the book — "... in her possession. Now you know everything I know. Have you seen or spoken to my sister?"

"No," Edmonds answered in a rush of air. "I apologize. I just ... you ..." He glanced at Drake, who was now sitting cross-legged in the middle of the floor and rapidly flipping the pages of a book on his lap. "You startled me and ..."

"Let's move past that."

Edmonds nodded. I pushed the book toward him. He touched its edges carefully, then rotated it so the text was right side up for him.

"You think because she has the knife and the book that she is interested in this demon summoning?" The sorcerer reached for his glasses and started to read the pages I'd indicated.

"It's the only clue right now," I answered. "I could be wrong. I often am."

"As we all are."

"Why can't I read this?" Drake asked, slapping the book he'd been glaring at closed with a boom.

"It's in German," Edmonds answered, unruffled by the outburst.

"I should be able to read German," Drake declared.

"Obviously not," Kandy said with a smirk.

Drake narrowed his eyes at the green-haired werewolf. Then, apparently up for the challenge, he reopened the book.

Edmonds flipped a page of the demon history to confirm he'd finished the entry, then flipped back to read it a second time. "I've heard of this story," he said. "Supposedly the unfortunate murdered woman was one of Jack the Ripper's victims."

"Supposedly?"

"Most sorcerers aren't so careless with a victim's remains. My understanding is that the Ripper murder of November 9th was particularly brutal. The crime ... unnecessarily violent."

"To raise three demons?"

"To supposedly raise three ..." — he referenced the book — "... of the lesser fallen. The author of this history uses Christian classification."

"Because he believed that demons were born from fallen angels."

"Or are the fallen angels themselves."

"That belief doesn't negate the possibility that three demons rose from a sacrifice performed with that knife. A knife now in the possession of my sister."

"Witches do not usually —"

"She's gotten a taste for it."

Edmonds fell silent. Kandy pulled out her phone and started texting. Drake was attempting to sound out words with a German accent.

"You don't believe in demons," I said, figuring out that his resistance wasn't just the inherent reluctance of a sorcerer to share information with a witch.

"They're a construct. A way of justifying the great evil man is capable of."

I nodded. I wondered if Edmonds — a sorcerer that Blackwell had identified as powerful enough to draw Sienna's attention — would be capable of raising a demon, or if his disbelief of this aspect of magic would cause such a spell to misfire. Magic was all about intention.

Edmonds rotated the book back toward me and pointed at the second picture in the entry. This was a depiction of the three demons raised that evening in 1888. Squat, scaled beasts with flat faces and broad shoulders, they were somewhat reminiscent of the guardian lions that were a constant motif in dragon decor, but without the manes. The professor tapped the page. "You've seen such as these?"

"No."

"But you've seen something you call a demon. Manifested by Blackwell?"

Now that was a loaded question. I wasn't sure how the sorcerers governed themselves, or what their version of the witches Convocation was. I also wasn't sure if Blackwell was a member of this governing body or if raising demons was a no-no for sorcerers. I imagined it probably was, just like blood magic was for witches.

Now … did I want to get Blackwell in hot water? Hell, yes. But could I afford to get the asshole in deep shit before I managed to neutralize Sienna? No. And yes, I was now thinking of 'murdering my sister' as 'neutralizing' in my head.

I looked at Edmonds, who'd already indicated he wasn't the London liaison for visiting Adept. I opened my dowser senses and tasted his magic more thoroughly. He shared the base earthy sorcerer quality that Blackwell had, but it was more like wild mushroom risotto with mild sausage than deep cabernet. Blackwell could kick his ass.

I smiled, and started to speak, just as something slammed into and took the hinges off the door behind me. The door canted sideways and crashed onto the sofa.

I swiveled, my knife instantly in my hand, to see a six-foot-four-inch light-blond werewolf blocking the door with his arms askew. Kandy, who'd been thrown forward at his dramatic entrance, held up one hand toward me and one hand toward the werewolf at the door. She had placed herself between the newcomer and Drake, who — miraculously — was just peering around her legs rather than tackling the intruder.

The male wolf lifted his chin and scented the air. The green of his magic rolled across his eyes.

"Control yourself," Kandy snapped.

Some of the alertness eased from the blond wolf's stance.

"May I help you?" Edmonds asked. He'd jumped to his feet and was now casually twirling his wand between his fingers.

I slipped my knife back into its invisible sheath and hoped no one had noticed me pull it out. I was really glad I hadn't accidentally stabbed the werewolf. I was jumpy.

The newcomer looked startled, as if he hadn't seen anyone but Kandy in the room. Then he flushed. "Excuse me," he said. His accent was full of rounded, musical vowels. Nordic, I guessed, which explained the height and the hair color — neither were typically British as far as I'd seen. "I … I —"

"It's me," Kandy said. She didn't sound too pleased. "I'm … I must be … ovulating." She spat out the final word like it was the bane of her existence.

The Nordic wolf flushed even deeper red and stuffed his hands in his pockets.

"Oh," I said, because something had to be said and I had no idea what to say.

"I'll … I'll fix the door," the blond werewolf stuttered. "Of course. I'm so sorry —"

"Maintenance will fix the door," Edmonds said. He returned to his seat and his perusing of the book.

"I'm Drake," the fledgling guardian said, as if nothing odd was in the process of occurring.

"I'm Jorgen. Nice to meet you," the Nordic werewolf said. Then he looked hopefully at Kandy.

"I'm not going to breed with you," she said, then rounded on me. "Some warning would have been nice."

"I was confined in a small room with you. And he moves quickly."

Jorgen smiled broadly. "I do. Fastest in the pack."

"No one cares," Kandy said.

"You are American," he said. He was completely unruffled by her aggression.

"I'm not interested," she answered.

His smile widened. I could feel his magic gathering around him.

"She really isn't," I said, to be supportive. "You're not her type —"

"How would you know?" Kandy snarled.

I threw my hands up in the air. Apparently there was some sort of werewolf game going on here that I didn't understand.

"Give me your number," Kandy said as she handed her phone to Jorgen. "Then go away."

He — still smiling — punched his number into her phone. "Nice to meet you," he said to the rest of us. He then backed out of the office, awkwardly pulling the broken door behind him and keeping his eyes on Kandy until the very last moment.

The green-haired werewolf glared at him with her arms crossed, then she rounded on me. "Well?" she prompted. "Demons exist. We saw one raised. A pack mate of mine was sacrificed with that knife. It looked like the devil with four horns and huge fucking feet."

The sorcerer's jaw dropped.

"I cut off its horn," Drake added helpfully. He jumped up to replace the book on the shelf, then crossed to peer down at the chronicle open on the desk.

"You did not," Kandy said.

"I'm sorry," I interrupted. "I get that the demon is important and everything, but who the hell was that guy?"

"Footballer," Edmonds answered.

"Some wolf," Kandy said dismissively.

"He didn't look like a football player."

"Soccer," Edmonds said.

"Right."

"The demon?" Edmonds then prompted.

"Here's the thing, professor," I said. "We think we might only have one day, and I'd love to chat about demons and such with you ..." — yeah, that was an utter lie — "... but we're on a schedule."

"I see. November 9th. Dates are important to your sister?"

I shrugged. "Magic is intention."

"Not exactly," Edmonds said. "These demons — if you believe in such things, and particularly in this story — have been summoned and vanquished. They cannot be raised again. In fact, some historians would argue that the location itself is closed. That the spot between the underworld and the mortal world was weak enough —"

"If you believe demons to be fallen angels or to rise from hell, sure," I said.

"And what do you believe, Jade Godfrey?"

I smiled and dodged the question. "What we're trying to figure out is what my sister believes, and whether or not she has allies or accomplices in London. Whether she's here at all actually, and what she's planning to do."

Edmonds nodded.

I closed the demon history book. He wasn't the sorcerer we were looking for. "Thank you for your time."

"Wait," he said. "The other two names that Blackwell gave you. Perhaps I can help you locate them?"

Yeah, sure. I was starting to figure out why so many of the Adept were so cagey all the time. Edmonds could totally want to honestly help. Or he could be collecting information on fellow sorcerers who Blackwell felt were capable of raising a demon, and who therefore had the power Sienna might be seeking.

Edmonds smiled at me. I was pretty transparent. He pulled a pad of sticky notes out of his desk and jotted down two names and phone numbers.

"That isn't a book of power," he said as he wrote. "The book itself wouldn't be an aid to a witch, even one who is blood crazed."

"I know."

"Yes, I see that you do." He handed me the sticky note.

"Perhaps these names will be duplicates, and perhaps they will just be extra. I'll call to let them know you spoke to me."

"Thank you." I stood, leaned over, wrote my cell number on a blank sticky note, then passed the pad back to him.

Kandy propped open the busted door, then she and Drake stepped into the hall. They moved together as if in some sort of collusion, which was worrisome. It was weird that I noticed, though. Branson had been berating me about 'being aware' for three months. I guess it was sinking in.

I stepped back toward Edmonds only to find that he'd approached without me realizing, so that I nearly bumped into him. I took a step back when he didn't, then said quietly, "Is it common knowledge that you don't believe in demons?"

"I would have thought so."

"Let me just warn you, then. Sienna won't be difficult to miss. She can't possibly sneak up on you, but I wouldn't stop for a chat."

Edmonds twisted his lips in a smirk that looked ill-placed on his face.

"Please," I practically begged, discovering that I liked this man despite the fact he was a sorcerer. "I understand that no sorcerer thinks a witch could best them. But Sienna had a rather lackluster talent that she's somehow made formidable and deadly."

Edmonds nodded. "I'll keep an eye out."

"And mention it to your ... Guild?" I guessed at the name of the sorcerers' version of the witches' Convocation. He didn't correct me. But then he wouldn't just give that information away.

"If you wish."

"I do. You know how to text, don't you?"

"Do I know how to ... how old do you think I am?"

"Pretty old."

"Ouch. I thought Canadians were infinitely polite."

"Well, I've been hanging out with the wrong sort."

Edmonds' gaze flicked over my shoulder, undoubtedly to Drake. I could see every question written across his face. I wondered what sort of Adept the sorcerer thought Drake was. I didn't know if sorcerers could qualify magic or just sense power. Drake was a lot of sheer power.

"Zebrafish?" the fledgling guardian asked hopefully.

I glanced at the sticky note in my hand.

"Surely you have a few minutes. It's an impressive facility," Edmonds coaxed.

"Thank you, professor," I said.

"Any time, Jade Godfrey, granddaughter of Pearl, Convocation chair, and baker of cupcakes. I hope we meet again."

I nodded and turned away down the corridor. I felt badly about not shaking his hand, but the Adept weren't all over casual contact.

"Are we going to be accosted by any more ruggedly male werewolves?" I asked Kandy as she matched my stride.

"Very funny coming from someone screwing around with an alpha," she said.

"Three months ago."

Kandy snorted.

"Just heavy petting."

"Uh huh."

"But not again. The life debt bond thing bothers me."

"You'll get over it."

"Heavy petting what?" Drake asked. "Sex, you mean?"

"I thought you wanted to see zebrafish, Drake." I suddenly wished I had a cookie with which to distract him. I'd become way too comfortable with all the Adept in my life, so my guard was low and my tongue loose. But I really didn't know how to be any other way.

A text message from Kett informed me that I was to meet him outside the building at the southeast corner of Stamford Street and Cornwall Road. Yeah, I was in London for the first time in my life. I wasn't sure how to get out of the building, let alone which way was southeast.

However, I did the mature thing and texted back.

On our way.

I figured I could pick up the vampire's magic on the street … or try to access our life debt bond. Except he'd feel that on his end, and I wasn't sure how he might respond.

Drake had surged ahead of us down the hall. He moved with a confidence a thirteen-year-old wouldn't normally display, as if he owned everything around him even as he was experiencing it for the first time.

Kandy was texting with someone, probably updating Desmond. How had the world functioned before cellphones? Crises must have come and gone without anyone knowing.

"Is it always like that?" I asked Kandy. "With wolves? Does that ovulating thing happen often?" My head was all over the place, and not just today.

"No," Kandy answered. "When you first join a pack, maybe. Or infringe on a new territory."

"For you?"

"First time. Unless they're of the same rank, most wolves see me as the alpha's enforcer, and that's fine with me. I don't want to play their games anyway."

"And … it's not like you're interested in that."

"In what, mating?"

"Yeah."

"You think I never want to have kids?"

"No … I mean, not with a guy."

Kandy bared her teeth at me in that nonsmile of hers. The one that informed me I was about to cross some line and she'd be glad to put me back in my place.

"I thought … I mean …" Okay, I was confused.

Kandy let me off the hook, sort of. "Just because I like human girls doesn't mean I'd choose to mate with a female werewolf. God, no." Kandy shuddered. "Can you imagine?"

I couldn't, but I had an idea my reasons were different than Kandy's. "I just meant that visceral connection. Have you … is that what it's always like for a shapeshifter?"

Kandy stopped walking. I continued a few steps, then awkwardly turned back. The green-haired werewolf stood with her arms crossed, glowering at me from the middle of the hall.

"I told you he wouldn't marry you," Kandy said.

I sighed. "And I told you I wasn't interested in marriage."

Kandy cocked her head to one side and waited. I glanced over to Drake, who had managed to lead us back to the front entrance. He was eyeing an art installation in a way that was making me nervous.

"Fine," I said. "I get that sex can be — should be — fun. That it doesn't have to be about love and marriage, but … God, I feel so freaking shallow even having this conversation right now —"

"Just get it out. Then it won't haunt you so much."

"Won't it?"

Kandy offered me a sad twist of a smile. "You know what I meant."

"Yeah, it's hard to keep all the emotions separate. Before I knew who I was — biologically I mean, because I sure as hell don't know who I actually am yet —"

"That's easy. You're Jade. You're cupcakes, trinkets, and deadly magic. Like that knife you carry. Pretty green stone, tasty magic, and deadly."

I smiled. "Well, thanks for sorting that for me."

"Any time." Kandy laughed and I felt blessed by the rare sound. Sure, she snorted and sneered a lot, but a full laugh was unusual.

"Desmond is going to find that connection with another shapeshifter someday, and I'll just sit there and watch him be blown away. If he's even talking to me after three months of silence."

Kandy shrugged. "Cats are different than wolves."

"It's the magic of it. The chemical reaction. Some humans think that's all love is, chemicals mixing perfectly."

Kandy nodded. I glanced back at Drake just as he reached for the first steel crossbeam of the installation.

"Drake!" I yelled.

He snatched his arms back to his sides. "What?" he asked, perfectly nonchalant.

"Don't climb art," I said, closing the distance between us.

"Is that what this is?" The fledgling dragon stared at the installation again.

"Yeah ... I think it's a fish."

"A zebrafish?"

"There's a plaque right there," Kandy said. "Or can't you read English now?"

"Kett's waiting," I said as I stepped between the werewolf and the fledgling. Drake was grinning at Kandy like he was microseconds away from seeing how far he could toss her.

"I know, I saw him circle the block twice already." Drake reached over my shoulder and tagged Kandy on the forehead with a flick of his finger. "Front seat!" he yelled, and then he took off for the doors.

"Shotgun!" Kandy yelled after him. "You're supposed to call 'shotgun'!"

Drake laughed, managing to not kill any students as he exited the building.

"He can't sit in the front seat," I said, slowly moving after him. "That's way too close to the engine."

"Hey," Kandy said. "Aren't I supposed to get chocolate if you're going to force girly talk on me?"

"I'll buy," I answered, crossing my heart with my index finger. "Your choice, ASAP."

"I'll use my Google-fu while you compare lists with the vampire and find another sorcerer for us to freak out."

I laughed. "Good plan."

Jorgen, the Nordic werewolf, was waiting for Kandy on the steps to the street. His back stiffened and he plucked the earbuds from his ears when we were ten steps away from him. He turned and grinned at Kandy.

She glowered at him in return. His grin widened. And then, to my surprise, Kandy smiled back at him.

"Hi," he said.

"Hi," she answered.

My heart pinched, right in that sore spot I'd been carrying for Sienna for over six months now. I pivoted away, crossing diagonally toward Drake where he leaned against a brick planter at the base of the stairs.

"See you later?" I heard Jorgen ask behind me.

"Maybe," Kandy answered. Then she jogged a few steps to catch up with me.

"That was a quick mating dance," I muttered.

"Nah, the dance hasn't started yet." Kandy actually sounded cheerful.

Kett, in a completely new, pristinely white luxury SUV, pulled past us on the street. We hopped into the vehicle while it was still rolling. Did Bentley or Rolls Royce make an SUV? If so, this was one of those. Even I could see the difference an extra hundred thousand dollars made. I felt bad placing my feet anywhere near the floor mat. Who would be insane enough to spend this sort of money on a car? Right, an elder vampire.

I settled into the passenger seat beside Kett — I'd shouldered Drake away from the front — and glanced over at the vampire. He looked pale. He shouldn't look pale, because he was always pale. More pale was a bad sign.

"Everything cool?" I asked him as we pulled into traffic.

He nodded but didn't look at me. The edge of the neck of his sweater was twisted, and I reached over to smooth it without thinking. It was stretched actually, the delicate cashmere fibers torn in places.

Kett snatched my hand away from his neck, crushing my fingers in his grip. He glared at me, red whirling in his eyes. The SUV lurched into the other lane, and a squeal of wheels indicated we'd narrowly missed being hit from the side.

"You're going to break my fingers," I whispered, trying to not wince from the pain of him grinding the small bones of my hand against each other.

He released my hand and returned his attention to the road.

"Touchy, touchy, vamp," Kandy said from the back seat. Her warning was obvious. She took her protection duties seriously.

"We got two more names from Edmonds, but he hasn't seen Sienna," I said. My even tone sounded forced as I pulled Blackwell's list from my satchel and compared it to the sorcerer's sticky note. "Same names."

"We'll head to the bookstore as planned, then." Kett's remoteness sounded perfectly natural.

Kandy and Drake started digging through some brown paper bags they'd found in the back hatch area. Kett had gone grocery shopping.

"You need to feed," I whispered to Kett without looking at him.

"Are you offering?" He snapped the question back at me, full of anger and indignation.

"No. I —"

"Then it's none of your business."

Drake passed an apple over my shoulder and I gladly took it. It was cold, as if it had been in a refrigerator. I pressed it against my cheek and stared out my window as the city of London creeped by. Kett didn't speak further, didn't ask for directions. I didn't make any more observations.

I'd always had a hard time keeping or finding friends, except Sienna. I didn't like acknowledging that hard spot lodged in my heart. And the fact that the spot was still there after all Sienna had done told me so much about myself that I didn't want to know. That I was stupid, and slow, and loyal to a fault.

Just like I was being stupid about how the vampire's pissiness bothered me. Not that Kett was a friend. He'd never pretended to be, and my reactions were my own, not dictated by him.

I bit down on the apple and sucked the tart juice from the flesh. I reminded myself that this trip to London wasn't about seeking revelation. I didn't need any more insight. What I needed was resolution; otherwise I was going to be caught in limbo between the two halves of myself — of my life — forever.

Chapter Seven

The bookstore Kett referred to was in the basement of a posh brick building in the South Kensington area of London. Once again, I had no idea where I was, but if I had been really into high-end shopping, this would obviously have been the place to come.

The bookstore owner — Clark — had been listed second by Blackwell and first by Edmonds. He didn't seem to have a phone, but that might have been a magic thing. Why some Adepts could use phones or other electronic devices while others couldn't didn't seem to be completely dependent on sheer power, so I wasn't sure yet what made the difference. How an Adept carried or used their magic, maybe?

Kett hadn't needed the GPS to find the bookshop, which was tucked between a shoe store and a clothing boutique. One look at the shoes let me know they cost more than the monthly rent on my bakery. And the clothing wasn't up to the sword-and-sorcery lifestyle I was currently living.

The bookstore was actually below ground. The front door — heavily warded — sat at the base of a narrow set of stairs. McGrowly, with his insanely broad shoulders, wouldn't have fit through it.

Why were my thoughts so constantly haunted by powerful people who I wasn't sure had my best interests at heart these days? Life was much simpler when I just needed to worry about matching my nail polish to my newest cupcake creation. The question looming before me was whether I wanted to go back there. To the simplicity. And could I do so now even if I wanted to?

A placard on the sidewalk declared that the store was open and called 'Books, Tomes, and Other Publications.' A bright orange arrow pointed down the stairs. Clark had as much flare for naming things as I did … as in, opting for the very obvious.

Despite the sign, though, the store wasn't open. At least it wasn't open for us, or for unknown Adept in general. Also, we belatedly realized as we crammed down the stairs together that we didn't actually all fit on the small landing in front of the entrance and the side window.

Runes were carved into the wood of the doorjamb. A playbill for *Wicked* was displayed in the window, through which I could see a book-covered bench. Other than that, all I could see inside was shelves upon shelves of used books.

"There's a bell," Kandy prompted. She was still on the stairs behind Kett and me. Drake was between her and us … the better to keep an eye on him.

"I've been here before," Kett said.

"And yet you hesitate to enter. That bodes well. Not," I said.

Kandy snorted.

Ignoring us, Kett closed his hand on the door latch. The silvery-blue magic of the runes shifted. They tasted of cloves and nutmeg … gingerbread cookies, actually, with that earthy sorcerer undertone.

The door opened. Kett flicked his ice-blue eyes to me. The blood I'd seen whirling in them in the car was gone.

"Try not to eat anyone we're looking to get answers from," I said, hoping he would be willing to move past whatever was currently standing between us.

The vampire offered me a toothy grin and then slipped silently into the bookstore. So I guess we were okay. Maybe I'd been overreacting. I wouldn't be surprised. I was on edge about everything.

The door closed behind Kett. I couldn't taste or feel anything beyond the runes of the doorway.

"Wouldn't books get musty in a basement?" I asked.

"Easy to defend," Kandy said.

"If there are two exits," Drake added.

"The guy's a sorcerer. He probably fled out the back the moment he knew we were here," Kandy said.

"I don't think we triggered any spells on our way down," I said.

"There are probably spells to prevent mustiness," Kandy offered.

The door reopened, and Clark — or so I assumed since I couldn't feel his magic beyond the wards — stood smiling at us. I couldn't see Kett. Clark couldn't have gotten more typically sorcerer if he'd tried. Unlike with Edmonds, I suspected he didn't bother to be anything other than what he was — a sixty-plus, gray-haired, round-bellied, magical bookstore-owning sorcerer with a comb-over.

"Jade Godfrey?" His British accent was so thick it took me a moment to recognize my name.

"Yes," I answered. "Pleased to meet you, Mr. Clark."

"Just 'Clark,' there's no mister here," he responded. "Yes, yes. The vampire says you have a book I might be interested in."

"We aren't selling," I said. "But we have questions."

"Yes, yes. We will see, won't we?" He stepped back from the doorway. "Come, come. Let's see what you have."

Clark had just stepped beyond the first bookshelf when I cleared the ward that he'd opened with his invitation. The sorcerer stumbled, and Kett appeared from among the shelves at his side.

Drake stepped into the store with Kandy behind him. Clark twisted back to us, clutching the bookshelf and visibly paler. Kett was supporting the shelf instead of touching Clark.

"What?" Clark murmured. Then he snapped his mouth shut while he stared at us crowding the entrance to his bookstore. "I … I …" Clark started again but didn't continue. His smile was entirely wiped from his face. "You said … witch and werewolf," he finally articulated to Kett.

"Yes," Kett responded smoothly, lying through his perfectly white, straight teeth.

Clark straightened. His face was now closed and questioning. Not fearful or angry, but unsure and wary. "Well, let's see what you have," he said, then he continued farther back into the store.

Not everyone found my magic tasty or Drake's compelling, it seemed.

Clark crossed behind a book-strewn counter deep within the shop. After shifting a few volumes around, he found and pulled on his reading glasses. Thus bespectacled, he took another moment to take Kandy, Drake, and me in.

I tried smiling, but the sorcerer's earlier jovial nature didn't return.

He nodded, though to what I wasn't sure, then cleared a space on the counter and patted the worn wood before him.

I obligingly pulled Blackwell's demon history chronicle out of my satchel and placed it before the sorcerer.

He hovered his hands over the book for a moment, then touched its edges lightly to rotate it toward him. "Not the original," he said.

"No," I answered, though it hadn't been a question.

He flipped open the cover and perused the first entry. "A fine duplication."

"Yes?"

"Yes, well, Blackwell always employs the best." Ah, Clark recognized the book and its owner.

"Does he?"

Clark looked up at me and offered a grim smile. "Does he still have the original?"

"No."

Clark's lips tightened. "Have you left him alive?" he asked. Then he glanced over all of us again.

"Unfortunately," Kandy answered, standing to my right.

Clark smiled more genuinely in the werewolf's direction. "That's too bad. I was hoping you'd agree to auction the books in his collection."

"We have left the sorcerer and his collection unharmed," Kett said. He was half hidden in the shadows to my left. His voice was as neutral as it ever was, but something was still bothering him. I didn't like it when things bothered the vampire. It took a lot to get him riled, and it was damn difficult to rein him in after the fact. He'd once left a tooth in Desmond's neck. I wondered if it had grown back yet, not that I wanted a close look at his fangs.

"Are you seeking the original?" Clark asked as he returned his attention to the book.

"In a way," I answered. "We're looking for a witch."

"And you think she might have come to me? What do I have that would draw her?"

"Your power," I said, very aware that the gingerbread magic I referred to was swirling around him now like a cloak. His manner was understated but his magic was uneasy. My suggestion further agitated it.

"And what are you here to try to take from me, Jade Godfrey, who is not a witch?"

"Nothing, sir," I answered. "I just have questions about my sister, Sienna — or Valencia, depending on what name she is currently using — and the book. A specific entry in the chronicle."

Clark held my gaze. This time I didn't smile. He nodded.

"I have read this history, page by page. There are three incidents that take place in London. Is it to one of those you refer?"

"The witch we seek has the sacrificial knife that was used in the Dorset Street rising," I said.

"What good would such a knife do a witch?"

"I don't know. We're still in the finding-the-puzzle-pieces part of our investigation."

"Information such as you seek is something I usually trade for."

"All right," I said. Then I waited. I was getting better at waiting, because I had learned during my dragon training that waiting was also the state of anticipating … taking a pause to watch which foot your opponent shifted his weight to, or to notice where or to who his eyes flicked.

Clark glanced at Drake, but then quickly looked away. The sorcerer couldn't just openly demand to know what sort of Adept the fledgling guardian was, because not knowing made him look weak.

He then slid his gaze to take in Kandy, who'd become antsy by my side. She rolled up on the balls of her feet and rotated her shoulders.

The air in the bookstore wasn't musty in the least. I cast my gaze around while Clark decided what he would ask us in return for information. Once beyond the wards, I had expected to feel magic from the books Clark collected and sold, but most of the shelves contained completely nonmagical hardbacks written and probably purchased by humans. History dominated many of the shelves — broken down by year and region — but a smattering of fiction paperbacks held a prime spot by the front door. A large section in the back corner seemed devoted to London specifically.

I'd expected magic to be buzzing at me from various points around the room, but besides a couple of books on Clark's counter, all the magic was concentrated behind and below where the sorcerer stood. This area — another basement level, I surmised — was warded from detection. Obviously, I could feel those inner wards, but I shouldn't have been able to feel the books hidden by those wards at all.

My gaze fell on three rocks sitting on the counter between Clark and me.

The sorcerer was watching me again. "You won't consent to leave the book with me?" he asked, already knowing the answer.

I shook my head. "I have something more valuable to offer you, sorcerer."

Clark's eyes narrowed. He didn't believe me for one moment.

I grinned. I used to loathe being underestimated, but now I was becoming a bit of a show-off. It wasn't a great character trait by any means, but Kandy, Kett, and Drake didn't care. On a daily basis, they were far more sure of themselves than I ever was.

"You have a large — I'm guessing rare by the various tastes — collection of books in your basement, sorcerer. You've taken pains to hide them, but you haven't succeeded."

Clark, who'd been thoughtfully tapping the demon history book, stilled. Then, he covered this pause with an amiable smile. "Of course I have a rare book collection. I advertise as much." He gestured to the shelves behind him. Those shelves did indeed hold a variety of magical books, but their magic was dim, almost flavorless.

"I'm not referring to those tasteless bits of bound paper. I'm speaking of the hundred or so books that lie beneath your feet."

Kett slipped by Kandy to stand directly beside me. He was a big fan of hidden collections.

Clark's eyes flicked to the vampire and then back at me. A glimmer of magic drew my attention to a ring he wore on his left index finger. The ring, which had been invisible before, was now imbued with his gingerbread power.

"Can you cast with that ring, Clark?" I asked, derailed by the bright shiny object — yes, I was still me underneath all the sword training and dragon DNA.

Clark looked startled. Then he smiled. "Dowser," he said.

I gifted him with an answering smile. Yeah, if I was going to blather on about hidden books and invisible rings then I wasn't hiding much from anyone, which was fine by me. Hiding took too much energy, and I didn't have any to spare.

"I'm surprised Blackwell lets you out of his sight."

"Who says Blackwell has any dominion over me?"

Clark's smile broadened. Sorcerers were such power sluts.

"Have you seen or been contacted by this witch with the book and the knife?"

"No," Clark answered readily enough. "No witches at all. Just you, dowser. Not for about three weeks."

"She would be ..." — I wasn't sure if Sienna still looked all black-witchy and veiny like she had the last time I saw her — "... unmistakable."

Clark's smile faded as he nodded. "Dark?"

"Yes, and possibly accompanied by a fledgling necromancer."

"No necromancers either. But then, they keep to themselves and aren't fond of old books, or of London in general."

"Too many ghosts," Drake whispered behind me to Kandy.

"I got it," the green-haired werewolf replied. "I'm not an idiot, boy."

I leaned over and flipped the pages of the chronicle until it was open to the picture of the sacrificial knife and the demon rising of November 9th, 1888.

Clark peered down at the entry. "I still don't understand what a witch would want with a book about vanquished demons. They can't be raised again, knife or no knife."

"Would you be capable of raising a demon?" I asked.

Clark paused. His ring glowed brighter for a moment. I drew back from the counter and wrapped my left hand around my necklace. That caught his attention, and the glow in his ring subsided.

Going around asking sorcerers if they could raise demons was so asking to get my ass kicked.

"You said you had something valuable to trade, dowser," Clark said.

I glanced over at Kett. He was a far better poker player than I. He nodded.

I stepped back up to the counter and took a closer look at the three stones laid out across the edge closest to me.

At first glance, the stones appeared to be smooth, slightly flattened, hunks of granite in different shades. Perhaps they'd originally been collected at some river's edge. However, I could taste pulses of power coming from underneath them. This magic was a dimmer version of Clark's clove-and-nutmeg spiced gingerbread. Even without flipping them over, I was totally willing to bet that each stone was carved with a rune. And that the three runes — connected to each other — were the anchor for the inner ward over Clark's hidden book collection.

"The stones are in the wrong order," I said.

Clark bristled as if I'd just informed him that his child was hideous and stupid to match. "No witch knows runes better than a sorcerer," he snapped.

"See how the magic slides around but not over the middle stone," I murmured to Kett, completely ignoring the sorcerer. Clark looked as if he was gearing up for some extensive rant, flushed cheeks and all.

Kett leaned forward, but I knew he couldn't see magic as well as I could. "Perhaps," he said. Vampires hated being wrong. I was surprised he was willing even to come halfway.

"The rune magic paired with the natural magic in the stone wants to be helpful, wants to heed your command, but you have them fighting each other."

"Every ancient spellbook ..." Clark sputtered. "This is absolutely preposterous to suggest. That I ... that I ... a sorcerer easily forty-five years your senior —"

I reached out and shifted the middle stone out of alignment. Clark lunged for me. Kett's hand was at his neck before the sorcerer had gotten to within an inch of my fingers.

I tugged the left stone into the middle spot and replaced it with the one that had been in the middle before.

The magic settled over the three stones. Then it flowed in a loop over and around all three. The taste of the books stored beneath Clark's feet disappeared.

I looked up at the sorcerer with a smile.

One of his hands was pinned to the desk by Kandy, the other by Drake. I'd been too intrigued by the magic stones to see either of them move. The fledgling guardian looked far too interested in the sorcerer's ring.

Kett released his hold on Clark's neck so swiftly that he actually stumbled forward.

In a breath, all three — Kett, Drake, and Kandy — were arrayed beside and behind me once again.

Clark blinked his eyes rapidly a few times. Then he remembered to close his mouth. He let whatever spell he had called up in the ring drop with an exhalation.

"I didn't mean to bully you," I said. "I'm just not great at talking through magical theory."

Clark pulled his reading glasses off and peered down at the three stones. Then he rubbed his eyes and looked again. "I ... I ..."

"You're welcome. Of course, we four will always know what lies beneath your feet."

Clark blanched.

"I was joking, sorcerer." I turned to Kandy. "Have you noticed that everyone is so serious today?"

"Yeah," the green-haired werewolf answered. "And you're not even wearing the sword. The blade really ups your bad-ass quotient."

Clark swallowed. "Thank you, dowser," he said. "I see. I don't quite believe, but —"

"It works."

"Yes."

"Now, to my question."

Clark licked his lips. "Yes, I would be capable. But you must understand, it would be suicide. If the spell didn't kill me, then the demon would. Only the foolhardy would think they could control such a thing."

"Yeah, well, foolhardy is kind of my sister's thing."

"Have you, Clark Dean Adamson, laid eyes on or heard of the black witch?" Kett asked, evoking the sorcerer's full name in that formal way of his. The fact that he knew the sorcerer's name spoke of their history together. A history I didn't have the time or inclination to dig into right now.

Clark swallowed again. "I have not met her myself, but I can give you a name."

Of course he could. Sorcerers seemed really big on selling each other out. I would have thought such individualism would be a relief after coming to understand the almost enmeshed nature of the witches' Convocation. Every little thing a witch did was accountable to her coven, and all covens were heavily governed by the Convocation. Put one toe out of line and you were blacklisted and punished. Then, hunted — if you ran — as Sienna was now hunted. But a witch would never write the names of her coven members on a piece of paper and hand it over to Adepts of unknown power.

The sorcerers' individualism bred mistrust and competition. At least it was currently to my benefit. Hopefully, Sienna wasn't reaping the rewards as well.

Driving in London was an exercise in insanity. Thankfully, traffic moved slowly, because everything was twisted around and on the wrong side.

It also seemed as if there was a tube station every block or so ... that was how many people lived in London and took public transportation. When I suggested we leave the SUV and try out the tube to Piccadilly, Kett looked at me as if I'd lost it. I guessed that vampires and underground rail didn't mix.

While walking back to the vehicle from Clark's bookstore, I kept stepping off curbs after looking in the wrong direction. I'd already been saved by three Londoners from death by double-decker bus. Kandy had nearly torn the arm off the first guy who blocked me. Thankfully, she figured out he was trying to save my life before removing any of his limbs.

So we drove. Kett was at the wheel while Kandy pored over maps on the iPad in the back seat — orienting herself, she said. Drake was working his way through a dozen crumpets that I'd insisted we stop for, but then didn't feel like eating. Yep, my world was upside down.

This wasn't a vacation, though that didn't stop me from staring at Buckingham Palace when Kandy pointed it out through the buildings. I thought Kett was trying to keep to the back roads, except such a thing really didn't seem to exist in London.

"You don't like it here," I said as I watched Kett wring his hands on the steering wheel for the third time. The vampire wasn't big on extraneous movement. He barely turned the wheel to navigate the SUV.

"It's London," he answered.

I let it drop and changed the subject. “The sorcerers don’t seem very organized. Not as political as other Adepts.”

“They have their League, but I doubt they all meet more often than once a year, except in dire cases.”

“The magic is old here. Even with all the renovated buildings. It’s old and well used. Almost tapped out.”

“A witch would feel that way in any city with such history. Disconnected from the magic. There are not many witches of power that reside in London.”

“Because of the magic or because of the sorcerers?”

“The sorcerers are not the seat of power here.”

“No? There’s no League liaison we should meet?”

Kandy shifted forward in her seat, though she didn’t have to get closer to hear our conversation.

Kett stilled, his gaze on the road, and for a moment I thought he wouldn’t answer. He often chose to not answer. Information was power to vampires.

“There are many creatures of magic that call London home,” he finally said.

“Many different types of Adept?”

“These powerful few would not title themselves as such, yet it is their city. We have thirty-six hours before we must present ourselves. I suggest we be gone in less than twenty-four.”

Well, that was an oddly delivered and underplayed threat … if it was a threat.

“There aren’t many shapeshifters here either,” Kandy said before I could question Kett further.

“Just your wolf hunk all on his lonesome, eh?” I teased.

Kandy glowered at me. “He’s here for school.”

“Shapeshifters, like witches, prefer an environment where nature can be easily accessed,” Kett said.

"But not vampires," I said, bringing us back on point.

"No. Not vampires," Kett agreed.

"Because vampires are already magic," Drake offered from the back seat. "They don't need to tap into natural sources to replenish."

"Blood is pretty natural," Kandy said with a sneer.

"Exactly," Drake responded. "There's more blood in cities."

"So London is full of vampires?" I asked. As I peered out at the gray, drizzly day and the people swamping the sidewalks, it made sense.

"No," Kett answered. His tone was measured and thoughtful. "One vampire and his ... brethren, if they're in his good graces this century."

Something about Kett's even tone and careful phrasing made me shudder. I don't think I'd ever heard him search for a word before, not in mid sentence.

"Are you ... are you one of his brethren?"

Kett inclined his head. "I am connected to a child of his."

"Big vamp is your gramps?" Kandy asked.

"By blood," Kett replied, his tone clipped.

I was surprised he was still answering questions. I was scared, actually, that he was still answering questions. It meant he thought the knowledge was important ... and vampires only ranked life, death, and power as important, not necessarily in that order.

"So in thirty-six hours we have to go meet your blood grandfather?"

"No. One of his lieutenants."

"One of his children?"

"If you prefer to think of them that way. As long as you understand that he hasn't divided his power in over a millennium."

"I don't understand."

"Energy cannot be created."

"I know, only harnessed."

"Yes, so vampires do not ... breed often or successfully. Only the most powerful manage, and even they must be willing to lose something of themselves. To become lesser for a time."

"Vamps don't give up power easily," Kandy said.

"No," Kett answered. "And they often loathe the one they have created for that exact reason."

He pulled the SUV to the curb in front of a five-storey apartment building. Not that it looked like any apartment I'd ever seen before. It was ... very British. Hell, I had no idea how else to describe it. It was brick, stone, casings, and porticos or whatever ... big, cased, paned windows ... wooden door with a huge brass knocker. That sort of thing.

Kett turned to step out of the vehicle.

"Wait, wait," I murmured.

Kett paused.

Kandy and Drake, always eager to be moving, tumbled out onto the street. The wrong side of the street — for me, at least.

"What are you not saying?" I asked. "Is this vampire — the lieutenant guy. Is he your ... dad?"

"He is not my maker," Kett replied. He turned to look at me. I could see his magic dancing in his skin — glimmers of red shards — and in his icy blue eyes.

"Am I dragging Drake and Kandy into danger?"

"Most certainly."

"I meant with the vampires of London."

Kett grinned, showing off his perfectly white, straight teeth. He was getting far too comfortable with that particular human gesture.

"I know something happened to you while we were talking to Edmonds."

"You know me well." Kett's grin widened into a smile.

"Stop smiling at me. Is big bad vamp going to try to fang us all or what?"

Kett laughed. The sound was oddly husky for his usually cool tones. "No one will bite anyone without permission."

"But we need to be gone within twenty-four hours."

"Most definitely."

"Otherwise, there are many ways to obtain permission, right?" Yep, I wasn't dimwitted all the time. Kett only had the okay to be in London for thirty-six hours. After that, his companions would be considered snacks. My mind boggled. Witch politics had always seemed so complicated, but at least they didn't demand blood tithes.

"You can't tell me that every Adept in London allows the vampires to drink from them."

Kett sighed. It was a heavy, deliberate sound. Deliberate in the fact that he had to inhale to speak or sigh, but not otherwise. Heavy because he was choosy when using it. "You're not just some Adept, Jade. And yes, any Adept of power in London forms some sort of allegiance with the big bad — as you call him — or his brethren."

Great. London belonged to the vampires … or at least one particular vampire.

"Do they at least wear capes and turn into bats or fog? It would make them easier to identify."

"You're thinking of Dracula's crew. You need to go much farther east to run into them."

I'd been joking, but I wasn't entirely sure Kett was joking back … though his use of the term 'crew' made it seem likely.

"I can see you thinking, dowser," Kett said. "It looks difficult."

Yep, now he was teasing me.

"You're awfully peppy all of a sudden, vampire," I said, not feeling at all playful. "That worries me."

Kett nodded. "As it should," he said.

Then he climbed out of the SUV.

Yeah, that wasn't a joke either. I sighed and followed him out into the drizzly day.

Three months of serious training in the dragon nexus and I was still lagging behind … everyone. Being able to kick someone's ass — even potentially — didn't make it any easier to figure them out or find them.

Chapter Eight

Peter Sayers, the third sorcerer on Blackwell's list, the second on Edmonds' Post-it, and the name Clark had all too willingly given up, lived just off Piccadilly. I gathered, given the way Clark had phrased it, that this area was supposed to be famous, or at least well known. For me, all the streets and buildings in London were pretty impressive looking, no matter the neighborhood. Sayers' apartment building was one of those all-brick deals with white-painted trim and paned windows, five storeys high.

"Nice building," I said as I joined Kandy, who was leaning against a lamppost and ignoring the never-ending drizzle that appeared to be the sum total of London weather.

Kandy shrugged. "Looks all the same to me. Big, loud, and too many humans."

"Impressive, though. It must be expensive to live right in downtown London."

"I doubt he owns the entire building," Kett said as he stepped up to my left.

Yeah, vampires weren't any more easily impressed than dragons. I ignored him. "Shall we buzz?"

"Already did. You know, while you were getting cozy with the vamp," Kandy answered. "No one home, apparently."

"I don't feel any wards here," I said, ignoring the barbed edge of the werewolf's comment. "Wait … where the hell is Drake?"

Kandy pointed up and to the right.

Drake was scaling the building. The thirteen-year-old was jumping from ledge to ledge, pulling himself up on the iron railings that I was pretty sure were only for decoration.

Kett started laughing.

Kandy's eyes widened and her jaw dropped as she turned to look incredulously at the vampire.

Yeah, Kett laughing was more remarkable than Drake scaling a five-storey building in broad daylight in the middle of freaking London. London, England. With a population of seven million plus people. All of who seemed to be on the street at any given time.

I glanced around. Being mostly residential, the sidewalks weren't as crowded as South Kensington, but there were still people passing by carrying groceries, walking dogs, and parking their cars.

Kandy started laughing.

Oh, sweet Jesus. "It's not funny," I hissed as I fought the urge to literally start pulling out my hair. "What is he doing?"

Kandy stopped laughing long enough to answer. "Seeing if the sorcerer is home."

"We don't even know which apartment is his."

"4A. It's on the buzzer. Probably the fifth floor. According to the fledgling, Brits number funny."

For some reason this statement made Kett laugh even harder. So then Kandy started laughing again. When had I become the stick-in-the-mud between a vampire and a werewolf? My life had turned completely freaking upside down.

"We need to get him down," I said. "Before someone sees him."

Police sirens sounded from a few blocks over and I flinched. Jesus, I didn't even know what to do if Drake got arrested. He didn't have a passport, and he certainly didn't look or sound remotely British.

Any minute, a Londoner was going to glance up and see the thirteen-year-old jimmying the window on the fifth floor above their heads. That was, once they stopped staring at Kett and Kandy guffawing it up on the sidewalk. Anyone who passed gave us a wide berth. A woman with two toddlers in a double stroller actually crossed the street to avoid passing by the giggle twins.

Drake got in the window.

I waited, my hand on my knife, for some explosion of magic as the fledgling disrupted a ward or was confronted by an angry sorcerer.

Kandy was wiping tears from her eyes. She caught me glaring at her. "What?" she asked. "It's not like he was going to hurt himself."

Kett suddenly stilled and slowly twisted his head to the left, as a cat does when seeing a ghost, or whatever they stare at when they stare at nothing. I followed his gaze but didn't see anything unusual, besides the fact that we were in London in the first place. It felt like being in the latest Bond film or BBC's *Sherlock* — hmm, *Sherlock* — or a historical documentary.

The street running perpendicular to us was actually much busier, more of a main thoroughfare. Cars and people were momentarily backed up at the traffic light. They then surged forward a half-car length before the light changed to green. A woman who'd been standing among the curb crowd didn't move with them. She was channeling the Audrey Hepburn look as hard as she could behind thick, black sunglasses, a three-quarter trench coat, coiffed hair, and slim-legged pants. And, yeah, I know who Audrey Hepburn was. They used her in all those Gap ads a few years back and everyone freaked about tarnishing an icon.

"I'll meet you at the hotel, dowser," Kett said.

"What? Hotel?"

"Hotel 41." Kett tossed the SUV keys toward me. I only managed to catch them out of fear of them hitting my face. "See to the fledgling."

And before I could open my mouth to freak all over him because I'd been trying to do just that for the last twenty-four hours, he was gone.

"I hate it when he does that," Kandy murmured.

"It's a trick," I said. "I mean, yeah, he moves fast. Faster than you or me, but he can't teleport. He uses the shadows."

The Audrey Hepburn lookalike was also gone. I wondered if Kett knew her. It was too much of a coincidence otherwise.

Drake wandered out of the front doors of Sayers' apartment building, grinning like an idiot. The back hem of his Scotland hoodie was torn.

"No sorcerers," he pronounced as he sauntered over to us.

"You understand what covert means, right?" I asked.

"It was Kandy's idea."

I turned to look at the green-haired werewolf. She grinned back at me, but in an edgy way, not friendly — like some tension was underlying the expression. "I just mentioned that the corner looked climbable," she said.

"That's like giving a thirteen-year-old the keys to the kingdom."

"What are these keys?" Drake asked eagerly, completely proving my point.

"I have no freaking idea," I snapped.

"Well, it's not nice to mention them like that, then."

Kandy started laughing again. Everyone had seemingly taken some sort of happy pill, and I was pissed they hadn't shared.

"Why is your hoodie torn?" I asked Drake, hoping there weren't any bodies to clean up in the fledgling's wake.

"Dog," Drake answered with a shrug.

"A dog laid tooth on you?" Kandy asked. Then she actually doubled over to laugh louder.

Drake grinned at the werewolf. His ego was so huge it was hard to even poke at it … or maybe it was that nothing ruffled him, like life was a grand playground.

I could use some of that attitude. Right after I hunted down my sister and hopefully rescued Mory — though why Sienna would drag a fledgling necromancer around for three months I don't know. Right after I took care of Sienna … stopped Sienna … killed Sienna.

"Phantom dog," Drake elaborated. "Cool spell, but he didn't have the window covered, just the front door. So I didn't see it coming."

A phantom dog had appeared and bitten a fledgling guardian dragon in the ass while he was leaving the apartment he'd already broken into by the window.

I started laughing, then. I couldn't help it.

Thank god Drake was here. Otherwise, it would just be all blood-magic, demons, and doom all the time. A girl could get lost in that darkness … a girl had gotten lost in that darkness. My sister. My best friend.

I stopped laughing.

Kandy flung her arm around my shoulders. "You need chocolate, Jade."

"I so do."

Grinning, Kandy held the iPad up so I could see the screen. It displayed a Time Out London app page for Melt, an artisan chocolate shop.

"Hot chocolate blocks, melt bars, and sea-salted caramel bonbons," Kandy said.

"Where is Notting Hill? We need to be there, like now," I declared. "But we should probably leave a note for Sayers."

"Sure," Kandy said agreeably. "How about on his fridge? After we sniff around for the black witch."

"The fridge seems rather aggressive."

"Exactly."

"We don't even know him."

Kandy shrugged. "He's the last sorcerer on the list."

"How about on his front door?" I countered. "We'll mention we were concerned for his safety, hence disturbing the wards." I glared at Drake. He grinned proudly. "I can tell from the hallway if Sienna's been around."

"Whatever," Kandy answered. The green-haired werewolf spun away and crossed to the apartment's front door.

I sighed. Was I the only one not interested in creating an international incident? Gran would be seriously displeased if I pissed off the sorcerers' League. And the League would never believe that Sayers had potentially been in peril from a witch, no matter how black.

Hotel-freaking-41 was freaking amazing. And it wasn't just the six thirty-gram melt bars going to my head. I mean, I was buzzed, of course, but the hotel was freakingly amazingly insane.

Okay, part of my awe might have been the chocolate overload. Melt's smallest bars came in milk chocolate — one with raspberry and one with hazelnuts — then dark chocolate — one with mint and one with orange — as well as a white chocolate strawberry and tarragon bar. It certainly wasn't my fault that the milk chocolate with passion fruit, the milk chocolate banana, and the sea-salted caramel bar only came in the forty-five gram size. So I had to try those as well.

I mean, I wasn't completely insane. I saved the love bar, chili bar, and popcorn bar for later … they were ninety grams each. After all, a girl had to show some control. I wasn't going to count the peanut-butter-and-jelly, white-chocolate, raspberry-and-mint, apple-crumble, or champagne bonbons either. They were tiny tastes of utter heaven, handmade fresh daily … in freaking London, England. I picked up three boxes of eighteen as well, as gifts for Gran, Scarlett, and … well, me.

Yeah, I was aware I was speaking rather quickly and much louder than I needed to when checking us into the hotel, but I was having a difficult time modulating myself. According to the front-desk clerk, Kett hadn't returned yet, though if he didn't want to be noticed coming and going, a human certainly wouldn't see him. Kandy was off in one corner of the lobby, texting and giggling. She'd consumed twice what I did. Drake was the only one of us who seemed unaffected, but maybe that was just because he was always bouncing off the walls anyway.

Everything in the hotel lobby was either oiled dark wood — wainscoting, bookshelves, art niches — or black and white — tile, carpet, linens. Even the duvets, once we got to the room, were black-and-white checked. You name it, and it was black and white, not either/or.

Kett had booked us into the conservatory suite, and after seeing its glassed ceiling and the early-evening sky view, I was super glad this wasn't going on the credit card Amber had dropped off for me. Yeah, I'd left gold and the witch had taken care of the plastic. The dragons dealt in gold coin. Drake and I got allowances, like actual kids. After seeing Amber's reaction, I had a good idea that dragons didn't have much concept of money, or of what each coin was worth in the human world.

Anyway, we'd picked up our key cards at the front desk, all without anyone asking for money, so Kett must have it covered.

Funnily enough — seeing as this was where Kett booked us — there was nothing magical about the hotel. No other Adepts. No incidental glimmers of residual magic in the halls or rooms. This felt off to me — empty. I'd become accustomed to being inundated by magic, I realized.

Kandy was continuing to text like a mad woman — she had been all the way through finding the chocolate shop, then driving to the hotel — as she wandered behind Drake and I on our way to the suite. She barely glanced at the room before she dropped her bag in the front closet and announced, "I'm out."

At least she had a bag to drop. Drake and I were still in leathers covered by gas station hoodies. We'd hidden our swords underneath the back seat before we valeted the SUV.

"What do you mean, 'out'?" I asked.

Kandy shrugged. "You know, pub out."

"You're going on a date? Now?"

"I need to eat. You know, real food."

"But —"

"We've got over eight hours until midnight. The vamp is still MIA. You two need to sleep, and I'm hungry."

"We should be scouting, hunting. I thought —"

"Nothing is going to happen in the next four hours. Shower, sleep, eat. Wait to hear from the vampire and this Sayers sorcerer. You can't rush a demon summoning." Kandy said this last bit with a smirk.

I just stared at her. I couldn't quite wrap my head around her just leaving. "You're just leaving."

"You don't have exclusive rights over leaving, Jade."

"I'm sorry, are you referring to me saving everyone's asses by dragging the demon through the portal?"

Kandy bared her teeth at me. Anger edged the sharp line of her jaw and cheekbones. "I'm referring to you not coming back until you felt like it."

Drake, having finished inspecting every nook and cranny of the suite, sidled up to me. He peered at Kandy over my shoulder.

"I wasn't ... that's not how ... or why," I said.

Kandy grasped the door handle and yanked it open. "Don't worry, I know my duty. I'll be back before anything goes down."

"The wolf is angry," Drake said.

Kandy curled her lip at both of us, then walked out of the room.

The door slowly swung closed on its hydraulic hinges and then clicked shut.

"Did you know she was angry?" Drake asked.

"No ... I didn't realize ..." Kandy was angry that I hadn't walked back through the portal with Desmond and Kett three and a half months ago. Well, so was I. But with the memory of Chi Wen's vision still seared into my mind, I knew I'd had no choice.

"I had to be careful. To plan. To make sure I didn't accidentally fulfill ..."

Drake patted my shoulder. "The wolf will understand if you tell her."

I nodded and clenched my right hand into a fist. I could still feel the slick blood that had coated my skin and dripped off my hand in the vision. I could still taste Sienna's malignant black magic as it spread into the fresh blood of my dead or dying friends and family ...

"The wolf is a warrior. She will fight by your side without you asking," Drake said. "If you want her there as a friend, you will need to make the request."

"Thanks, baby Buddha," I said, putting as much snark into my tone as I could muster against the darkness of my memory.

"Food?" Drake asked.

"Yes," I said, and I shook away the feeling of blood coating my hand. "Let's order room service. That way, we can eat far too much and no one will notice."

Drake grinned. "I want a hamburger and fish and chips." He held out the room service menu to me, open to the page he was referencing. So he had found something valuable during his investigation of the suite.

"Good," I answered as I crossed to the phone where it sat on a side table, painted in a harlequin diamond pattern. "And I'm not ordering a salad .... well, maybe on the side of fries."

Drake slept, but I didn't. Neither Kett nor Kandy returned to the suite. I'd exchanged a few texts with Gran and Scarlett, updating them on our lack of progress, but I hadn't heard back from the sorcerer, Peter Sayers.

Before Drake nodded off, he and I had snuck into the underground parking and retrieved our swords. I didn't like being without mine, which was odd seeing as I'd only had it for a few days. I sat with the sword across my lap and tried to meditate, but to no avail. Branson had given me the scabbard privately after my father, Yazi, had presented the sword itself. The leather of the scabbard was black, but it was etched with a dark green floral design. It was a whimsical choice coming from the sword master, but it suited me perfectly.

I wasn't remotely worthy or ready to wield this sword.

I could feel the trickle of Blackwell's spell that I'd channeled into the sword underneath my fingers. The magic, now contained, felt almost benign.

This was the sword I was going to kill my sister with ... not in a cave outside of Portland, and not with my jade knife. That was the only way I knew how to stop Chi Wen's vision of the future ... except to just leave Sienna alone, which I also couldn't do.

This was the sword I was going to kill my sister with ... I'd known it the moment the blade had been handed to me, the moment my fingers curled around the hilt.

And with that terrible thought acknowledged, I slept.

Two hours later, with Kandy and Kett still MIA, and Drake still crashed out and snoring like a small volcano, I wandered down into the hotel restaurant.

I had a crazy craving I still hadn't quite satisfied. Yeah, I got that it would probably never be satisfied until I got my life sorted out, but I still enjoyed the act of feeding it.

I avoided the Leopard Champagne and Cocktail Bar — I really wasn't dressed for it, nor did I want company — and settled into a comfy barrel chair at a linen-swathed table for two in the empty lounge. They served dinner until 10:00 P.M., so I was just under the wire, but I wasn't there for food.

The server, who was a couple of years younger than me, sauntered over with a grin. Yeah, the place was dead and he was probably just a few minutes away from going home when I showed up — but most heterosexual men turned on the charm when confronted by my blond curls and ready smile. Even paired with the dumpy hoodie, I felt sure the laced leather pants were getting his mind whirling.

"Evening," the server said. His British accent was clipped and not as broad as Clark's had been. "Are you a guest with us, or are you waiting for a guest?" His smile widened invitingly.

I peered up at him. I couldn't quite figure out what he was suggesting with the second question.

His smile dimmed. "I apologize, I was just requesting your room number. We're encouraged to address our guests by name."

"Jade," I answered. "We're in the conservatory suite."

"I see." His smile dimmed further. I gathered that staying in the conservatory suite made me seem less available.

"I'll have one of each of these," I said, pushing the transaction along beyond the pleasantries and pointing at the dessert menu.

"Excuse me? One of each?"

"And a hot chocolate, unless it's made with a powdered mix and water."

The server stared at me for a moment, then he grinned as if he thought I was joking. I wasn't.

"Forget the cheese plate, but I'll have the melon créme brûlée, all six flavors of ice cream, the coffee ice cream sundae ..." — I ran my finger down the dessert list just to make myself clear — "... forget the fruit, definitely the white chocolate parfait, and the baked cheesecake with the raspberry coulis."

The server was blinking rapidly at me. I should have stayed up in the suite, but I'd needed to take a couple of steps away.

"So?" I asked. "Is the hot chocolate made from a powdered mix?"

"Ah, no," he replied. "Chocolate sauce, house made. Ah, whipped cream?"

"Made fresh or from a can?"

"Fresh."

"Fine. Good. Thank you." I tugged the cloth napkin out of its fan shape and placed it on my lap.

The server hesitated, hovering around the second place setting. "Are you expecting ..."

"No, thank you."

He quickly gathered the other setting and hustled back to the computer at the end of the bar.

So I wanted dessert? So freaking what? I inhaled as I fought to not go ballistic over something so trivial. Of course the server had reacted like that. Who wouldn't? Well, except me, of course. Or any of the shapeshifters ... or dragons. Dragons adored sweets. They just never seemed to have any chocolate around ...

A brown-haired man wearing a well-tailored suit stepped through the arched entrance of the lounge and stopped to scan the room. His hair was cropped short to look effortlessly styled, but I could tell it still took him fifteen minutes to fix every morning. He stood a couple of inches over six feet and had recently been wearing a tie. His buttoned-down shirt collar was designed to be worn with one, and the buttons were now undone.

He took one look at me and the pleasant smile he'd been sporting — the kind that made it look like you belonged wherever you were currently going, no questions asked — slid from his face.

He was in his early thirties, and good-looking in a pale English sort of way ... meaning he was tall but too slim for my tastes, and my cheekbones didn't need the sort of competition his would offer.

He was also a sorcerer. Oh, he wore something to disperse or diffuse his magic — a personal ward maybe, because I hadn't tasted his diluted Earl Grey tea magic until I'd seen him — but he was powerful.

He hadn't moved an inch as he continued to stare at me. The server, who'd turned to greet him, was getting twitchy and exchanging questioning looks with the bartender.

"Peter Sayers," I said invitingly. My voice carried easily across the room.

The sorcerer shook his head. Then, realizing the gesture probably looked like a denial of the name, he grinned sheepishly and bobbed his head in a nod.

He only tripped once as he crossed to me. The server, who was at Sayers' heels, almost ran into him, and then paused to straighten the table the sorcerer had bumped.

"Jade Godfrey?" Sayers asked when he got to within two steps of me.

I nodded, and for some reason — now that he was near — I reached underneath the table, pulled my knife out of its sheath, and laid it across my lap.

Sayers noted my movement and nodded in acknowledgment of it.

"Will you be joining the lady?" the server asked, much more brusque than he'd been with me.

Sayers looked to me.

"Yes, please do," I said. "Something to drink?"

"Macallan's ten. Water on the side," Sayers said as he sat across the table from me. He didn't take his eyes off me.

The server nodded but hesitated to leave. Yeah, something was off about Sayers ... in that perfectly pleasant, well-groomed serial killer way.

I smiled at the server. "Still only one fork though," I said.

He laughed and then headed back to the bar.

Sayers was still gazing at me as if I was some sort of gift from God. And maybe I was. Just not for him.

"I could sense your magic from the lobby," he said.

"I doubt it was solely mine. I'm not the only Adept staying here."

Sayers' eyes widened. Then he nodded as he got my underlying message — I'm not alone.

"You're still not what I expected," he said.

"I get that a lot. You spoke to Clark, then?"

He hesitated, then nodded. I wasn't totally sure that was a 'yes.'

"Why do you wear a diffuser?" I asked. "I doubt it contains your abilities — because that would be stupid — so it just tones down the taste of your magic. Why?"

Sayers went rigid, then tried to relax but didn't quite pull it off. "Dowser," he said, with a smile that was half the wattage of his previous attempt. "I run an importing/exporting business that would benefit from your services."

"The diffuser interests me, sorcerer," I said, ignoring the 'services' comment. I wasn't sure why I was pressing the issue so hard. I usually found I caught far more flies with honey — or cupcakes —than with outright demands. "What need do you have to hide your magic? From whom?"

The server stepped up to the table with a tray holding all four … no, five, of my desserts. Sayers and I didn't speak as the server placed each item down on the table and set my hot chocolate close to hand. The rapidly melting whipped cream was overflowing the mug and running down the sides. This pleased me.

"Thank you."

"Shall I identify the desserts for you?"

"No, thank you. I'm fairly certain I have it covered."

Before the server had completely turned his back, I had a bite of the cheesecake in my mouth. "Ah," I said. "Baked and served with a fruit coulis, there is no other way. I'm thinking of branching into mini cheesecakes."

Sayers' grin was back, but brimming with confidence. This grin said he'd figured me out — based on the excessive desserts — and liked what he saw. Boy, was he wrong. And, boy, was I going to get a kick out of proving it to him.

Like I'd said before, who the hell was I these days? I needed some of Drake's dragon Zen. Not all of it — it was a bit insufferable coming from a thirteen-year-old — but at least enough that I had a reserve of calm. I needed to bake or to make a trinket … maybe if I didn't exercise my alchemist powers frequently enough, my magic got caught up inside me until it desperately needed to discharge.

Magic ... I was thinking about magic, not sex. Though that could easily be the problem as well.

"I'm looking for my sister," I said. Sayers opened his mouth to answer, but I cut him off. "And you've seen her."

The sorcerer snapped his mouth shut.

"You're only the fourth sorcerer I've met, Peter Sayers, and yet you're all the same." I scooped a tiny ball of pistachio ice cream onto my spoon and held it in front of my mouth. Sayers' gaze fell to my lips, as I knew it would. "Sorcerers never do anything for free, and yet you came here voluntarily."

I allowed the ice cream to roll off the spoon and onto my tongue. Then I licked the spoon.

Sayers watched me, his clamped jaw betraying his mounting anger. He didn't like being played with, but he liked the game.

"What I don't know is whether or not you're aiding Sienna."

"A sorcerer wouldn't help a witch," he spat. "And I certainly don't know any Sienna."

I believed him. "Right, she goes by another name now. And 'aid' isn't the right word, is it? No, sorcerer. Perhaps you think you're using her."

"What would a sorcerer want from a witch?"

"Well, I could give you a list of spells, potions, and charms, but that would be boring ... and potentially embarrassing for you." I picked up the Pirouline, aka the cookie straw, from the side of the white chocolate parfait plate and twirled it in the air. Yeah, I was questioning his manhood.

He flushed angrily.

I tried out the parfait. It was sweet, as I knew it would be. But overly sweet — obnoxiously sweet — was exactly what I was looking for right now. Because everything else around me was in limbo — intangible, much like the magic of the sorcerer sitting across from me was diffused.

"Maybe it's the book," I said, around a second bite of the parfait. "Except the others didn't think it had much power, so why would you want it?"

The sundae was tasty. I'd scooped a large spoonful while Sayers was figuring out how to gain control of the conversation. I usually wasn't a fan of coffee, but I liked it in this form just fine.

"And what of the fledgling necromancer?" I asked.

"What necromancer?" Sayers snapped, and my heart sank.

I placed my spoon down, suddenly done with the desserts before I'd really begun. What a waste.

I couldn't tell if the sorcerer was lying or not. But he hadn't gotten up and left when I'd started interrogating him, and I wasn't sure why.

Sayers tugged lightly and needlessly at the wrist of his suit jacket. Then he placed his hands flat on the table before him. I wasn't sure how to read his body language either.

The server dropped off Sayers' finger of Macallan and the sorcerer took it without saying a word. Then he nodded the server away and added water to the scotch.

"I don't feel like interrogating you any longer, Sayers," I said.

"Thank God," he answered.

"But you're still here."

"Your magic is still intriguing."

"Have you figured out what you want from me yet?"

He raised his eyebrow and grinned at me wolfishly. I raised my eyebrow back at him and waited. I didn't believe he was interested in me like that for one moment.

He looked away and sipped his drink.

Yep, no follow-through. Man, that bothered me. What was the point of innuendo and flirting that never led anywhere?

I was a downer tonight. I took a sip of the hot chocolate, then sucked all the melty whipped cream off the top. Ah, that was better.

"Are we back to the interrogation?" Sayers was trying to flirt … again.

"No. You're going to leave me to my desserts, which I am going to eat, because I do have follow-through." I dug into the cheesecake.

Sayers frowned. "You contacted me."

"Right, right. One of my friends will check in with you. You'll be home later on tonight, yes?" My mention of friends deepened Sayers' frown. I might be wrong about him knowing Sienna. Maybe he'd come to the hotel after getting my note because he'd spoken to Edmonds and Clark and wanted to meet me for himself. And by me, I meant Drake, of course. Because what sorcerer was interested in a dowser — a power they already had in a limited capacity — when an unknown and unusual Adept was in town?

Kandy or Kett would make quick work of Sayers. They could both pick out liars before the actual lie was out of their mouths — by heartbeat for Kett, and I presumed by scent for Kandy.

It was coming up on eleven o'clock. At 12:01 A.M., it would be November 9th. I didn't know if Sienna was in London. I didn't know how literal she was preparing to be, but I did know that we were walking distance from the Dorset Street site. Well, walking distance for us

… Google Street View also informed me I had a warehouse and a parking garage to stake out. It would be easier to carry swords at night than by day as well.

All that was going to happen with or without Sayers' information … or lack of information.

"We've gotten off on the wrong foot," Sayers said.

"Have we? I'm not so sure."

"You asked me here —"

"I didn't, really. Not in a way that implied anything. If I'm wrong about you and Sienna, then I'm sure Edmonds or Clark filled you in … though maybe they didn't. Sorcerers don't seem big on sharing information." I looked to him for confirmation. He gave none, so I dug into the melon créme brûlée. It was too sweet. I relished every creamy bite.

"All right," I continued. "Here's the gist. My sister, a black witch in a blood frenzy, might be in London to raise some demons, even though logically she shouldn't be able to raise them. She kidnapped a friend of mine — a fledgling necromancer under my protection. And I will kick any ass in my path to get the fledgling back … unharmed."

Sayers opened his mouth, but I stopped him once more.

"Oh, and Sienna needs a sorcerer's power to do all this. Binding is her specialty. So if you do see her, turn the other way."

"Or she'll kill me?" Sayers asked mockingly.

Stupid, stupid sorcerers.

"Yeah, eventually. My ice cream is melting."

"I enjoy watching you eat."

"Oh, please. This is done. It never began."

Sayers lost his smile in a way that let me know it wasn't going to return. I could see him better without it, but I still couldn't quite tell what put me off about him. Was it just the diffuser he wore that bothered me? Had I blown this all out of proportion? Should I apologize?

Kett slipped into the lounge. His pace was oddly languid and yet deliberate … as if he might be drunk but hiding it. Vampires didn't get drunk, though. At least I didn't think they did.

Sayers turned to follow my gaze, but Kett closed the space between the entrance and the table before the sorcerer had fully looked behind his own shoulder. He flinched to find Kett standing next to him.

"Jade Godfrey," Kett whispered. Then he smiled in a way that sent a not-unpleasant chill down my spine.

Oh, shit.

"Kett," I said as pleasantly as possible. "You haven't met Peter Sayers. Importer/exporter."

"Pleased to meet —" Sayers began.

Kett stepped past the sorcerer, showing him his back, and stood alongside me. He reached down and touched his cool fingers to my inner wrist.

"Are you drunk?" I hissed.

"Are you?" Kett asked in return.

"No."

"Unfortunate." He dropped my wrist and stepped behind me, facing Sayers again. I really wasn't a fan of having an apparently drunk vampire behind my back, knowing he lusted after my blood — however cool and reservedly.

Sayers stared, open-mouthed, at Kett. I finished the coffee ice cream sundae.

We probably could have stayed like that — me eating my desserts and Kett and Sayers facing off — for the next hour, except my phone pinged.

I had a text message from Kandy.

Heading back.

I looked up at Sayers. "We're heading out now," I said. "Please don't get yourself killed. I know I've been oddly rude, but please don't ignore my warning."

"He's not powerful enough for your sister to take notice," Kett murmured.

"He's wearing a diffuser," I said, downing the last of my hot chocolate in one long swig. I could feel the sugar starting to course through my bloodstream. Soon, I'd be jittery with it. Good.

"Is he?" Kett's tone grew more intense and focused.

Sayers swallowed, just once. I gathered that he would have preferred to go unnoticed by the vampire.

"Why would you wear a diffuser to meet a dowser, sorcerer?" Kett asked.

"I'm fairly certain he's already met Sienna," I said as I ran my spoon around the depths of the sundae glass.

"That would make it an even odder choice," Kett said.

"Would it?" I asked. "Maybe I'm wrong. In any case, if he hasn't met her, we've warned him."

"And if he has met her and he's still alive, then his power is not what Sienna wants," Kett added.

We both looked at Sayers closer — at his magic, specifically. The sorcerer stared back at us, mouth still agape as we continued to discuss him as if he wasn't actually in the room.

"It would be nice to know for sure if Sienna is in town," I mused.

"I could take him back to the suite," Kett offered. His cool tone was completely nonthreatening, and yet the biting-to-extract-information implication was very clear.

"We'll know soon enough," I said as I stood, satisfied that I'd done justice to the decadent desserts. I wasn't so sure what was up with Kett and the vampires of London. Adding 'biting sorcerers' to any list of wrongdoings we were about to commit — if we were to confront Sienna — probably wasn't a great idea.

I walked away from the table and finally got the rise I'd been waiting for out of Sayers. Magic bloomed around his wrists, where he'd earlier tugged at his jacket sleeves. I hadn't been able to identify any specific magical objects on him before, because of the diffuser he also wore somewhere on his person. But he couldn't hide the magic he was triggering now — diffuser or no diffuser.

As Sayers stood to follow me — or perhaps to attack me — I turned into him. Wrapping my fingers around each of his wrists — over his suit jacket, so he wouldn't be able to lift his hands — I leaned into him as if we were kissing goodbye. That last part was for the benefit of the server and bartender.

"You don't want to cast against me," I whispered in his ear. Sayers twisted against my hold. I applied just a little more pressure and he winced. Yeah, I was strong … for just a dowser. "If you actively use these bracelets against me, then I have the right to relieve you of them. It's sort of my job."

"Is it?" Kett asked. He stood behind and slightly to the side of Sayers. Though he was about two inches shorter than the sorcerer, I could still clearly see his ice-blue eyes.

"Well," I answered. "It will be."

"Interesting."

"I have no idea what the hell you are talking about," Sayers said.

"Do you want me to take the bracelets, and the diffuser for that matter, or not?" I was still smiling prettily for the server's and bartender's benefit.

"No," the sorcerer answered begrudgingly. The magic of the bracelets he wore dimmed. I didn't know what spell he'd been calling up, but it felt like I wouldn't have liked it at all. No wonder Gran loathed sorcerers … in her entirely polite Canadian way. I let go of Sayers.

"Do you know Sienna or not?" I asked.

"No," Sayers answered as he rubbed his wrists.

I glanced up at Kett and he frowned. I took that to mean Sayers was actually telling the truth.

"I apologize then," I said as I stepped away. "Thank you for coming to see us. Please be wary over the next few days."

Sayers nodded and I turned away to sign the bill at the bar. A 12.5 percent tip was included, but I added another 10 percent.

Kett had a few more words with Sayers that I didn't bother trying to hear. Then the sorcerer hightailed it out of the lounge without another glance at me. I made more enemies than friends these days. It used to be the other way around … well, if I counted acquaintances as friends.

"Have a good evening," I said to the server.

"You as well, Jade," he replied.

Kett matched my step once I turned into the corridor to our suite. I had a feeling he'd stayed behind to make sure Sayers was out of the building.

"So …" I said. "You sober enough to go hunting?"

"Always," Kett replied.

"Tonight …"

"Yes?"

"Tonight we end this. If Sienna is there and Mory is in danger ..."

"You'll pick protecting the fledgling over containing your sister."

"Yes."

"I won't."

I stopped in front of our suite door. The black-and-white-check carpeting was a plush cushion underneath my feet, even through the leather soles of my boots. "Is it cowardly of me to ask this of you?"

Kett's magic danced within his skin and in his eyes ... every inch of him was magic, but I didn't ... couldn't let it distract me.

"I will kill the witch if you cannot," Kett said.

I closed my eyes at the pain that bloomed in my chest — pain so coated in anger now that I couldn't distinguish between the two emotions anymore. "It should be me."

"Why? You're not responsible for your foster sister's actions, Jade Godfrey."

"I feel like I am."

"This is a human weakness you feel. Misplaced guilt. Do you not think she deserves to die?"

"Is this a conversation you're morally qualified to have, vampire?" I opened my eyes to meet his once again. "How many people have you killed just to live?"

Kett smiled. The gesture was tight on his face. "The difference is, I have not broken any laws ... not since I was the one enforcing them. Sienna has, on multiple counts. And the number of deaths on my hands is not so large as you make it out to be."

"One is already too many."

Kett nodded and stepped back from our intimate huddle. I instantly felt bad. He was a vampire. I was pretty much condemning him for something utterly beyond his control. I knew that was naive.

"I will do it," I said. "I should be the one to see this through. But if I'm struck down or incapacitated —"

"I will step in and add to my tally. Which is already too long for your youthful morality, dowser."

"At least you won't be breaking the law." Sienna had been tried and convicted. Her life was forfeit and had been even before she'd learned to keep the powers that she stole from those she murdered. She already had five bodies on her tally, as the vampire called it — including Hudson, Rusty, Jeremy, and two other werewolves — and those were only the ones I knew about.

"But I would for you, Jade." With a terrible sadness, Kett brushed his fingers across my cheek and then stepped into the suite so quickly I almost didn't see him go.

Something was really up with the vampire. He wouldn't tell me what it was until it was past necessary for me to know. I just hoped we got out of London before whatever he was worried about also became an issue for the rest of us.

Chapter Nine

Kandy hadn't returned to the hotel by the time we were ready to go. We texted the werewolf our destination and then set out on foot. The balmy night had cleared enough I could see a few stars, despite the reflected lights of the city. It was a lovely evening for a walk, except for the hunting and potentially slaughtering my sister part.

As we neared our destination, we circled the two outer blocks twice to dowse for magical activity. There wasn't any. So it was just after midnight on November 9th when Kett, Drake, and I turned onto Duval Street, aka the former Dorset Street.

"Millar's Court was entered through a passageway between numbers twenty-six and twenty-seven, before it was demolished in 1920 to make way for a new fruit market," Kett said.

I glanced over at the vampire — making sure to constantly keep the overly excited Drake in my peripheral vision — to note that his magic was actually glowing within his skin. It should have been dimmed by the fact that the street was well lit.

"Did you read the wiki page, or is that a firsthand accounting?" I teased.

Kett gifted my brilliant repartee with a quirk of his lips.

Drake stepped out of my field of vision and I snagged him back by his hoodie. The hood pulled back from his dark-haired head and exposed the hilt of his sword, which he wore underneath. The gold of the hilt caught and refracted the overhead street light back at me. Drake grinned over his shoulder and dutifully fell into step beside me.

"I don't see a fruit market," I said. The north side of the street was dominated by what looked like offices over warehouse storage. A five-storey open-air parking lot occupied the south side. Each level of the structure looked like a long stretch of balcony, with white aluminum railings and everything. That was odd. Maybe the parked cars liked to have a view?

I paused midway down the block. Kett slipped into the shadows to my left and dampened his cool peppermint magic further. Drake, all honey and almond magic, placed his back to mine, as we'd practiced in training so many times now. Behind me, his magic was muted from my dowser senses … well, as muted as dragon magic could ever be. But this placement, along with how familiar I was to the taste of his magic, helped me focus ahead and around me.

I used my eyes first, noting the small brass plaque on the door to my left. "Importing/Exporting. Now who do I know who supposedly makes a living doing that?" I asked rhetorically.

"Sayers," Kett replied. His voice was just a breath of wind, but Drake and I could hear him perfectly well.

"Yep. You'd think one of the other sorcerers might have mentioned he keeps offices near the site of the Dorset Summoning." I turned to look up at the parking lot across from me. I couldn't taste any other magic nearby. I would have thought London would be full of magic. Glimmers, at least, or people who maybe didn't even know they were a quarter or an eighth magical. But it wasn't. Centuries of humanity dominated here, perhaps whitewashing all the natural magic in its wake.

"This was a stupid guess," I muttered, more to myself than anyone else, even though the other two could hear me just fine. "This is too complicated for Sienna. If it's even possible. She's probably in Barbados. We always wanted to go there ..."

It was anger, not pain that stopped me up. So much anger it squeezed the air out of my lungs. Sienna and I had plans. We'd loved life ... together. At least that was what I thought. How had it gotten so far astray? With me in London, vampire and dragon in tow, hunting my sister? My best friend?

Magic — bitter dark chocolate and something smoother, closer to semisweet chocolate but not so bland — came from the parallel street, opposite the direction of the hotel.

"Kandy and her Nordic werewolf, Jorgen," I murmured, right before they jogged into view.

Kandy tucked her chin — she'd previously been sniffing the air — and glared in our direction. Jorgen was grinning, maybe a little manically.

"Well, the good guys are all here," Drake said. "Time for the bad guys to show and try to outnumber us."

"This isn't a movie, Drake," I said.

"We doubled back. Didn't smell anything," Kandy said as she and Jorgen jaywalked across the street.

"Us as well," I said. "There's nothing here. Just go back to your —"

Then I tasted it ... just a hint of magic ... dark, oily, blood-soaked earth magic.

"Sienna," I breathed. "There." I slowly lifted my hand to point across the street.

"The car park?" Kett asked.

Jorgen flinched. He hadn't known a vampire was hiding in the shadows.

"Odd," Kett murmured. "I would have thought that the warehouse was closer to the historic location."

"Which floor?" Kandy asked.

"I have no idea," I said. "Why can't I taste her more clearly?"

"She's in a protection circle as before?" Kett asked, stepping out of the shadows and startling Jorgen even more. His wolf momentarily rippled across his face and hands, teeth and claws appearing and disappearing in the same breath. Well, that was cool in a completely amped-up freaky way.

"No," I said in response to Kett. "Wouldn't I taste the magic of the circle?" I wrapped the fingers of my left hand through the wedding rings on my necklace, and set my right hand at the hilt of my invisible jade knife. This often helped focus my dowsing magic, but I didn't need it this time. The hint I'd caught before bloomed on its own.

"She's here," I said. I darted across the street, but then realizing the magic was continuing to build, I cried out.

"Down!"

We all flattened ourselves as magic exploded out of the parking lot.

"What is it?" Drake asked. "Has she summoned the demons?"

"No," I answered, peering around the garbage can I'd crouched behind and feeling rather stupid. "Just … um … fog."

"What?" Kandy snapped. We all straightened to stare at the fog that now filled the balconies of the parking garage.

"Sorcerer," Kett spat. Yeah, that was a big reaction from the vampire, but I'm guessing Blackwell's fog spell was an unpleasant memory.

"Not that kind of fog," I said.

With the other four at my heels, I crossed to the entrance of the lot to get a closer look.

"I think I left my oven on," Jorgen blurted, and then spun away.

"What?" Kandy asked, grabbing his arm.

"My oven," the blond werewolf repeated. He tugged his arm against Kandy's grip.

"Perimeter spell," Kett said. "To keep the magically lacking away."

Kandy slapped Jorgen across the face.

The werewolf shook his head and then grinned. "Thanks."

"What is that?" I asked, pointing to a line drawn perpendicular to my feet. "Sand?" The fog was neatly contained on the other side of the line.

Jorgen hunkered down to sniff the sand. "Not beach," he said.

"Break the line, break the spell?" I asked Kett hopefully.

He shook his head, but didn't share his thoughts.

"I can't see through the fog," I said. "Kandy?"

"Me neither."

"Kett?"

"No," the vampire answered reluctantly.

I reached up, palm forward, and extended my hand beyond the sand line and into the fog without resistance. "Not a ward, but ..."

"But?" Drake prompted.

"I can't taste anything beyond the fog. Like all the magic I felt before is diffused now. Evenly distributed through every molecule of fog or something."

"Distributed?" Kett asked.

"Yeah, I can taste magic all around. But I can't distinguish the tastes or pinpoint where the magic is emanating from. Nor can I grab or hold it, which means I can't channel it into the sword."

I turned to look at Kett with an irritated smile.

"Impressive spell," he acknowledged.

"Yep, made specifically for me. And Sienna wouldn't bother cloaking her activities, so I tipped our hand somehow. I'm sorry." This fog spell was obviously the work of a sorcerer who knew my powers, and I'd rather flagrantly displayed my dowsing ability to three sorcerers today. If one of them hadn't been in league with Sienna then, they were now.

"We saw a similar type of magic this evening," Kett said.

"Sayers' diffusing spell, or magical object, or whatever."

"We shouldn't have bothered warning anyone," Kandy spat. "Then they wouldn't have known we were coming."

"I didn't know you were coming at all," I said.

"I said I was." Kandy turned her glare from the fog to me.

I looked over her shoulder at Jorgen. "This isn't a great idea for a first date. What's in this fog could get you killed."

"In the fog itself?" the Nordic werewolf asked.

"No, it seems harmless enough." I swirled my hand within the entrance. I knew there should be a ticket booth and a gate about a car length ahead, but I couldn't see it. "But the black witch has only one reason to be here. She's going to try to raise three demons."

Jorgen smiled manically. "Sounds like fun."

Kandy laughed.

"You talk too much, warrior's daughter," Drake said. Then he stepped into the fog.

"Damn it, Drake," I cried after him. "We need some sort of plan."

"Kandy and Jorgen," Kett said. "First floor, west to east. I'll take the second. Drake and Jade start at the third. We meet together at the fourth and continue together to the top, unless one of us finds something before that." Kett followed Drake into the fog.

"No, splitting up is a bad idea," I said. Kett didn't respond. "And that's only half a plan! What happens if we do run into something and we've split up?"

"Looks like the fog was going to separate us anyway," Kandy said. "This way we won't be worried we've lost each other. See you at the top." She and Jorgen were swallowed by the fog as soon as they moved beyond the sand barrier line. And I was alone for the third time since stepping out of the portal.

I waited for screams, but none came. I waited to see if I could feel the magic of my friends moving through the fog. If I could feel Sienna's magic again … but it had been such a brief taste. What if I was wrong?

"Well, Jade," I said out loud. "Something magical is happening here either way. Why not wade in … it's what you do best anyway." Great … now I was talking to myself.

Drake reached out of the fog, grabbed my left wrist, and pulled me over the sand barrier.

Well, that was one way to make a decision.

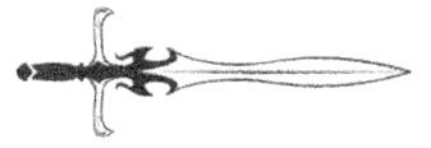

I could barely see anything within the fog, nor could I taste any magic other than the diluted strains that floated all around me. It was as if the fog spell took all the Adepts within its borders, mixed their magic together, and then diffused it throughout the parking lot structure.

"I don't even like breathing in here," I muttered.

"So don't breathe," Drake said.

Helpful, wasn't he?

"The stairs are over here." The fledgling guardian tugged me farther through the fog to the right. He opened the door to the stairs so swiftly that it crashed into my shoulder.

"Ouch! Watch it, Drake!"

"Sorry, didn't see you there."

"You're holding my hand!"

"Yeah, not your shoulder, though."

I sighed, realizing as I did so that in that frustrated expulsion of air, I sounded exactly like my Gran. Damn it.

I pushed past Drake and headed up the stairs.

The fog was thinner in the stairwell, as if it had only gotten in because we'd opened the door. "The fog must have spread out from one place," I said.

"Can you track that?"

"Probably not."

We rounded the stairwell to see a giant number one painted on a blue door.

"The door on the ground floor was green," Drake said.

"Great. Now you won't forget where we parked our car."

"At the hotel. And the valet parked it, not —"

"I was being sarcastic."

"I don't get it."

"It's all right."

The third floor was indicated by a giant number two on a red door. Yeah, the Brits were weird when it came to counting floors.

"Ah, I see. The red line on the floor stops here. As the blue line did at the second floor."

"Yep," I said as I placed my hands on the door and tried to sense any magic from the other side of it. "I've got nothing." Damn, this was frustrating. I didn't realize how much I'd started to rely on my dowsing senses until they were gone. "It would be nice to have a witch around," I said.

"To counter the fog spell?"

"Yeah."

I flattened myself against the wall beside the door and Drake did the same next to me. Yeah, just like they did in the movies. I pulled my jade knife, switched it into my left hand — though I wasn't exactly ambidextrous — and awkwardly reached across to open the door with my right hand.

In one breath, Drake and I spun through the door, crouching low and to the sides. We waited. The fog was thicker again. I could no longer see Drake. The door snapped shut behind us. Nothing else moved or sounded out. Everything was muffled by the fog.

Think. Think. Think. Wandering in the fog was just plain stupid, but I couldn't channel its magic into my sword because I couldn't feel the source of the spell. I was also worried I might end up trying to pull all the fog's diffused magic — Drake, Kett, Kandy, and Jorgen included — into my sword. If that was even possible.

"A fan would be great," I muttered. I peeled myself away from the door and stepped sideways — hand extended — along the wall. "I figure we can follow the wall around the entire floor, back to the door we came out of."

"Okay," Drake said, far too agreeably. I grabbed the back of his hoodie and continued moving. We found the first car right after we hit the white aluminum railing I'd seen from the street, which made sense. Drake leaned over the railing, legs in the air, as he stuck his head out through the fog.

"Can you see?"

"Yes. It's clear here like it was at the entrance."

I crouched down and looked closer at the bottom of the railing. The line of sand appeared there as well. "It must have taken hours to set up this spell," I murmured. Hours that overlapped Sayers chatting in the hotel lounge with me? Maybe I'd been wrong. Or had he spent all day setting the spell, then come to the hotel?

I resisted the urge to scrape away the sand to see if that would release the spell. I was terrified by the thought that a fog like this would just spread and spread until it enveloped the entire city, and then country, perhaps only caged in by the ocean.

Then we'd really need witches, and it would be my foolish, foolhardy fault. "Not this time," I muttered to myself. Then to Drake, I asked, "Anyone on the street?"

"No. The perimeter spell must be keeping the humans away," he answered, then pulled his head back in from over the railing. "There are two floors above us."

"Great," I said, continuing along the white railing in front of a long line of cars, front bumper after front bumper. This must be long-term or overnight parking.

As we neared what I guessed was the center front of the parking lot, I thought I heard something. I paused and lost Drake as he took off in a swirl of fog. Damn it, I'd loosened my hold on him when I crouched to check the sand.

I was going to have to follow him. His hearing was better than mine, so obviously the noise meant something to him.

Knife drawn and back in my proper hand, I darted forward between two cars. I crossed the center lane and stepped between two other cars, which were parked facing the other direction.

Then I nearly fell through the center of the building.

Well, that was an exaggeration. I would have had to leap a four-foot-high concrete wall to fall through, but it was still a shock. The parking lot was built in a rectangular spiral that left the center open through all five storeys, a space about twelve feet across.

Of course, that wasn't as much of a shock as seeing Edmonds suspended in the air directly in front of us, three storeys up. He was held by thick ropes that formed a pentagram, lashed to the columns in the very middle of the open well at the heart of the building.

The fog was thinner here, but I still couldn't see more than a few feet below or above Edmonds. I guessed I could only see the unconscious sorcerer because whatever spell coated the ropes of the pentagram also kept the fog spell at bay. He looked way younger than his forty plus years and vulnerable without his tortoise-shell glasses or elbow patches.

Drake stepped out of the fog to my left. He was walking along the edge of the short wall that had stopped me from falling through the center of the building, as if he'd just circled the perimeter.

"I can't tell if he's alive," the fledgling guardian said. His voice was unnaturally grim.

"He's alive." As I watched the too-pale sorcerer, I saw his chest slowly rise and fall.

"Spelled?"

"Most likely. As is the rope."

"So we cut the ropes and free the sorcerer."

"Right. Except we don't know if the spell is anchored here or below or above. Also, we don't know that if we cut the rope, we won't trigger the spell." I called to Edmonds. "Ummm, Professor? Professor, can you hear me?"

The spelled sorcerer didn't respond.

I narrowed my eyes and desperately tried to anchor my dowsing senses in my necklace and knife. I thought I could see a line of magic running up and down from Edmonds, as if bisecting him through his heart. "Do you see that?" I asked Drake. "That line of magic, blue-black? There! When the fog shifts?"

He peered where I indicated, but then shook his head.

"Okay," I said, preparing to come up with some plan. I was way, way out of my depth here, and feeling just as lost in the fog as was intended. I didn't think my next confrontation with my sister would go like this … I thought I had prepared, trained.

I peered up and then down over the short concrete wall and through the ropes, but I couldn't see the next floors. I looked at the concrete pillars on either side of me, to which the pentagram was lashed. They were smooth and free of handholds, which made total sense safety-wise but was still a bitch. Drake might be able to jump up from floor to floor. Hell, the fledgling might be able to jump off the top floor and land without hurting himself, but I couldn't. Not without seeing where I was going, at least.

"Back to the stairs?" I didn't like leaving Edmonds, but I also wasn't sure I could rescue him without finding the origin of the spell. "The source is probably on the first floor, where they could actually anchor it to the earth. At least, that's how witch magic would work."

But if it was, then Kandy and Jorgen would find it — if they could sense the magic once they got near enough, despite the diffusion of the fog spell. I pulled out my cellphone, half-heartedly hoping it worked in the fog. It didn't. I sighed. "Or it's a series of pentagrams suspended over open air from here to the top floor."

"You've seen this magic before?" Drake asked as we cut through the fog directly west, or maybe it was east, to find the door. I assumed there was a second stairwell at the opposite side from which we'd come, so either direction worked. They'd both lead up. The car bumpers made it a little easier to find our path through the fog quickly.

"No," I replied. "I'm just guessing. Three demons, three pentagrams."

"All with sorcerers in them."

"I hope not."

"Your sister is powerful enough to capture or compel three sorcerers?"

"I hope not."

We found the stairs to the fourth floor and headed up. Thankfully, Drake kept his mouth shut — and kept to himself his dragon philosophy about the futility of hoping for something you already knew wasn't possible.

For a moment, as we approached the center of the fourth floor, I was able to hope I was wrong about my multiple-pentagrams-all-connected-by-a-single-spell theory.

Then, with my hands set on the low concrete wall as I peered ahead, the fog parted and I saw Clark spread-eagled and trussed up in a roped pentagram suspended across the open air, directly above Edmonds. Not that I could see Edmonds below.

For some reason, seeing the older man strung up like that — his comb-over fallen to the wrong side of his head — made me even angrier. It was so undignified. So unbelievable that my sister would come into London and treat people like pieces on her own personal chessboard.

"Pawns," Drake said, stepping out from the fog after walking the perimeter of the concrete wall.

"What?"

"Like pawns on a chessboard."

"Was I talking out loud?"

"Yeah. You do that a lot."

Shit. "Is the pentagram set up the same way?" I shelved the discussion of my sanity for later, but was really hoping I didn't have entire conversations out loud. Especially not conversations with my sister.

"Looks like it. Tied to columns at five points. Magic on the rope."

"No fog within, though," I said.

"So the pentagram is sealed with a spell?"

"Above and below, I think. And the same column of magic rises out from Clark. See directly above and below his heart?"

I could see the deep blue line more clearly now. Either I was more in tune with the magic, now that I knew what to look for, or the fog was dissipating.

Drake shook his head. Not counting the exceptional power of Pulou the treasure keeper, all dragons could see or feel magic, and the fledgling was able to identify specific types of Adept easily. My dowsing abilities seemed to be connected to my witch magic more than my dragon side, though.

I peered upward but couldn't see to the next level. "Want to bet on door number three?"

"Four," Drake answered. "We're going to the fifth floor next, right? The doors were numbered from the ground floor up."

"I meant … never mind. It was on the edge of sick and twisted anyway. Door number four it is."

Except it wasn't Sayers as I thought it would be, strung out in the pentagram within the empty space of the fifth floor.

It was Mory.

The fog had parted as it had each time we'd neared the well. Drake stepped up on the ledge to walk the perimeter, just as I laid eyes on the fledgling necromancer.

Mory wasn't spread-eagled and tied into the rope pentagram like Edmonds and Clark. Her hands and ankles were trussed with what looked like the same rope, but she was perched with her legs cradled to her chest in the center of the pentagram. She wore the necklace I'd made to protect her from malicious magic. Unfortunately, it didn't prevent kidnapping.

"Mory!" I cried.

The black-swathed, army-boot-wearing, pale-skinned fifteen-year-old scowled at me. "Stealthy, Jade," she said.

"Where's Sienna? What's going on?"

"What does it look like, duh?"

"Hello, necromancer," Drake said cheerfully as he crouched on the four-foot wall beside me.

Mory's hair dye had grown out two inches or so. The lavender tips were washed out and scraggly. She looked like she hadn't eaten since I'd last fed her. My heart constricted, and for a moment, I couldn't speak past the pain of it. I thought the feeling might be joy, but I didn't remember joy hurting so much before. "I thought … I worried …"

"Yeah, well, maybe I would have been better off dead," the teenager said.

"She's not a happy person," Drake said.

"She's a necromancer," I answered.

"I see." Drake nodded, projecting Chi Wen's sage quality again.

"Who the hell are you?" Mory snapped.

"Drake," the fledgling guardian replied with a wide grin. "Jade's friend."

Mory's scowl deepened. "Good luck with that, Drake." The necromancer managed to make the thirteen-year-old's name sound like a curse word.

Yeah, teenaged angst at its worst. Thank God she was okay.

"We're going to cut her down," I said.

"But you said —"

"I know, but —"

"You aren't going to cut her down." Kett's voice came out of the fog to my left. Drake actually flinched. I felt the proximity of the life debt bond Kett owed me a second before the vampire spoke. Even the fog couldn't dissipate that, it seemed.

Kett stepped forward to observe Mory like she was a bug caught in his web.

"Great," Mory groused. "You brought the vampire."

"He's been hunting for you for three months, Mory."

"Actually," Kett said, "I've been looking for the witch."

"Whatever," Mory snapped. "Took you all way too long. And now if you cut these ropes, we all die.

And if you don't cut these ropes, we all die. Or some sorcerer shit like that."

"Sayers."

"Who knows, some guy. She found him online. They don't talk in front of me."

"So we counter the spell," I said, turning to Kett.

He nodded. "It's anchored on the first floor."

"But if we cut the anchor ..."

"This all collapses."

"So we still need the source."

"Try the roof, morons," Mory said.

I took a deep breath. "Where are Kandy and Jorgen?"

"I sent Jorgen for reinforcements. Kandy is with Edmonds."

"Three witches would be nice."

"We'll have to settle for werewolves. If they get here quickly enough."

I peered up and saw hints of the starry night sky. The fog was thinning the closer we got to open air.

Magic thrummed through the ropes of the pentagram.

Mory gasped and scrambled to her feet. She was now standing in the very center of the pentagram, which as I'd suspected was sealed from below. She looked across at me with wide eyes, all her belligerence washed away by fear. "She ... she ... can't drain me because of the necklace."

The fledgling necromancer twined her fingers around the necklace resting on her collarbone. I'd made this necklace specifically to protect Mory from Sienna, and from Mory's brother Rusty. Or his ghost, rather. His spectral energy or whatever he was. The necklace was presumably also the reason the necromancer wasn't sleep spelled like the two other sorcerers. I imagined that Sienna had deliberately left Mory ungagged. It was just another twisted way of hurting me further. This time with Mory's own words.

"But she can siphon off bits of my magic," Mory continued. "She thinks she has enough now, and that with the anniversary date and the location, she can raise and control those demons with the knife that raised them before."

"This isn't even the correct location," Kett said.

"All that matters now is what Sienna thinks is true," I said. "And what she's willing to do to make something happen. Drake, stay with Mory." I turned into the fog.

"Jade!" Mory cried after me.

I turned back. "You're not going to die today, Mory. I'm sorry I left you before. I'm really glad you're alive, even if you hate me forever. But you're not going to die today."

To Drake, I added: "If the spell comes down before I neutralize Sienna, or Sayers, whoever is casting — you cut the rope."

Drake nodded. He pulled his broadsword out in a flash of gold that I could see clearly despite the fog.

"No," I said, "with this." For the first time since I'd crafted it, I willfully handed over my jade knife to another person.

Drake took the blade with reverence. He nodded solemnly.

"No, Jade," Mory said. "If you cut the rope, the spell will backlash and everyone might die."

"Not Drake, Mory. Magic can't kill him. He is magic." I sounded way more sure of myself than I actually was. "Drake, you cut the rope, you grab Mory, and you head for the nearest portal."

Drake frowned and started to protest.

"Not for you," I said. "For Mory."

He nodded.

I turned away, not sure whether my knife could even get through the spell on the rope while it was in Drake's hands. The fog prevented me from fully assessing the magic of the pentagram. The knife had cut through Blackwell's wards, though, so all I could do was hope.

Because I couldn't send anyone else after Sienna. I was the only one who could resist her magic … unless she had new tricks and new magic. Then she was going to kick my ass. Though I also had a shiny new sword, so maybe we'd be even.

"You take the sorcerer," I said to the fog, knowing that Kett was somewhere near. "Unless he's casting. Then I will take him." I felt naked without my knife, but at least I still had my katana. This was my sword's destiny, after all.

"As you desire, warrior's daughter," the vampire replied from out of the fog. He sounded far too pleased. But then, I was still in denial about that part of me. The part that wanted to kick Sienna's ass way more than I wanted cupcakes, chocolate, or pretty new trinkets.

My sister brought out the darkness in me.

Chapter Ten

I stepped out onto the roof of the parking lot. It was completely open to the night air, and the fog was thicker around my knees than my head. Which was good, because I was going to need my eyes.

Sienna was waiting for me. She and Sayers were standing in a roped pentagram rigged at the top of the parking lot's central open well.

It hurt to look at Sienna with her bulging black veins and inky eyes. She wore a fabric bag slung across a tattered cloak. She was going for bag-lady chic now. I was also unhappy to note that she was wearing what looked like three of my trinkets. I hoped she'd had a stash, because I really didn't like thinking that she'd gone back to Vancouver for them. Sayers was still in the suit, which made it more obvious he'd come directly here from the hotel. I guess the sorcerer had wanted a look at me before he tried to kill me. I couldn't figure out if that was polite or insanely rude.

Sayers, as best as I could see, was putting the final touches on the pentagram spell, because unlike the three below us, it wasn't sealed. Within the thinned fog, I could taste the sorcerer's sugared Earl Grey essence and Sienna's old blood-drenched earth magic.

I tamped down on this nausea-inducing combination, and — just for a moment — wished I hadn't given my knife to Drake. I had a clear shot at Sienna, but I couldn't throw the katana slung across my back the way I could throw my jade knife.

"Hello, sister," Sienna said. She was holding the sacrificial knife she'd used to kill Jeremy. The anger that had been on a low simmer in my belly now ramped up, until I felt like my heart might be on fire.

I didn't have any witty words. I didn't want to trade quips with my evil best friend. I just wanted this to be over, over, over.

Kett stepped into my peripheral vision. Sienna's black-lipped smile widened at the sight of the vampire. This stretched the black veins snaking across her face in such a way that my belly rolled with a different kind of queasiness, but I didn't look away.

"Back for more, vampire?" Sienna purred. Then she snapped her teeth at him. Yeah, that was my sister now, cheesy and evil. In a strange reversal of roles, she had drunk Kett's blood in the basement of my bakery six months ago ...

Wait.

Blood.

Sienna's blood spreading across the altar in the vision Chi Wen shared with me ...

"Don't drink her blood," I hissed to Kett.

He furrowed his brow.

I could clearly remember Kett slumped off to the side of the cave in Chi Wen's vision, as if it was my own memory. But what could possibly kill — or at least incapacitate — the vampire in that version of the future?

"I saw ... I was shown something," I said, sorting quickly through my thoughts. Sienna had cocked her head to one side as if trying to hear our conversation.

"In the nexus?" Kett asked with an involuntary shiver. Yeah, vampire and dragon magic really didn't mix.

"Yes, by the far seer."

Kett nodded as he slipped off into the fog to my left. It hardly even swirled in his wake. I reached for my sword, pushing Chi Wen's vision — and the way Sienna's black blood had spilled from her body and mixed into the blood of my loved ones — out of my mind. I focused on the tip of the sword as I brought it forward to point at Sienna.

Three leaps — now that I could vaguely see where I was going — was all it took to cross the space between my sister and me. I pulled the sword back over my head, ready to strike. And for a moment, right before I tried to lop her head off, I held Sienna's surprised gaze.

Yeah, I could come up with new tricks in three and a half months as well. Like speed and strength and a shiny new sword.

Sienna threw up her hands. Black magic sparked between them, but she was too late.

Still in midair, I swung the sword, twisting it slightly right over my shoulder and across.

I hit a magical barrier.

Sayers had sealed off the pentagram.

My katana crashed against the ward in a multicolored flare of magic, which threw me — still twisted in strike pose — back the way I'd come.

I slammed into a parked car fifteen feet away, blowing out its windshield and caving in its roof with my landing.

Ouch.

Sienna was laughing, though I couldn't see her as I was once again swallowed in fog.

"Pretty sword, Jadey!" she cried as she clapped her hands.

I peeled myself off the crushed car, glass tinkling to the concrete all around me. I felt badly for the owner. Hopefully his insurance covered acts of God, because I wasn't sure how else he'd explain it.

I crouched low beside the passenger-side front tire — noting it had exploded — and placed the flat edge of my blade across my left wrist. I held the sword close to my eyes in an attempt to examine it in the fog. It seemed unscathed.

"You okay, sis?" Sienna called, which confirmed she couldn't see me in the fog either.

I sheathed the sword over my shoulder and ran through a quick series of downward dogs and planks to make sure I hadn't broken any bones. Any aches sustained from the magical backlash and my trashing the car eased.

"We need her to trigger the spell," Sayers hissed. I could hear him clearly through the fog.

I eased forward, staying in my crouch, and made my way back to the pentagram.

"I know, sorcerer," Sienna spat. "It's my idea, isn't it?"

"But I had to seal the pentagram prematurely. We have to drop and then reinitialize the spell."

I started laughing. Then I laughed some more. I'd seen fewer cars on the roof than below, but my laughter hit and bounced off all of them to reverberate through the fog.

"I warned you, Sayers," I said. Then I laughed again.

Somewhere on the other side of the pentagram, hidden within the fog, Kett started laughing. Dear God, I hoped I didn't sound quite as creepy as he did. I was seriously glad he was on my side tonight, because that laugh was going to haunt my dreams.

"Shut up!" Sienna screamed. She always did have a low breaking point. Once sealed in the pentagram, I assumed that she and Sayers wouldn't be able to cast outward, so screaming was all she could do to Kett and me.

"She played you, Sayers," I called out as I stepped around another car. I could feel Kett doing the same on the other side of the pentagram, through the life debt bond and through his magic. The fog wasn't diffusing that magic as much up here on the roof. "She had no intention of triggering the spell with my blood."

"What is she —" Sayers began.

"Shut your stupid hole, Jade," Sienna said. "You're just embarrassing yourself, again. Don't listen to her."

For some reason, Kett found this doubly amusing. His laughter ramped up accordingly.

I rose out of the fog, facing Sayers, who'd moved to the final point of the pentagram when he'd sealed the spell. If there hadn't been a ward between us, I could have reached out and smacked him.

He flinched at my appearance. I raised a finger to my lips and smiled at him. This confused him, as it should have.

Sienna was standing with her back to us. Her lips were moving as she bowed her head over the original copy of Blackwell's book.

She was already starting the ritual.

I tried a bit of sign language with Sayers. I tapped my ear and then my chest — 'Listen to me.'

I brought my hands up in the universal shrug meaning 'Why?' Then I showed him four fingers. Why four? Why four pentagrams, I meant, for three demons?

Sayers' confusion deepened.

Stupid freaking sorcerers.

Sienna marked her place in the book with the sacrificial knife, then put the book in her fabric bag. Up close, the bag was actually just a burlap sack tied at the two upper corners with rope. This … this was baffling from a girl who'd once put a Louis Vuitton bag on layaway for over a year, and then slept on my couch so she didn't have to pay rent at the same time.

A little more frantically now, I gestured toward Sayers — 'You' — then slashed my hand in the air and pointed at my chest again — 'Not me.'

You not me.

"What?" Sayers asked.

"Jesus Christ," I snapped as I watched Sienna spin around. "You stupid freaking sorcerer. Four pentagrams for three demons?"

"The fourth triggers the spell —"

"No, idiot. A sorcerer triggers a spell … or a black witch with the powers of a sorcerer. This pentagram is for her spell. You know, for when she drains your magic. Duck, asshole."

Sayers ducked as Sienna lunged toward him with a small switchblade she'd had hidden in her cloak.

The sorcerer spun away but got his foot caught on the ropes of the pentagram. The spell sealed it from underneath, but the thick rope was still difficult to walk on.

"Been taking your smarty-pants pills, hey Jadey?" Sienna sneered.

It doesn't take much intelligence to outsmart you was on the tip of my tongue, but I kept my mouth shut. I didn't want to address her. I didn't want to treat her like a person.

As Sayers fell, he raised his hands, muttered something under his breath, and cast a spell. I still couldn't taste the magic, but I could see it. The unknown spell hit Sienna, slamming her back against the ward that kept her just out of my reach.

Sayers scrambled to his feet as Sienna fell to her knees.

Kett rose out of the fog beside me. "It was smart to play them off each other," he said.

"Excuse me?" I answered in mock surprise. "Did you just compliment me?"

Kett leveled a cool I'm-not-amused look at me. I grinned back.

The black witch and the sorcerer continued to do battle within the pentagram.

"She'll kill him eventually," Kett said.

"Yeah. We need to counter the connection to the other pentagrams before that. I gather we can't do it the same way we did in the cave?" Kett and I had collapsed the pentagram in the Sea Lion Caves by using the magic in his blood as a catalyst, which I then triggered with my knife.

"No, not with four pentagrams tied together."

"If collapsing this one triggers the others, then we take them out of order. Get Mory out first?"

"You would kill Edmonds and Clark to rescue the necromancer?" Kett asked the question without judgement, but with a lot of curiosity.

"Okay, fine," I said.

Sayers had been holding his own, but Sienna's spells were hitting him harder and harder as the fight progressed.

"Sorcerer," I called. "Take down the ward. We'll spare your life."

Sienna slammed Sayers with her fireblood spell. He was able to scream, so I gathered it didn't hit him at full strength.

"We have to counter the ward," I hissed at Kett.

"Without witches at each pentagram —"

"Stop naysaying and come up with something."

"When the sorcerer dies, any spell solely constructed by him will fall as well."

I turned from glaring at Kett to watch Sienna looming over Sayers. He was dragging himself away from her, toward Kett and me. He was more than half dead already.

"Sienna," I said. "Stop this. I don't understand any of this. Why are you doing it? To what end?"

"Oh, so now you want to talk to me? Now you want to know why?" Sienna answered. "There is no 'Why.' No 'Because.' There is only today and then tomorrow. And tomorrow, I shall be more than I was today."

Sayers rolled over on his stomach, locked eyes with me, and reached for the point of the pentagram that I was closest to. Sienna yanked the sorcerer backward by his hair as his fingers brushed the point where the ropes intersected.

The ward fell.

Kett and I lunged forward just as Sienna slit Sayers throat.

Blood spurted across my face and chest. My sword was in my hands. I drew back to swing. Sienna's magic was everywhere. I could taste it as it swirled around Sayers, as if it might be lapping at the lifeblood pumping out of him.

My blade was inches from Sienna's neck as my foot landed on the top edge of the concrete wall.

Everything went black.

Sienna had trapped the wall.

Kett would have called this touch-triggered spell inspired. I just called it crazy painful, and was super pissed at myself for missing it within all the magic-diffusing fog and Sayers' magic literally gushing out of him.

I knew it was Sienna's work, because when I did finally wake — sprawled with my ass on the hood of another car and my head crammed against the short concrete footing of the exterior railing — her magic was all I could taste. Trigger-released spells not tied to a magical object, which I'm sure I would have sensed, were impressive. I mourned for the witch who had to die for Sienna to learn that trick.

I tried opening my eyes, but all I saw was black and pinpoints of light … then a flashing light? A plane. I was staring at the night sky.

I rolled off the car and just lay on the concrete for a while. I couldn't feel my legs. I was really hoping the foot that had triggered the spell hadn't been blown to bits. I'm not sure my dragon-inherited healing worked on missing limbs. I cranked my neck sideways to look. Nope, I still had two feet.

The fog was gone. So Sayers was dead.

I reached out with my dowser senses — struggling to get the taste of Sienna's dark blood magic out of my mouth, and nose, and head — and tried to find Kett. I couldn't sense him, but when I cranked my head in the other direction, I could see the buckled and trashed railing to my left. I guessed he'd gone off the roof. Lucky for him that he was already dead, so the five-storey fall couldn't kill him.

A whole hell of a lot of magic was boiling up from the center of the parking lot. I managed to sit up and look as more of my body came under control. I could taste Sayers, Edmonds, Clark, and Mory, as well as Sienna. My sister's magic overrode all the others.

Sienna stood with Sayers obviously dead at her feet. She was reading from the demon history book. The asshole sorcerer who'd written the chronicle had included the incantation used in 1888. Freaking arrogant sorcerer. I could see Sienna's lips move, but I couldn't hear her.

Yeah, that really was a wicked stunning spell.

I managed to get to my feet, even though I still couldn't feel the right one, and reached for my sword. It wasn't on my back.

Damn.

I looked around, but Sienna was raising the sacrificial knife above her head now. Though I had no idea what she was going to do with it, I ran at her.

She turned and saw me coming. Just as I leaped for her, she simply dropped the knife into the pool of Sayers' blood at her feet.

I crashed into her and we flew onto the empty pavement behind the pentagram, rolling ass over head until we slammed against the metal door to the stairs. The force of our tumble actually caused the door and its concrete housing to buckle and collapse.

From behind me, I sensed dark, dusty cemetery-tasting magic. Then dank, rotten graveyard magic spread down deep, as if reaching into the crap-filled bowels of the earth.

"Drake," I screamed, "cut the rope!"

I untangled myself from Sienna, who thankfully appeared to be knocked out. I tossed off the clumps of concrete that hindered me and made it to my feet for a third time in less than ten minutes. I ran for the pentagram, feeling the magic grow as it hit the anchor point five storeys below. It then sprang back to hit the first pentagram. Edmonds started screaming as if he was being ripped apart. Sayers must have cast the sleep spells, but now with him dead, they were nullified.

Oh, God …

My right foot wasn't working properly. I hadn't noticed before, but now — waiting to hear Mory start screaming — I felt like I could barely move, as if I was stuck in masses of marshmallows or molasses.

I made it to the pentagram and peered over the short wall and through the ropes, seeing Mory and Drake one floor below. Drake was hacking at the rope with his broadsword.

"My knife!" I cried. "My knife!"

"Didn't work," Drake yelled back as he slashed at the spelled rope a couple of inches from Mory's feet.

The necromancer looked up at me. She was clutching her necklace, and her eyes were way, way too big for her pixie face.

Then she smiled, just to break my heart further.

A demon literally ripped through and out of Edmonds' corpse three-storeys below. It was mottled gray, looked vaguely like a Chinese guardian lion without the mane, and was the size of my bakery walk-in fridge. That is if my fridge suddenly grew seven-inch claws and double-fanged teeth. Buying us a few seconds, the demon helpfully stopped to eat Edmonds' corpse as its first meal in the human dimension.

Though where the hell Sienna had actually summoned it from — seeing as demons turned to dust when killed — I had no freaking idea. My sister had obviously figured out a way to substitute the sorcerers' corpses for the nonexistent demon corpses. Then, combining sorcery, necromancy, and black magic, she'd raised the vanquished. So did that mean that demons left spectral energy behind when they were killed? That idea didn't help at all with the terror that was currently controlling my brain.

Clark — still strung up directly above this first demon — had managed to twist his head enough to see it rise through Edmonds' corpse. He began to shriek in anticipation.

The screaming grew worse as the magic moved up another level and hit the portly sorcerer. He would be a good-sized snack for his demon. Oh, God. That was a sick … sick … utterly terrified thought.

I locked my gaze to Mory's. Drake was barely denting the magic of the pentagram ward with his sword. I could see new slash marks each time he brought the blade down, and he wouldn't give up before he broke through, but it was going to be too late.

An eerie calm settled over me. Then I did the only thing I could do.

Without even looking, I bent down and picked up the sacrificial knife, which was now coated in Sayers' blood. I could sense that the knife was still tied to the demon spell, but I had no idea how to use that. I wasn't that kind of witch.

I was an alchemist.

I took all the magic I could feel still in Sayers' blood — Sienna hadn't even siphoned a third of it — and used my magic to bind it to the residual magic of the knife and the remaining magic of the summoning spell. I fortified the blade with everything I had at my fingertips. I informed it that it could now cut through any magic.

Then I hacked through the blood-soaked rope at my feet like a crazy person.

Yes, I was performing blood magic without even pausing to worry about the consequences. Yes, I created a knife of terrible power filled with the blood magic of a sorcerer almost as powerful as Blackwell — again without even worrying about it.

I couldn't get to Mory quickly enough any other way.

The rope gave way and I fell, hit the ward that was still actively holding Mory prisoner, and rolled off it to Drake's side. Sayers' body fell as well, but it didn't roll off the dome of the ward. Instead, it hung rather grotesquely suspended over Mory.

The Edmonds demon shook its head — the only remaining evidence of the creature's host were the grisly bits caught in its maw — and leaped upward in an attempt to grab hold of Clark, or at least the rope holding Clark. It couldn't get a hold, so it shrieked, opening its mouth terrifyingly wide. As in, the width of a fridge door.

Drake pressed the jade knife into my hand but I ignored him. Clark stopped screaming below us. That wasn't good.

I brought the transformed sacrificial knife down on the rope of the pentagram.

The second demon tore through Clark's corpse fifteen feet below us, then immediately started gorging itself on the dead sorcerer even before its hind legs had fully emerged.

Drake thrust his arms forward just as the ward, and then the rope, collapsed underneath Mory's feet. He snagged the fledgling necromancer's bound wrists just as the Clark demon — still finishing off Clark's corpse — grabbed Mory's legs.

The displaced magic of the pentagram ricocheted through the severed rope and hit the Clark demon, which was hanging off the rope with one hand and straining to eat Mory with the other.

The Clark demon shrieked and lost its hold on Mory.

The unfinished spell hit Sayers' corpse, which was tangled in the rope still tied to the other side of the low concrete wall. As Drake pulled Mory over that wall, the third demon erupted from Sayers' corpse, covered in blood and intestines. It didn't pause to eat Sayers, though — not when I was alive and breathing and within easy reach.

The demon hit me. Its claws raked through my hoodie and scored my leather vest underneath. We tumbled backward, smashing into Drake, who had time only to wrap himself around Mory to protect her.

I wrestled frantically with the demon, which was only two feet taller than me, but felt like it weighed a hundred tons. It was striking me faster than I could heal, and I was already slick with my own blood.

But we'd managed to rescue Mory. Everything else would be okay now. My heart rate steadied and my mind cleared.

I jammed the sacrificial knife into the demon's maw, managing to get both my feet underneath its chest to throw it off me. It hit a car across the way and slid off the trunk, shrieking and batting at the knife wedged in its mouth. The idiot had bitten down, puncturing its upper jaw and nose with the blade.

I rolled to my feet.

Across from me, Drake was defending Mory from the Clark demon. It was still somehow wearing the sorcerer's knit cardigan, the sweater tangled around the small horns or ridges of its head. For some reason, this sight made me crazy angry.

Drake swung his broadsword and slashed the demon's shoulder, cutting deep. The demon scrambled away, just out of reach of the blade. Drake couldn't press it because Mory — clutching my jade knife in both hands — was hunched against a car. She was shaking violently, maybe going into shock. But she'd cut the ropes binding her wrists and ankles at least.

The Sayers demon decided to ignore the knife embedded in its mouth and leaped for me, but I was ready for it this time. I met its lunge with a forward chest kick and followed through with a knee underneath its jaw. This drove the knife farther into what should have been the creature's brain, but caused it only to stumble.

"Drake," I called. "Behind you on three."

The fledgling guardian didn't respond as the Clark demon took another swipe at him, but I knew he heard me.

"One ..." I said, lunging forward with my left foot. "Two ..." I leaped into the air, bringing my right foot — which I still couldn't totally feel — forward. "Three ..."

I slammed this foot into the Sayers demon, driving it back toward Drake. In a spectacular move, he spun, severed the neck of the demon with his broadsword, and then continued his spin to once again face off with the Clark demon. He'd kept himself between the demon and Mory the entire time.

The Sayers demon's head slipped sideways and hit the ground in a shower of ash.

The Clark demon shrieked, scurried back to the collapsed pentagram, and leaped for the severed rope hanging down from the roof.

I crossed to and picked up the sacrificial knife. Its dark magic thrummed against the skin of my palm. I dusted the ash off it and hoped I could unmake what I'd made.

Drake was dragging Mory to her feet when the Edmonds demon, looking rather slashed and bruised, climbed up the concrete column and leaped from ledge to ledge toward the roof.

Kandy — in full half-beast form — climbed after him, using the ropes of the severed pentagram and the ledges. She was favoring one arm as she did so.

"Wait," I cried after the werewolf, but she was gone. "At least they're heading for the roof and not the street." I realized my mistake as soon as I said the words. Sienna was on the roof. "Drake, you need to move Mory to safety."

Dank magic blew by me like a blast of wind. My ears sealed and then unsealed with a pop. "Shit," I swore. "She's awake."

I looked toward the open railing and could see a ripple of magic in the air. A ward. "She's used Sayers' sand boundary for the fog to seal us in."

Damn it. My sister was way too strong. And Kandy was up on the roof alone.

"Stairs," I hissed at Drake. Sienna might expect us to climb up after the demons. Maybe the stairs gave us a bit of a chance at surprising her.

Drake got Mory's arm over his shoulders. The petite necromancer was so much shorter than the fledgling guardian that her toes barely touched down in this position. Which was fine, because Drake had no issue with practically carrying her as we ran for the stairs.

The top of the stairs were shattered from Sienna and me smashing into them from above. That the two of us together could crush this much concrete and steel was a scary, scary reality, so I just pushed it out of my mind.

I climbed up first, staying crouched at the upper level and hopefully out of sight. Then I reached down for Mory. Drake lifted her to me and I hauled her up. Jesus, her wrists were going to be bruised to hell from all of this, but she didn't make a sound as I settled her beside me in the rubble.

Drake joined us.

I reached behind me and touched the jade knife Mory still clutched. She tried to press it into my hand and I shook my head. I pushed my magic into the blade and whispered, "No one can take this away from you, except me."

Mory nodded her understanding as the magic settled into the knife.

I couldn't get her out of the parking lot — not quickly, at least — and I couldn't take on two demons and Sienna without Drake, so the necromancer would have to stick with us. The thought made me sick, and I tamped down on the emotion. Guilt wasn't going to make any of this go away.

"If you happen to see my sword, let me know," I said to Drake.

He nodded, and as one, we sprang out of our crouches and onto the roof.

Chapter Eleven

Without the fog, the night sky was clear, though it had been raining all day. The surrounding buildings were a well-lit background. Though not many seemed to be residences, I imagined the police would be alerted to our disturbance soon, if they hadn't been already.

So, yeah. Clear night.

So clear I had no problem seeing Sienna standing on the far side of the parking lot with her foot on Kandy's chest and the demons on either side of her. And yeah, she had my katana.

"I see your sword," Drake said, not a hint of humor in his tone.

"Yeah, me too."

Mory climbed out of the rubble behind us. I could taste her toasted marshmallow magic gathering behind me.

"Is Rusty here?" I asked.

Mory nodded.

"Would he like to come out to play?" We needed all hands on deck, including the ghost of Mory's brother who had a special hate for Sienna — seeing as how she murdered him. Rusty wasn't exactly an innocent himself. But then, none of us were anymore. Again, thanks to Sienna.

"She figured out how to counter him," Mory whispered.

That made sense. Even Sienna couldn't put up with being constantly attacked by the spectral energy of her ex-boyfriend for long. A boyfriend she'd killed and drained of magic.

"She's using large amounts of magic tonight. If Rusty bides his time, I imagine he'll find an opening."

Mory nodded and set her jaw in determination.

Sienna was grandstanding, spinning the sword around with her wrist. Everything was a show with my sister. Hey, I liked a great presentation as much as anyone, but she took it way too far.

Drake and I stepped closer. In two swift movements, we had halved the distance between us and Sienna. Mory stayed behind.

I wasn't sure at first that Kandy was breathing, but her magic bloomed and then twisted around her. She transformed back into her human form and curled into a ball at Sienna's feet. She looked worse than before with her cuts, bruises, and torn clothing, but I knew the transformation was a way her magic helped to heal her.

Sienna looked startled to see us suddenly so close. She laid the tip of my sword on Kandy's neck.

Drake casually reached underneath the bumper of a smashed car — my ass was indented into its hood — and pushed it out of his way, opening up the field before and around us.

Sienna's eyes widened. She laughed like a little girl getting an unexpected gift.

"If you clap your hands, you'll find this knife in your throat," I said. I raised the sacrificial knife before me as if ready to throw. I was bluffing, though. The knife's balance was totally off. The accuracy of a throw would be chancy, and then I'd be weaponless.

The demons pawed at the ground and snorted. I had no idea how Sienna was controlling them — technically, I was holding the knife — but I wasn't sure how she'd constructed the spell in the first place.

"Three against two, Jade," Sienna said. "I'd watch your mouth and start begging."

"You always were terrible at math, sister," I said.

Sienna started to sneer, but her retort was cut off by Kett rising — all red-eyed and fanged — out of the darkness behind her and latching onto her neck.

Damn it! I'd told him not to bite her. Some sort of spell exploded around them — the dark magic buffeted me as I charged forward — and they tumbled sideways.

The demons shook their heads like dogs shaking off water. Then they fell on Kandy.

Drake and I attacked as one, dropkicking different demons. Drake's sword flashed and his demon shrieked. I rounded on mine, but the damn thing scampered away and flung itself at the wrestling mess that was Sienna and Kett.

Sienna had dropped my sword by Kandy. I reached for it as Kett managed to fling the demon off his back and over my head. His back was scored with claw marks that instantly healed. Unfortunately, in order to toss the demon, Kett had removed his teeth from Sienna's neck, giving her just enough time to fling out a spell. They were situated in the middle of the rest of us, and Sienna somehow managed to cast in all directions at once. Her trusty fireblood spell hit me, Kett, Mory, Drake, and Kandy, but unfortunately not the demons.

Pain seared through my brain, but I knew this spell. Though Sienna was stronger than ever, it didn't bring me to my knees. It did, however, cripple Kett. Kandy was probably lucky she was already passed out.

The demon Kett threw had landed near Mory. It pulled its hind legs underneath it to leap on the necromancer, who was shuddering in pain despite wearing the necklace I'd made for her. The necklace obviously needed to be reinforced.

Drake stumbled, winded as the spell hit him. But he didn't drop until the demon he'd cornered knocked him over, latching its massive maw onto the fledgling guardian's shoulder.

I threw the sacrificial knife, and despite my misgivings about its balance, it skewered the demon as it leaped for Mory. In the same motion, I dove over Kandy and came up on two feet with my sword in hand.

The skewered demon stumbled sideways. Sienna — the veins in her face bulging with black magic — grabbed the sacrificial knife out of its head. It turned, confused now like a rabid dog, and leaped over Kett to latch onto Drake's other shoulder. The fledgling dragon went down a second time. The three of them rolled, crashing through the few cars in the lot and pushing them aside like a wrecking ball.

Sienna flipped the knife in her hand. Blade down, she plunged it toward Kett. I dove, my katana extended to block Sienna's thrust, but ended up face down across Kett's chest. Sienna grabbed my hair and twisted me up onto my knees. I felt the sacrificial knife ghost across my throat, but then Sienna screamed and freed me.

Mory had buried my jade knife into Sienna's thigh. My sister backhanded the necromancer across the face, and the fledgling flew back onto the concrete rubble at the top of the stairs. Her body, sickeningly limp, slammed down and was still.

I felt the shallow cut across my throat heal.

Sienna stumbled back and yanked the jade knife out of her thigh — quickly dropping it to the ground as it seared her hand. I gained my feet and brought my sword into play.

Sienna got the sacrificial knife up to block my first blow. She left herself open though, so I slammed a kick into her chest and she flew backward.

I stepped over Kett to stalk my sister, feeling him rise to his feet behind me. Sienna couldn't maintain the fireblood spell and fight me.

My sister threw some malignant spell at me and I stepped sideways, feeling Kett mirror my movement. It barely touched me.

"It's over," I spat, stepping within striking distance.

"Not yet, sister," Sienna said. Blood speckled her lower lip and chin, so she wasn't invulnerable … yet. I was surprised to see it was red.

Then the two demons who'd been clawing Drake both hit me at once.

I lost track of Sienna with four sets of claws raking me from all directions. I was vaguely aware of Kett fighting alongside me. I threw an elbow and knocked one of the demons back, but felt something snap in my arm. I dropped the sword.

The other demon clawed me across the shoulders and I fell to my knees, rolled, and came up with the jade knife in my left hand — my right was still useless. I slit its throat. It stumbled. I stood.

Kett had the other demon cornered. I took another slash at my demon's neck with my left hand and managed to drive it farther back.

In the blink of an eye, Sienna was before me with the sacrificial knife.

The demon latched onto my left shoulder. I tried to block with my right, but I wasn't going to be fast enough.

Sienna thrust the knife toward my heart.

Kett appeared suddenly in front of me and took the blow.

Sienna screamed in frustration.

I willed the jade knife into my right hand and slashed across my body to slice the demon's neck for a third time. It shrieked and let me go.

Sienna shoved Kett away from her while keeping hold of the sacrificial knife.

Kett fell as if he was mortally wounded. Except that wasn't possible, because he wasn't mortal.

I reached for my sword where it lay at my feet.

Sienna started laughing. "Nice knife, Jade," she said. "I'll trade this for the stupid necromancer."

I grasped the hilt of the katana and brought it around to finally lop off the demon's head.

It crumbled into dust.

I was bleeding from multiple wounds. Though my arm was working, it ached like it was filled with molten lava. And Sienna was still freaking laughing.

The final demon — its head down to charge me — stepped between my sister and me. Sienna was obviously still controlling it.

Then I felt the life debt bond between Kett and me disintegrate. It took all my breath away. I stumbled. I twisted back to Kett, who was lying staring up at the night sky, not a hint of red in his eyes now.

Sienna glanced around the rooftop. She casually ran her fingers over the ridges of the demon's head as if she were petting a cat. She looked utterly satisfied.

"I'll leave you to it, sister," she said. Then she twirled the knife I'd made with blood magic — a knife powerful enough to kill a vampire who'd walked the earth for centuries. She grinned at me. "You give me such pretty presents. Maybe I'll be lucky and you'll make it out of here alive. I'd like more presents like this one."

I stepped toward her. The demon reared up.

"Everyone is dying," Sienna whispered as if it was a delightful secret. "I should know. I can feel it when it happens now."

Then Rusty — the ghost of Mory's brother — attacked her. His timing was getting better and better. Sienna shrieked and raised the knife against this invisible force, but knives were nothing to ghosts.

The demon snarled, but without direction from Sienna, it didn't seem to know what to do.

If Rusty was in play then Mory was still alive.

I spun and brought the sword to the demon's neck. It leaped up and over my blow — clearly, self-preservation trumped all.

Behind it, Sienna stumbled back, her magic rolling up and around her as she somehow countered Rusty's attack. Even so, his assault drove her back toward the broken railing where Kett had fallen off the roof earlier.

She fell.

Heedless of the demon somewhere behind me, I ran to the edge of the roof and peered over the broken railing. The ward had fallen. Sienna must have at least lost consciousness, then. But I couldn't see my sister in the darkness pooled between the streetlamps. Why weren't they spaced closer?

Mory was sobbing. I didn't want to acknowledge the devastation behind me. I had to finish it. I had to make sure that —

Dragon magic hit me like a blow to the head. I stumbled, turned, and fell to my knees by Kett's prone form.

My brain scrambled, then refocused.

Suanmi the fire breather stepped out from the crumbled stairs.

"Suanmi," I breathed. I didn't know if the guardian had felt the presence of the demons in her territory or if she'd simply tracked Drake here, but hope flooded my system, clearing my senses.

The elegant, refined French woman curled her lip at me and barked, "Drake, avec moi!"

The demon leaped for the guardian. Though only a quarter of its size, Suanmi caught it by the throat and breathed the words, "Meurt, rejeton du diable" into its ear. Assuming it had ears.

The demon disintegrated into dust. Suanmi, her nose crinkled, brushed it off her classic Chanel pant suit, with the pink-piping-edged jacket and all.

"Suanmi, please," I cried. "My sister."

The fire breather stalked toward me. "What have you done with Drake, half-blood?" she asked in her heavily-accented English.

The few cars that had been parked on the roof were crumbled together in the far corner of the lot. These shifted as Drake stumbled out from underneath them.

Suanmi sighed, just as I had taken to sighing at the fledgling. I whispered a silent prayer in thanks that the thirteen-year-old was on his feet.

"Sorry, guardian," Drake said.

"Avec moi, Drake," Suanmi said. Then she turned away.

"No!" I cried. "I need your help."

Suanmi whirled on me, fierce and full of anger. Her magic hit me like a sledgehammer. My heart skipped a beat or two. "Clean up your own mess, Jade Godfrey," she sneered. "And don't come back before you do, or I will grant your wish and make all your troubles go away."

"But guardian ..." Drake protested.

Suanmi snagged him by the ear. He instantly quieted.

"Such petty disputes are beneath a guardian, Drake," Suanmi said. "We shall discuss your punishment just as soon as we get out of London."

Drake swallowed and nodded.

"See to your pets, half-blood. They are dying." Suanmi's smirk was refined and spiteful. It was amazing she could pack so much nuance into one expression. But then, she'd had a half-dozen centuries to practice.

Still holding Drake by the ear, the guardian of Western Europe spun away and stepped into the stairs.

"It was fun rescuing you, Mory," Drake called over his shoulder.

Then they were gone.

I felt utterly lost without the dragon magic I'd had by my side for the last three months.

"Jade."

Mory was crying. I wasn't sure how long I'd been kneeling there feeling sorry for myself.

I looked up. Mory had crawled to Kandy and was cradling the werewolf in her arms. The necromancer was bleeding badly from her forehead. Half her face was covered in her own blood.

I had to check on Kandy. I had to check on Kett.

"I don't know any healing magic," I whispered.

And Sienna. Sienna might be lying dead in the street below. I could still taste her blood-soaked earth magic, but it was mixed in with all the residual magic throughout the parking lot. I couldn't pinpoint her location with my senses alone.

I pulled myself closer to Kett. The wound in his chest from the sacrificial knife hadn't healed. This wound had severed the life debt bond between us. So, according to the magic of the bond, this blow would have killed me if Kett hadn't stepped in. I couldn't even begin to wrap my head around the idea that Kett might have sacrificed his immortal existence … for me.

Ribbons of charcoal — or ash, maybe — were spreading out from the wound. They ran slowly up Kett's neck as I watched.

I reached out to touch his face, but then hesitated. Pushing through the shock that had obviously taken hold of my adrenal system, I switched hands. I hovered my left hand over Kett's mouth and brought my jade knife up to slice my wrist.

"Stop!"

A woman's scream was followed by a crushing blow to my shoulder. She knocked me sprawling over Kett and to the edge of the roof before I even laid eyes on her.

A woman as pale skinned as Kett stood crouched over him, baring her wickedly fanged teeth at me. Her fangs were at least an inch longer than Kett's. Her eyes were not only filled with blood but swirling with magic. And her magic — a sharp, pungent peppermint — was almost an exact replica of Kett's.

No. I had that backward. His magic was a duplicate of hers, and nowhere near as strong.

This was Kett's maker, who also happened to be the Audrey Hepburn lookalike I'd seen on the street that afternoon.

I cradled my left arm in my right as I staggered to my feet. "I think he's dying," I said. No. I pleaded. "I was just trying to feed —"

"Dragon blood," Kett's maker snapped. "If he isn't already lost to me, he would have been."

"I'm not … I don't think …"

"That is obvious. Take your friends and go."

"I can't."

"Now." The power in her voice made me shiver, made me want to obey her unquestioningly.

"He's my —"

"I swore not to touch you, Jade Godfrey." She spat my name like it insulted her to even know it. "If he dies, I will suck the marrow from the werewolf's and necromancer's bones and make you watch. If he doesn't die, you have eighteen hours left. After that, if you set even one foot in London, I will take everything from you."

I believed her. I also believed, as wounded and depleted as I was, that I probably wouldn't be able to stop her. She might manage to kill Mory or Kandy before I could get in her way.

So I left Kett.

I was doing that a lot. Leaving people who might be dead or dying, and saving those I could. I was doing it over and over and over.

I hefted Kandy over my shoulder, hoping Mory could walk just holding on to me, and ran for the stairs.

The werewolf was still breathing. Thank God. But I needed to get both her and Mory to a hospital and then figure out later how to explain what had happened to the human authorities. I was already in epic shit with the Convocation and the Conclave, not to mention the sorcerer's League. The shapeshifter Assembly would have my head if the hospital took blood samples, but I wasn't going to let Kandy die if I could help it.

I managed to get Kandy and Mory down to the ground floor without having our hearts ripped out by Kett's maker. It was slow going, and I kept frantically glancing back. My dragon healing abilities had been seriously tested, and my right foot and left arm still didn't feel fully under my control. Kandy was heavier than she looked, and Mory just stopped moving halfway down. I had to ferry both the werewolf and the fledgling necromancer one at a time for the last two flights of stairs.

I tucked them both inside the entrance ticket booth — Mory was still conscious but not speaking. Then I drew my jade knife and went to look for Sienna.

The sidewalk was empty — no blood on it or anything. The pavement was cracked, but that could have been due to Kett's fall.

Kett.

My chest constricted and I stepped back to look up at the roof. The railing was crumpled and hanging off the edge, but the building looked remarkably undamaged from the outside.

'Clean up your own mess,' Suanmi had said. But I had no idea what to do now. Everyone I knew in London was either dead or dying.

Call Gran.

I pulled my phone out of my hoodie pocket in pieces. A phone call to Gran was really going to have to wait. I was losing it, starting to shake. My mind was blank … I didn't know what to do.

"Jade?"

Kandy. It was barely a whisper, but I heard it. I turned back to her and Mory, still scanning with my eyes and my dowser senses for Sienna … nothing. I couldn't even taste any residual magic out on the street.

Kandy's phone might have survived the … what should I call it? Fight? Destruction? Triple demon summoning? Getting our asses handed to us?

Her phone hadn't survived. But that was okay, because just as I was thinking that I was going to need to steal a car, the werewolf cavalry descended on us.

Jorgen was back and brought a pack with him. He'd also brought a witch.

Thank God for werewolf hormones.

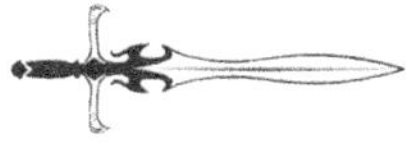

Jorgen hustled off with Kandy. It was difficult to protest this when I was surrounded by five werewolves who all looked like they could seriously kick my ass. Plus, the green-haired werewolf was in serious need of healing, and I had no idea how to help her.

The witch — who pretty much refused to identify herself to me — dumped a bunch of healing magic into Mory, then started ordering Jorgen's werewolf buddies around. A couple of them had police uniforms on that looked real to my completely uninformed eye.

The witch was a dark-haired woman in her forties with a charming British lilt. She didn't offer to heal me. That was okay, because she was pretty magically spent after working on Mory, and I also didn't know how my magic might react to hers anyway.

"An investigative team is on the way," she said quietly. She glanced over at me sitting on the sidewalk at her feet, with Mory slumped against my shoulder. "They were nearby. On the trail of the … black witch." She looked up at the car park for a long moment, then frowned darkly. "Don't leave the hotel without permission." Then she walked off without another word.

One of the werewolves hauled us around the corner and flagged down a cab. It was obvious that they wanted us as far away from the scene as possible, and who was I to argue?

My foot sorted itself out before I hit the hotel lobby. This was good because Mory, who still hadn't spoken, collapsed in the elevator and I had to carry her to the suite.

I tucked her into bed and made a beeline for the en-suite bathroom. One glance in the mirror and I was surprised the cab driver hadn't refused to take us. I actually looked worse than I felt, and I felt like a pile of shit scraped off the bottom of my sister's shoe and left to fester on the roadside.

I left the door open so I could hear if Mory woke, then turned the water to hot in the walk-in shower.

I stripped off my ruined leathers. Though they'd somehow held together on my body, they fell to shreds on the bathroom's black-and-white hexagon-tiled floor.

Every surface of my body — neck to toes — was scored by still-healing demon claw marks. My left arm was mangled as if it had been chewed on. The skin was newly pink, but underneath was a knotted mess of muscle and tissue.

Three and a half months of training and a shiny new sword, and this is what I looked like after confronting Sienna. I hadn't even gotten to use the sword, really. That said a whole lot about how I really didn't deserve to wield it.

And speaking of blades ...

I stepped into the hot shower and tried to not weep over the sacrificial knife that I'd transformed with blood magic into something far more deadly — and then had pretty much handed it to Sienna. A knife that could kill a centuries-old vampire ...

"Please don't be dead," I whispered. Blood washed down my body and pooled around the drain at my feet. My toenails — unpainted for the first time in years — took on a pinkish hue. "Please don't be dead."

But the life debt bond had broken ...

I started to cry, great ragged sobs that were violent and involuntary. I hunkered down underneath the hot stream of water and pressed my hands over my mouth, so as not to wake Mory.

And I sobbed.

I sobbed until my legs gave out and I curled up on the tile. I sobbed until I hurt myself, until blood vessels broke in and around my eyes. I sobbed for my stupidity and failure.

I sobbed for my sister.

And I cried for Kett … my mentor, my friend, and my protector, who I'd scorned in the hallway of the hotel not three hours ago for killing in order to live. And then I killed him myself, with my naiveté, stupidity, and recklessness.

By the time I stopped crying, I was unsure of how long I'd been taxing the hotel's boiler … but I felt guilty about the wastefulness so I turned off the water.

I still sat on the shower floor, soaking wet until the steam had cleared from the room and I began to shiver.

Mory said something in the other room, talking in her sleep. I lifted my head so that my wet hair hit my face. It was far cooler than my skin, and I realized I was running a temperature. My body was probably burning off the residual magic of Sienna's spells, and also probably whatever crap was in demon spit.

"Rusty, no," Mory murmured from the other room.

I stood up and grabbed a towel. That was enough uselessness for one evening. I had Mory to look after and Kandy to check up on.

And Sienna. There was no way Sienna was sitting in a shower bawling like a brat. No, Sienna had a new toy she was undoubtedly eager to try out.

Chapter Twelve

Just before dawn, a knock at the suite door pulled me away from watching Mory sleep. I'd been worrying that she hadn't woken yet, but was also fretting about waking her to feed her if she needed the sleep to heal.

I'd ordered food the second the kitchen had opened, so I thought the knock was room service. Instead, I opened the door to find a dark-blond woman around twenty-five standing in the hall. She was a couple of inches shorter than my five feet nine inches. Her hair was pulled back and up in a French twist that wouldn't last an hour on me, and every well-tailored piece of clothing on her dripped money — all without my recognizing a single label, because there weren't any.

"Jade Godfrey?" she asked politely, already knowing the answer. Her slight accent identified her as American.

I met her gaze and flinched. Her blue witch magic curled and coiled behind her eyes so tightly that I couldn't distinguish their actual color.

She furrowed her brow at my flinch. I transferred my gaze to her hands where her magic also pooled, though not as intensely as behind her eyes.

"I know you," I said, and I met her gaze without flinching a second time. Her magic was heavily doused in nutmeg — which wasn't a scent I associated with witch magic — along with the sweet floral tones I would have expected. Sweet nutmeg was an odd combination.

"Yes," she answered. "I'm Wisteria Fairchild. The reconstructionist."

Right. We hadn't actually met during Sienna's trial, but Wisteria had presented a YouTube cube thing that somehow played back the scenes of Hudson's and Rusty's murders. The reconstructionist somehow collected residual magic and then transformed it into a visual presentation. This was the most damning evidence against Sienna. Until I saw it at the tribunal, I didn't even know that such magic was possible.

"Wisteria. That's an ... unusual name. I imagine you go by something else?"

"No."

Chatty witch. Not.

"The Convocation thought it best if someone who knew your magic ... and your family was here."

"I'm confused. You're here because?"

"An investigative team has been called in to contain, examine, and clean the area of last night's incident."

I stared at her. My brain was obviously low on processing power this morning. "That was less than six hours ago."

"Yes, well. It's rather a mess, isn't it? Best to move quickly. Will you be inviting me in? Or shall we continue to discuss such a sensitive topic as the morning newspapers are delivered door to door?"

I nodded and stepped back — still too overwhelmed and naturally polite to take exception to being bullied by a woman not much older than me. The room service waiter turned the corner of the hallway just as Wisteria stepped into the suite.

The reconstructionist settled into a plush love seat in the sitting area, placing a large designer bag on the floor at her feet.

The waiter rolled a tray laden with enough food for five big eaters into the room.

"I didn't know ... I haven't ordered for you," I said to Wisteria.

She nodded and addressed the waiter. "Tea. Herbal. Mint if you have it, not chamomile."

The waiter nodded and crossed to a set of converted antique cupboards. Once opened, they revealed a coffee and tea station, as well as a mini fridge and sink.

He set the water boiling and then stepped back to have me sign the bill. I barely glanced at it closely enough to calculate the tip. He then served Wisteria her tea in a china cup — I assumed the mugs were reserved for coffee — and left. I had a feeling he was still half asleep.

The door clicked shut and I rounded on the reconstructionist. "You were in London?"

"No, Seattle."

"Six hours ago."

"The Convocation arranged transportation."

"Excuse me?"

Wisteria tilted her head and looked at me. Her magic boiled behind her eyes. It was unnerving. As far as I could taste, she was nowhere near as powerful as Gran or my mother, Scarlett. And yet magic usually flowed throughout a witch's physical body, not concentrating in such specific areas. Wisteria Fairchild was very good at controlling her magic. Brilliant at it. But I really, really didn't want to be around if she ever lost that coiled control.

Wisteria sipped her tea. It was too hot. She sucked in her breath to ease the pain of the burn. It was the first purely human thing I'd seen her do. Then I suddenly realized I made her nervous. I'd never thought about that before — never thought about how it must feel to be the most powerful person in the room. The extra responsibility made me momentarily heady. I wasn't sure I could carry more weight right now.

I grabbed the top plate of food, not caring what it hid beneath its warming dome, and sat down on the couch opposite Wisteria to eat.

"I have passports for you, the fledgling necromancer, and the werewolf … Kandy. The Convocation wasn't sure you still had access to yours. I also have airline tickets. Your flight leaves in four hours. You need to be at the airport in two, but you cannot leave the hotel without an escort."

"I can't leave —"

"You will leave. There is a bounty on your head — directly from the vampire elder himself — that goes into effect in less than ten hours. You're to leave the country and are not welcome back."

"What? Because of Kett? Is he … alive?" I stumbled over the last word from emotion — but also because I still wasn't exactly clear on whether vampires were alive or not. To me, they looked like pure animated magic — especially Kett's maker.

Wisteria waved her hand dismissively. "I don't know all the details. I don't normally operate as a point of contact. I'm sure I'm stepping on many toes here, but the Convocation will smooth everything out eventually."

"Gran … you mean 'Pearl Godfrey,' when you say 'the Convocation.' "

Wisteria smiled that tight smile of hers that didn't go anywhere near her eyes — a learned gesture of polite conversation. "There are thirteen board members. It takes seven to reach an agreement, but there wasn't a single dissenting vote in this matter. The witches are firmly on your side, in this circumstance at least."

"But why you?" I asked, stuffing the pancake I'd just folded in quarters straight into my mouth. "Not that I'm not glad you're here, but why didn't Gran or Scarlett use this miraculous transportation?"

Wisteria tilted her head to regard me a second time. I gathered my ignorance of witch magic confused or maybe intrigued her. I couldn't quite tell which. She was difficult to read with her magic held so tightly in her eyes.

"Gateway transportation can be tricky. My magic seems to accept it, though it is not ... pleasant. It's also disruptive to the natural flow of magic, so its use is limited. It took me three hours to get into Vancouver and five minutes to arrive at the designated point in the parking lot."

"And Gran didn't come because her magic doesn't like ... moving like that?"

"I gather. And she was casting, of course. And the investigative team is currently without their reconstructionist. So I had a valid reason to be here."

My grandmother was capable of moving a witch through space from Vancouver to London — the thought was awe-inspiring. The grid point portals were anchored in deep wells of natural magic. Other portals, such as the one in the Sea Lion Caves, were tied to the specific ability of one uber powerful being, Pulou the treasure keeper. Blackwell's amulet was constructed by a formidable alchemist. But a witch who could gather enough magic from the earth and channel it in order to transport another witch? All without the support of a full coven? I had no idea Gran was capable of such a thing. That any witch was capable of such.

Mory wandered out of the bedroom and toward the food without acknowledging either Wisteria or me. Her magic was barely discernible. She leaned over to look through the four plates remaining on the cart, lifting and lowering the domes until she found waffles.

My gaze dropped to the necklace that sat heavily on the necromancer's collarbone. Something about it was off — discordant with the rest of its magic, but not necessarily dangerous — as if it was dented and the flow of its magic restricted.

I half rose out of my chair to look at it closer. I was reaching toward it when Mory snapped, "Don't touch it."

I flinched at the utter hatred in her tone. "I was just —"

"Never mind," the teenager said. She all but dropped her plate of waffles onto the glass coffee table, then proceeded to douse them in syrup.

"This is Wisteria —"

"I know. Where's Kandy?"

"She's …" I glanced up at the reconstructionist.

"Healed enough to be going over the events of the evening with the lead investigator," Wisteria said. "I gathered the reconstructions before I came here, so the crew could start cleaning."

"Covering up the mess Sienna made," Mory said mockingly, her mouth full.

"That was much more than a mess," Wisteria said. Her tone was even but stern.

Mory nodded, somewhat appeased by this assessment.

"Your mother would like to talk to you," Wisteria continued as she pulled a cellphone out of her huge bag.

The fledgling necromancer snatched the phone and her plate, then booked it back to the bedroom, slamming the door behind her.

"Your sister has cut a swath of destruction across the United Kingdom. The investigators tasked with finding and stopping her have identified a number of missing witches, and now three sorcerers. The fledgling necromancer will need to testify."

I nodded, still staring at the closed bedroom door. "She'll hate me forever."

"She's lucky to be alive," Wisteria said, not a hint of compassion or understanding in her voice. "One day she'll realize it."

I changed the subject. "Was one of the missing witches skilled in delayed or triggered spells?"

"Azure Dunkirk. Her coven reported her missing from Manchester two days ago. The investigators were following up there when they heard from Maize."

"Maize?"

"The witch that the werewolves contacted. She's a well-known healer, and actually the only witch who makes her home in London. Luckily, one of the werewolves had prior contact with her."

I nodded, not even remotely absorbing the information. I leaned forward and set my empty plate on the coffee table. "I did something last night … I made something …"

Wisteria held up her hand, palm toward me. "I'm not your confidant or your judge. As far as I saw, you did what you thought necessary at the time. Those demons … your foster sister …" Wisteria frowned and shivered slightly.

"I'm sure you've seen worse," I said.

The reconstructionist met my gaze. "I've never seen worse than what your sister has done, and I was certified at sixteen. The youngest ever. I've been practicing in North America for almost ten years now."

I shut up. My stomach rebelled against the pancakes and eggs I'd just eaten. But I wasn't going to throw up perfectly good food over freaking Sienna.

Wisteria leaned forward and spoke softly. "I've never seen magic like yours, Jade Godfrey, or the boy who was with you. You both gleamed gold within the darkness your sister conjured. Pure gold. You lighter, blue-tinged. The boy darker, an almost rose tone."

I felt tears threaten to overwhelm me again. I hadn't known that … I couldn't see my own magic. I wiped my cheeks and nodded.

Wisteria returned my nod and rose to her feet. "Now, I gather you and the fledgling will need clothes. If you give me your sizes, I'll see what I can do. The concierge in a hotel like this should be able to get us anything, no matter the hour of the morning."

I glanced down at my attire. I'd stolen a tank top and a pair of Lycra workout pants from Kandy's clothes, but the pants were too short on my legs. The werewolf's jeans hadn't even remotely fit — like, not even over my thighs, even with all the dragon training. I'd thrown a hotel terry cloth robe over it all.

"What, this?" I asked. "Not good enough for Heathrow Airport?"

Wisteria laughed and handed me a pad of paper from the writing desk in the corner. Her laughter was a reserved, refined sound that offered a glimmer of lightness to my heavy soul.

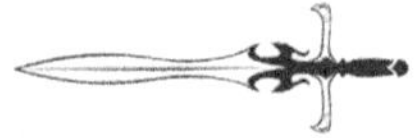

The next few hours were a whirlwind of phone calls — Gran and Scarlett — and answering questions as guardedly as I could when the lead investigator showed. Mory continued to completely ignore everything, though she gushed over the clothing Wisteria brought for her.

The lead investigator was an uppity British witch who was seriously pissed that we'd been hunting Sienna in London without telling anyone. How we were to know to report our suspicions and activities to her team, I wasn't sure. When I informed her that we contacted the sorcerers and the so-called vampire elder, she just curled her lip at me and continued with the questions.

It seemed that the Adept had no problem asking hard questions when investigating a crime.

Wisteria — who outright refused to let me call her Wist or Wisty — sat next to me and squeezed my arm every time she wanted me to gloss over an event. I gathered that her reconstruction — the YouTube cube thing she was carrying around in her bag — showed what happened at the parking lot but not what led up to the disaster. Interestingly, Wisteria also refused to hand the cube over to the lead investigator until after the Convocation had seen it. She had actual written directives to back this up. Her handbag was that large for a reason. And here I'd thought it was a fashion statement completely at odds with the rest of her well-kept, minimalist appearance.

I should have slept, but I didn't want to relax anywhere other than in my own bed, no matter how far away that was at the moment.

I asked about Kett.

No one had answers.

Wisteria scored me some MiH jeans, a green cashmere sweater, and white patent three-quarter Doc Martens boots with roses etched up the sides that totally screamed 'limited edition' to me. I was ready to make her my best friend for it. She didn't seem on board with that plan, though.

The reconstructionist used our impending flight as an excuse to haul Mory and me out of the hotel suite and into a rental car before the investigator had finished her interview. By the deadly look this garnered, I really hoped Wisteria wasn't stepping on too many toes for my sake.

She barely said a word to us on the way to the airport. And, of course, Mory was also honing her impression of a rock in the back seat, so I just kept randomly flipping radio stations when a song came on that I didn't want to hear. I tried a lot of radio stations. It seemed I wasn't interested in listening to music or talking.

The reconstructionist pulled up to the international departures section of Heathrow, and once again I was really glad I wasn't driving. The airport was huge and sprawling.

"I'm surprised we aren't under heavy guard," I said jokingly as I stepped from the car.

"You are," Wisteria said. Then she pulled away without saying goodbye.

I reached for Mory, not wanting to lose her in the pressing crowd. She deftly avoided my touch, almost knocking over a toddler with her dodge.

Fine. I'd let her get lost at the freaking largest airport in the United Kingdom … I already was.

I moved — slowly in case Mory did want to stay with me — toward the revolving doors, happy that I only had my satchel and katana, and wasn't dragging the huge bags hindering the other travelers. Portals were decidedly less intimidating. Well, if I didn't include having my life threatened by one of the nine guardians of the world if I used one … or returned to the nexus.

Kandy appeared out of the crowd. Her hair was freshly dyed green but in a slightly different shade … darker, I thought. It almost perfectly matched the green glow of magic that rolled across her eyes when she met my gaze, saw my smile, and didn't return it.

Mory flung herself at the werewolf as if I were the one who'd kidnapped her in the first place.

Something in my chest broke. I was surprised there was anything left to break so close to my heart. But I felt it snap, right in that place where I had stored all my pain over losing Sienna.

Then the anger rose to patch the crack.

I shoved the two extra airline tickets at Kandy's chest. She stumbled back and almost dropped them.

"Don't worry," I snarled. "I'll get my seat reassigned."

Then I walked away, leaving Kandy and Mory staring after me. Yeah, maybe it was childish. Yeah, maybe I deserved their nasty shit, but I wasn't going to take it.

No one had any freaking idea what I was feeling. No one had any idea what it was like to hunt your own sister, your best friend, and fail to bring her to justice — even though according to the investigators, that wasn't my job. It was my responsibility.

And you know what? I didn't drag Kandy, Mory, or Kett into any of this … I'd walked through the Loch More portal two and a half days ago with every intention of finding Sienna on my own. And maybe, just maybe, if it had been me facing her alone, all that other terrible shit wouldn't have happened.

Now we'd never know.

I paused. The airport was teeming with people. Glimmers of magic floated all around me, but nothing substantial. We Adepts were a minority by a long shot in this world. I was one of a kind. I could walk through portals. I didn't need to sit on a plane for eight hours. I could be home in minutes.

If I knew where the London portal was ... if I could get away with using it. I was under the impression that Pulou could block portals against certain users if he so desired. For the doorways he'd specifically structured, at least. So the Loch More portal would be open ... and Suanmi had more important things to do than sit in wait for me to use a portal. There were, after all, only nine guardians for the entire world. They were overworked if not underpaid. But then, I wasn't entirely sure how guardian powers worked or even what abilities they encompassed ... the London portal was exclusively Suanmi's — I'm sure it was how she'd arrived in the city last night, so she'd probably know the second I used it.

Kandy stepped up beside me, her face tilted to the departure board above us. "Looks like the plane is on time," she said.

"I'm not interested in playing shapeshifter dominance games with you," I said, not looking at the werewolf. "If you're here by my side, then you're here as a friend, not as a follower and not as a protector."

Kandy, still not meeting my eye, bared her teeth. But then she seemed to shake off whatever reaction had seized her. She nodded. "Check-in is this way," she said. "They have to pack up your sword and special check it."

"Yeah." I wasn't happy about handing the katana over. At least security would be unaware of the invisible jade knife at my hip.

Mory pressed against my left side as we cut through the crowd after Kandy. Her ears barely came up to my shoulders. I didn't acknowledge her further. I'm sure she had a lot of shit to work out. I could lead her through this crowd, but I couldn't heal her.

"My necklace is broken," she said to the back of my left shoulder.

"It's just dented, not broken," I responded. "I'll fix it."

"Okay."

"Okay."

And that was that.

We checked in, boarded the plane, and left London. Supposedly, I was to never return. Part of me hoped that Sienna was still somewhere beneath me as I looked out the window at the airport green space and then the houses and buildings of London growing smaller and smaller. Maybe the investigative team would find her.

Except she would kill them all, and probably become more powerful than ever.

No. Sienna was on her way to her next target, and I had to get in her way … somehow.

Kandy and Mory undid their seat belts, lifted the arm of the seat between them, and curled up together to sleep. Thankfully, Kandy didn't seem to have a scratch on her that I could see. But then, my wounds had healed on the outside as well, so that was no way to tell, really.

I pulled Blackwell's duplicate demon history book out of my satchel. Then — starting with page one — I began memorizing the bloody thing. I had no idea if Sienna would return to the same source material, but it was the only lead I had within my grasp.

Thankfully, the steward had Lindt chocolate on board. It wasn't Valrhona or Amedei, but it would do. I bought every bar over 60 percent cocoa that he had, ignoring his flabbergasted response.

I had work to do, and it was time I started applying myself as diligently as possible to the job. Chocolate was damn fine at focusing me.

The moms were waiting at the international arrivals gate just beyond customs at Vancouver International Airport. And though I was twenty-three-going-on-twenty-four, I was relieved to see Scarlett's strawberry-blond hair seconds after I cleared customs. When the taste of my mother's magic hit me — strawberry and white chocolate over her grassy witch base — I knew I was home. Which was odd, because Scarlett hadn't really raised me.

Mory's mom, Danica Novak, opened her arms — her face already puffy with previously shed tears — and the teenaged necromancer flung herself, sobbing, into them.

"She made me. She made me," Mory said.

Danica's eyes reminded me of Rusty's, but her hair was a shade lighter. The taste of her magic — sugared violets — was a more pungent version of her son's. The necromancer powers were usually strongest in the female line.

I reached out for a brief but fierce hug from my mother. Scarlett then turned and hugged Kandy, a gesture the green-haired werewolf accepted more enthusiastically than I would have expected.

Gran stepped around Scarlett, and I was shocked to realize I hadn't seen or felt her beneath all the other magic around me. She grabbed me and didn't let go.

"Your magic," I cried before I could stop myself.

"It's all right, Jade," Gran whispered. "You're home."

That didn't answer my question, so — still captured in Gran's grasp — I looked to Scarlett.

My mother smiled one of those tight smiles edged in sadness that she was getting too good at. "The transportation spell. It's not really my kind of magic, so Pearl took the brunt of it. Normally, we'd gather a coven, but time was tight."

"I didn't realize … I'm sorry, I didn't mean …"

Scarlett interrupted my confused apology. "Don't be silly, my Jade. We did what we wanted. It was the least we could do … we couldn't … didn't … We wanted you home."

Gran pulled back from the hug and cupped my face in her hands. Her silver hair was pulled back into a loose braid, which fell down to her lower back. "I'm so proud of you," she said. Her tone was defiant and fierce, as if she was ready to argue against anything I might try to say.

Tears welled in my eyes and slipped down my cheeks. I couldn't do anything to stop them.

"No, no," Gran said. She wiped her strong, capable fingers across my cheeks to dry my tears. "A batch of cupcakes will sort out my magic, and a good sleep will do you some good."

She linked her arm through mine. Scarlett did the same on the other side, and together they pulled me out of the airport toward the short-term parking lot across the main road.

"A grilled cheese sandwich would be nice," I said as we dodged traffic and Scarlett stopped to pay the parking fee.

"With ham," Kandy added. The werewolf was striding alongside Gran. Mory and her mother were trailing along behind us, still quietly weeping.

"What? No. Gross," I said.

"I'm sure we can figure out something for both of you," Scarlett said as she led us toward the car.

Gran squeezed my forearm, then released me to dig around in her purse for her keys.

We paused at Gran's car and I watched Ms. Novak settle Mory in her car, two spots farther down from us. She looked up, caught my gaze, and nodded. Well, that was a step in the right direction. I'd been worried about her proficiency with death curses for over three months. Not that anyone would confirm or deny whether such a spell were possible, even for a necromancer of power. I wasn't sure how powerful Danica or Mory were, because I didn't know any other necromancers with which to compare them.

"I need to cast a circle tomorrow," I said quietly to Scarlett before she slipped into the driver's seat. It was the first time I'd ever seen Gran not drive. My mother nodded and ran her fingers down my arm, leaving the soothing tingle of her magic behind.

"Pearl and I will come to you. I gather you have a plan?"

"The start of one. A guess, based on something Blackwell said."

Scarlett pursed her lips but then nodded. Blackwell was not her favorite subject. "Tomorrow morning. After sunrise to allow Pearl's magic another cycle to replenish."

We climbed into the car and Scarlett drove us home.

Except for the new orchid plant on the granite countertop of the kitchen island, my apartment looked exactly the same as it had before I'd taken off for Portland. Scarlett hadn't added a thing in the three months I'd been gone, even though she'd bought something new every week in the three months previous to that. Though my room was suspiciously cleaner than I remembered.

I skipped the grilled cheese and slipped into my bed, only stopping to remove my boots. It took me longer to fall asleep than I expected. I lay there for a while, feeling Kandy's, Scarlett's, and Gran's magic in the kitchen and the comforting magic of my apartment wards all around me.

I wondered where Sienna was tonight.

No loved one had picked my sister up from the airport. No grandmother had been willing to drain her magic to send aid her way. No sister was there to whisper secrets in the dark … but then, Sienna didn't have any secrets anymore. She only had whims, and she left only devastation in her wake.

Chapter Thirteen

I woke up around five o'clock, so I guess I must have eventually slept. The time change should have been confusing, but over the three and a half months I'd spent in the dragon nexus, I was never actually sure what time it was anymore, so it didn't affect me.

I wiggled my toes into some flip-flops and promised myself a mani-pedi later that day. I made sure to not glance at my nails. I didn't need to melt down over nail polish right now. I exchanged my crumpled jeans for an older pair of Sevens. I needed to cinch the belt down two holes. Well, that was a silver lining in an otherwise tumultuous and painful few months.

My room was rather tidy, not that I was generally messy. But it had a stale, unused feeling about it that I hadn't felt in the rest of the apartment last night.

I pulled on a heathered navy T-shirt the logo was a T-Rex trying to do push-ups — over my tank top and padded through the living room and down into the bakery.

I didn't stop for breakfast. I already knew what I wanted to eat. Oh, yes, cupcakes.

The bakery was closed today — Sunday — now that Bryn, my very accommodating and definitely underpaid employee, had stepped up to cover all my baking shifts. Sales had slowed a bit but not drastically — according to Scarlett, who'd taken over the books.

Yeah, everyone was stepping up while I was stepping out to kill my sister. I pushed the nasty thought away, clipped my curls into a twist at the back of my head, and retreated into the pantry.

Surrounded by the delicious smells of chocolate, vanilla, and spices, I just breathed for a moment, willing everything to be okay. Even though it wasn't, and I was fairly sure it never would be again.

I hauled all the ingredients I needed out of the pantry and set them down on the long stainless steel workstation that I'd had custom made to accommodate my height. The stacked ovens and walk-in fridge were behind me. I immediately did up a batch of *Lust in a Cup* — dark chocolate cake with dark-chocolate cream-cheese icing — because if I only had time for a single batch, it was going to be my favorite.

While those cupcakes were baking, I did up a batch of *Cozy in a Cup* with bananas Bryn had set aside. They looked perfectly ripe for the banana chocolate chip cake. I followed that up with an experimental recipe I'd been half-heartedly thinking about, something that combined the honeyed almond of Drake's magic and a hint of the spices of Shanghai, such as peppercorn or cumin. I only had ground coriander, so I had to settle.

Something was wrong with the *Lust in a Cups*. They were almost too perfectly formed, and darker brown than I remembered. I checked the cocoa packaging, but Bryn hadn't changed brands or percentages. I let them cool before frosting, thinking I was just out of practice.

Except … the *Cozy in a Cups* looked more like *Puck in a Cups*. Was the baking soda old?

I was peering anxiously at the experimental cupcakes as they baked when Kandy wandered into the bakery kitchen from the back alley exit.

"Thought I'd find you here," the green-haired werewolf said as she snagged one of the newly frosted *Lust in a Cups*. I liked to wait until the icing hardened just a little before eating. That wasn't insanely picky when it was your own baking.

"You're up early," I said, not taking my eyes off the oven window.

Kandy shrugged. "Time change." She took a bite of the cupcake.

Then she spat it out.

Spat it out.

I stared at her, utterly aghast.

"Um," she mumbled as she crossed to the fridge and drank directly out of a container of milk. "I think you forgot something."

I reached for a cupcake, broke it in half, and tried a bite. "Sugar," I moaned. "I … I made an entire batch without sugar?"

"The frosting is good." Kandy licked the dark-chocolate cream-cheese icing off the remainder of her cupcake.

"I forgot the sugar?" I repeated, because it was an unprecedented event and bore repeating.

Kandy was now peering suspiciously at the batch of *Cozy in a Cup* that I'd just transferred to a cooling rack. "What are these?"

"Cozys," I answered, feeling a little weak at the knees.

The timer buzzed. Dreading what I was about to see, I pulled the experimental batch out of the oven and put them on the counter.

Kandy and I stared at the tray.

"They don't smell right," she finally said.

I started crying. I had been fairly certain I was done with the tears before we left London, but I obviously wasn't.

Kandy wrapped her arms around me. Her magic tingled against the skin of my arms and filled my mouth with the taste of berry-infused dark chocolate with a fine bitter finish. She hugged me fiercely and didn't speak.

I got the tears under control much quicker this time.

"God, I feel so weak," I blubbered when I was capable of forming words.

"Yeah," Kandy muttered, her voice heavy with unreleased emotion. "I'm upset about the cupcakes too."

Then the green-haired werewolf released me. She shoved the mixing bowl of dark-chocolate buttercream icing for the *Puck in a Cup* into my hands, along with a spatula.

"Who needs a spoon?" I muttered as I crammed a mouthful of frosting in.

"Exactly," Kandy said as she reached across the counter to retrieve a second spatula.

"London was a royal fuck-up," I said. Kandy didn't give a shit about my language, and I used the word with utter vehemence.

"Well, if you're going to go royal, there probably isn't a better place."

I laughed. My tears had dried on my face and my skin felt like it was going to crack, but I threw my head back and laughed.

Kandy rescued the bowl of icing, but not before I got another scoop and — in between weirdly inappropriate guffaws — stuffed it into my mouth.

"I can feel the chocolate coursing through my system," I said.

"That's the sugar. The chocolate hit comes later," Kandy said, sounding rather sage.

This statement renewed my laughter.

"I like your T-shirt," Kandy said. She was wearing one with a kumquat and an apple. It was obscene, as usual. I often wondered how she wore those T-shirts in public. I guess she just didn't care at all who she offended … or scarred for life.

I sobered and locked my gaze to the green-haired werewolf's. I offered her a sad smile, and she returned it along with a bump of her shoulder.

"I almost got you killed," I said.

"Nope."

And that was it. She just outright absolved me of any responsibility for London.

"It's going to happen again."

"Yep."

I took a deep breath, more for the oxygen to clear my head rather than a true sigh. "I need to go downstairs."

Kandy stiffened.

"I'm not leaving," I murmured, and the werewolf relaxed. She thought I meant the portal in the bakery basement, when what I really needed was a place to cast. A place accustomed to my magic. I was a terrible witch — spell-wise — I needed all the help I could get.

Kandy's eyes gleamed the green of her shapeshifter magic, and she bared her teeth in her predator smile. "A spell?"

"Yeah."

"Then you'll bake again? Because this shit is unacceptable."

This time when I laughed, Kandy joined me.

We were still laughing as we wandered upstairs to wake Scarlett and retrieve Blackwell's demon book.

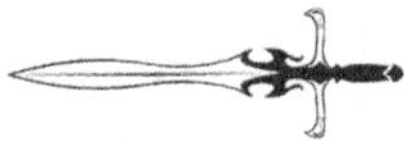

"Explain it again," Gran said. Her tone — though carefully measured — sounded full of doubt.

I sighed.

Gran, Scarlett, Kandy, and I were seated around the witches' circle I'd inscribed in the hard-packed dirt floor of the bakery basement with a broom handle. The portal on the east wall at my back thrummed sleepily, but I didn't need it today. Boxes that predated the bakery were piled neatly on wooden pallets to one side. The ceiling was low enough to touch, and the walls were concrete-patched brick. Gran hadn't allowed me to renovate the basement when I'd taken over the lease and opened the bakery. I hadn't understood why until I'd discovered the portal's existence — or rather, Sienna discovered the portal and then tried to torture me into opening it.

"I know it might not work," I said. "But it's the only clue we have right now. And the sorcerer said —"

"Blackwell," Scarlett spat.

"I know no one likes him, but you can't deny he is powerful, and —"

"Too powerful," Gran interrupted. "And with an agenda where you are concerned."

"Right," I muttered sarcastically, "he's figured out a way to capture me, or drain my magic, or hypnotize me with this stupid duplicated demon book just as soon as I cast a spell."

"Well, that seems far-fetched," Gran said.

Kandy started laughing. Scarlett grinned, and suddenly all the tension diffused from the basement storage room. Yeah, that was my mother's magic and it packed a lot of mojo.

"The dowser is still pissed about the cupcakes," Kandy said. She was sitting cross-legged in the dirt on the west side of the witches' circle. Sienna's spot. You know, from before my sister became all blood crazed and power lusty.

"You would be too," I snapped at the werewolf. Then I smiled.

Gran gave a soft 'humph' and I knew we were settled enough to move forward.

My grandmother sat at the north side of the circle and Scarlett sat at the south. Gran had been waiting for us in the bakery kitchen after we'd managed to drag Scarlett out of bed. She'd been frowning in the general vicinity of the cupcakes. As soon as I had a moment, I needed to hide the evidence before anyone else saw the disaster in the bakery, and the dumpster out back was the best choice.

I placed the book of demon history in the middle of the circle and then nodded to Kandy to light her pillar candle. We each had a candle sitting on the edge of the circle, but not touching. Kandy, Scarlett, and I sat cross-legged. Gran had brought a yoga block to perch on. It was a great idea, which I might appropriate. You know, if I ever tried to cast again.

"There was this witch in Scotland, Amber —"

"Cameron," Gran interjected as she lit her candle with the taper Kandy passed to her.

"Yeah. She carried these ancestral stones with her, which got me thinking about my witch magic and how it's way stronger here, I think. You know, beneath my home. Near the portal."

"Ancestral land," Gran said. She sounded exceedingly intrigued by my mention of the stones. I was probably in for an interrogation later.

"And with the addition of you and mom here, I thought I just might be able to cast a seek spell for Sienna."

"With a book." Gran was back to doubting without sounding at all doubtful.

"I'm just looking for a hint. This book is tied to the original by a thin thread of magic, and maybe the original is aware of where it is?" The question fell on hesitant ears, though Scarlett did smile encouragingly. Yeah, I got that the book was an inanimate object.

I lit my candle and passed the taper to Scarlett.

"Don't we need a map?" Kandy asked. "Wouldn't that help?"

"Magic is rarely literal," Gran said.

With Scarlett's candle lit, we all raised our pillars and blew a breath through the flame toward the circle. Not hard enough to snuff out the flame, but just enough to pass some of our magic into the circle.

There was a chance none of this mattered … the circle, the candles, the breath of magic. But this was how casting a circle worked for me, so this is what I did.

For a brief moment, Kandy's eyes glowed green as Scarlett's and Gran's glowed blue. I felt their combined magic whirl around in the circle. I presumed mine was in the mix — though I couldn't taste it — and the circle closed. The combined magic whirled in a storm of green and blue before me, dancing over the book and testing the edges of the circle like a capricious child.

"I seek — as I have done before — my sister, Sienna." Though speaking out loud wasn't actually necessary, I found it easier to make my intention clear through vocalization. "She holds this book. Where is it?"

The magic dipped and swirled around the book. I could imagine it tasting and testing the residual duplicated magic of the sorcerer who wrote the demon histories collected within the leather binding.

Nothing else happened.

"She seeks something in this book. Something interests her in this book," I said.

The book flipped open, the pages fanning back and forth. The magic intensified and dipped again, tasting, testing, seeking. Then the pages settled.

The four of us leaned forward.

"Thank you," I murmured, like the magic was a dutiful puppy.

The book was open to a tale of a demonic summoning that had happened on the west coast of a large island. It included a sketched map, which looked a lot like the Pacific Rim National Park on Vancouver Island. Or, specifically, Long Beach, which ran between Tofino and Ucluelet.

"Sea demons?" I asked. "What does that have to do with —"

Gran gasped. I flinched. I'd never heard that sound from her before, and it had shocked me right in the pit of my frosting-filled stomach.

The magic of the circle snapped and was gone.

"What is it?" I asked, already dreading the answer.

Gran held out a shaking hand to the inked picture that accompanied the tale. It depicted a long wooden shaft with a hand-carved stone arrowhead and feathers on its butt end. It looked like it was of First Nations design.

Scarlett moaned.

Then it hit me. Gran owned this spear. It hung in her study, almost hidden behind the mountain of books.

"Your grandfather," Gran said, then faltered. She held a shaky hand to her mouth and looked over at Scarlett. I'd never seen her look to her daughter for support before … and neither had my mother. Scarlett absorbed the responsibility quickly.

"Is it still in the study?" Scarlett asked.

"I … I'm sure it is," Gran said, not sounding at all sure.

"Did you change the wards, Gran?" I asked.

She looked at me with tear-filled eyes and shook her head. Sienna would have unhindered access to Gran's home. She could come and go without Gran knowing as well, because Gran couldn't taste residual magic like I could.

"How many?" Kandy asked. She steadied her voice. "How many fucking demons?"

I glanced down at the book. It was still open to the specific chronicle, but I had already practically memorized every story already.

"Dozens." I was feeling dizzy, though I was still sitting down.

"Impossible," Scarlett said.

I locked my gaze to Kandy's. I'd never seen the werewolf look frightened before. I imagined that terror was echoed on my face.

"Okay," Scarlett continued. "First, we need to figure out if the spear is gone. With all due respect, I've never seen a seek spell work like this —"

"Jade's magic is not to be underestimated," Gran said.

That should have felt like praise. It should have felt like support — but it felt way more like a warning.

Damn it all to hell ... which was exactly where we were all going if the magic and the book were correct. Hell on the gray-sand beaches of beautiful Tofino.

The four of us stood staring at the blank space on Gran's study wall that had once held the native spear. Not that I'd even really taken notice of it before today, before it was gone. But Sienna would have. My sister had always been far more interested in magic than I was. I imagined how gleeful she must have been when she'd recognized the drawing of the spear in the chronicle. I wondered when she took it. Did she risk coming back to Vancouver with Mory in tow? Or did she return after London? After she'd test run the triple demon summoning?

I couldn't taste any residual magic in the study other than Gran's. But then, when Sienna wanted to pass unnoticed she knew how to hide her magic from me.

Scarlett was poring over the entry in Blackwell's demon history book. Her strawberry-blond hair formed a waterfall all around the black leather binding. I was fairly certain she'd read it at least four times now.

"Does it have a date?" Kandy asked. "Sienna seemed big on the anniversary in London."

Scarlett shook her head, making her curls dance. I wasn't sure Kandy caught the gesture, so I spoke up. "No date. Not even a season. And I'm guessing at the location —"

"No," Scarlett said. "You're right ... a beach discovered by James Cook ... called Nootka Sound. That's 1778 or so."

"Yeah. It was the description of the long beach on the Pacific coast that solidified it for me." My sarcasm fell on preoccupied ears, and that was okay because it wasn't terribly witty.

"Native spear. West coast of Vancouver Island," Kandy said. "Standard Adept protocol is we contact the skinwalkers."

"What? No," I said. "No. No. They don't want protocol or to be interfered with —"

"That's a good idea, Kandy," Scarlett said, continuing to ignore me.

Gran sat down heavily on an antique chaise lounge that I wasn't sure had ever been used before. Her magic was sparking off her in a way that unnerved me. I'd been trying to ignore it.

Gran's movement drew Scarlett's gaze from the book, but not her full attention. "Will you go?" she asked Kandy.

"Already gone," Kandy said as she headed for the door.

"Wait," I cried. "They'll see it as protecting their territory. They will want to come —"

"I hope so," Scarlett said, grim and matter-of-fact about it. "We'll wait for Desmond and however many shifters he can rally quickly, then we'll head for the ferry."

Kandy nodded and left. I sat heavily on the end of the chaise and stared at my mother. Some power shift had happened and I wasn't sure when … or what was actually going on.

"Desmond?" I asked weakly.

"Yes. Kandy's been texting with him since you came back from London. Well, since London, I think. He's just been waiting for word."

"I've been so wrong ..." Gran was whispering behind my back, so I swiveled to look at her. "So wrong about how I raised you and Sienna —"

"That's not needed right now, Pearl," Scarlett said.

I whirled back to stare at my mother. She looked strong and defiant. Her magic rolled across her eyes as she reached over to tuck my chin up. Yep, I'd been hanging my mouth open.

Scarlett held her fingers underneath my chin and smiled at me, that tender smile she reserved for me alone. "Will he come?" she whispered. "If you ask, will he come?"

It took me a second to figure out who she meant. Yazi, my father. God, I wondered if it hurt her to ask me. We hadn't discussed him much during our hurried conversations the few brief moments I'd managed to step out of the nexus. He was too epic for a phone conversation — epically life-altering ... and yet not, because Gran and Scarlett were and always would be my family. I believed Scarlett loved him — though they'd only had that one night together — but his sheer power frightened her as well. This was why she and Gran had kept me so cloistered my entire childhood. The fear of what I was capable of and what attention that would draw from other Adepts — like Blackwell — who'd try to take advantage of my magic.

"If we can't stop dozens of demons from rising on the west coast, he'll come," I said. "One black witch isn't a big enough threat to draw the guardians' attention. They oversee the entire magical and human world. But dozens of demons would be."

"But he ... Yazi might come if you asked," Scarlett said.

"It's my mess." Suanmi had really driven that home for me, like a spear through my heart ironically.

"No, Jade," Gran interjected. "It's beyond that now. It never was your fault."

"Fine," I said. "He'd come. If I could find him quickly. And if the world isn't ending somewhere. He doesn't exactly have a cellphone. The guardians aren't gods. They're not even all nice people. But it's Haoxin's territory. She might come."

"Ah. That explains this entry," Scarlett said. "He … your father is the warrior that the sorcerer makes note of." She looked back down at the book in her hands. " 'And at the side of Haoxin, a warrior with a golden sword came to the aid of the beleaguered natives.' The writer goes on to assume they were sorcerers."

"Of course he does."

"So this Haoxin —"

"Different person."

"Sorry?"

"It was 1778, right? Best I've been able to figure, Yazi would have just become a guardian then. The Haoxin I've met is newly … I don't know, ordained, ascended. Like only a hundred years old or so."

Scarlett was staring at me, the book all but forgotten in her hands.

I changed the subject. "The sorcerer doesn't say how the demons were summoned or what triggered the rising."

"No," Scarlett agreed. "Which hopefully means Sienna won't know either."

"But it also means she'll try everything she can think of." My mind flashed to the memory of the altered sacrificial knife in my sister's hands.

"Will you ask him then? Or Haoxin, if you can't find your father?"

I pushed past the dread settling in my stomach — the dread of what that knife might do in Sienna's hands. "I could go through the portal in the basement, but …"

"You might not make it back in time."

I nodded. Suanmi's warning had been very, very real, and it resonated with my own guilt.

"I left spur of the moment," I said. "I was afraid they wouldn't let me go, not that they would force me to stay, but it's just … Chi Wen's vision."

"I know, my Jade," Scarlett said. She touched my shoulder, and her magic brushed against me soothingly. We might not have spoken about my father, but I had recounted the vision to my mother. I'd needed her and Gran to understand why I hadn't returned.

"I didn't want the far seer to show me anything else. I didn't know I wasn't going back right away. I'm so sorry."

"You always do your best," Gran said.

I didn't believe her, not deep in my soul. London weighed on me.

"We'll call the necromancers," Scarlett said, rapidly changing the subject.

"What? No," I said. "The skinwalkers are bad enough. The necromancers have no defensive magic. They're both practically human."

"You said the demons were previously vanquished."

"It should be impossible," Gran said with a sigh.

"Yes, but —"

"Then we'll need the necromancers. And Pearl, how many witches are near enough to be here for the last ferry tonight?"

"Three," Gran answered. "With two more already on the island."

"Wait!" I cried. "You … you're talking about an army."

"Yes," Scarlett said. "It's too bad the sorcerer is not to be trusted and that Kett is … dead." She ran her fingers through my curls, then went back to reread the chronicle again.

I turned to look at Gran, utterly aghast. "But —"

"This affects all of us, Jade," Gran said. "What will Sienna do with a horde of demons?"

"I don't know," I whispered.

"The blood magic has her now," Gran said. "I'm so sorry I didn't see it. I never thought her capable."

"You never thought me capable," I said. I wasn't sure why I needed to return to that sore point now, when Gran was already deep into self-flagellation.

Pearl Godfrey, who'd been the most powerful person I'd known for twenty-three years — and was still the most powerful witch I knew — nodded sadly.

Then she rose to help her daughter, a witch whose powers were focused on charm and charisma, plan a war.

By the time I made it back to the bakery, Mory was in the kitchen eating the *Pucks in a Cup*. Apparently, the necromancer had no taste buds … and an iron stomach.

"Stop that," I said, dumping everything in the garbage and offering the fledgling necromancer a banana instead.

She looked at this offer skeptically. I'd just fallen a few notches of cool in her estimation. I hadn't been aware I could actually go farther down.

"You said you'd fix my necklace," Mory said.

I nodded. "Does your mother know you're here?"

Mory shrugged, but it looked more like a 'yes' than a 'no', so I let it go.

I reached for the necklace and Mory backed up a step while clutching the chain to her chest. "I don't want to take it off."

I tried to smile but the expression just twisted on my face.

Mory dropped her gaze from mine.

"Let's go upstairs," I said. "I'll fix it there. No one can get through the wards without my permission." I, unlike Gran, had changed my apartment wards six months ago. Maybe it was a good thing to underestimate yourself sometimes. Gran's confidence had practically handed Sienna the spear … though before I got too high and mighty, the knife I'd pretty much gifted Sienna with was probably far more deadly than the spear.

"Are there cookies upstairs?" Mory asked as I led her to the back stairs.

I folded the wards around her as we climbed.

"There will be," I said, figuring I'd be more successful baking for Mory than for myself. Yeah, I wasn't totally thick about my magic all the time. I knew I'd ruined those cupcakes because I felt I didn't deserve them.

"My mom's been on the phone all morning," Mory said. "A bunch of people are trying to fly in."

"Yeah," I answered as we entered the apartment living room and I prepared to invade my mother's privacy. Though to be fair, she was the one who'd taken over my craft room in the first place. I needed supplies to fix Mory's necklace. "The Adepts of the West Coast are building an army."

Mory nodded sagely and allowed me to lift the necklace off over her head. She'd showered and was once again outfitted in her not-goth-not-army-brat-but-almost clothing.

My desk — tidied but relatively undisturbed — was still situated underneath the north-facing windows. Normally, this offered a breathtaking view of the North Shore mountains, but today all I saw was fog. The world looked like it ended a block north of my apartment building. I shuddered, laid the necklace on the desk, and resolutely started digging through the far-too-tidy drawers for tools.

"Nice bed," Mory muttered, not a hint of sarcasm in her tone.

My mother favored silks and vibrant colors. I wasn't sure how she kept her duvet quite that poofy, or how she had so many pillows perfectly piled on the queen-sized bed she'd crammed into the room. I suspected magic.

"The shapeshifters and witches are coming?" Mory asked.

I nodded as I inspected the oddly tarnished gold chain.

"And the vampires?"

"No."

Mory nodded, not as relieved as I thought she would be. None of the Adept got along with vampires, but least of all, necromancers. There was some history there that Kett had only hinted at — something about how vampires had been created in the first place, and how powerful necromancers could control the undead. All the undead.

"But there will be cookies, right?" Mory asked as she threw herself down on Scarlett's neatly made bed. "Before we all go to fight Sienna and probably die?"

I laughed. Trust a necromancer to be blasé about impending death. It was also the first time I'd heard Mory refer to my sister by name. I took that as a good sign. A sign of healing.

I began to polish the necklace. The tarnish came off easily underneath the cloth, with a little help from my magic. I let my eyes unfocus and my fingers move beneath my conscious awareness, while I thought about everything I'd put off thinking about.

I thought about Blackwell's fog spell, the one I'd trapped in my sword. The spell had held Kett until he'd transformed himself … or allowed himself to go bestial to counter the sorcerer's magic. I thought about the dampening collar in Blackwell's possession, and how I was going to have to survive to do something about that. Then I thought about Sienna slowly siphoning necromancer powers from Mory, despite the protection of the necklace.

"How long did it take Sienna to learn to block Rusty?" I asked.

"What?" Mory answered sleepily.

I glanced at the perfectly polished necklace in my hands, then at Scarlett's alarm clock by the bed.

It was 11:34 A.M. More time had passed than I'd thought.

"After Sienna learned to block Rusty, she could start siphoning your magic?"

"Bit by bit, in both cases," Mory answered as she flopped over onto her stomach and propped her chin in her hand to look at me. "Why?"

"I'm not sure yet … but it won't happen again."

I stood up and gently lowered the necklace over Mory's head. The necromancer patted the chain and then smiled at me.

"I don't hate you," she said.

"Well, that's good," I answered. "Because I'm going to need your help with the cookies. If the shapeshifters are coming, we're going to need dozens."

"Dozens?" Mory echoed. Then she asked, "You want me to bake with you?" as if I'd just asked her to marry me.

"Yeah," I said, returning the smile. The fledgling necromancer was going to be all right … until we met Sienna again. There was no chance we'd manage to keep Mory at home without spelling her.

Chapter Fourteen

So I waited … and baked. I flinched as each text came in on my phone — until Mory muted it, after which I jumped each time it vibrated on the counter.

One text announced Kandy's arrival in Squamish. I gathered that her demanding to see the old lady with all the beastly kids didn't go over well with the band. We'd inadvertently trespassed on the skinwalkers' territory three months ago. Unfortunately, at the time they were kidnapping us, we didn't get actual names to go with the animals the skinwalkers would cloak themselves in. At least Kandy and I didn't. Kett might have, but obviously that knowledge was lost now …along with all the knowledge and truth he'd collected over centuries of life. Yeah, I was hanging on the precipice of maudlin … still.

A second text announced the first of three witches arriving — as summoned — to Gran's house. Scarlett was sending out cc'd messages now. I wasn't even aware my phone could do that.

The third and fourth texts were about necromancers — it seemed Mory was 'missing again.' This forced me to pick up my phone and communicate her location — my apartment — and activity — baking peanut butter and chocolate chip cookies.

Unsurprisingly, after this second round of text messages, the first knock at the door wasn't the one I'd been dreading. Though had I known it was coming, I probably should have been worried. I opened the door to reveal Mory's mom, Danica. The necromancer looked more put together than she had at the airport, but she didn't actually smile until she laid eyes on Mory over my shoulder.

"Jade," she said, and though I thought she was going to launch into some speech, she rather awkwardly didn't continue.

"Would you like to come in?" I asked, stepping back and reaching out for the magic of the wards.

"No." She beckoned for Mory. "We don't have much time before the seven o'clock ferry. I understand we're all trying to meet there."

Um, yeah. I hadn't gotten that text yet.

Mory stepped by me and handed her mother three fresh baked cookies wrapped in paper towel.

Danica's gaze fell on Mory's necklace. "You fixed it, then?" she asked.

"Yes."

"Thank you ... I know what it does, what it protects her from. Thank you."

She meant Rusty, her own son whose ghost had almost managed to kill Mory the first time he'd tried to go after Sienna. I still wasn't sure about Rusty myself, but it must pain Danica incredibly to know such terrible things about her son.

I nodded, pushing away the tears that seemed to be constantly on the edge of falling these days.

"We — the necromancers and I — will need to know more about the demons in London. Mory says they were somehow reanimated?"

"Yeah. Previously vanquished and supposedly impossible to summon. Mory, Kandy, and I were all there. We might have all seen different things."

"But you felt their magic and the magic that was used to … reanimate or resummon them?"

"Yes, but I hope to God Sienna doesn't try to use the same spell. She somehow substituted the sorcerers' corpses for the demons' bodies, I think. They were like … vessels, maybe."

Danica's jaw tensed at my mention of my sister. Yeah, if she'd killed my son and kidnapped my daughter, I'd become very proficient at death curses if there was such a thing.

"There aren't enough sorcerers to sacrifice in the world," Mory said as she broke a piece from one of the cookies her mother held. "There are going to be dozens of demons this time."

Mory's blasé attitude threw me again. I was still haunted by seeing the demons in London tear their way out of the corpses of the sorcerers, then eating their hosts.

"We'll just have to stop the summoning beforehand this time," I said. Yeah, that sounded weak and pathetic to my own ears as well.

"I'll need as many specifics as you can give me, of the spell, the rising, and of the demons," Danica said. "If we're to have any hope of controlling what your sister raises."

"Of course," I said, though I had to swallow past the lump in my throat to speak. "It was a sorcerer spell, so I might be guessing at some parts."

"I'll speak to the werewolf, Kandy, as well," Danica continued. "We'll see you on the ferry."

The necromancer turned away. Mory followed, turning back to wave before she hit the front stairs.

I closed the door and quickly crossed back to the kitchen to start packing up the cookies as I waited for the final batches to bake. I concentrated solely on this task, and despite Danica's request, attempted to not remember the demons of London any more than I already did.

I needed to pack as well, but other than my sword, I didn't have much to bring that I wasn't already wearing. I never took off my necklace, and my jade knife was almost always strapped across my right hip. I looked down at my jeans and flip-flops. My dragon trainer, Branson, would be appalled about me going into battle like this ... I might have an old pair of leather pants somewhere ...

The second knock on the front door — the one I'd been dreading and yet anticipating — came after a text confirmed the plan to be on the seven o'clock ferry. Another text informed us that Kandy was on the way to the ferry terminal now with a contingent of skinwalkers.

I opened the door to find Desmond leaning against the frame, looking back over his shoulder. I had a heartbeat to absorb his impossibly broad shoulders, tawny short-cropped hair, and chiseled jaw before he turned his green-flecked golden-brown eyes on me.

"Desmond Charles Llewelyn," I breathed.

"That's alpha to you, alchemist," Desmond drawled. He wasn't a drawler, though — he was attempting to be playful. A little of the metaphorical weight that was crushing me eased.

"Hi, Jade," Lara called, drawing my attention over Desmond's shoulder toward Kandy's apartment across the way. Last time I'd seen Lara, who was one of Desmond's enforcers, she'd been a breath away from dying because my sister had wanted my undivided attention.

"Hi, Lara."

As I watched, the lovely werewolf grabbed Kandy's spare key out from underneath a seventy-pound planter. I was seriously glad to see her on her feet. Even if her purple-glossed bee-stung lips made me insanely jealous.

"You take too much on yourself, Jade," Desmond said, pitching his voice low. He'd been watching me watch Lara, who entered Kandy's apartment and disappeared from my sight.

"Well, that's the kettle talking, isn't it? Alpha?"

"No. I take responsibility only for my own. You seem to think that nothing bad happens without your stirring of the pot first."

I squared my shoulders and jutted out my chin. "I had nothing to do with that tsunami that happened last month."

"Are you sure? I heard you batted your eyelashes at some sorcerer in Hawaii."

"I would never," I exclaimed with mock indignation. Yes, Desmond Llewelyn, Lord and Alpha of the West Coast North American Pack was flirting with me.

We really were all going to die.

"Let me in, little witch," he murmured. "I like the pants."

I was wearing a pair of red leather pants. I couldn't find anything else remotely as sturdy. I'd found a high-buttoned black leather vest in the back of my closet that I was guessing was actually Sienna's because it was rather tight across the chest. I'd planned to throw on a T-shirt and my 7th Heaven Zachary boots — black lace-up Fluevogs — but was glad I hadn't yet when

Desmond's gaze snagged on my breasts. Finally, someone found me more interesting than my necklace.

"What about the rest of the outfit?" I said, not budging from the doorway.

"Looks like it's restricting your breathing," Desmond said, his face full of concern. "I can help you with that."

I laughed. "We have to leave in fifteen minutes. It's a forty-five minute drive to the ferry."

Desmond swore under his breath, then offered me a grin. I'd never seen him this relaxed. Going to war suited him … or perhaps it was the threat of impending death.

"Later, then," he promised.

I nodded. "After the life debt is resolved."

He tilted his head to look at me and then shrugged his shoulders. "It makes no difference to me, but if it would make you more … settled, fine."

"You were going to say 'easy,' and I think that's already been established in your case."

He laughed.

"But yeah, it would make me feel better. And …" I hesitated. He hadn't asked me why I hadn't called in three months. He hadn't asked me why I didn't walk through the portal after him. I wasn't sure, with his currently relaxed flirting, if any of that even mattered to him or if somehow he already understood.

"And … I didn't call."

"No, you didn't."

"I … I saw something in the nexus."

"Is that where we were?"

"Yeah."

"You saw something that made you not call?"

"Yes, no. I didn't know where we stood."

"Outside your front door apparently," Desmond drawled, but he wasn't exactly amused.

I didn't want to talk about the vision Chi Wen the far seer had showed me any more than Desmond wanted to listen, so I took the opportunity to shut my mouth.

"Want to help me carry the cookies?" I asked, as seductively as I could when actually talking about baked goods.

"Hell, yes," he replied as he stepped through the wards. I folded the magic around him to allow him entry into the apartment.

"I figured we have time for a hello-haven't-seen-you-in-three-months-kiss as well," I said to his broad shoulders as I closed the door behind me.

He turned and pulled me to him before all the words were out of my mouth. "Yeah, I got that," he said, right before he laid a blazing kiss on me.

I wrapped my arms around his shoulders and the back of his neck, and opened my mouth to his tongue and his delicious magic. Smooth, dark chocolate — more citrusy than Kandy's berry, and without the bitter finish — rolled over all my senses … taste, smell, and touch. Desmond's magic curled over and around me. His skin was hot underneath my roaming hands.

The kiss was brutal — almost punishingly so. Eons away from the playful way he'd teased me in the bakery kitchen three months ago. As if he was punishing me for being gone so long and welcoming me home at the same time.

I aligned my body all along his. He was only a couple of inches taller than me, and my legs were long enough that we matched up in all the right places. He wasn't dampening his magic now.

His tongue darted against mine. His stubble was rough against my upper lip.

He groaned as I tugged his T-shirt out of his jeans and had my way with the skin of his overly muscled back. His magic sparked underneath my hands like the shock of static electricity.

I briefly contemplated how quickly I could get my clothes off, find a condom, and get to the bed — or any surface with a bit of give, actually — then orgasm and get dressed again.

"We don't have enough time," I muttered against his lips.

"We're waiting, remember?" he answered. Then, with an effort that he made seem Herculean, Desmond pulled himself away from me and crossed — walking rather uncomfortably — to the kitchen sink.

I flushed further — heat spreading up my chest to my face — as I remembered why his gait was so hindered. I'd seen and felt that region of his body very clearly during our first make-out session in the Squamish forest, three and a half months ago.

Desmond poured a glass of water and downed it.

Then he pierced me with a stare that made me estimate my ability to clear the kitchen island in a single bound.

He laughed, shook his head, and poured another glass of water.

I laughed too — a little sadly, because the moment of sexy reprieve was over. Then I grabbed a T-shirt, a knit hat, and my sword from the bedroom.

It was going to be a terrible day … or evening … or tomorrow, whenever. If that was going to be my last kiss … well, I kind of wished Desmond had gotten into town sooner.

I grabbed a two-pound bag of 72-percent Valrhona chocolate — Araguani, a single origin from Venezuela — out of the bakery pantry before we climbed into Desmond's SUV, which he'd parked illegally in the alley beside the dumpster. The chocolate was quickly proven completely unnecessary, because there was a custom box of See's Candies waiting for me in the passenger seat. Yep, filled with my favorites and miraculously untouched by the werewolves.

"I'm really glad you didn't lead with this," I teased Desmond as he climbed into the driver's seat beside me. I stopped to inhale the intoxicating aroma of the opened box. "I would have had to have you on the kitchen floor."

"Shit," Desmond responded. "I'll remember that for next time."

"Make sure you do." I grinned at him and popped a *Scotchmallow* in my mouth.

Both sets of back doors opened. Lara climbed in behind Desmond and Audrey climbed in behind me. Delightful. I wasn't exactly friendly with Audrey — a striking brunette werewolf, who always looked sleek and perfectly-coiffed whatever she was doing. She also had a habit of fawning over Desmond in a way that really irked me. I'd seen her made Desmond's provisional beta three months ago. She couldn't hold a candle to Hudson — Desmond's previous beta who Sienna had murdered because I'd drawn his attention. She didn't have an ounce of Hudson's charm or diplomacy, but I gathered she didn't even bother trying.

"Don't share," Desmond whispered as he started the SUV.

"Now that wouldn't be like me at all." I held the box out for him.

He grinned and selected a dark chocolate caramel — my second favorite.

Then I passed the box back to the werewolves as Desmond, shaking his head at my stupid generosity, turned right out of the alley and headed down the hill in the direction of Burrard Street Bridge.

"Time to hunt," Audrey said, far too gleefully for my taste.

"It's a seven-hour trip," I said, just to shut her up. Beta or no beta, she totally got under my skin.

She bared her teeth at me in the rearview mirror while Desmond was checking his blind spot, so the feeling was mutual.

But she'd still fight and kill at my side.

My sister was an unintentionally unifying force. The Adept of the West Coast would never be the same. If, you know, any of us were alive tomorrow.

We didn't exactly drive in tandem with the witches and necromancers, but with the text messages flying around the SUV, we might as well have been. We sped over the Lion's Gate Bridge, climbed the North Shore to reach the Upper Levels highway, and arrived at the ferry terminal with thirty minutes to spare.

Despite the fact that it was practically pitch dark at 6:30 P.M., and I was nestled in the huge SUV with a box of chocolates as my comfort blanket, I still felt the moment Kandy arrived with the skinwalkers. They were parked in two cars about twenty cars behind and one lane to the right of us. The witches — Gran, Scarlett, and three others I'd never met — were parked ahead. I didn't sense the necromancers until we were loading onto the ferry.

It was going to be a rough ride surrounded by this much magic. And the questions … I imagined everyone would have questions.

Desmond brought thirteen shapeshifters with him. That, added to three necromancers and the fledgling Mory, five skinwalkers, seven witches — including the two already on the island — plus Kandy and me made thirty-two Adepts.

Deep down in my heart — or maybe that was my soul — I knew it wasn't going to be enough.

All the different magic I was feeling had me jittery and off balance. I stayed in the SUV on the car deck while the shapeshifters cleared the restaurant out of food. I gathered the skinwalkers opted for the cafeteria, and the necromancers stuck with coffee from the onboard Starbucks. Even Kandy was distant, prowling around as if securing enemy territory. All of us on the same ferry, headed toward the same destiny, and still the Adept didn't intermingle. They even took turns — dictated by some unwritten schedule I didn't have a copy of — visiting me.

First, the elder skinwalker crossed the three lanes of parked cars between us. I saw her and started to open the SUV door, but she waved the gesture off as she approached. I unrolled the window instead, glad I didn't need the car keys to do so because Desmond hadn't left them with me.

Kandy slipped up to stand beside my window. The elder eyed me for a moment and then looked pointedly at Kandy.

"Elder Thomas," Kandy said.

"Call me Rebecca," the elder said as she dipped her head toward me. The raven feathers she wore almost disappeared against her dark hair, which was shot with steel gray, center parted, and pulled to the sides in two braids.

"She doesn't like being referred to as 'raven,' " Kandy cautioned me. Rebecca could indeed wear the guise of a raven when it suited her to do so — like when she was encouraging her skinwalker children to chase me through the woods and scare me into a river.

"Ms. Thomas, thank you …" I began, but she cut me off with a raised hand.

"The spear shouldn't be in the hands of a black witch," she said. "And many of our people live in the area where your mother fears the demons will walk. We will protect them tooth and claw, if necessary."

"All right," I said. "It's just —"

"We take responsibility for our own. We're not as weak as you think."

"I don't think that."

"Then trust we will do our part, but not be stupid about it."

I nodded and glanced over the elder's shoulder. A man and a woman stood behind her, close enough to hear our conversation but far enough away to stay out of it. He was in his mid-thirties and, if memory served, cloaked himself in the guise of a grizzly bear. I thought his younger sister, the resemblance was obvious, was the skinwalker who cloaked herself in the guise of a black bear.

The elder followed my gaze and smiled. "My son, Gord, and daughter, Drew," she offered.

I exchanged nods with the bears. I didn't see the red fox or the coyote, but I could feel their magic nearby. The skinwalker magic was similar in color to the shapeshifters', but tasted of wild onion and huckleberries.

"And your granddaughter? Has she been chosen by her spirit animal yet?" I knew it was on the edge of rude to ask after the private magic of the brave teen I'd met in the Squamish forest, but I needed to know. I needed to know that the skinwalkers would survive and thrive, and that Sienna wouldn't ruin — couldn't ruin — everything.

The elder smiled in a tight, fleeting gesture. "The raven blessed our family for the second time, but I have a feeling that Maia will walk in whatever skin she pleases by the time she is my age."

"She is not with you."

"At home with her grandfather," the elder answered. "You see, Jade Godfrey, we're not careless."

I nodded, pissed that people were short with me whether I cared too much and worried, or if I just barreled into situations without thinking. I didn't say anything, though. I knew when to respect my elders.

"I brought cookies," I said.

"No cupcakes?" the elder teased with a much more honest smile.

"No. For those, you'll have to come to the bakery," I said, repeating my invitation from months before.

Kandy opened the back door and reached into the inner hatch to extract one of the bakery boxes I'd packed with cookies.

The elder took the offering, then turned away to the stairs that led up to the passenger deck without another word.

"One down, twenty-nine to go," Kandy murmured, referring to the other Adepts onboard the ferry with us.

"God, I hope not," I said. "Want to share a box of those with me?"

"Hell, yeah."

"Grab the cowboy cookies."

Kandy climbed into the back seat and dug through the boxes of cookies while I watched another group of Adept approach through the rows of cars. I was pretty much trapped in a large, steel box over freezing cold ocean, miles and miles away from land. It was going to be a long trip.

"Necromancers, twelve o'clock," Kandy muttered behind me. Her mouth was already crammed full of cookie.

"Geez, you could have shared before chowing down." The coconut — paired with chunks of dark chocolate and oats — was what made the cowboy cookies supremely tasty.

"This is my second … nope, third one." Kandy chortled to herself as she stepped out of the SUV, facing off with Danica and her crew as they neared our vehicle.

These questions were going to be harder. At least Mory wasn't with them. I really didn't want to recount the demon summoning in London while the fledgling watched me. I shivered and tugged my knit hat lower over my ears. Why the hell I'd grabbed a hat and not a coat, I have no idea. I decided to blame Desmond for my forgetfulness and felt immediately better.

After an hour on the ferry, I felt drained of information. After an hour and a half, I felt like I had nothing left to give. Right before the ferry docked at the Departure Bay terminal in Nanaimo, Kandy rescued me with a piece of terrible cafeteria cheesecake that I gobbled up. Then I licked the plastic container. There was a lot of my childhood wrapped up in ferry cheesecake, most of it spent with Sienna, but I didn't dwell on that any longer than it took me to eat.

It was past time to put that all behind me. Not in a denial sort of way, but in an acknowledged 'that happened, that made me who I am, let's move forward' way. You know, like a real adult ... with a shiny new sword.

Chapter Fifteen

Tofino was one of my favorite places in the world, not that I got there more than once every three years or so. I usually loved every minute of the drive. But normally it wasn't so dark that I couldn't see the view, and I wasn't driving with a maniac shapeshifter who liked to double the posted speed limits on the hairpin turns.

We were winding through the mountain pass that separated the east and west coasts of Vancouver Island. I shrieked — for the second time — at the cliff face barreling toward me, inches from the front bumper in the headlights.

Desmond laughed, delighted at my reaction. He even managed to not crash the vehicle.

"Just because your reactions are faster than a human's doesn't mean a car is meant to be driven like this," I snapped.

"The GL550 is a high-performance luxury SUV," Desmond responded, still chuckling.

"Sure, like an army tank. It's not a sports car."

Desmond looked affronted. Then he grinned and stepped on the gas as if to prove his point. Shapeshifter games. Why did I keep stumbling into them … and why wasn't I traveling with the witches? Oh, right — because they asked too many questions, thinking I was one of their own so interrogating me wasn't a breach of etiquette. The shapeshifters weren't a wordy bunch.

"Shouldn't your beta be riding in a separate car? You know, in case you kill us all with your insane driving?"

Desmond glanced up at Audrey in the rearview mirror. "Beta-elect," he said, as if that should answer my question.

The road went down to a single lane and the cliff on the righthand side of the SUV dropped off into inky darkness. Desmond finally slowed, though he still sped on the straightaways or passing lanes. I guessed he'd proven his point and thankfully didn't actually want to drive us off a cliff.

"So tell me," Desmond said quietly in the dark between us. "Tell me what you haven't told the others."

My stomach bottomed out. I hadn't been deliberately lying to anyone, but the fact that I was an alchemist was still closely guarded, need-to-know info. Only a handful of people knew … if I didn't count the dragons.

"I made something," I said.

"In London?"

"Yes. With the knife that Sienna used to kill Jeremy."

Desmond twisted his hands, but then deliberately released them when the steering wheel groaned in protest.

"The sorcerers were dying," I continued, pushing past the fear of telling him, the fear of them all hating me before the night was over. "I might have been able to get Mory free with my knife, but …"

"It would have taken too long," Kandy said — blunt but kind — from the back seat.

"Yeah," I agreed. "I took what magic Sienna hadn't drained from the sorcerer Sayers, combined it with the knife, the residual ritual magic, and mortared it with my own magic … and, honestly, my desperation."

"Blood magic," Desmond murmured.

"Undeniably," I said.

"Feeling at all psychopathic now?" Desmond's smile was a flash of white teeth in the dark of the car interior.

"Not in general," I answered, but I couldn't bring myself to be light about it. "You have to understand, I'm not actually sure what I made. Except it cut through the sorcerer's magic like butter … and … and …"

"Jade thinks she killed Kett with it," Kandy said.

"The life debt bond," Desmond said. "Did the vampire actually step between you and a killing blow?"

"The magic thinks he did," I whispered. Then I turned to stare out at the dark view and blink my tears away. Silence fell as we all thought about the ramifications of such a knife in Sienna's hands. Audrey was the only one of the four of us who hadn't seen my sister in action yet.

"A blood magic-sharpened sacrificial knife," Desmond said. He glanced up in his rearview mirror. "We'll just have to take it away from the black witch."

"Consider it done," Audrey said, a wolf growl edging her declaration. For someone so put together and prissy, she was also rather toothy. I wouldn't want to get between her and anything she truly wanted. Hell, I wouldn't want to be in a room alone with her … she really didn't like me. Or, rather, she really didn't like the idea of me with Desmond.

Which brought up a complex problem that I had no brainpower to think over at the moment — namely, that Desmond was alpha of a pack, and therefore no relationship with him would ever go anywhere. I wasn't pack. I wasn't a shapeshifter.

"It won't be easy to get near the black witch," Kandy said, bringing my thoughts back on point. "Even Jade had a difficult time in London, and you know magic doesn't affect the alchemist the same way it does the rest of us."

"Jade was rescuing the fledgling necromancer and defending her fallen companions," Desmond said evenly. Kandy had been one of those fallen. "Here, she'll have us all around her, the witches at our backs, and the necromancers to hopefully counter the summoning magic."

Yeah, all I had to do was get through a horde of demons, overcome Sienna's defenses, and kill my sister.

Easy as freaking pie.

And I'd always made terrible pie. I brushed off my inadequacy by claiming that there just wasn't enough chocolate in pie to hold my attention. But I was way beyond denial and disclaimers now.

We'd caught the seven o'clock ferry, which docked at 8:45 P.M. in Nanaimo, from which it was a three-hour drive to Tofino. The dashboard clock was glowing 11:07 P.M. when we hit the junction of Highway 4 and had to either turn north or south. Ucluelet was eight kilometers to the south and Tofino was thirty-three kilometers to the north. Yeah, I was good at reading big green highway signs, even when they were only illuminated by headlights. The concern was we didn't know exactly where the demon rising had taken place in 1778. So even if Sienna had a couple of days' lead time on us, I hoped she'd gotten hung up on this point too.

Desmond pulled over when we reached the junction. As we waited for everyone else to catch up, I climbed out of the SUV and took a few steps away to see if I could sense any of Sienna's magic ahead of us. Any glimmer to let me know which way we should turn.

I clutched my sheathed katana in my left hand, not bothering to strap it in place across my back, but ready to draw. I was careful to not step out of the wide beam of the SUV's headlights. Knowing me, I'd slip on the road base at the edge of the highway, twist my ankle, and tumble into the dark woods that spread out on either side of us.

Desmond stayed in the SUV. His stern face was frequently lit up as text messages came in on his phone. Audrey and Kandy slipped off into the forest in opposite directions. Twisted ankles weren't high on their list of concerns. I guessed they were scouting, but — by the taste of their magic — they didn't go far.

The first two vehicles to join us were the remainder of the shapeshifters. Other than Lara, I didn't recognize a single other person among them, and they didn't approach me for introductions.

The witches, necromancers, and skinwalkers arrived in tandem.

Car doors slammed and gravel crunched, but no voices cut through the darkness. My mother crossed out of the night, passing Desmond's SUV to join me in the wide beams of the headlights. By this light, her hair was a fiery red rather than its usual strawberry blond.

"Anything, my Jade?" she asked.

I shook my head. She nodded, her arms crossed against a chill I didn't feel, and turned to climb into the passenger seat of Desmond's SUV.

Danica appeared and offered me a sad smile as she climbed into the seat behind Scarlett. Then Rebecca, moving silently along the paved road, climbed in behind Desmond after the necromancer.

I inhaled and willed the peaceful evening to settle around me, just for a moment more.

Scarlett, clearly lit by the interior cab light, looked up at me expectantly. The blue of her witch magic rimmed her eyes. Desmond followed her gaze. None of the four Adept in the SUV spoke to each other. They were waiting on me.

My mother had convened a war council on the side of a highway in the deep of the night — and I somehow, someway was their key weapon.

I sighed. Then returned to the SUV.

"First, the witches will join Olive at her home in Ucluelet," Scarlett said as I crammed myself in the back seat behind her, forcing Danica to scoot to the middle. "We will cast a seek spell for Sienna with the hairbrush Jade retrieved."

I'd successfully used the residual magic in the hair from this brush to find Sienna over six months ago in Vancouver. She'd been in a protection circle next to Rusty's half-eaten body.

"Her magic is radically different now," I said. A seek spell, even one powered by seven witches, was 90 percent guaranteed to fail.

Scarlett nodded and then continued, "Rebecca will continue through to Tofino and approach the elder of the local band to see if he or the other elders might know of the location of the demon rising in 1778."

"The government and the residential schools erased much of our history when they tried to destroy the First Nations way of life," Rebecca said. "I don't know how much the Tla-o-qui-aht have retained of their history or their connection to the earth, but I will ask."

Yeah, no one in the SUV was going to bitch about the band's ability or inability to help us. Whether or not they could help didn't rank very high against the list of atrocities committed in the name of reformation, education, and religion — also known as a greedy-ass land grab by an invading force.

"The necromancers will try to determine if there is any unusual spectral activity in the area," Danica said. "Once we have a better understanding of the situation, we will be able to formulate a response." She didn't elaborate further and that was fine by me. I didn't know what was involved in necromancy, but I was satisfied with that blank spot in my education.

"Jade?" Scarlett prompted. I guess it was my time to share.

"I'll dowse," I answered. "For Sienna and Blackwell's book." And the sacrificial knife, I didn't add. The SUV was getting stuffy with magic and my head was already aching.

"The shapeshifters will back the alchemist," Desmond declared.

"I can't accurately dowse when surrounded by too many Adept."

"We will determine the space you need and move forward from there," Desmond said. I wasn't entirely sure we were talking about dowsing any more. "We will continue to keep in contact by text message."

"When magic starts being thrown around in large enough quantities, the cellphones won't be reliable," I said.

"By then we will be making a stand together, my Jade," Scarlett said. "Because none of us will attempt to confront Sienna alone."

My mother twisted around in her seat and held my gaze until I nodded my agreement. Then she exited the vehicle, quickly followed by Danica and Rebecca. None of us, it seemed, were comfortable in each other's company for very long.

Desmond turned around to stare at me.

"What?" I snapped.

"You will not attempt to go off alone, dowser."

"I already agreed."

"Did you?" he drawled. "Or did you just lie to your mother?" He tilted his head as if scenting the air, as if he'd smelled me lying. Freaking shapeshifters.

I glared at him.

He grinned back. It wasn't a nice smile.

I looked away. "Fine. Kandy can come with me. I know her magic well enough."

He snorted with satisfaction. Then he asked, "As well as you know mine?"

And, we were back to flirting … hell, maybe the dominance games were all part of the mating dance for him as well.

"Well, I haven't licked the inside of her mouth, if that's what you're asking."

Desmond chuckled. The doors opened and the SUV shifted as Audrey climbed in the front passenger seat and Kandy climbed in beside me.

"What's up?" Kandy asked.

"Desmond's getting off on the idea of you and me in bed together," I answered. My voice dripped with as much derision as I could muster.

"Who wouldn't?" Kandy said.

"What?" Audrey screeched.

Desmond laughed louder at that and Kandy joined him. Audrey glared at me in the rearview mirror. The green of her werewolf magic ghosted over her eyes.

Still laughing, Desmond put the SUV in gear, pulled onto the highway, and turned toward Tofino.

I wanted to laugh too, but I couldn't find the capacity to do so.

I was numb — though maybe 'mentally drained' was a more accurate description — as I stepped out of the SUV in the first parking lot we came to off the main road. Highway 4 cut through Pacific Rim National Park on the way to the town of Tofino.

This time, I slung the katana across my back and cinched it too tightly in place. At least this pinch of pain registered, if only fleetingly.

The park was a well-maintained collection of beaches and hiking trails and lookout points. Long Beach was the most likely location for a demon summoning, just due to its size. At least, I hoped we'd started looking in the right place, because farther north along the beach the homes and hotels started right at the edge of the park and extended all the way into Tofino. Even in November, Tofino was a popular tourist destination — a world-class beach resort. And, being a Remembrance Day long weekend, I imagined the hotels and B&Bs were very full.

The Wickaninnish Inn was one of those hotels, and one of my fav places to stay when I could afford it. They had these thick white cotton sheets, heated bathroom floors, and tubs overlooking the crashing surf. And the food was great. They even made the strawberry jam they served in the morning with their fresh croissants.

Unfortunately, this wasn't one of those trips.

As planned, the skinwalkers left us when we pulled into the parking lot, heading farther into Tofino to the native reservation. The witches had turned into Ucluelet at the junction to meet at the home of a witch by the name of Olive. That way, they'd have an established witches' circle with which to cast the seek spell. They would be at half-coven strength tonight, and that was a lot of firepower for a simple spell. They'd know right away if it worked or not.

The necromancers had followed us into the parking lot, and began setting up some sort of spell of their own to communicate with any of the local ghosts who might be interested in chatting. Yeah, creepy, but it was a fantastic idea.

I was just fine with walking away from all that, heading through the woods and onto the gray sand beach.

Desmond and the other thirteen shapeshifters intended to follow Kandy and me by scent, staying back far enough to not overwhelm my dowser senses. Half of them were stripping out of their clothing as I was heading through the trees. Actually, I tripped over a log looking back to see if I could catch a glimpse of Desmond's ass. Unfortunately, he seemed to be keeping his clothes on.

"Eyes front," Kandy said. She was walking ahead of me on the path. "Last thing you need is a broken ankle."

Or heart, I thought. I hated when the wolf was right.

We stepped out onto soft sand, but it became hard packed a few feet away.

Long Beach stretched for miles in each direction. Other than a few randomly spaced outcrops, nothing impeded the twenty-foot waves from relentlessly pounding the beach. It had been raining on the drive here and continued to mist now even though the night was quite clear.

"Wow," Kandy said. The view, even by the light of the crescent moon, was breathtaking, but we weren't here for the atmosphere.

"The tide gets even lower than this," I said. "Can you tell if it's going out or coming in?" Kandy could see better than me in the dark.

She didn't answer right away. Her eyes glowed green as she scanned the vista. I took about ten steps to get to the hard-packed sand, which was still wet but easier to walk on. I waited there to see if the next wave reached me as it came thundering in ... it didn't.

"Out," Kandy said.

"This reminds me, sickeningly, of Oregon," I said.

"Nah, that was caves. This is beach."

"Still, one of those rogue waves could grab us and pull us all the way to China."

"I doubt the current would take you even half that far."

"So not the point, werewolf."

Kandy laughed, soft and husky. "All right, time to play. Do your thing, dowser. Right or left?"

I inhaled, attempting to ignore the mass of magic in the parking lot, as I tasted the area around and beside me. It smelled of sea, sand, and wet seaweed with cedar in the mix — probably from the fallen trees that had been stripped of their bark by the ocean and tossed to shore to form a border between the beach and forest behind us. No magic.

Oh, there was natural magic all around us. The area was abundant with it. Not as much as I'd felt at the grid point at Loch More, but the earth here was old and wild. Compared to Vancouver or London, it was untouched by humans.

"No clue," I answered Kandy. "The witches are north. Let's go south. I think open beach is more likely, no?"

"Who the hell knows?" Kandy said, but she followed slightly behind me as I moved southward, parallel to the surf. "No lights," she murmured after a few steps.

"It's all parkland here," I said. "Long Beach Lodge overlooks this beach at the very end of the park. If we don't find Sienna before then ... well, there'll be a hell of a lot more people to protect." I didn't even want to contemplate dozens of demons rising fifty feet from homes and hotels.

We walked.

We got wet.

My hair began to stick to my face. And still there was no hint of Sienna.

I was cold and hungry. Chilled actually. And I was so going to ruin my boots and leather pants in the rolling surf and sand. I didn't much care about the pants except that it was wasteful, but hunting Sienna was putting a nasty dent in my prized shoe collection.

"What if we're wrong?" I whispered into the moonlit darkness around me. The crashing surf whipped my words away, but Kandy still heard me.

"If we're wrong, we'll figure it out. Also, Mory has been following us for the last mile."

"I know," I said with a sigh. "I'm trying to figure out whether or not we should acknowledge her."

"She's fallen twice. And she's bleeding from the scrapes."

I stopped walking.

"I'll go get her," Kandy said.

"All right."

She turned back. The bitter chocolate taste of her magic receded quickly behind me.

And then I was alone on the beach.

"Now would be a good time, Sienna," I whispered into the crashing surf. The wind, which had picked up in the last few minutes, lashed my damp curls around my face. "Just you and me."

Nothing happened.

Kandy returned carrying a disgruntled fledgling necromancer over her shoulder. The green-haired werewolf dropped Mory to her feet in front of me. She looked like a defiant pixie with the moonlight washing across her face, glaring up at me through her shaggy, purple-edged bangs. Though the purple looked more gray in this light. Her hands were on her hips. It was like having an imp inexplicably mad at me.

Kandy's cellphone pinged before I could acknowledge Mory verbally. The werewolf glanced at her phone. "The witches are out."

Yeah, I saw that coming. "I'm surprised it took them so long. They must have tried multiple spells."

I opened my mouth to chastise Mory, but she beat me to it. "I've saved your ass just as many times as you've saved mine."

Kandy laughed.

"Yes," I replied, slightly surprised that I had to agree. "But if you didn't keep putting your — as you so delicately phrased it — ass in situations where it needed saving, my own ass wouldn't be in jeopardy so much."

I was rewarded for my wittiness with a chin jut from the angry imp.

Kandy's phone pinged again. "The skinwalkers are out. And, man, that old lady raven has a mouth on her."

I glanced at Kandy's phone. "That's a typo."

"Ah, yeah. That makes more sense."

I scanned the beach before us, then I turned to look out at the surf. We'd been walking for maybe forty-five minutes, but it felt like longer. Desmond and crew were catching up behind us.

"Rusty says …" Mory began, but then faltered when I turned to look at her. Rusty and I had an uneasy truce going on, but only because I had no idea how to actually get rid of him.

Mory straightened and fixed her gaze over my shoulder, which made me quickly step sideways.

"I don't like him sneaking up on me," I cried.

Mory laughed, and slammed her hand across her mouth to muffle the sound. "He's a ghost. All he does is sneak." Her words were garbled behind her hand and laughter.

"Still, creepy all around," Kandy said, commiserating with me.

"Rusty says what?" I asked, weary but not stupid enough to ignore a potential lead.

Mory nodded, but not to me, to the air to my right. I forced myself to not step farther away.

"Rusty says that he might be able to find her … Sienna. Though he calls her … by another name." Mory corrected herself awkwardly. She had no problem swearing like a drunken trucker, so I gathered this censorship was for the benefit of my feelings.

"What's stopping him?" Kandy snapped her teeth on the question mark. The werewolf hated standing around and talking.

Mory looked to me, her eyes suddenly pleading for understanding.

"He wants you to take the necklace off," I said. "To strengthen your connection."

Mory nodded and bit her lip. "I knew you wouldn't want me to, Jade, but …"

"If he's right …"

"Yeah. Plus if you're with me, you can put the necklace back on … if … you know."

I leaned down to lock eyes with the necromancer. "Yeah, I know. If your ghost brother tries to kill you again."

Mory puffed out her mouth, but then swallowed the protest and nodded.

I straightened and looked over at Kandy. The green-haired werewolf shrugged, seemingly uncaring, but I could tell by the tense way she held herself that she was wary and unhappy.

"Did your mother say no?"

"Yes."

Jesus. At least she was being honest with me. So when I said yes — because no matter what, Sienna had to be found and stopped — at least I knew ahead of time everyone would be pissed at me … again.

"Will he … remote project, or should you follow him?" I asked. My understanding of how necromancy worked was really basic.

Mory was already lifting the necklace from around her neck. "Both. He talked to the ghosts. The ones who wouldn't talk with mom, so he thinks she's close. But she's not on the beach."

"In the forest," I groaned. I really wasn't a fan of running for my life after midnight in the freaking forest.

"I like the forest," Kandy said with a wicked smile, as green rolled over her eyes.

"Yeah, you and the skinwalkers."

Kandy laughed and unzipped her hoodie.

Tofino was about to have a new pack of wolves. Delightful.

Chapter Sixteen

Mory — well, Rusty via Mory — led us through a thick stand of trees that separated the beach from the highway — not that the road looked like a highway here, but it was still officially Highway 4 through to Tofino. We darted across the road, not because there was any traffic to be seen but because something about the wide expanse of asphalt made me feel exposed.

A newly paved bike path ran along the east side of the highway. Mory, pausing and murmuring to Rusty — or so I assumed — wandered along this path until she came to a perpendicular trail marked with a provincial park sign. The sign outlined hours of operation, no campfires allowed in the park, and that sort of thing. It also showed a map depicting a web of hiking trails, which pretty much meant nothing to me. I'd have to rely on the wolves to get me out of the forest even if we stayed on the path. I had a terrible sense of direction, and no idea how to identify landmarks in the dark to lead me back.

But then, I had known this might be a one-way trip … even if I hadn't admitted it out loud yet. My sister had kicked my ass in London. I was alive because she wanted me to be.

While Mory paused at this crossroads, her head tilted slightly as she listened to something I couldn't hear or sense. I reached out beyond the multitude of werewolf signatures hidden all around us in the forest and tried to find a hint of Sienna to the east. I had just assumed I should look on the beach …

Mory swayed in front of me, calling my attention back. It was dark, but the fledgling necromancer looked paler than normal in the moonlight.

"Where's Rusty?" I asked. I didn't want to touch Mory while she was actively trying to use her necromancer powers, but I also wanted to make sure she was okay and not too drained. Her toasted marshmallow magic tasted as if it was still at normal strength, though. Not diluted.

"Through there," Mory said. She nodded toward the dirt path that cut through the woods to my right.

"There is no way Sienna would be in the woods," I said. "Not when there's a beach nearby. She's probably checked into the Wickaninnish and sleeping peacefully in gloriously thick white cotton —"

Mory held up a finger to silence me. Yeah, I loved being bossed around by a fifteen-year-old.

"Rusty says this way," the necromancer murmured after listening to the air for a bit.

Have I mentioned how freaky it is to me that I can't feel a drop of magic from ghosts? That just doesn't equate in my head, because they're magic, right? What else could they be other than some form of magic?

"Why?" I asked, touching Mory's shoulder lightly to stop her from blindly following Rusty into the woods. "Why would Sienna be in there?"

"I don't know, Jade," Mory answered. "He can feel her there … she calls to him."

"I'm sorry? 'She calls to him'? Yeah, that doesn't sound great."

"Because she killed him. Drained his magic. They'll always be connected."

Jesus, that was epically deep in a way I didn't have a lifetime to wrap my head around.

Mory stepped onto the forest path and I followed, feeling the still-unseen wolves shift around us. Kandy with her bitter chocolate magic stayed close, but the others kept their distance so as not to overwhelm my senses. But with them even as near as they were and Mory pumping out her toasted marshmallow magic in front of me, my dowser senses were pretty compromised already.

"Dowsing is not a terribly useful skill when surrounded by Adepts," I muttered. I hated feeling useless, and being led around by Sienna, pretty much clueless until I figured everything out way too late —

Wait.

"Wait," I said to Mory's retreating back. I could barely see the fledgling necromancer in the woods, though the moonlight was trying to filter through the swath the path cut through the trees. "Wait, wait," I repeated.

Mory turned back to me, then swayed again as if the movement made her woozy.

"He's taking too much," I said, meaning that Rusty in his eagerness to find and punish Sienna was draining too much of Mory's magic.

"It's fine," Mory sighed. "I think we're almost there."

"Just a second … I'm thinking."

"You don't have to blow a gasket about it."

"You don't even know what a gasket is."

"So?"

"So don't use phrases you don't understand."

"It's old speak. You — being old — get it."

"I'm not even in my mid-twenties," I snapped.

"Actually, you are."

"We've stopped." Desmond's curt voice came out of the dark forest to my right.

Mory flinched, and despite being pissed at her, I felt a little bad I hadn't warned her. I, of course, had felt Desmond approaching from miles away.

"Has the fledgling lost the connection?" Desmond asked. I could tell by his vocal quality that he hadn't transformed into McGrowly. I was fairly certain he also couldn't talk in full mountain lion form. Wrong type of vocal cords.

"No," Mory snapped. "Jade is thinking."

I waited for Desmond to make a snarky crack, or at least laugh. When he didn't, I shifted on my feet, worried I was delaying us for nothing.

The silence in the forest felt packed with more performance pressure than I'd ever felt before.

"It might be nothing," I said. "It's just we … I just barreled into … London. And I thought I had a plan, and …"

"Plans change," Desmond said, curt but not unkind. He stepped onto the path a few paces beyond Mory. His eyes glowed full green — probably trying to enhance his human vision with his cat's — but as I thought, he hadn't transformed.

I nodded to acknowledge him and looked at Mory. "This tie you mentioned, like how Rusty is tied to Sienna."

"Yeah, so what?"

"So," I said, trying to be patient and not simply rip Mory's head off and dig out the information I was seeking, skipping the dripping sarcasm and teenage ennui. "Remember when you saw Blackwell in the park in Portland?"

"Asshole sorcerer."

"Yeah, when you saw him that first time at the Jazz Festival, you said he was surrounded by shades." Actually, the necromancer had been so freaked out by whatever she'd seen hovering around Blackwell that I had to practically carry her out of the park.

Mory shrugged.

"Is Sienna surrounded by shades in the same way?"

"No," the necromancer answered, but then she thought about it a bit more.

"Before she learned to block Rusty from using your magic to hurt her?"

"Yeah, I get the question. Maybe. But she kept me drugged, you know, so that kept me from using my powers while she figured out the blocking thing."

"She sleep-spelled you through the necklace?"

"Nah, human drugs. In my food. I had to eat something."

Oh, freaking hell. That was information my already damaged soul wasn't going to absorb neatly.

"She had to back off on the drugs when she wanted to travel, but by then she'd figured out how to block Rusty. She had some of your trinkets. Maybe they helped."

"It must be something that comes naturally to necromancers. Blocking shades or ghosts. Something you probably do without even learning," I said, steadily putting things together. "She was slowly draining you and slowly learning the power."

"She's no necromancer," Mory spat. "She can't see ghosts, or talk to them."

"But she can do necromancer spells and summonings."

"Maybe."

"If she was surrounded by the shades of all the Adept she's killed, could your mom communicate with them?"

"They're not like Rusty. They'd just be residual energy. Shadows."

"Shadows all focused on the object of their death," I said, and I looked up to meet Desmond's gaze. "If Rusty can sense Sienna ahead, and they're connected because she killed him, then everyone she's killed might still be … around."

"I'll let the necromancers know," Desmond said. He stepped back into the dark of the forest.

"I don't get it," Mory said.

"I don't either. Maybe it's not important. Maybe your mom already knows. But what if Sienna can use the shades somehow? Like stored energy? Magic is energy. Maybe the necromancers can disrupt that connection if it exists. We need all the defenses we can build."

"Can we continue then?" Mory asked. Her snark was firmly back in place. It tended to drop when Desmond was around. She wasn't a big fan of the alpha, and seemed to try to stay under his radar. Once, I'd felt the exact same way … during a much safer and calmer period of my life.

"Lead on," I said.

Mory huffed out a breath and continued down the trail.

Almost thirty minutes and three twists in the trail later, Mory, via Rusty, had led us to what appeared to be a caretaker's or park ranger's hut. The hut, along with a public outhouse — currently closed — water tap, and message board, was dead center in a small clearing in the forest. Trails led to and from this clearing in four directions. A water-stained picnic table and benches stood on the opposite side of the hut, directly across from the outhouse.

I wished the moon was fuller, and therefore brighter. I could really only just see the outlines of the structures in the clearing.

"Rusty can't get inside," Mory said. Not taking her eyes off the hut, she shuddered as if cold. It looked like just a chill, but I worried her shiver meant more than that.

We were hunkered down in the trees at the edge of the clearing. I pulled Mory's necklace off — it was a tight squeeze around my head — and noted that it was glowing with a light blue tint of magic, as if being entwined with my necklace had charged it somehow. I dropped it back in place over Mory's head.

"Hey!" the fledgling necromancer exclaimed, though she immediately curled her fingers around the thick gold and silver chain.

"Next time, you learn to strengthen the connection with Rusty using the magic of the necklace."

"I'm not a witch," Mory sneered.

I shrugged. "Fine. Don't, then."

I stepped around Mory and stumbled through the woods with Kandy in wolf form at my side — off the path — until I'd walked the perimeter. I stopped when I was once again facing the front door of the hut.

"No magic," I whispered into the surrounding trees. "Not that I can taste or see. I should get closer to confirm."

"No," Desmond growled. He was standing at my back suddenly, though thirty seconds ago, he'd been much deeper in the forest.

"I'm not going to argue with you about it," I said as Scarlett, led by a wolf I didn't recognize, stepped up to meet me. I could taste other witches nearby now, and the skinwalker magic just at the edges of my senses. The troops were gathering ... again.

"Key weapons don't waltz into apparently empty clearings after being led there by a ghost," Desmond said.

"He has a point," Mory whispered.

"Don't take sides," I hissed at the fledgling.

She shrugged and stroked her necklace thoughtfully. It was an unconscious gesture, but backlit by the magical glow, her fingers looked skeletal. I looked away.

"Danica understood your thoughts about the poor souls Sienna has killed," Scarlett said. "She and the other necromancers are trying to figure out if they can make use of it. Thankfully, their magic seems compatible with cellphones, so they're calling friends and family for guidance."

I nodded, but my attention was fixed once again on the hut. "Something's not right," I said.

"Rusty wouldn't mislead us," Mory insisted.

"That's not it."

"Audrey," Desmond called softly into the darkness. A gorgeous, dark gray wolf stepped up beside Mory. The necromancer flinched. The wolf dropped its jaw open in a toothy smile ... or like it was about to take a bite out of the fledgling.

"I suppose you won't allow me to go?" Desmond asked hopefully.

The gray wolf lowered its head and a growl rumbled out through its now aggressively bared teeth. Mory squeaked and pretty much threw herself into my lap, knocking me off my haunches and onto my ass in dirt, dried leaves, and ferns.

I hadn't seen it coming, but I'm fairly certain I should have been able to take a hit like that and stay on my feet. I sighed. "Don't run. Only prey runs," I said to Mory, attempting to be stern and comfort her at the same time.

The fledgling necromancer disengaged from the hug I was now forcing on her and climbed in between where Scarlett was standing and me. "I am prey," she whispered.

"Only if you see yourself that way," Scarlett admonished.

"Yeah, claws and teeth beat ghosts any day." Mory's snark was seeping back.

I looked at Audrey, who'd backed off a step at the mention of ghosts. "Don't be so sure," I said to the fledgling.

"You'll need thumbs," Desmond said, either oblivious to or bored with the drama taking place at his knees.

Audrey took another step back and her green magic rolled around her so brightly I had to look away. Still on all fours, she transformed into her human form. Her completely naked human form.

Audrey straightened from her crouch, unabashedly displaying the most gorgeous female body I'd ever seen — long muscled legs, high breasts, and a slim waist that curved down into perfectly proportioned hips — as if I hadn't already hated her clothed.

She stepped by me — I was still sprawled on my ass like a street urchin in the dirt — and out into the clearing.

At the same time, a ring of green-glowing eyes moved a step forward to the edge of the trees, surrounding the hut and the outhouse. All the shapeshifters' attention was fixed on Audrey.

"What's on the picnic table?" I murmured, not expecting an answer. I'd noted the dark shadow there when I'd done my perimeter walk and brushed it off as a water stain … except it had been raining all day, so a water stain shouldn't show up like that on wood.

"Blood," Desmond answered. His remote tone suggested he was utterly focused on Audrey as she picked her way past the table and reached for the handle of the hut door.

Blood, blood. A pool of blood soaked into wood. Why was that ringing —

"Wait!" I cried.

Mory and Scarlett flinched beside me. Audrey froze with her hand an inch from the doorknob.

"Wait, wait," I muttered, fiercely trying to focus my thoughts. Everything was moving too fast … like London …

"Sayers," I whispered.

"The sorcerer?" Scarlett asked.

"Yes," I breathed as it clicked into place for me. "We're forgetting what Sienna does."

"I think that's rather difficult to forget," Scarlett said.

"No, I mean, she binds power —"

"Steals," Mory spat.

"Exactly. And the last Adept that I know of who she stole power from was Sayers."

"You said you couldn't feel any magic in the clearing," Desmond said, a pissed-off growl edging his statement. I got that he didn't like being thwarted. Actually, I got that he wanted to be in the clearing instead of his beta-elect, but protocol or whatever kept him standing in the woods behind me.

I straightened and pulled my jade knife. In the moonlight, the green stone of the blade glowed almost the same hue as the shapeshifters' eyes that still ringed the clearing across from me.

"I feel no magic in the clearing, and yet there's natural magic all around us. It's dim, touched and eroded by humans and Adepts alike. It's like the magic I find in the jade."

"Sayers' specialty," Scarlett murmured.

"I thought it was just a magical dampener he wore, but then the fog spell that covered the parking lot dampened and diffused magic within it."

"Sienna siphoned this sorcerer's power?" Desmond asked.

Audrey remained standing perfectly still in the clearing. Her dark hair cascaded down her bare back. Her skin glowed in the pale moonlight.

"She got some of it. Enough to trigger the demon summoning — a spell Sayers set up — but I bound the rest." I let this painful admission hover in the darkness between Mory, Scarlett, and Desmond.

"In the knife?" Desmond asked. "Which the black witch now has?"

"Yes."

"She's learning too fast," Scarlett said. "Impossibly fast for someone previously so unskilled."

"No," I said. "She's just trying everything. You understand? She would always try everything once. We just have no idea what she tries that doesn't work."

I stepped forward into the clearing. Desmond, Kandy, Mory, and Scarlett followed. The shapeshifters — not all of them wolves, I now saw — stepped forward to tighten the perimeter but stayed in formation.

Desmond's form was a mountain lion, so I knew his pack would contain other species of shifters besides the wolves I'd met. I saw at least one coyote, what appeared to be some type of fox, and a smaller cat that was maybe a lynx out of the corner of my eye as I crossed to the hut.

Audrey turned and sneered at me as I approached. "I don't smell any magic."

"Go ahead, touch the door," I said, smiling at her sweetly.

"Jade," Scarlett admonished.

Audrey raised her chin and gazed over my head to look at Desmond, her expression now welcoming and receptive. She was like a porcelain statue in the moonlight, except for the dark nipples and trimmed triangle of dark pubic hair. She didn't seem to have the problem Kandy had with body hair growing back after she transformed. I guessed that was a refined shapeshifter ability, similar to their half-beast forms. I wanted to slap her silly … repeatedly.

Instead, I stopped beside her and looked at the door. I still couldn't feel any magic. "Still nothing."

Scarlett bent down, and with a flick of her fingers called up a dimmer version of her light spell. Even though the blue ball glowed with less wattage than usual, the shapeshifters and I flinched from it.

After a few rapid blinks, I could see the line of coarse salt along the underside edge of the door.

"Definitely spelled," Scarlett said. She straightened and opened her palm to send the blue ball of light over the picnic table. "No magic in the blood?"

"No," I answered.

"Animal?"

"No," Desmond answered. His nostrils flared, and then he scrunched his nose. "Human, a few hours old."

"The sacrifice for whatever spell she's working?" I asked, speaking more to myself than the others. I turned back to the door. "The dampening spell wouldn't need a sacrifice ... No, she used it to mask whatever is inside."

I reached for the handle but Audrey knocked my hand away and grabbed the doorknob herself.

Nothing happened.

The werewolf strained. Then with a grunt and a flash of shifter magic, the handle popped off in her hand.

The door swung slightly open on loose hinges.

"Impressive," I said. Without breaking a sweat, Audrey had countered some sort of ward on the door that I hadn't even felt.

I touched the tip of my jade knife to the door and pushed it the rest of the way open.

Audrey stiffened and moaned ever so quietly. I couldn't see what she saw within the darkness.

Scarlett sent her light spell to hover over my shoulder. I reeled away from the carnage that lay in the one-room hut even before my brain had fully processed what my eyes had seen.

My mind refused to acknowledge the image imprinted there as I turned to block Mory's view, actually lifting the fledgling and carrying her — kicking and protesting — away.

I heard Desmond step forward and absorb the scene in the hut with a pained grunt.

"How many?" Scarlett asked, her voice thin and unsteady.

I suddenly very much wanted my Gran. I wanted the life she'd carefully directed me toward — keeping me away from magic, keeping me ignorant and safe, and not forever haunted by my sister's deeds. I wanted her to wrap her arms around me as I was now holding Mory, who quieted once she figured out what I was blocking her from.

"Jade," Scarlett called to me. "I ... we need you to look at the magic."

I nodded and turned back to the hut. Kandy, in wolf form, brushed by me and stood in front of Mory, exchanging places to watch over the fledgling.

Scarlett and Desmond stood at the door and watched me approach. Audrey stood to one side with her arms crossed protectively and her head bowed. She wasn't so confident and cocky now, but I couldn't take pleasure in this change because the hut was full of dead bodies.

A pile of dead bodies. Their blood soaked into the pentagram inscribed on the wooden slat floor.

"Magic?" Scarlett prompted. She was trying to steel her tone and failing.

I scrubbed my foot along the coarse salt at the entrance. Scarlett gasped. Yeah, that was lazy of me, but I was pretty sure — seeing how the blood beyond was pouring over the edges of the pentagram — that whatever spell Sienna had worked was finished here.

The putrid smell of Sienna's dark magic, now released to linger in the air, turned my stomach.

"I think the salt was to anchor the damping spell," I finally said. "If we looked for it, I'd guess there's an outer ring as well, around the clearing."

"The spell inside?" Scarlett prompted.

I shook my head. "I don't know. Not only witch magic, I don't think. And she didn't kill all these people for a dampening spell. The pentagram isn't sealed. I assumed that meant the spell had been completed, but maybe we interrupted her?"

"I'll get a necromancer to look at it," Scarlett said.

"No!" I cried.

Scarlett laid her hand on my arm and tugged me away from the door. Desmond stepped over to talk to Audrey.

"I didn't mean Mory," Scarlett said. "I just meant your Gran and Danica should take a look. If it's not solely witch magic … or sorcerer, as far as I can tell."

"No," I answered. "It's Sienna's magic. It's chaos unleashed."

Scarlett was still stroking my arm. Usually her magic soothed me, but it didn't now. Perhaps I didn't want to be soothed.

"She can't come back from this … killing humans," I whispered. "This many people can't go missing from Tofino without an explanation …"

"You didn't think … Jade. My Jade …" Scarlett's voice caught. "You didn't think Sienna could be saved?"

I shook my head and stepped away from my mother. But yes, deep in my heart I had still hoped … utterly stupidly, utterly blindly hoped.

Audrey had crossed to the shapeshifters. They tightened their ring until they were gathered around her. If I was an artist, I would have been struck by the dangerous beauty of the scene. A naked woman surrounded by predators.

But I wasn't an artist.

I turned to Mory, whose eyes were dark saucers on her too-pale face. She had the fingers of both hands twined through her necklace, as I normally would have myself.

But I didn't. My necklace and knife weren't the kind of shield my raw soul needed now. Such a balm didn't exist.

Just as Sienna's magic shouldn't exist.

Just as I — born of witch and guardian dragon — shouldn't exist.

"No ghosts, Jade," Mory whispered as I crossed to her.

"Could they have passed over?" I asked hopefully.

"No," Mory moaned. "I mean, not the shades, not from such a violent death. We should ask my mom … but no."

I looked back at the hut. Scarlett was working magic — creating some sort of shield around herself in order to step inside. The blue of her magic illuminated the stains on the floor, running over the edges of the pentagram and soaking into the dry wooden slats …

Oh, God. Damn it, Rusty. The ghost of Mory's brother had led us to the biggest concentration of Sienna's magic that he could feel. Sienna herself could block him, but not while she was expending large amounts of magic. Such as the amount it would have taken to perform the sacrifice in the hut. I guessed dampening spells were only effective against the living, not shades or ghosts. Though the ward had kept Rusty out of the hut itself.

"Tell your mom about there not being any ghosts here," I said.

Mory nodded and chewed her lip.

"Now, Mory. Call her now!"

I looked down at Kandy, who was still in wolf form at Mory's side. She obviously wasn't subject to Audrey's orders, and hadn't gathered around the werewolf with the other shapeshifters. "And stay with Kandy."

"What?" Mory cried. "Why Jade?" The fledgling had her phone to her ear.

Desmond, Scarlett, and Audrey turned to look at us.

"She's already completed the sacrifice. Maybe only moments before we got here," I said to no one in particular. "With the knife, you understand? She's completed the sacrifice, and she has what she needs to activate it. Maybe in the knife or tied to the spear. It's a two-part spell."

Then I turned and ran into the forest, back toward the beach, knowing I was too late.

Again and again. Always too late to stop Sienna.

Chapter Seventeen

I ran, heedless of the undergrowth blocking my way or the branches scraping my face. I ran, not bothering with the path, not bothering with direction, knowing, knowing, that any second, any breath, I would taste Sienna's magic. It would rise up and overwhelm me. But I would fight.

It was never going to be any other way.

I lengthened my stride until my legs burned — not with pain, but with magic. The shapeshifters were behind me, moving as one unified force. The witches were mixed among them, and the necromancers were already ahead of me … perhaps still in the parking lot.

Magic flared along a long line to my left. For a moment, I saw it warp through the thick cedar trees. Someone behind me screamed — a witch, I thought, but I didn't stop. I corrected my course to follow this thick line of death magic — all blood and earth and dankness. It — as I had feared — was a delayed spell tied back to the park ranger's hut. Sienna had gained that ability in England somewhere, by killing a witch named Azure Dunkirk. It seemed important to remember such things now, instead of being constantly surprised by everything happening around me.

This was the path I was walking now. There was no denying it any longer.

Well, I was running, actually.

The forest broke open before me. The night wasn't as dark now, though nothing had actually changed. Nothing except me … fundamentally me …

I crossed the highway in two strides. A stand of trees, maybe fifty feet across, was all that stood between me and the seething mass of magic I could now feel on the beach.

Dense peppermint magic bloomed to my right and then barreled into me. I twisted off my feet and slammed into — actually, slammed through — a cedar tree. It cracked and snapped in half. I tumbled, throwing my hands out to slow myself. I dug troughs through the earth and ferns and cedar needles, ending up elbows deep before I stopped.

"I taught you to fall better than that," a cool voice whispered from right next to me.

I pushed up off the ground, spun in midair, and came up to my feet holding a blond, too-pale, blue-eyed vampire by the neck.

His magic was different. It didn't dance in his skin any longer. It still tasted of peppermint but it was richer and darker now, and the other spice that had always eluded me was more present. His eyes were rimmed in red, his fangs longer than before.

"You can't barrel into this fight alone, alchemist," he said. "You're always running for trouble rather than away." Then he laughed. Or, rather, he gurgled, as I was still holding him aloft by his neck.

"Kett," I whispered. "Not dead?" Yeah, I had my Captain Obvious hat on.

I set him down on his feet but didn't loosen my hold on his neck. What with the red eyes and fangs, I wasn't an utter idiot.

The shapeshifters fanned out behind and around us, hidden within the trees but near. I could also sense that the necromancers had moved to join the witches.

Kett tilted his head, thinking. "More dead, perhaps," he said. I couldn't tell by his tone if this secondary reincarnation was a bad thing or not. "You look … appalled, alchemist."

"I … I saw …"

"Yes."

"I felt …"

"Yes. I shall miss the life debt bond as well." He grinned. The expression was so utterly human on his completely inhuman face. "Did you really try to feed me your blood, Jade?"

I felt his breath brush across my cheek and ear … damn, he was faster than before.

I wrapped my arms around his shoulders before he could step away again. I pressed a kiss to his lips. He was like holding cold marble. His lips were unyielding. He brushed his fingers through my hair, and something broken in me healed.

"With or without the bond, I'll always be able to find you, Jade Godfrey," he whispered against my lips, answering my unasked question.

"I'm glad you're alive," I said, still clutching his shoulders. I was slightly worried now that he was just an apparition.

He raised an eyebrow. His fangs were nowhere in sight suddenly.

"Okay," I said. " 'Alive' might be the wrong word. I'm glad you're here."

"You saved me from the true death a second time, warrior's daughter. My master prevailed on her maker to bequeath his blood, but only after she named my connection to you. As your friend …" — Kett laughed as if amused by the idea — "… I am valuable to the Adept. Not just vampires. Not just the Conclave."

"Because I'm an alchemist or because I'm half-dragon?"

"Both," Kett answered. "Shall we renew the life debt?" He nodded toward the beach.

He was joking. More than just his magic had undergone a transformation.

I threw my head back and laughed. It was completely inappropriate timing, but I needed to laugh … or to cry.

"You hightail it off into the forest without an explanation," Desmond said as he stepped through the trees. "And I follow, only to find you wrapped around a vampire."

This statement — as much as Desmond's utterly disgruntled tone — reinforced my laughing fit. Kett joined me.

"I thought you were barreling into a shitload of trouble —" Desmond said.

"She was," Kett interrupted. He turned toward the beach, loosening my hold on him. I figured that if Desmond could see him, then he was real. I let him go.

"The black witch has triggered a rather elaborate spell on the beach," Kett said.

"You don't have to sound so impressed, vampire," Desmond muttered.

Desmond and I followed him through the trees until we had a view of the shoreline, but were still sheltered by the forest.

I looked out at the scene Sienna had once again constructed. The rest of the shapeshifters, witches, necromancers, and skinwalkers gathered behind and beside us. No one spoke. We were beyond the planning stages, the gathering of information. It was time to react and hope that, combined, our individual skills prevailed.

Sienna was standing on a jut of rocks a few feet out into the surf. The tide was lower now. As far as I could see, she was simply standing on a rock, holding the native spear above her head and chanting. No pentagram, no book.

Magic churned in the ocean all around her. Blood — her own — streamed down from her slashed forearms. The sacrificial knife was stuck in a belt that rode low across her hips. She wore a simple calf-length black dress. Her legs, arms, and feet were bare. Every vein in her body stood out black against her pale skin.

Kett shifted to my left. Desmond stood on my right and slightly behind. The shapeshifters — most of them already in half-beast form — spread out around us.

Scarlett stepped up to my shoulder. I didn't look away as she murmured, "The necromancers say she has the souls somehow trapped above her. Dozens of them. Mory is having trouble keeping Rusty from answering her summons."

Shit.

"She's fueling the spell with the souls of all the people she murdered in the hut?"

"And everyone she's ever killed. You were right. The necromancers will try to disrupt this connection. The skinwalkers will guard them as they cast. The witches will provide shielding …"

"And we'll barrel through," I said.

"Yes, but —"

"It's okay. That's what I do best."

"The shapeshifters and the vampire will get you through. And you … you will …"

"Try to get past her shields."

"Yes. I love you, Jade."

I turned and met my mother's gaze. Our indigo eyes were the same color, but hers shone bright with witch magic.

"I love you, mom."

Scarlett nodded and turned away. Her movements were stiff, as if her limbs wanted to be doing anything but walking away.

I looked back through the shapeshifters and sought my Gran's gaze. She looked stern, reaching for Scarlett's hand and adding her daughter's power to the linked line of witches. A tall witch with light brown hair had a nasty cut on her cheek. I gathered she'd been the one who'd screamed in the forest when the delayed spell snapped into place, but she didn't falter now. None of us could falter now, not with what was happening on the beach.

Dark magic literally boiled the water around Sienna, turning the white surf black in the moonlight. I couldn't feel or taste the energy she drew from, but I could imagine what the necromancers saw. The trapped, tortured souls of Sienna's victims coiled around my sister's head.

"We have to go," I whispered.

"Not yet," Kett said. "We wait for the witches."

I unsheathed my sword, bringing the two-and-a-half-foot blade up over my shoulder and in front of me.

"We stay in formation," Kett called out. "The alpha here, me here, and Kandy just behind the alchemist. No one steps in front of the warrior's daughter. Protect her on both sides at all costs. We move across the beach as one."

I glanced back at Desmond, waiting for some growled retort about being ordered around by a vampire. He simply grinned at me, and — in a flash of explosive magic — transformed into his half-beast form.

"Hello, McGrowly," I said. "Fancy meeting you here."

McGrowly chuckled. It was a terribly unpleasant sound, which probably scared every small animal within hearing range to death.

Naked, Kandy wrapped her arm around my neck from behind. She must have transformed out of her wolf form somewhere in the forest, maybe in order to carry Mory. With a hug that would have choked a human, she pressed a kiss to my temple. I squeezed her arm with my free hand and she let go.

A rush of magic flashed behind me — all bitter chocolate and berries — and Kandy transformed into her half-beast form. McGrowly grunted, impressed. I guess he didn't know Kandy had been practicing.

I could feel the witch magic now, first seeping along the ground at our feet and then slowly rising up in front of me. They were creating a shield. Impressive, but I wasn't sure how long it would hold against the putrid, boiling magic I could taste from fifty feet away across the beach.

I stepped forward, out from the shelter of the trees. I twirled my katana — completely unnecessarily — to loosen my wrist. Then I straightened my arm and pointed the blade toward my sister.

"Sienna!" I screamed. My voice knifed across the sand.

Sienna opened her black eyes, like two yawning chasms carved into her face. Then she smiled.

A fifteen-foot black-crested wave crashed onto the beach. It receded, but left a horned demon in its wake. Standing six feet at the shoulder, it lifted its snubbed snout in the air, opened its blood-red eyes, and bared its fanged teeth in our direction.

Another wave crashed in, depositing a second demon beside the first.

"Mutt," McGrowly spat behind me. The demons did look reminiscent of mastiffs. You know, if mastiffs were covered in gray scales and weighed about … I don't know … five hundred pounds each.

"No one likes a mutt." The words were mangled by McGrowly's fangs, but the shapeshifters all around us understood him perfectly. They growled in unified agreement.

Another wave brought another demon mutt, then another and another. They shook and stretched their boney backs.

"Come and get me," Sienna cried. She was so freaking typical, like all the freaking time.

I curled my other hand under and around the bottom of my sword hilt, rotating my body into an offensive stance.

The witch magic snapped fully into place in front of me.

I took a deep breath, settling into my stance as I exhaled. I tasted the moment. It tasted of death.

"Now," Kett whispered.

My muscles contracted, propelling my body forward. The soft sand shifted underneath my feet, but it didn't shake me. I flew toward my destiny, lifting my sword up over my head as I pivoted into a spinning leap to take the head off the first demon that jumped at me, snarling.

Its blood splattered my arms and throat even as it dissolved into ash … no, sand. I could feel the grit against my skin and taste it on my lips. I was aware that I was screaming — the pain of it tearing at my throat — as I flipped my katana up over my opposite shoulder, lunged, and took off the head of the next demon that leaped at me.

I was still running, carving my way toward Sienna. The demons were nothing but an obstacle to cut through. Sienna was the goal. My sword would be at her neck next.

The demon horde stopped us halfway across the beach. I was only aware of the demons in front of me, and Desmond and Kett beside me. If I looked at them too closely, those monsters at my side were even more terrifying than the demons. McGrowly would reach out, snatch a demon, and rip its head off. This wasn't a clean, simple process. He was coated in demon blood that burned its way through his clothing and seared his skin. If he noticed, it didn't slow him down.

Kett flitted in and out of my peripheral vision as a seemingly demonic version of himself — though not quite the mess of chaos that had freed itself from Blackwell's spell in Scotland. This incarnation was graceful and bestowed with deadly claws. Instead of ripping off heads, he sliced them off. Yes, with his bare hands.

The space between Sienna and me was filling with more and more demons impeding my ability to swing my sword and cleanly deliver killing blows. I could see a dozen in front of me alone, with more and more rolling out of the surf behind. How many people had Sienna killed? Was each demon a reanimation of those souls? I pushed this traumatizing thought out of my mind and pressed forward, hoping I was freeing their spirits as I vanquished each demon before me.

The shapeshifters were getting hit hard around us. The witches' spell offered some protection, but it wasn't entirely demon proof. Sienna wasn't able to cast any extra magic through it, though. I'd felt at least three fire-blood spells hit the shield and fizzle. So that was a good thing.

I could still feel Kandy, Audrey, and Lara near me, but the witches' shield spell wasn't wide enough to block the demons to our left and right.

I tried to ignore the screaming. I tried to ignore the faltering witch magic. I just swung my sword as I inched forward.

"Jade!" Kett yelled.

I had missed the second demon climbing over the shoulder of the one I was currently facing. This demon sprang at me, too close for me to get my sword up and between us. I tumbled backward, knocking Kandy and Audrey aside where both were wrestling their own demons — literally.

The first demon gleefully leaped over the second. For a brief moment — with me pinned underneath them — they tussled over who was going to rip my throat out first. Unable to free my sword, I managed to pull my jade knife out and jammed it into the eye socket of the first demon, just as the second took a swipe and caught my neck with its claws.

I nearly blacked out from the pain. My blood spurted all over the second demon. But instead of lapping it up, it shrieked and reeled back. This shifting of its weight pressed the first demon farther down onto my jade knife. The creature dissolved into sand that flowed around me, mixing with the blood still pumping from whatever artery had been severed in my throat.

I tried to roll to my feet but didn't make it up. The second demon was still scrambling back from me as others closed in to take its place, ready to finish me off.

Kett stepped in front of me and took the head off the second demon. Then he turned and smiled at me. "I guess that answers that question." I had no freaking idea what he was talking about. His smile faded as my vision blurred. "Jade?"

Everything went momentarily black. Note to self: Getting my throat gouged out was not a good idea.

I came to and found Kett and Desmond standing over me. I sat up and shakily retrieved my sword. It was covered in blood and sand. That seemed so disrespectful.

I felt magic building up behind me …

The necromancers …

"Duck," I tried to scream, but it came out as a gurgled whisper. I'd stopped bleeding but my throat was still healing.

The necromancers unleashed their spell. It flew across the sand. It flew toward us. It flew toward Kett. Necromancy and vampires didn't mix.

"Duck," I screamed for real as I surged to my feet.

Kett flattened himself to the sand in front of me. The necromancers' spell blew through and around me. And just for a flash, I could taste sugared violets.

"Rusty …" I whispered.

The spell hit the churning well of energy that had built up above Sienna — the power source I couldn't feel or taste. My sister shrieked and collapsed to her knees.

The demon before me shook its head as if shaking off an invisible leash. Sienna had momentarily lost her hold on the horde.

Another flash of magic flew in from behind — the witches. This spell also blew by me, tasting of fresh-cut grass, lilac, and strawberries. It ignited inches in front of me, burning through every demon in my path.

Before me, the witches' shield collapsed, but I was already moving. I sheathed my sword and gripped my jade knife. The sand of the disintegrated demons hung suspended all around me … or maybe I was just moving so fast it hadn't fallen to the ground yet.

I felt my mother fall, her magic so dim I could barely sense it. This was the same spell she'd used against the demon in the Sea Lion Caves. Then, it had been more powerful than I had ever thought her capable of. Now, backed by a half-coven of witches, it was astonishing. And so filled with magic it could be deadly for the caster. I willed myself forward despite the terrified feeling that I might be losing her.

The skinwalkers, who'd been waiting behind the witches, leaped into battle.

The demons broke through the shapeshifter defensive line.

More screams, more dying.

I kept moving forward.

I hit the surf. I leaped over the next wave — and there was no demon within this one. The necromancers had stopped the generation of new demons by freeing the souls, or energy, that had been fueling Sienna's summoning, but not the already risen horde. At least a dozen demons remained on the beach behind me.

I had left everyone else behind me. I leaped up on the rock. Sienna was still on her knees. She looked up and smiled as I thrust my knife forward into the ward that shielded her from magic.

From magic, but not me.

Except the jade knife met no resistance. Off-balanced by this, I fell forward, stumbling to kneel before Sienna.

She'd opened the protection circle, just for that single breath. It snapped closed behind me.

And I faltered.

Sienna's magic was too powerful. It was fully unleashed within the circle. It owned the circle. It rejected me, momentarily scrambling my senses.

Then I became aware of a dark burning deep within my gut — and of the seething, terrible magic searing into me.

I looked down. Sienna had stabbed me in the stomach with the sacrificial knife as I fell. A knife that I had created to cut through magic, a knife capable of killing a vampire.

"That's the third freaking time," I muttered. I could taste blood in my mouth.

Sienna laughed. "Ah, Jade." She reached out to stroke my hair. Her hand came away bloody, and she looked for a moment like she was contemplating licking it.

"I wouldn't do that," I murmured. I could feel my magic fighting the power of the knife — and claiming it … because it was already my own creation. "The demon didn't like it much."

Sienna giggled. "No matter. There are always other ways."

Then she kissed me. Hand cupping my head, knife twisting into my gut, she kissed me.

I screamed. And screamed.

She was pulling my magic out — somehow dragging it from me through my lips.

I was dimly aware of more screaming outside the circle, followed by a crack of magic as Kett or Desmond tried to break through Sienna's wards.

But Sienna — who had killed and bound the magic of so many Adepts — was too powerful.

I slumped sideways and she guided me back onto the rocks, still kissing me, still siphoning my magic.

Now she'd be unstoppable. The horde would kill most of the Adepts arrayed against her, and then she'd step out of the circle and kill the rest. With my magic.

My friends, my family … all dead, just like I'd seen in Chi Wen's vision.

Except … this wasn't the cave. And that wasn't my destiny.

My mouth, clamped shut against Sienna's assault, was filled with blood.

I spat this mouthful into Sienna's face.

She screamed and reared backward. As it had been with the demon before her, the magic in my blood was incompatible with Sienna's black magic — or maybe it was that my dragon magic was the antithesis of demon or dark magic — I didn't know. But it distracted Sienna for just a moment.

Still barely able to move, I wrapped my hand around the sacrificial knife that was poisoning me with its blood magic and yanked it from my belly. The toxic magic was already in my system, slowing me as I rolled to my side to avoid a spell Sienna half-heartedly tossed at me. This spell — an ice-based variation of her fireblood spell — hit my shoulder and actually helped steady me rather than freezing me in place.

"What have you done?" Sienna shrieked, desperately wiping my blood from her face. But the damage was already spreading. Her veins — filled with black magic — had burst open. These oozing wounds stank of the dark putrescence of that magic.

I wrapped my hand around the hilt of my sword over my shoulder. Sienna hadn't tried to disarm me — she learned from her mistakes, knowing not to touch anything I might have claimed, such as my jade knife, which had burned her so badly in the past.

I unsheathed my katana with Chi Wen's vision focused in my mind. I remembered Sienna sprawled dead on the altar in the cave, but with her deadly, intoxicating magic still alive.

"It can't be destroyed," I whispered.

I swung the sword around, its tip striking sparks of magic wherever it grazed the inner edge of Sienna's protection circle.

Sienna screamed and flung up her hands as I brought the sword to her neck.

But I didn't cut off her head.

No, I reached around her, over her shoulder, and grasped the blade exactly as I shouldn't. The sword sliced into my hand, my blood coating its razor-sharp edge.

Sienna wrapped her hands around my neck and tried to strangle me. Black dots immediately appeared before my eyes — my throat was still wounded from the demon's claws.

With the last of my strength, I bent the unbendable blade around Sienna's neck — smoothing the metal with my magic when it wanted to crack and break — until it encircled her shoulders.

I couldn't breathe. Sienna's nails dug into my skin. Her blacked-out eyes were fierce. She was screaming with rage.

Then, remembering the blade's purpose and how the magic of Blackwell's circlet worked, I sucked all the magic out of Sienna and into the sword.

Well, it wasn't quite that easy.

At first, her screams turned from rage to pain. She let go of my neck and brought her hands up to the blade in an attempt to push it off over her head. She severely sliced her hands doing so, which only served to intensify the magic I was trying to work. My blood and her blood mingled. I smoothed this combined magic out over the entire sword, then pulled and pulled and pulled all of Sienna's magic after it.

I fell to my knees, unable to support myself and work such a terrible alchemy.

And it was terrible. It was a terrible, terrible thing to do to another person. A fate worse than death for any Adept.

The veins on Sienna's face split wider as the magic drained out of her.

She stopped screaming.

Her eyes cleared and returned to their normal cappuccino brown. "What have you done?" she whispered through cracked, black-bleeding lips.

I kept pulling, even as I felt my own magic faltering … I guess even I had limits.

The black magic drained from Sienna's veins. Her face began to heal.

"Stop, Jade … Jade …" she begged.

I didn't stop. I knew I couldn't stop. I went beyond the blood magic, beyond the black magic. I took her witch magic — the familiar taste of it made me weep. I took the binding powers, because if I didn't, the cycle would just start again.

"Stop … Stop …" Sienna was crying now, sobbing.

I didn't stop until I fell. The magic of the protective circle crashed down around us, and I dropped to the rock with Sienna across me.

I'd given it my all.

On the beach, and through the forest beyond, the demons were winning.

I couldn't do anything about it.

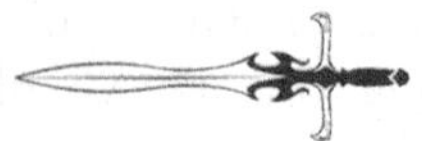

Portal magic washed over me as a doorway opened on the rock behind me. This was the treasure keeper's magic. Pulou was the only one of the guardian dragons who could open doorways that weren't permanent.

I felt, rather than saw, Yazi step through this doorway and lean down over me. My father brushed his fingers lightly on my cheek, and said, "She's alive." I'd never heard him sound so serious. Normally, his magic was an intense experience for me, especially when he touched me. Now I could barely taste it blended among the magic of the portal and Pulou.

"Of course she is," Pulou said. He was somewhere above and behind me, but I still couldn't open my eyes.

"Will the healer come?" Yazi asked.

"To kiss your daughter again? I imagine so."

Yazi straightened. I imagined he was surveying the massacre on the beach. "Will you ask him to attend us, treasure keeper?"

Pulou huffed out a sigh. "I'm to be your errand boy today, I see."

Yazi laughed, but the sound carried none of his usual exuberance. "Who else am I to ask? Drake is still sequestered. I figure it will be fifty years before the fire breather loosens her reins again."

"The fledgling is far too clever for that," Pulou said. He was chuckling.

I held on to the residual touch of dragon magic — my father's magic — that he'd left on my skin. This wasn't healing magic, of course, but if I could just get my own magic to mirror his, maybe I could remind my body how to heal itself.

I opened my eyes.

My father was standing over me, fully armored in some sort of hard-shell samurai gear. His face was utterly serious as he gazed toward the beach. The breeze tousled his sun-kissed curls around his ears. Supposedly, I was a feminine replica of him, but I doubt I could ever look so fierce … or golden godlike.

The door shut behind us as Pulou stepped back into the dragon nexus, or so I assumed.

"Hey, dad," I whispered.

Yazi glanced down at me sprawled across the rock at his feet. He smiled. His face looked more natural this way.

"Is this the black witch?" he asked.

Sienna laid utterly limp across my torso. "Yeah," I said. "Well, not anymore."

"Yes, I see. Good. Shall we have some fun then?"

Um, I could open my eyes and move my mouth to talk, but I wasn't actually moving any substantial part of my body. "Sure," I answered, a bit faintly. I hated to say no to anyone, and I really couldn't say no to my newly discovered father.

Yazi drew his sword out of thin air. The golden magic of it hit me like a sledgehammer to the chest. This I could thankfully still feel, even though everything else was deadened around me. The magic was a spicy chocolate that was fresh and potent. It was an intense incarnation of the warrior's power, unique to my father.

The warrior turned to face the beach. Slowly, painfully, I rotated my head to see what he was seeing.

The shapeshifters — at least the ones still standing — and a couple of skinwalkers were still fighting. I could see Kett and taste witch magic, so not all the witches were dead yet.

Yazi bellowed. The noise actually flattened the waves as they crashed before him. It stirred the sand and ruffled the trees beyond.

Everyone on the beach stopped fighting, including the demons.

Yazi bellowed a second time, sounding a little pissed now.

The rock vibrated painfully under my head, so I lurched up just in time to see and hear every demon on the beach and in the forest shriek an answer to Yazi's challenge. Then the demons charged … right toward me. And I couldn't fully lift my arms yet.

Yazi laughed and took one step off the rock into the rolling ocean. He brought his gold broadsword around — no fancy moves or anything — and cleanly lopped off the heads of the first three demons.

"Holy shit," I muttered.

Yazi took another step. He was knee deep in the ocean now — the waves didn't even budge him — and lopped off three more demon heads.

The portal magic bloomed behind me as the remaining dozen demons realized they'd made a mistake accepting Yazi's challenge and turned to flee.

Kett and the remaining shapeshifters threw themselves after the demons, chasing the creatures across the beach as they scattered into the forest. Yazi entered the fray. The witches — not including Gran or Scarlett as far as I could see — immediately ran to the fallen on the beach.

Pulou stepped out from the open portal and looked down at me. A bear of a man, his girth was only emphasized by the full-length fur coat I never saw him without. He spoke with a British accent, though his territory was Antarctica. Yeah, that was odd, but I guessed one of the guardians needed to oversee it.

I met Pulou's gaze. Then his eyes flicked to Sienna, who lay across my lap now. Specifically, he was looking at the sword still twisted around her neck. Then he looked back at me.

The ruined katana glowed, tasting of all the magic Sienna had stolen, as well as her own. It was impossible to distinguish any one taste over another.

"I've made something," I said.

"I see." Pulou didn't sound judgmental, but I knew an object of great and terrible power when I created it.

"Will you keep it for me?" I asked.

"That would be wise."

I gently pulled the twisted sword off Sienna's neck and held it up to Pulou. He took it carefully, holding it just by the tips of his fingers as he slowly rotated it. Different colors of magic swirled in the folded steel.

In Pulou's hands, the sword morphed, shrinking to the size of a bracelet. Then the treasure keeper opened his fur coat. More magic than I'd ever felt before hit me, scrambling my brain and blurring my vision. Pulou placed the shrunken sword in a pocket within his coat, then buttoned it up again. Something crazily metaphysical and dimensional had just happened, and I had no context in which to understand it.

Qiuniu, the guardian healer, stepped out from the golden doorway that stood open just behind Pulou. If any of the witches — and maybe even some of the shapeshifters — had been near enough, they would have instantly swooned at the sight of the Brazilian guardian dragon. He was that beautiful … if you liked that sort of thing.

He smiled down and nodded where I was sprawled at his feet. "Warrior's daughter."

"Guardian," I responded.

His eyes flicked to Sienna, barely registering her. Then, frowning, he looked past us toward the beach.

"I cannot revive the dead," he said.

"That's certainly up for debate," Pulou said. "I remember your predecessor —"

Qiuniu glanced in Pulou's direction and the treasure keeper put up a hand in surrender. "The warrior certainly wouldn't expect or desire such a thing from you, healer."

Qiuniu nodded, then smiled at me again. "I shall be back for you, Jade Godfrey. You will live. Others … their magic is very faint."

He stepped into the ocean before us and headed to the beach and the multitude of bodies lying scattered there.

I moaned and looked away. I looked down at Sienna, who still lay across my lap. I couldn't taste even a hint of magic from her. I actually wasn't sure she was even alive until I saw her chest rise with breath. Unconscious like this, and with her skin clear, she looked sixteen again.

The sacrificial knife lay across her chest.

"The knife," I said to Pulou.

He just shrugged and said, "A trifle. Not for you to wield perhaps, but not meant to be locked away."

I opened my mouth to protest — and then realizing who I was about to argue with, I snapped it shut.

Yazi laughed from somewhere deep in the forest. He was chasing down the remaining demons that had broken through our defenses, then continued on into the human world without Sienna to direct them.

"We've won," I murmured.

"Have you, alchemist?" Pulou said. "Not everyone is rising at the healer's touch."

I turned to look back at the beach. I could see Kandy, in human form, standing by Qiuniu as he leaned over a gray wolf on the beach. The green-haired werewolf was scratched and bruised, her hair was back to its natural dull brown … but that wasn't the point. She was on her feet.

I couldn't see Desmond or Kett among the fallen.

Reaching out with my dowser senses, I could taste witch magic but not specific witches. "I can't find Gran or my mom," I said, voicing the fear I could feel wedged like a rubber ball in my throat. I was surprised I could speak through it.

Pulou nodded. "Your magic is faint. Depleted."

I looked down at Sienna and thought about that for a moment. Everything had been so much easier … so much nicer, before I'd known I was an alchemist. Before I'd known I was half-dragon and not just half-witch.

"Will it come back?" I finally asked.

"Of course, warrior's daughter. Most likely stronger than before. Living through great trauma usually has that effect … on all of us."

"But not on Sienna," I murmured.

"No. You've taken every last drop. I have never seen or heard the like. Perhaps this is best kept between us."

"The Adept wouldn't understand."

"Oh, they would understand. And they would fear you."

I looked up at the treasure keeper. He smiled and patted my head like I was a toddler … and to him, I was.

"A conversation best left to tomorrow," he said.

"Tomorrow?" I echoed.

"Yes. When you come to treasure hunt for me." This was a statement, not a request.

I nodded. His smile deepened.

"I must go. Haoxin is calling," he said. "Tell your father and the healer I will be back when they need me."

I nodded again. I guess I'd run out of words. I was really, really tired.

Pulou stepped back through the portal and it snapped closed behind him, taking the comforting warmth of the dragon magic with it.

Qiuniu, still a dozen feet away on the beach, acknowledged the portal closing with a glance and then returned to healing. More shapeshifters were being helped to their feet. I tried to be glad of that, and to not dwell on Qiuniu shaking his head to Rebecca, the skinwalker elder, as he crouched over the body of Gord. He had reverted from his grizzly bear form in death.

The skinwalkers should never have been on the beach, but they stepped up without question when the witch magic fell. And the witch magic had fallen because of the spell the witches used to get me to Sienna.

My sister was looking at me.

Her eyes were once again the color of cappuccino robbed of its foam.

"Hey," I said.

"Jade?" Sienna asked. Her brow furrowed. "You're covered in … in … are you okay?"

Utter hope spread through my chest, warming me from within. The painful spot that had been lodged there — always hurting, never easing since that terrible night in the bakery basement and all its terrible truths — melted.

Maybe it was going to be okay —

Sienna's frown deepened. She lifted her hand and flexed her fingers. "Jade." Her tone sharpened. "What have you done?"

I opened my mouth to soothe her … to plead with her … to make her see —

"Jade!" Sienna shrieked and rolled off my lap to rise shakily to her feet. The sacrificial knife fell to the rock between us. I placed my foot over it as I stood as well.

Sienna watched me do so and then lifted her hateful gaze to mine.

"It's not going to be okay," I said — to myself, not my sister.

"No, it's not!" she shrieked. Then she attacked me.

She raked her nails across my face — I barely felt it.

She pummeled me in the stomach and kicked me in the legs — I didn't move. I didn't even raise my arms to stop her.

I felt magic spark from the beach and looked over to see Mory and her mom, Danica, stumbling toward us, supporting each other. Mory's toasted marshmallow magic took flight and zoomed toward us.

I willed my knife into my hand and easily batted the spell out of the air before it hit Sienna. I recognized the magic without having felt it before, without ever knowing it might be real. It tasted like a death curse — or at least an attempt at a death curse.

I shoved Sienna, still kicking and screaming, behind me. "Mory! No!"

The second spell — a much, much stronger curse — came from Danica. When I slashed this out of the air before me, it shattered all the bones of my right hand.

Danica fell to her knees in the sand. A wave crashed against her. Mory screamed, then began to drag her mother away from the water's edge.

Desmond was suddenly beside me. He'd taken human form. I started to smile at his grimness. I started to reach out to him with my undamaged hand, to tell him —

He reached by me, yanked Sienna forward between us by the hair, and snapped her neck.

My sister hung suspended upright for a moment while her brain informed her body that she was dead. Then she fell to the rock at my feet.

The life debt bond between Desmond and I dissolved into a painful puddle of mush at the bottom of my heart.

I stared at Desmond in disbelief. He gazed back at me impassively.

"I … I …" I murmured, not sure what I wanted to say, not sure I was even reacting at all.

"You weren't going to do it, Jade." He pitched his voice low. His use of my given name was meant to be intimate.

"She was my sister."

"She killed my pack mates. I'm alpha. It was never going to be any other way."

Gran, flanked by Scarlett and Kett, pushed through the crowd of half-healed shapeshifters who'd gathered around the rock on which Desmond and I stood … on which Sienna lay dead.

"This is witch business," Gran snapped.

The shapeshifters parted. Gran waded through the water and climbed up onto the rock with Scarlett and two other witches I didn't know.

Gran reached for me, but then didn't actually touch me. Her white-gray hair was wild, flying around half out of her braid. Her eyes were rimmed with magic that I could still barely taste.

"Gran …" I felt the tears start to stream down my cheeks.

Gran nodded. "Let's go home."

I nodded.

Then she looked down at Sienna lying dead at my feet and sighed.

Scarlett reached around Gran and brushed her fingers down my arm.

"Mom ..." I said. I just wanted her to make everything right again. It was an impossible wish.

Gran leaned down to Sienna, snapping a curt "No!" to Desmond when he also bent. "She is my responsibility. Witch responsibility."

The four witches gathered around Sienna. I stepped back as they lifted my sister between them and carefully carried her off the rock and through the surf.

"Jade," Desmond murmured, still beside me.

I shook my head and wiped the tears from my cheeks.

Then I very deliberately locked eyes with him and placed my fingertips to his chest. He looked momentarily pleased, until I started to push. I pressed with just the tips of my fingers. I didn't flatten my hand or lean in with my shoulder. When he didn't immediately yield, my feet slipped back on the wet rock. I anchored my stance to continue pushing. I kept my eyes locked to his and then — as surprise flashed over his face — he moved. Just a step back, but involuntarily, as he'd been resisting my push.

I turned my head toward the beach and dropped my hand. He was no longer in my peripheral vision.

Message sent and received.

I am stronger than you.

I stepped off the rock and into the crashing waves to follow my sister's body as it was carried across the beach.

Yazi appeared at the edge of the forest, not a scratch on him though his armor was pockmarked by demon blood and covered in sand. I saw the moment my father laid eyes on my mother for the first time in twenty-four years. I saw the sorrowful smile they exchanged among the chaos and carnage of the dark early morning.

I took another step and fell, feeling Kett's magic as he caught me before the waves swept me away. For the briefest of moments, I wished he'd let me go.

Then I didn't see anything for a long, long while.

Chapter Eighteen

When I woke up, I was in my bed, in my apartment, staring up at the ceiling. The room was dim, but only because the curtains were drawn.

I felt as if I'd just stepped from the beach into lying on my bed, except I was healed again … in body and magic, if not mind. Though I thought I'd already proven to myself on multiple occasions in the last six months that I was capable of healing my mind as well, I was just slow in that general area.

I reached out with my dowser senses to test the wards around my apartment, then instantly reined them back in when that tiny taste was rather intense.

I turned my head to observe the sacrificial knife sitting on my bedside table. It was resting on Blackwell's demon history book — the original, by the taste of it — and it exuded pissiness. Which was worrisome, as inanimate objects really shouldn't have moods. Someone had put me to bed and brought the knife and chronicle home as well. I wondered what else had been cleaned up while I was unconscious … I guessed that depended on how much time had passed.

I rolled out of bed — literally, since I wasn't completely sure I was ready to be on my feet. But I stood steadily enough to pull on jeans and my red 'Smart Ass University' T-shirt over my tank top and underwear.

I noted in the mirror that I didn't have a scratch or bruise on me. Even my hair looked amazing — gleaming and perfectly curled. I narrowed my eyes at this suspiciously. I suspected magic. Witch magic, probably from the witch currently puttering around in my kitchen.

The jeans were loose — damn dragon training, they were my favorite pair — so I cinched on a belt as I wandered down the short hall to the main room of the apartment.

By the light filtering through the windows, it was midmorning. The North Shore mountains were snow-capped and stark against a light blue, cloud-free sky. A nonrainy day in Vancouver in November? Odd. Maybe I'd lost more time than I thought.

Gran was making waffles in the kitchen. I didn't own the waffle maker she was using, so it must have been another addition courtesy of Scarlett.

"Good morning, sleepyhead." Gran gifted me with the blinding smile that she had only ever bequeathed for an A-plus on my report cards. I wouldn't have seen many of those smiles while growing up if I hadn't been good in home economics.

"How did you know I was awake?" I asked as I pressed a kiss to her temple, then poured myself a glass of orange juice. It looked freshly squeezed.

"How I always know," she replied.

"You spell me?"

"Of course," she answered without shame. "Sit. I'll serve."

Gran loaded two waffles onto a plate — I could smell the cinnamon in the batter and was already trying to not salivate.

I took a swig of orange juice and crossed around the kitchen island to hop up on a stool. The juice was freaking amazing. The taste practically exploded in my mouth. "What are these, magical oranges?"

"Olive grows them in her greenhouse," Gran answered absentmindedly.

I'd been joking. "Olive?" I echoed. "A witch with a plant affinity?"

"You met her," Gran said. "She held the protection circle over Scarlett when she fell." Gran looked up at me, utter pride in her voice. "I would never have thought Scarlett capable of such a spell, even backed by six other witches. She was magnificent."

Gran was referring to the spell that had cleared the path for me through the demons once the necromancers had countered Sienna's summoning spell.

The orange juice turned sour in my mouth. I set the glass down and fiddled with my fork. Gran had set two plates.

"How many ..." I started to ask, but then stopped myself. I wasn't sure today was the day for such questions. Instead, I watched Gran spoon strawberries and whipped cream on the waffles, eagerly taking the plate when she offered it. I was starving.

Gran settled in beside me and we ate. Then I helped myself to seconds. She hadn't finished her first plate yet

"Where is Scarlett?" I asked between mouthfuls of goodness.

"With your father."

That stopped me midbite. "Err, really?" I said. "Where? Here?"

"They've gone for a walk, apparently," Gran said. Her tone implied exactly what she thought of this improper walk.

I wasn't prepared to think of my parents together. That was disconcerting in a life-altering sort of way. "You think they'll bring back ice cream?" I asked.

"If you ask, I believe they will both do anything." Gran squeezed my knee, and I kept my suddenly teary eyes on the kitchen sink across from me. "We all would."

"Gran —" My voice broke with the emotion once again choking my throat. I never remembered being like this before — so racked with emotion and constantly on the edge of tears — not even as a teenager.

"Not as many as you would think, Jade." Gran answered my unasked question. "We slowed the demons. They became unfocused once you penetrated Sienna's circle. Then the blindingly gorgeous Brazilian man who seemed to appear from nowhere healed many I would have thought already beyond the veil."

Excuse me, grandmother? Blindingly gorgeous Brazilian? Up to that point, I would have told you that my Gran didn't even notice people's gender … just whether they were Adept or not.

"Qiuniu," I murmured.

"Oh, yes," Gran said — and then she actually rested her hand on her heart as if it was beating too fast. "You should have seen him run to you when you fell."

"I think that was Kett," I said dryly.

Gran waved this comment off. "After that. And the kiss! I could actually feel the magic moving from him to you."

"I gather I'm not the only one he kisses like that, Gran."

"No matter," Gran said as she stood to clear the plates. "Even if you're one of the few he kisses like that, it's good to remember."

Oh, God! I could see the matchmaking wheels turning. Gran now saw me married to a guardian dragon. One of the nine. The idea was utterly terrifying.

"Leave it," I said to Gran. "I want to bake."

Gran looked pleased — it didn't always take a gorgeous Brazilian to turn her head — and I wandered back to my bedroom for some sneakers and a hair elastic.

The bakery was open and full of customers. Bryn squealed and threw her arms around my neck when I entered the kitchen from the apartment stairs. Her dark hair was longer than I remembered — the bob now brushed her shoulders.

"Missed you," she whispered into my hair. Bryn didn't have a drop of magic in her, but I swore she was related to the skinwalkers. The brave, practically-human-themselves skinwalkers, who had defended the necromancers with their lives.

I pushed my rising tears away — again! — and tried to not hug Bryn too fiercely.

"Are you back?" she asked.

I looked up and saw Gran over Bryn's shoulder. She'd paused halfway through the kitchen on her way to the storefront — paused to hear me answer Bryn's question.

"Will you stay?" Gran asked.

"Yes," I answered them both.

"Perfect!" Bryn declared. Then she squealed again and said, "I have something for you to try." She ran out of the kitchen. The swing doors, which I often kept open while I was baking so I could see a slice of the bakery and street, swung closed behind her.

"Hot chocolate," Gran said. "She's been testing recipes with your ganache as a base. Dark and semisweet."

"Nice," I said. That was a great idea for the fall season. It was obvious the bakery would be okay without me, but I wasn't ready to walk away from everything I'd worked so hard and spent so many early mornings to build.

I ran my hand over the pristinely clean stainless steel counters and smiled.

"You'll stay," Gran said.

"I can't promise not to travel."

"Why not?" Gran said with a shrug. "There's a portal in the basement only you can use." She laughed, not a hint of fear in her face. I'd been wrong. I thought she'd be afraid of my dragon half. "You were brilliant, my Jade," Gran whispered. "I'm so proud of you."

My heart constricted. My thoughts were on the knife upstairs, and on the blood magic I'd performed. Gran couldn't forgive that. She would never be proud of that.

She stepped back to me and touched my hand where it still rested on the workstation.

"There's this knife I made," I whispered.

"I've seen it," Gran said, completely matter of fact.

"The treasure keeper wouldn't take it, but he also didn't think it was for me to wield."

"Interesting. He was the bear of a man … dragon, I mean … in the fur coat?"

"Yeah."

"Well, we'll talk more about that later, shall we?"

"Will there be a tribunal? For London, or Tofino?" I wasn't quite ready to simply brush it off yet.

"No," Gran said, her tone unassailable. "It's done. The price has been paid."

Sienna was dead, she meant. And oddly, she didn't sound completely happy about it. Perhaps Gran hadn't buried every hint of love she'd held for her foster child.

"The knife," Gran continued. "And … anything else isn't anyone's business."

"The end justified the means?"

"Today, yes. Maybe not tomorrow."

Well, it was hard to argue with that.

"And Sienna's … body?"

"Cremated."

"And the human victims?" I asked.

Gran sighed. "You wanted to bake."

"When I was in London … when I thought Kett was dead and Kandy was dying. And Mory … I didn't know what to do. I should know what to do."

Gran nodded. "The Convocation employs investigative teams. For Tofino and London there was no investigation, just cleanup."

"You covered up a mass murder in Tofino?" I didn't know how I felt about that.

"Restaged."

"With someone else taking the blame? One of the humans?"

"Yes. At a campsite."

Silence fell between us. Gran waited patiently for my next question, but no matter how many questions I asked today I wasn't going to feel any better. I understood that the Adept had to limit their exposure to the nonmagical world, had to protect themselves … but I didn't have to like it.

"I think I shall have Todd make me a latte," Gran said.

She turned away and I let her go. I was wearier than I'd thought when I first woke.

The healing of my soul would obviously take the longest of all.

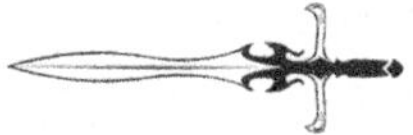

Kandy wandered into the bakery kitchen via the back alley just after lunch. I was shocked to see her arm in a sling, but tried to not show it.

"Purple?" I asked, referencing her newly dyed hair.

Kandy bared her teeth in the nonsmile that usually preceded claws also being bared. "Lara thought she'd be funny," she spat, "seeing as how I'm currently unable to wring her neck."

Lara was alive then — thank God — and she was obviously still mad about purple.

"I don't like it as much as the green," I said, hardly believing that to be the truth even as it came out of my mouth.

"Give me two or three days," Kandy said. "I'll fix it."

"And is Lara's neck still in jeopardy?"

Kandy shrugged and ran her finger around the edge of a bowl I'd filled with warm chocolate ganache. Bryn's hot chocolate idea had galvanized me to try a recipe I'd always deemed too difficult to serve and too costly to charge for.

"Gone," Kandy said, answering my question about Lara. "Back to Portland. All of them."

The last sentence was heavy with implication. Desmond, she meant, was back in Portland. Fine. That was where he belonged.

"And yet, you're here," I said.

Kandy shrugged again, then leaned around me to see what I was making.

"Grab a couple of stools from the office," I said.

She obligingly wandered off into my tiny, windowless back office and came out with two stools. She plunked them down on the opposite side of the steel workstation across from me.

I crossed to the freezer and pulled out the ice cream I'd put in there to set. I'd never actually used the ice cream maker before, but found it upstairs in a cupboard when I thought to look. Thank you, Scarlett.

"What are you making?" Kandy breathed with anticipation. She lifted her nose and scented the air.

"Just wait," I said with a glance at my oven timer. I poured a circle of chocolate ganache — it was thick but still pourable — on two plates. "Are you staying in Vancouver?" I asked the purple-haired werewolf as I carefully sliced two strawberries.

"Why not?" Kandy answered. Her grin wasn't as nonchalant as her tone.

"Shouldn't you be with the pack?"

"They'll get along fine without me."

"But I won't?"

"Nope."

A warm mushy feeling bloomed in my chest and I grinned at Kandy like an idiot.

"Ice cream?" she asked.

I laughed, then pulled a teaspoon through the ice cream twice to collect two tiny scoops. It could have used another hour in the freezer, but Kandy wouldn't care.

"The kid is upset."

"Mory?"

"Yup."

"But alive."

"Thankfully."

"Is she angry I didn't let her kill Sienna?"

"She tried to kill the black witch?"

"Yeah."

"Shit. No, she's mourning Rusty."

So I had felt Rusty's magic along with the necromancers' spell as it passed over me to break Sienna's hold on the souls she'd collected. "He carried the spell?" I asked, my prep momentarily forgotten.

"Yeah. It was the only way they could figure out how to get it through to the black witch. He was already tied to her."

"And he hasn't come back?"

"Nope. Moved on, they're saying. Might be for the best though, you know?"

Yeah, I knew. Mory didn't need to have her dead brother, who might also be a serial werewolf killer, hanging around for the rest of her life. But the fledgling necromancer wouldn't see it that way.

"A lot of people sacrificed themselves to save the day."

Kandy nodded.

"How many?" I forced myself to ask the question.

"Desmond brought our thirteen best fighters. All volunteers, all capable of half-beast form. Trained, Jade, to defend the pack at any cost."

"How many?"

"We lost two, Jamie, a fox, and a werewolf, Tina."

I'd seen Jamie in fox form just outside of the park ranger's hut, but never met him or Tina in person. I inhaled deeply and then held my breath to stop myself from crying. Then I asked, "And who survived but won't ever be the same again?"

"That dragon healer is crazy powerful. He brought back three that I thought were already dead and Audrey."

"Audrey?"

"Yeah, she was a goner. The healer brought her back, but she was still crazy injured. Desmond finished the job by making her beta, tying her to the collective power of the pack. Tore a big chunk out of his arm and fed it to her right there on the beach. An accession is usually a bit more formal."

I stared at Kandy.

She shrugged. "The bitch saved my life. She's going to be totally insufferable about it."

"So now the truth comes out. Audrey's staying in Portland, so you're staying here."

Kandy grinned. "Something like that."

The oven buzzer sounded.

"Ready?" I asked.

"Always."

Pushing away all the things I knew I would grieve over for months — even years — to come, I focused solely on the task before me. I pulled the cupcakes out of the oven just as Kett wandered back from the storefront and settled onto the stool beside Kandy. I'd known he'd been pretending to drink coffee with Gran out front, though I doubt they'd exchanged a single word. The werewolf didn't acknowledge the vampire. Her eyes were firmly fixed on me as I flipped the hot cupcakes onto the cooling rack. I'd only baked two to start, because they had to be served warm. Gran would have to wait for the next round.

"I gather we have a circlet to steal from Blackwell?" Kett asked as I placed the piping hot cupcakes on the ganache in the center of each plate.

"It isn't stealing when the retrieval is dragon certified." I quickly poured the remaining ganache over the hot cupcakes, then dropped the mini scoops of ice cream on top, along with the fanned sliced strawberries.

Kandy snickered and Kett nodded sagely, as if he'd known I was going to take Blackwell's circlet and give it to the dragons for safekeeping all along.

I pushed the plate across the table to Kandy. She gazed at it in awe.

"This is not a cupcake," she said. Her tone was reverent, as if confronted by some miracle.

"It is," I answered. "It's a molten dark chocolate cupcake covered in ganache and served with a dollop of mint ice cream."

I found a fork and took a bite. It was utter heaven in my mouth.

Kandy didn't bother with a fork. She picked the dripping cake up off her plate, smearing warm chocolate all over her fingers, and wedged a quarter of it into her mouth.

"I'm thinking of calling it *Unity in a Cup*."

"Screw that," Kandy said, her mouth full. "It's a freaking orgasm in a freaking cup."

I laughed and took another bite, closing my eyes to savor this one. "It's like you and Kett had babies," I said, my mouth full of insanely good goodness that tasted almost exactly like Kandy's and Kett's magic combined … except sweeter.

"That's disgusting," Kandy sneered. Then she lifted her plate and licked it clean … literally.

Kett threw his head back and started to laugh.

I took a third bite and melted into the perfectly molten moment.

Acknowledgments

With thanks to:

My story & line editor
Scott Fitzgerald Gray

My proofreaders
Pauline Nolet
Leiah Cooper

My beta readers
Ita Margalit and Joanne Schwartz

For their continual encouragement, feedback, & general advice
Patrick Creery, for the French
Gertie, for the cupcake holders
Heather Doidge-Sidhu, for double-checking everyone
My lovely bloggers, for reading and reviewing
The Retreat, for letting me play in your sandbox

For her Art
Elizabeth Mackey

ABOUT THE AUTHOR

Meghan Ciana Doidge is an award-winning writer based out of Vancouver, British Columbia, Canada. She has a penchant for bloody love stories, superheroes, and the supernatural. She also has a thing for chocolate, potatoes, and cashmere.

For recipes, giveaways, news, and glimpses of upcoming stories, please connect with Meghan via:

Newsletter, http://eepurl.com/AfFzz
Website, www.madebymeghan.ca
Email, info@madebymeghan.ca

Please also consider leaving an honest review at your preferred retailer.

ALSO BY MEGHAN CIANA DOIDGE

Novels

After the Virus

Spirit Binder

Time Walker

Cupcakes, Trinkets, and Other Deadly Magic (Dowser 1)

Trinkets, Treasures, and Other Bloody Magic (Dowser 2)

Treasures, Demons, and Other Black Magic (Dowser 3)

I See Me (Oracle 1)

Shadows, Maps, and Other Ancient Magic (Dowser 4)

Maps, Artifacts, and Other Arcane Magic (Dowser 5)

I See You (Oracle 2)

Artifacts, Dragons, and Other Lethal Magic (Dowser 6)

I See Us (Oracle 3)

Catching Echoes (Reconstructionist 1)

Tangled Echoes (Reconstructionist 2)

Unleashing Echoes (Reconstructionist 3)

Champagne, Misfits, and Other Shady Magic (Dowser 7)

Misfits, Gemstones, and Other Shattered Magic (Dowser 8)

Gemstones, Elves, and Other Insidious Magic (Dowser 9)

Demons and DNA (Amplifier 1)

Bonds and Broken Dreams (Amplifier 2)

Mystics and Mental Blocks (Amplifier 3)

Idols and Enemies (Amplifier 4)

Instincts and Imposters (Amplifier 5)

Endings and Empathy (Amplifier 6)

Misplaced Souls (Misfits 1)

Awakening Infinity (Archivist 0)

Invoking Infinity (Archivist 1)

Compelling Infinity (Archivist 2)

Novellas/Shorts

Love Lies Bleeding

The Graveyard Kiss (Reconstructionist 0.5)

Dawn Bytes (Reconstructionist 1.5)

An Uncut Key (Reconstructionist 2.5)

Graveyards, Visions, and Other Things that Byte (Dowser 8.5)

The Amplifier Protocol (Amplifier 0)

Close to Home (Amplifier 0.5)

The Music Box (Amplifier 4.5)

Moments of the Adept Universe 1

Misson Recon: Bee (Amplifier 5.5)

TRINKETS, TREASURES, and other BLOODY MAGIC

MEGHAN CIANA DOIDGE

TREASURES, DEMONS, and other BLACK MAGIC

MEGHAN CIANA DOIDGE

INVOKING INFINITY

MEGHAN CIANA DOIDGE

COMPELLING INFINITY

MEGHAN CIANA DOIDGE

Made in the USA
Las Vegas, NV
12 April 2025